Painted Veil

Also by the author
Interrupted Aria

To receive a free catalog of Poisoned Pen Press titles, please contact us in one of the following ways:

Phone: 1-800-421-3976
Facsimile: 1-480-949-1707
Email: info@poisonedpenpress.com
Website: www.poisonedpenpress.com

Poisoned Pen Press
6962 E. First Ave. Ste 103
Scottsdale, AZ 85251

Painted Veil

The Second Baroque Mystery

Beverle Graves Myers

Poisoned Pen Press

Poisoned Pen Press
6962 E. First Ave., Ste. 103
Scottsdale, AZ 85251
www.poisonedpenpress.com
info@poisonedpenpress.com

Printed in the United States of America

For Megan

"Lift not the painted veil which those who live call life."
Percy Bysshe Shelley
Sonnet, 1818

Part One

Acqua: Water

Chapter 1

"Sometimes it takes another fool to show you the error of your ways."

I was alone in my dressing room at the Teatro San Marco, addressing my image in the oval mirror flanked by unlit oil lamps. Morning sunlight streamed in a high window, glinting off the gold-threaded costume hanging on the wardrobe door behind me. To celebrate the upcoming marriage of the Doge's eldest daughter, the Savio alla Cultura had commissioned an opera filled to the brim with pomp and pageantry. Our director, Maestro Rinaldo Torani, had chosen to rework the score of a minor composer who had long since disappeared into obscurity in one of the more unpronounceable German states. The subject of the nuptial opera was the great Roman general Julius Caesar's adventures with Cleopatra Queen of Egypt. Torani was planning to dazzle Venice, and her foreign visitors, with an unprecedented display of vocal fireworks and spectacular stage effects.

We'd been deep in rehearsal for *Cesare in Egitto* for the past week. Those seven days had passed at the cadence of a funeral march. My funeral, it seemed. I had been cast as a nefarious Egyptian prince, the brother of Cleopatra. Not an insignificant part, but not the *primo uomo* role of the title. That honor had gone to Francesco Florio—the vain, arrogant, impertinent fool who was goading me to take a serious look at my own sorry behavior.

Florio and I belonged to a class of men who inspired ecstasy in the audiences of the day. We were *castrati*—male sopranos—the rulers of the opera stage. I had made my professional debut in Venice three years earlier. Since then, I had sung the plum roles at the San Marco, Venice's state theater, and been in demand for civic festivals and court entertainments all over the north of Italy.

I admit that I'd let the sweet wine of success go to my head. I had squandered too many hours of valuable practice time in dining with patricians who only wanted to parade Venice's latest rage before their guests. Their fawning had only escalated my conceit. Eventually my tailor saw more of me than my family, and I noticed that old friends were avoiding me. I knew I was behaving like a fool, but I couldn't seem to stop. The adulation enticed me like a drug. I shook my head at the mirror. A pale face with smooth, boyish cheeks shook back. The shadowed eyes that had seen too many late nights forced me to be brutally honest. Maestro Torani's casting decision was just. My voice had suffered from my dissipations; it no longer merited top billing.

I dropped my chin to fiddle with the grease paints littering the dressing table. Trying to evaluate my demotion in a calm fashion, I instead found my hands snapping a stick of bisque pink clean in two. Why Florio, for God's sake? I could have stood losing my position to almost anyone but him. And why had Maestro Torani not warned me?

The first week of that wet, windy May of 1734, returning from giving a concert in Florence, I had been shocked to find Venice in a state of great excitement over Florio's upcoming appearance in the wedding opera. Born Francesco Florio in a village near Bologna, the vocal wonder had acquired legions of admirers who had taken to calling him Il Florino. If I was scaling the lower slopes of fame in my native Venice, Il Florino stood on the heady, international heights. His luscious soprano and never-ending notes had conquered London, Vienna, Dresden, and every noteworthy opera house in between. We had clashed from the moment he'd set his beautifully shod foot on the San Marco stage.

"Maestro Torani, you must excuse my late arrival," he had said that first day, striding onstage, waving a plump, bejeweled hand at the musical director. "My worthless servant failed to scent my bath water. By the time the fellow ransacked my trunks for the proper oil, the water had cooled and he was obliged to start all over again. So tiresome."

The statuesque singer unhooked the clasp on his cloak and stood in an attitude of anticipation. Lace ruffles poured down his chest, and a watch chain loaded with charms and medals spanned his considerable mid-section. Torani opened and shut his mouth several times, then motioned for a pair of theater lackeys to remove the garment of crimson silk. Tenor Niccolo Galiani and flamboyant contralto Rosa Tiretta led the pack of secondary singers watching Florio with intense interest. Niccolo's gaze was worshipful, Rosa's frankly appraising.

Emma Albani, our veteran *prima donna*, came forward bobbing her head in the suggestion of a curtsy. "You probably don't remember, Signor Florio, but we sang together in Dresden years ago."

"But I do recall, Signora. We shared several ensembles." Florio brought her hand to the vicinity of his mouth, kissed the air, then said so loudly the stagehands on the catwalks above the stage could hear, "For pity's sake, do try to keep up to tempo this time."

The soprano snatched her hand back, and a flush crept over her doughy, powdered cheeks. Our Emma prided herself on her cordial disposition. Other leading ladies might renege on contracts, refuse to sing arias which failed to suit, or come burdened with spendthrift husbands or meddlesome mommas, but not the lady who had been dubbed "the sweet angel of song" by her fellow Venetians. Of course, that appellation had been given more than a few years ago. The angel's voice had lately developed a wobble in the high register, but Emma contrived to keep herself in work by being supremely agreeable. Besides amusing us with clever jokes, she never argued with fellow singers and never said no to theater management. I had always enjoyed working with her. When Florio's needlessly cruel remark erased Emma's pleasant smile and replaced it with a look of embarrassed confusion, the visiting *castrato* slipped yet another notch in my estimation.

After Emma had retreated to the dark sanctuary of the wings, Torani cleared his throat and pressed me forward with a nudge to the small of my back. "Signor Florio, allow me to present Venice's finest *castrato* and favorite son, Tito Amato."

To my surprise, Florio bowed, declared himself enchanted to make my acquaintance, and made theatrical small talk while Torani got the delayed rehearsal underway. Throughout Emma's opening recitative and aria, Florio kept a smile pasted on his broad, flat face. He nodded indulgently as he waved a finger to keep time with her music. Something about that haughty smile nettled my pride. My stomach churned as it had when I'd first heard that Florio would be singing the lead, and an unfortunate compulsion gradually took possession of my mind. By the time it was my turn to sing, I was burning to prove my worth and show Florio how hard he would have to work to captivate the audience for his own.

From the moment my lips parted I ignored Maestro Torani's direction from the harpsichord and went my own way. Though the operatic conventions of the day called for singers to decorate the written melody with their own improvisations, the judicious performer showed his artistry with a discreet application of musical ornamentation. In my zeal, I dumped discretion and good taste out the window like a fishwife hurling slops into the canal. I packed the lilting measures with an excess of *fioritura* and trilled where I should have paused for breath. Torani was shaking his head, slicing the air with an increasingly agitated hand. I ignored him and ended with a sustained cadenza that was wonderfully extravagant, but totally out of character for the piece. Emma stood in the wings, alternately chewing her thumbnail and throwing me sympathetic glances.

During Torani's ensuing rant, Florio could barely contain his chuckles. "So," he muttered, as he strolled to center stage to take his turn, "that is what passes for vocalizing in Venice these days."

Thoroughly disgraced, I crept into the wings to join Emma and the other singers. Torani played the instrumental interlude that led to Florio's first aria. The singer struck a graceful posture with one hand curved on his hip and the other holding a sheet of music at chin level. Gradually, almost imperceptibly, Florio began to puff himself up with majesty. The man seemed to be growing before our eyes. He sounded the first note with amazing delicacy, a perfectly formed crystal tone that somehow filled the vast, empty theater. Then Torani struck a chord and they were off. Florio's penetrating soprano flew through Caesar's triumphant aria, his pace challenging the director at the harpsichord to keep up with him. Yet, the singer's intonation remained pure, his trills brilliant, and his improvisation elegant. Even had I not been neglecting my vocal exercises, I knew I had met my master. Florio demonstrated what the voice maestro at my Naples *conservatorio* used to tell us before every class: "Any singer can sing, a *castrato* must astonish."

The latch on my dressing room door clicked and pulled me away from my musings. From down the corridor, an indistinct uproar met my ears. Over a medley of sobbing and whining, a man's harsh voice scolded and a woman defended herself in strident tones. My manservant, Benito, squeezed through the door carrying a large box which he laid reverently on the sofa. With quick, deft motions he untied the cord, lifted the lid, and unwrapped layers of silvery-gray tissue. He gave me an excited grin as he placed an elaborately constructed headdress on a china stand.

"What do you think, Master?" he asked, his delicate hands fluffing the plumes that had been flattened by the tissue.

"I think they are terribly loud. There couldn't be more of a rumpus if someone had been murdered."

"That's just Signor Carpani taking the seamstresses to task over a missing bolt of cloth. I'm asking you about the helmet. Isn't it a beauty? This is what you will wear with your battle armor. Do you like it?"

I fingered the gold trim on the nosepiece and ran one of the soft ostrich plumes through my hand. If the ancients had actually worn something like this into battle, the bright trims would have made exceedingly fine targets. "It will do, Benito."

"Do?" My manservant's carefully plucked eyebrows shot up. "It's a masterpiece, every bit as nice as the one made for Signor Florio. I saw to that. I stopped by the Jews' shop every day to make sure they didn't stint you."

"You need not have worried. The Del'Vecchio clan does beautiful work. They have always provided quality headdresses for the theater."

"Still, it doesn't hurt to make sure." Benito frowned. My manservant was a small man, a *castrato* like myself. But while I possessed a eunuch's typically long arms and legs and had to constantly curb my appetite for fear of developing a paunch like Florio's, Benito remained as delicate as a sparrow no matter how many generous dinners he consumed. In his younger years he had played the female characters in the opera houses of Rome, where papal decree banned women from the stage. When his youthful looks abandoned him and singing engagements became few and far between, the clever *castrato* offered his services elsewhere. Benito had long possessed a knack for discovering people's needs and finding ways to fulfill them.

I had first encountered Benito during the disastrous weeks that surrounded my Venice debut and had not expected to continue the acquaintance once those sad events had reached their startling conclusion. Yet our paths seemed destined to cross. The little *castrato* had soon popped up to assist me in another matter, and when he offered his services on a permanent basis, I found myself surprisingly keen. Benito had been my servant for several years now, and tended to pout if his efforts weren't appreciated.

I turned to face him over the back of my chair. "*Grazie,* Benito. The helmet is splendid. It's just that, at this moment, I am more concerned with matching Signor Florio's vocal skills than competing with his wardrobe."

My manservant shrugged and took up my hairbrush. Tending to avoid wigs whenever possible, I'd left the house with my hair loose about my shoulders. Why a man with a perfectly good head of hair should borrow another's mane and wear it on his head like a piece of sod was a mystery to me. Benito disapproved of my informality. More in tune with the reigning style than I, my manservant strove to dress my locks at the height of fashion. He reached for a stand that held a trim bag wig the color of my own dark hair. "Will you wear this for the rehearsal, Master?"

"No. Just arrange my own hair. Simply." I ignored his exaggerated sigh and settled back before my mirror to enjoy the gentle pull of the brush through my locks. "And tell me what the argument in the hall was about."

"Signor Carpani accused Madame Dumas of purloining a bolt of figured velvet meant for one of Signor Florio's costumes. She denied it, but can't produce the fabric."

"Madame Dumas is an unlikely thief. She must have served this theater since before I was born. She left Paris in the last days of the old King Louis and has been the costumer here ever since."

"Well, she's argued herself hoarse and her girls are in an uproar. Carpani is threatening to have them all tossed out on their pretty behinds."

I shook my head. "That's ridiculous. The bolt must have been mislaid."

Benito gave me a dubious glance in the mirror. "Have you not lifted your eyes from your songbooks this long week? Signor Carpani has stuck his nose in every closet and cupboard of this theater. I'll wager he has the location and value of every paper of pins written down in that big notebook he carries under his arm. If the missing fabric were in the theater, he would have found it."

I grunted as Benito worked at a tangle with the brush. "That clerk has been worrying Maestro Torani to death."

"Why have we been saddled with this *cretino* of a penny pincher all of a sudden?" my manservant asked in his irreverent way. I had never tried to tame my servant's mouth. In some matters I had set fast limits, but Benito knew he was free to say what he liked.

I answered, "One compelling reason—profit. Since the Republic appropriated the San Marco for its state opera house, the Senate has been pouring ducats into the theater with only meager rewards. Maestro Torani is more interested in making beautiful music than making sure the account books add up. And he has let the scene designers run wild with their spectacular effects."

"The public love it. The last opera that brought the horses and chariots onto the stage packed the pit and the boxes every night."

"Yes." I grimaced, recalling the backstage stink and mess. "But the box office can't bear the cost of such stunts. With the considerable sum paid to engage Il Florino, the Senate has called a halt. Thrift has suddenly come into vogue."

"Hence Signor Carpani."

"And Signor Morelli," I murmured, closing my eyes as Benito began to curl my hair with a wand he had warmed on his little alcohol stove.

The Savio had appointed Leonardo Morelli, a dour patrician, to oversee theater expenditures and curtail waste. The Morelli family had once wielded considerable influence in government circles, but had been knocked down a peg or two when a profligate Morelli lost the family's Rialto warehouses at the faro table. The new Ministro del Teatro might be short a few ducats, but as a gentleman of standing, he could not be expected to tally the accounts himself. For that, Signor Morelli had recruited an exacting clerk who seemed to revel in figures and ledgers. It took only a few days for Signor Carpani and his notebook to become as much a part of the San Marco as the painted curtain that separated the everyday Venice with all her charms and foibles from the idealized pageants we played out on the theater's stage.

Benito passed me a hand mirror, and I turned my head to admire his work. Rehearsal would soon begin. From neighboring dressing rooms, Rosa's dusky contralto moved up and down the scales, echoed by Niccolo's mellow tenor. I made a silent vow to my newly coifed reflection as Benito whisked a clothing brush over my shoulders. If any difficulties threatened the upcoming opera, they would not be caused by me. I would imitate Emma Albani and become the soul of congeniality. I would turn a deaf ear to Florio's pompous pronouncements, reapply myself to my music, and try to regain the confidence of Maestro Torani and my fellow musicians. The great occasion that *Cesare in Egitto* would celebrate demanded no less.

Chapter 2

I left Benito polishing shoes and started through the maze of corridors that led to the stage. Audiences would be surprised to see how much space lay behind the backdrop that they thought of as the "back" of the theater. The dressing rooms were down a hallway that led to the right, well behind the stage. A larger, intersecting corridor held workshops and studios. With less than two weeks until opening night, this area was bustling. Carpenters were knocking scenery flats together, and machinists were tinkering with the intricate contraptions that brought the eye-popping stage effects to life.

The project of the morning was nothing less than the River Nile. As described in the libretto, the first act curtain of *Cesare in Egitto* rose on the open-air atrium of a palace outside Alexandria. The contentious brother and sister, Ptolemy played by me and Cleopatra played by Emma, awaited a barge carrying the Roman hero, Julius Caesar. The scene designer had submitted a model depicting a series of columns and arches topped by statues of Egyptian deities. The river appeared through the wide arches as a trio of horizontal waves set before the backdrop. These could be made to simulate the rolling waters of the Nile by a team of burly stagehands turning cranks which slid the waves back and forth. As Caesar, Florio would make his first entrance singing from the prow of a barge bedecked with flags and streamers pulled in on a track behind the waves. For every enthralling but seemingly effortless entrance of this type, there was an army of stagehands straining at ropes, winches, and pulleys in the wings and below stage.

I paused to stick my head in my favorite workshop: the scene painter's studio. Luca Cavalieri, the principal artist, always had a vast canvas hanging from the ceiling, covering one entire wall. I loved watching it progress. Luca started with a lightly outlined sketch, painted a rough background, then added layers of perspective to create a vista that seemed to stretch for miles. This morning, the studio was an island of quiet in the backstage sea of banging, clanging activity. The smell of oily paint and pungent turpentine hung in the air, but the huge canvas was untended. Luca was nowhere to be seen.

An exclamation of disgust floated up from behind a waist-high counter. I investigated. Several of Luca's assistants were kneeling on the floor throwing dice. They jumped to their feet.

"Ah, it's you, Signor Amato," said the taller one, whose name I could never remember.

"Yes, just me. You can go back to your game." I grinned. They were accustomed to my stopping by to admire their work and knew that I, as a singer, had no authority to fuss about their idleness, even if I had been the fussing type. "Where is your master? He is usually up to his elbows in paint by now."

The shorter, broader artist rattled the dice before answering with a touch of irritation. "Who knows? Signor Cavalieri keeps his own hours these days."

His fellow painter seemed more anxious to defend the studio's supervisor. "He'll be strolling in any minute now. You know Master Luca. He's always busy with something. When he's intent on a project, he forgets everything else, even what hour of the day it is."

"Does his latest project have a charming smile and a bosom to match?" I jested, but the painters passed a cautionary glance. With elaborate shrugs, they turned their attention back to their game.

Before I could take a good look at the large canvas and the other half-painted flats leaning against the walls, someone bellowed my name out in the corridor. It was Aldo, the stocky, pugnacious stage manager who did hold authority over the entire backstage crew. Luca's assistants swept the dice from the floor, jumped up, and reached for paint-stained smocks. I signaled for them to relax and went out to find Aldo pacing the corridor like a racehorse eager for the starting flag. A self-important smile stretched his thin lips across his round, alpine face. With his pale complexion and light brown hair, he appeared more Austrian than Venetian, but I knew his family as long-time residents of the parish next to my own.

"I've wasted ten good minutes looking for you, Amato. Maestro Torani wants a word with you before rehearsal." Aldo rocked back on his heels and searched my face for signs of the curiosity he thought his message would produce. He was disappointed. As part of my determination to distance myself from my old, careless ways, I was keeping my emotions on a tight rein. The stage manager continued with a scowl, "In his office. Right away."

The director's office lay on the opposite side of the theater. The San Marco was a venerable opera house. It dated to the middle of the last century when it first occurred to a small group of noblemen that people might pay to see the intoxicating new spectacle that combined song, dance, and visual delights. Throughout the years, several families had owned the theater and exploited it to the utmost. When the Senate took over, the roof was leaking, the gilt on the boxes was flaking, and plaster was falling in hunks. Even the boards that floored the stage had warped. During the long-overdue refurbishing, Torani had claimed a quiet corner as far away from hammering, sawing, and vocalizing singers as the layout of the building would allow. The summons to his private sanctum came as a surprise. If Torani had anything to say to a musician in private, he generally used Aldo's cubbyhole by the stage door.

To avoid my colleagues gathering on the stage, I crossed behind the blank batten and canvas backdrop that stretched into the yawning gloom above. The hall outside Torani's office was empty. I rapped on the door. The director didn't make me wait; the door opened as if he had been standing right beside it. I began to worry. Was I guilty of some unknowing but serious transgression? Had I run afoul of Signor Morelli or the ubiquitous Carpani? I knew Maestro had not summoned me to indulge in social pleasantries. Rinaldo Torani seldom socialized with his musicians. He always said that the director of an opera company could not afford to get involved in personal entanglements with theater employees. He was probably right. I had seen company intrigue scuttle more than one promising career.

Torani closed the door, careful to make sure that the latch caught. He motioned me to sit, then lowered himself into a high-backed leather chair behind his writing table. An inkwell had overturned, leaving a black stream that meandered over and around wrinkled papers, dirty crockery, and spent quills. He pushed at the debris in a half-hearted attempt to impose order, finally giving up and throwing his heavy-bottomed wig on top of the whole mess. A wig made sense for a man who retained so little of his own hair, but unless he was conducting an opera in front of an audience, our director could never manage to keep one in place for more than a few minutes.

"How are you this morning, Tito?" he began, running a hand through the frizz that ringed his balding pate.

"I'm doing well, Maestro."

"Finding Ptolemy's cantabile aria a bit challenging are you?"

"I've been working on it at home. I think you will be pleased."

He nodded and shifted his weight in his chair. "How are you getting along with Signor Florio? Not crossing swords too much, I hope."

"I find that there are things I can learn from him," I replied, choosing my words with care.

"I wouldn't be surprised if there was some tension between you. Florio can be... a difficult colleague." The director used soothing tones. He cocked his head. Was he inviting a confidence? Maestro Torani had always reminded me of a determined sheepdog herding an untidy flock of singers and musicians. If we were late to rehearsal, Torani barked in quick, clipped phrases. If we dawdled in learning our words, he snapped at our heels until everyone fell in line. This new show of fatherly concern had me baffled.

I cleared my throat. "I do wish I had known that Florio would be coming to Venice to head the cast of *Cesare* before I heard it in the coffeehouse."

"Ah, yes. I must apologize for that." Torani bowed his head. "If you had been in the city I would have made sure you were informed. As it was, the Savio sprang the news on me while you were in a coach on the road between here and Florence. It took but a few hours for all Venice to be buzzing about it."

I spread my hands in a gesture of resignation. "What's done is of no consequence now. We all know our places and rehearsals for *Cesare* are progressing."

"I detect a note of bitterness, but I can't blame you. I suppose I'd feel the same if I were in your position." Torani rose and crossed to a sideboard holding a large pewter pot and some mismatched cups and saucers. "Will you take some chocolate? I have some every morning."

I nodded, more bewildered than ever.

He served me a cup, poured one for himself, then leaned against the front of the writing table with his legs crossed at the ankles. "Florio has been accused of overweening vanity. I'd be foolish to argue against that charge, but it might help you to bear him if you knew something of his background."

Torani contemplated the frothy liquid he was swirling in his cup, then continued. "Our new star did not study at a *conservatorio* as you and most of your fellow singers did. He was trained for the stage by private tutors. The director of a choir in a small chapel outside Bologna discovered Florio's voice and recommended him to a music enthusiast in that city. That gentleman arranged for his, em…" Torani sent me a quick glance. "…arranged for his surgery, and spared no expense to school him, not only in music, but also in the social graces that a singer moving in exalted circles is expected to possess."

"I've been told that he was only fourteen when he first sang in public."

"True. He was pushed to the stage early, but debuted to unprecedented acclaim. In the span of one evening's performance he exploded from complete obscurity into the brightest star in the heavens."

"Unlike the stars that remain fixed in the night sky, Florio's fame continues to spread and brighten."

Torani nodded. "The man is feted and showered with gifts wherever he appears. In London, the Prince of Wales was so enthralled that he had a medal struck in Florio's honor, as if he were a general who had just saved the empire."

"I've heard the story. When some of the courtiers objected, Florio said that when an English general sacrificed as much as he had for his voice, then he would gladly give up his medal."

Torani gave a dry chuckle. "Florio has a sharp tongue, but few men could bear such unremitting adulation without it marking their characters for ill. Do you know he doesn't even have a home? He talks of using his riches to build a *palazzo* fit for a duke in the Umbrian hills, but he has never stopped traveling long enough to find a suitable estate."

I smiled to myself. Here, at last, was something I possessed that my rival did not. My home might lie on an out of the way *campo* in the Cannaregio, a modest quarter far from the Piazza San Marco with its magnificent Basilica and government buildings, but it suited me well. I had been born in that house, learned to play ball in the square, and had my first music lessons at the parish church down the *calle*. Since our father died, I had been sharing the house with my brother and sister.

My sister Annetta was the heart of our small family. She minded the house and was responsible for all our comforts. A mistress of detail, she thought of everything from sprinkling our sheets with lavender water while they dried in the sun to rising at dawn to have her pick of the freshest fish at the *pescheria*. In age, she stood between my older brother Alessandro and myself. Other matters tended to put her in the middle as well. I admit Annetta was often called on to play the role of peacemaker.

Alessandro still didn't know what to make of his eunuch brother. Simply put, we lived in different worlds. My brother was a merchant seaman who hearkened back to previous generations of sturdy adventurers who had made our city-republic the center of Mediterranean trade. He was probably one of the few Venetians who had no use for opera. Alessandro considered music a frivolous career for any man and the doctoring done to preserve my perfect soprano an offense to reason and nature. He refused to believe my protestations that I had made peace with my condition and might even have chosen it if my ten-year-old self could have been granted the wisdom to understand the gains that would spring from the pain and the loss. We had not argued the matter for several months. Alessandro was away on a trading journey, probably haggling over a cartload of goods at some exotic *suk* even as Maestro Torani regarded me over the rim of his cup.

The director bit his lower lip. He started to speak, frowned, then said in a rush, "Tito, I must tell you why I called you here. I have a rehearsal to supervise."

Finally. "Yes, Maestro?"

"Have you had a good look at the scenery lately?"

"I looked in on Luca's studio this morning. The backdrop for the first act is much the same as it was two days ago."

Torani took a sip of chocolate and let it linger in his mouth as if he still had doubts about confiding whatever it was he had on his mind. At last he said, "The work has come to a complete halt. The canvas in the studio should have been ready to fly above the stage days ago. The others are in a similar condition, only partially complete. The background painters have done as much as they can without Signor Cavalieri's direction."

"Where is Luca? Has he fallen ill?"

"No, he's not ill. I've sent messengers to his lodging. He's simply disappeared." Torani leaned toward me. A thin sheen of perspiration had formed on his prominent forehead. "Tito, I need your help. I want you to find Luca Cavalieri and get him back here to finish the sets."

His request drew me up in my seat. "Maestro, why do you ask this of me? Luca is a pleasant fellow, but we are hardly friends. I rarely see him outside the theater."

Torani ignored my question. "I've already made a few inquiries," he said. "I've talked to Luca's assistants. And Aldo. Sometimes they go to a café or a wineshop after the show."

"But, Maestro…"

The director forged ahead, his eyes intent on mine. "The last time anyone at the theater saw him was night before last. Luca and his two background painters worked late that night. They've been tearing through the oil and the candles. I can tell you, Carpani has been on my back about that."

Torani turned and deposited his cup on the desk top with such force that the handle snapped and chocolate splashed over the jumbled papers. He grabbed a few sheets, moved them to safety, and dabbed at the muddy rivulets with his handkerchief. I offered him mine, but he shook his head and sat back down behind the writing table with a profound sigh.

"You see how it is here. Morelli's long-nosed clerk is choking the life out of me. It was a black day when Morelli hired that clerk away from Probate Court. Carpani insists that I account for every *soldo* in the most excruciating detail. He's suffocating me with piles of lists and requisitions. What's worse, his meddling is keeping me from my real work. I haven't even had time to block out the scene we are to rehearse today." He put his hands together in a prayerful position. "I don't have time to run from pillar to post to look for Luca. Please, Tito, you can do this. You uncovered a murderer for us once before. Finding a scene painter who's decided he needs a holiday should be child's play."

I hesitated. "Perhaps something's happened to Luca. He might be in a hospital, unable to tell anyone who he is."

Torani shook his head quickly. "Do give me some credit. That was one of the first things I checked. No, Luca's inconstant ways have made him forget he's a working man. You find him, and I'll make sure he never forgets again."

"Then why not send Aldo, Maestro? He knows Luca much better than I do."

Torani gave me a long look over the tips of his fingers, then said, "I've already quizzed Aldo. He knows nothing and is busy with his other duties. You are the one I want for this job. I trust you, Tito. We've weathered many storms here at the San Marco and you've always done everything I've asked of you. I know this is different than my usual requests, but finding Luca would be a great help to this theater. And to me personally."

I squirmed in my chair, remembering the vow I had made in my dressing room only minutes before. Tracking Luca down shouldn't be too difficult. The man was known for his artistic talents, not restraint in the face of Venice's many temptations. Balls, all-night gambling, rich food and drink, and the more private pleasures that could be found in dim *casini* all over the city: Luca had fallen victim to each of these on many occasions. I was sure to find him in one of his haunts, already regretting a two-day bout of Venetian excess and ready to return to his canvas.

"All right," I answered, only dimly aware of how easily I'd been herded to that decision. "I'll do as you ask, Maestro, but you'll have to see that I get out of rehearsal in good time. And I'll need Luca's address."

Torani's pinched face relaxed. He smiled and rubbed his hands like a hungry man about to carve a mouthwatering joint of beef. He hastened to give me the details he had gleaned about the last time Luca was seen. These were sparse in the extreme. A little after nine on the evening before last, Luca had given his assistants their leave and bidden them a cheery goodnight. They expected to see him the next morning at their usual time. A few minutes later, Aldo asked Luca to go have a drink with him, but the painter declined, saying he had a few more things to do. When Aldo returned to finish locking up, Luca was gone and hadn't been seen since.

"One more thing, Tito," the director said as he tore a scrap of paper from a sheet on his desk and wrote out Luca's address. "You must be discreet. Signor Carpani hasn't realized that the work on the sets has been delayed. I'm praying you can get Luca back to the theater before he finds out."

Chapter 3

Signor Carpani was annoyed. Not only had rehearsal started at quarter of eleven instead of half past ten, but Torani immediately undertook to drill Niccolo, our Neapolitan tenor, leaving the other singers free to lounge in the green room downstairs or watch Niccolo's struggles from the floor of the auditorium. Unfamiliar as he was with the often inscrutable workings of an opera company, Carpani raised an objection.

"Maestro, can't these other singers be given something to do?" The clerk's high, nasal voice carried from the floor of the auditorium up to the figures on the stage.

Torani turned and answered with a fixed smile, "Do, Signor Carpani? I don't understand. They are doing what they need to be doing."

"But they are wasting time. Signor Florio is holed up in his dressing room complaining of a headache. Signor Amato is sitting here with his feet up. And I have just come from downstairs. One of the women is knitting." He made this last observation in astonished tones more appropriate to announce that the bronze horses above the doors of the Basilica San Marco had jumped from their perch and were galloping around the Piazza.

"I suppose filing wills and court documents didn't prepare you for theater work." A pent-up sigh escaped the director's lips. "But you must understand, Signor Carpani, singers can't sing all day. Their throats won't take it. I'll get to the others in due time. Meanwhile they may study their music, learn Niccolo's aria along with him, or simply rest their voices."

Carpani harrumphed, and his shoulders gave a frustrated twist. He might have gone on, but Torani had already snapped his fingers and commanded Niccolo to "take it from the beginning, once more, *con molto spirito.*" As the tenor complied and filled the auditorium with a martial tune, the wiry black-clad clerk prowled back and forth with his hands behind his back. After a few minutes, he settled into a chair with a lap desk balanced on his knees and a pair of spectacles perched at the end of his long nose. Copious notes poured from his quill. I was glad he had chosen a seat far enough from mine to make conversation inconvenient.

Niccolo's aria was melodic and rousing, and the tenor managed to produce a few interesting embellishments, but my mind began to wander on the third run-through. I stretched my arms above my head, stifled a yawn, and looked around the opera house, my second home. Carpani and I were sitting on the floor of the auditorium, facing the stage. Its elegant proscenium arch was formed by double columns on each side and above by symmetrical swags of plasterwork which met at a huge cartouche bearing the lion of St. Mark. The orchestra pit, set slightly lower than the rest of the auditorium, curved out from the stage and was connected to it by a short flight of stairs at each end. The auditorium itself was embraced by a horseshoe of luxuriously appointed boxes rising tier upon tier. The wealthy aristocrats and merchants who engaged these boxes for the season gazed down on the stage and also had a bird's eye view of the populace who could afford only a *soldo* or two for their night at the opera. Those striving to sound elegant would use the French term and say that the poor watched the opera from the *parterre*, but most Venetians used the more descriptive word—the pit.

The theater had recently ordered benches so the rabble could sit rather than stand or mill about. Backless and roughly made, the benches had been designed to be moved aside for cleaning. That morning they were stacked against the walls; Carpani and

I had settled in comfortable chairs borrowed from an unlocked box.

During performances, I'd learned to keep a sharp eye on the pit. Especially the gondoliers. No one enjoyed the opera as enthusiastically as Venice's boatmen. They didn't simply listen; they strained forward, swaying to the tune and drinking the music in with every pore. If they were pleased, applause was nothing. They stomped, yelled, and demanded endless encores. But if we failed to entertain, out came the hard candle stubs and soft tomatoes. Even the most talented singers among us soon grew adept at ducking.

Of course, in song as in dining, one man's meat is another man's poison, so it was inevitable that fistfights between the supporters of rival singers would break out. Then the beautifully dressed aristocrats would show their true colors. With card games and intimate suppers abandoned, hisses and catcalls would spill out of the boxes. One great lady had even been known to overturn her chamber pot on the brawlers in the pit.

I turned my attention back to the stage. After some work on his intonation, Niccolo finally managed to produce a rendition of the aria that satisfied Maestro Torani. The director released him and announced a scene from Act One. That was my call. I left Signor Carpani to his notes and ducked under the Doge's box and through a door that led backstage. The scene we were to rehearse took place in Caesar's encampment. A military tent of yellow and blue striped silk was planned for upper stage right. For now, the stagehands were positioning a pair of benches to denote its place. A row of officer's tents that was supposed to stretch into the distance on the backdrop existed only in the mind of the missing Luca Cavalieri.

As I came through the wings, Florio approached from the back corridor. He was flanked by his manservant and his manager, Ivo Peschi. Ivo looked after the star's travel arrangements and business interests. He was a middle-aged man with a blue-gray wig that stood up like a brush and ended in a rat's tail tied with a limp bow. His creased face wore a frown. Florio's valet, a wispy fellow with a perpetually hangdog appearance, carried Caesar's battle helmet as if it were a tureen of hot soup. Except for the colors of the plumes, the helmet was a duplicate of the one Benito had deposited in my dressing room earlier that morning. I sighed. Something told me that not much singing would be accomplished in what was left of the morning.

Florio and I came out of the shadowed wings and stepped into the glow of the footlamps at the same time. Torani, manfully trying to ignore the obvious, was ready with stage directions.

"Ah, Signor Florio, if you would be so good. As the curtain rises, Caesar stands before the entrance of his tent. In a short recitative, he voices his suspicions of Ptolemy's scheming character, then sings his aria vowing to frustrate the prince's evil designs." Torani indicated Florio's mark with a determined smile, but the singer didn't budge.

A flurry of low, excited whispers swirled behind me. In the wings opposite, workmen laid down their tools and moved closer to the stage. The old theater hands could smell a scene brewing and didn't want to miss any of the action.

Florio wore a coat of plum-colored taffeta. Though the day was not particularly cool, he had wrapped a long scarf of yellow silk several times around his throat. As usual, he stood with one foot turned out to show off a muscular calf encased in an immaculate white stocking. All eyes were on his colorful figure as he faced Torani's wilting smile.

"The aria will have to wait, Maestro."

"Wait? But our rehearsal schedule is particularly tight today." Torani's smile disappeared completely.

"I have discovered an unfortunate matter which requires immediate attention." Florio indicated the plumed confection in his valet's hands. "My man tells me that Caesar and Ptolemy's battle helmets are virtually identical."

"Are they now?" Torani said slowly, before turning to me with an apologetic look. "Could we have a look at yours, Tito?"

Someone must have alerted Benito. He was already bringing my headgear onto the stage.

"Look, Signor Florio, the colors are different. The helmets match your costumes. The audience will have no difficulty in telling your characters apart," Torani observed.

"That is not the issue. Ivo?" Florio sniffed delicately and took out a handkerchief that he waved toward his manager before pressing the linen square to his temple.

Ivo Peschi launched into a diatribe more worthy of a court advocate than a singer's nursemaid. "I have Il Florino's contract here," he said, unfolding a bulky sheaf of paper that he had been harboring in an inside pocket. "It clearly states that his 'helmets, swords, and similar accoutrements will not be eclipsed in majesty or dignity by those of any other player.'"

Torani nodded as the recitation of clauses and stipulations droned on. Finally, the manager stopped to draw a breath.

"Well, what would you like me to do, Signore?" Torani addressed the singer.

Florio measured my height with his gaze, then came to stand right in front of me. He put his hand flat to the top of his head and kept it level as he moved it toward mine. His bejeweled fingers stopped in the middle of my forehead. "You are at least two inches taller than I am," he said accusingly. Then to Torani, "I'll need five or six inches added to my helmet. More plumes, taller plumes. Blue ones, I think. Blue always shows up well under the lamps."

Torani's face was turning red, but he kept his voice even. "Certainly. We'll just order another one. There's still plenty of time. Shouldn't be too difficult. Now, let's get back..."

A shrill voice interrupted. "No, Maestro, absolutely not. Those helmets have been bought and paid for. They cost four ducats each." Signor Carpani ascended to the stage, shaking his finger at Torani like a nursemaid admonishing a naughty child. "Further expenditure is out of the question."

Florio whirled furiously. "What? Is my contract not to be honored? Am I to be treated like some unknown, some unknown..." He flapped his handkerchief uncertainly, then caught sight of Niccolo. "Like some unknown *tenor*?"

"There is no money in the budget for further costuming. The helmet will have to be worn as is, by Signor Florio or someone else," Carpani replied firmly.

The singer's jaw dropped. "I was employed to bring the highest level of distinction to this production. The Savio assured me that only an artist of my caliber could make this opera an occasion fit for the marriage of the Doge's daughter. Are you telling me my services are no longer required?"

Carpani shrugged, Torani mopped his perspiring brow, and Ivo Peschi shuffled papers. The wings and the catwalks above were filled with stage crew regarding the impasse with mounting excitement. Then, there came a shifting movement in a group upstage and a slender, skirted figure pushed through the workmen. I recognized Liya Del'Vecchio, a daughter of the Jewish family that crafted headdresses and masks for several theaters in the city.

Many of my countrymen favored a singularly Venetian type of beauty: dainty features, hair bleached to a red-gold, form sleek and plump as a sparrow, manner demure yet accommodating. There was something in that, but Liya, with her exotic looks and forthright demeanor, attracted me more than any other woman I'd met at the theater. Or anywhere else, for that matter. It didn't hurt that the Jewess displayed a fertile intelligence behind her quick tongue—I found women who offered only flirtation and gossip as tedious as a concert on a poorly tuned violin. To my sorrow, I had to admit that Liya had never been particularly attentive to me, but nevertheless I had always followed her doings with the greatest interest. What was she up to now?

Seemingly calm and unaffected by the tense atmosphere and numerous pairs of staring eyes, Liya crossed the wide stage. Her dress was drab and utilitarian, but her fine dark hair was done up in plaits wound with a red scarf and held in place by an array of gold pins. The striding heels of her neat boots resounded through the silent theater. She ignored Florio, spared a brief glance for the feathered helmet in his manservant's arms, then greeted Torani with a graceful nod. Before taking my helmet from Benito, her expressive black eyes sent my valet a decidedly irritated look.

"There's no need to order a new helmet, Maestro. I can make an adjustment to Signor Amato's," she said, carrying my helmet over to Torani. "You see where these ostrich plumes are tacked down. I can remove the feathers and replace them with a row of dyed horsehair. That would remove about six inches of height from Ptolemy's helmet and make Caesar's appear taller by comparison."

"Horsehair?" I spoke for the first time. Horsehair was a poor material for a principal singer. The trainbearers and spear carriers had to make do with those common bristles, but must I? Had my value sunk that low?

"Yes. We have some back at the shop. I'll bleach the hair and get a sample of your costume fabric from Madame Dumas. After it's dyed, the crest of horsehair will match your costume and stand up about so." She ran her hand over the top of the helmet. "I can make it look right."

I was seething. I kept telling myself that it was only a helmet and it shouldn't matter so much, but it did. Florio already had the lion's share of the crowd-pleasing arias and I had been left with precious little music that would stir the gondoliers and their followers. Did the expensive star have to upstage my wardrobe as well? I realized that my answer lay in the question itself. Too many ducats had been spent to bring Florio to Venice and too many people were anticipating his performance for me to imagine that his contract stipulations would be ignored. If Torani did not indulge Florio's vanity, then Ministro Morelli or his superior, the Savio, would find a director who would. I swallowed hard. I saw I would have to accept the change, but nothing could make me like it.

Carpani adjusted his spectacles and inspected the helmet as if he had just been appointed Savio in charge of millinery. "You won't be paid any more," he cautioned the seamstress. "In fact, since you are replacing valuable ostrich plumes with an inferior material, the theater should request a partial refund."

"The replacement will involve a good deal of labor." The girl spoke as firmly to Carpani as the clerk had to Florio. "My mother and I can ill afford the time. We have a large order of masks to finish for the new comedy at the Teatro Sant'Angelo." Carpani frowned as the girl went on. "But because this theater has been such a loyal customer, we will undertake the job at no extra charge."

Torani spread his hands in a conciliatory gesture. "Surely, Signorina Del'Vecchio presents the perfect solution. Let's have her take this cursed helmet back to her shop and get on with rehearsal."

Carpani handed her the helmet with a sharp nod. As he passed in front of me on the way back to his notebook, he muttered under his breath. Several phrases carried: "What can you expect if you deal with Jews? Cut-throat dogs the lot of them."

"Signor Florio?" Torani asked with a tentative smile. "Will these arrangements be suitable?"

The haughty *castrato* glanced at his manager, who still clutched the thick contract in his sinewy hands. After receiving a judicious nod, Florio acquiesced with surprising cheerfulness and moved to his rehearsal mark as if nothing remotely unpleasant had just occurred. It was as if he had been playing the scene for dramatic effect, just a bit of fun to enliven an otherwise boring rehearsal.

"Tito?" At least Torani had the grace to ask my permission, even if the alteration was a foregone conclusion. I agreed with a great show of amiability, sternly reminding myself that one costume was not worth getting upset about. After all, I had other things to think about. I had a wandering painter to find.

Chapter 4

True to his word, Torani released me with plenty of time left in the day to search for Luca Cavalieri. The theater sat at the confluence of two narrow canals, midway between the Piazza and the Rialto. Of all the open spaces in the city, only the vast square before the glittering, domed Basilica and its soaring bell tower enjoyed the designation of Piazza. Any other square, no matter how many homes and shops might enclose it or how grand a church might adorn it, was only a *campo*. Along with the Doge's palace and the Senate's headquarters, the Piazza San Marco boasted a number of cafes and taverns, but I remembered Luca mentioning a favorite drinking spot in the warren of alleys and *campi* that made up the commercial district of the Rialto.

I went out by the stage door and turned left toward the marketplace to look for the tavern called The Four Winds. After enduring several weeks of cool, rainy days, the populace welcomed the sun with buoyant spirits. The porters and messengers who haunted gondola landings hoping to pick up a bit of work had rolled up their sleeves and lounged against bridge railings with their faces turned up to the clear, azure sky. Gondoliers without fares sang snatches of tunes or bantered with water girls who passed by swinging their hips, shouldering wooden yokes with copper buckets suspended from each end. All along the narrow walkway by the canal, people loitered in shop doorways, too infatuated with the gentle sun and the warm, southern breeze to go inside and see to their work.

Presently, the pavement dumped me onto a broad *campo* with an ornately sculpted well at one end. The water girls clustered around its steps, drawing up bucket after slopping bucket. As an island surrounded by the undrinkable salt water of the lagoon, Venice relies on these public wells for its cooking and drinking water. The incomparably pure, sweet water is a gift of the sky and untouched by human hands. It comes from rain that falls into grills set in the paving stones and filters through a bed of sand into the deep, cool cisterns that underlie every *campo*. Throwing refuse into a well is punished as a major crime; even habitually neglecting to replace the wooden cover can earn someone a hefty fine. Every *campo* has a troupe of girls who earn their bread by delivering their liquid cargo to neighboring houses and shops. Four *lire* buys a daily supply of water for the month and releases a housewife, or her maid, from the never-ending chore of water hauling.

Expecting to find The Four Winds on the opposite side of the *campo*, I skirted around the water carriers, likewise the woodmen offering bundles of kindling for stove fuel. Halfway across, a crowd gathering before the church steps blocked my way. A mustachioed man in a coat of balding purple velvet was clambering onto an upended barrel with the help of several women. The speaker was short, potbellied, and totally unprepossessing, but his voice had a commanding ring.

"Come one, come all," he shouted from his makeshift rostrum. "Prepare to be amazed. See the marvel that has thrilled princes and sovereigns throughout the length and breadth of Italy."

The showman had the swarthy complexion and jet black hair of a Sicilian but spoke in the Venetian dialect. He had chosen his place with care. The wide arch of the church's paneled doors provided an impressive backdrop, and a shaft of sunlight threw his dramatic gestures into full illumination. By contrast, most of his onlookers stood in the shadow of a tall building to the left of the church. I had no time for this mountebank, but the swelling crowd herded me inexorably toward him. I ended up in a raised doorway with a good view of the speaker, but on the opposite side of the square from where I wanted to be.

Glancing around the *campo*, I saw only one person who was familiar to me. On the fringe at the other side of the crowd stood a tall Englishman I had met at one of Count Monteverde's tedious dinners. The man's name escaped me, but I couldn't fail to remember his face. His open, good-natured countenance under a shock of untidily arranged blond hair had made a sharp contrast to the elaborate curls and weary, dissipated features of the other guests at table that afternoon.

The showman was exhibiting a white dove, holding the bird aloft on an uplifted wrist. At a chirp from a tin whistle, the dove flew in an arc just over the heads of the crowd and landed on his opposite wrist. Two chirps and the dove reversed the procedure. The crowd watched intently, but I suspected that the bird would have to demonstrate fancier tricks than this to hold their interest. The showman did not disappoint. In eloquent phrases, he described his feathered companion's chief talent: fortune telling. Despite my errand, I was intrigued. I didn't believe his spiel for a minute, but I was curious to see how he was going to convince the onlookers to part with their hard-earned money.

With the dove on his shoulder, the man held up a ring the size of a dinner plate with a flat disk inside. The disk was rigged so that a tap from the bird's beak would make it spin. One side was white, the other black. This was the meat of the routine: for one *soldo*, anyone could ask the bird a question that would be answered by a spin of the disk. If the disk came to rest on the white side, the answer was *yes*. Black signified *no*.

A man immediately stepped forward to test the bird's skill. I thought his southern face very like the showman's, only thinner and younger. A brother, or perhaps a son? He tossed a coin in a basket held by one of the women. "Is my name Giovanni Goretti?" he asked with a wide grin. When the disk came up black, he registered a look of studied astonishment. "What a marvelous thing. The bird knew I was trying to trick him. Goretti is my cousin; I am Pietro Batista."

People nudged each other and muttered excitedly. No matter what common sense must be telling them, most of the crowd appeared ready to believe that this ordinary bird could answer their heartfelt questions. Was it the appeal of a tantalizing mystery that promised to enliven a humdrum day? Or perhaps an ancient, primitive way of thinking that we're all prey to given the right circumstances? I didn't have the answers, but there was no doubt in my mind that the showman was manipulating the crowd as surely as he did his trained bird.

A careworn woman lugging a bundled infant could hardly wait to add her coin to the basket. "My baby has an ailing chest. He coughs all the time. Will he get well?" She had to raise her voice and repeat her question over the cries of "poverino" and "Dio santo" from the sympathetic crowd. The bird man held up his hand for quiet and twisted his head to give the dove a questioning look. Apparently satisfied that the bird understood the question, he lifted the ring to shoulder level. The dove's sleek, snowy neck stretched out to give the disk a sharp peck. The disk was a blur of gray as it spun, but the mother's anxious face broke into a smile as it came to rest white side forward. Wild applause and whistles of admiration broke out. The showman had his audience in the palm of his hand.

I glanced at the big Englishman across the square. Somehow I thought a member of his stolid race would be immune to such foolery, but he was applauding as loudly as the credulous Venetians.

Something else caught my eye. The man who had asked the first question was weaving in and out of the thickest part of the crowd. A knot of dandies in silk coats and gold-trimmed hats pushed one of their number forward to ask a question, and the prowling rogue pressed himself into their midst. Laughing, the chosen fop rolled his eyes to let his friends know that the game was beneath him and drawled toward the dove, "Master Fowl, will I find luck at the faro table tonight?" When the disk turned up black, he shook his fist at the bird in a gesture of mock revenge.

The crowd roared. Many hands competed to offer coins, and people in the rear shoved to the front so they could take a turn. No one paid any attention to the arm that was diving in and out of pockets like a slippery eel. I grunted in realization. So this was the real game. The fortune telling dove was just a bit of side business to draw a crowd and keep them amused so the showman's confederate could separate Venetians from their pocket money.

Remembering my original reason for visiting the *campo*, I stepped off the doorway stoop and began to shoulder my way through the crowd. People pushed back with groans and curses, but I was determined to get to the tavern. After throwing a few rough elbows, I made it to the fringe on the other side just as the pilfering henchman made a dive for the Englishman's pocket. The rogue had a quick arm, but my arm was longer.

"No, you don't," I shouted as I grabbed his wrist and shook it to make him drop the purse of clinking coins.

His quarry wheeled around with a bewildered look but had the dexterity to catch his purse before it hit the ground. The pickpocket bent to my restraining hand and gave my thumb a vicious bite. Dropping his wrist with a squeal of pain, I unwillingly allowed the rogue to disappear into the dense mob before either of us could lay another hand on him.

As we put a few paces between ourselves and the crowd that was still enthralled with the magical bird, the Englishman hastened to wrap his handkerchief around my bleeding thumb. "I say, that's a nasty bite. We must get it seen to."

"Take no heed of it. It will be all right. At least the villain didn't get your money."

"Precious little he would find in my purse." The blond haystack shook as he laughed, then eyes of the clearest blue gave my face a second look. "I know you, you're Tito Amato, that singing fellow. We met at the house of that disgusting Count. And I went to see you at the opera last month. Damn fine show. I don't know how you do it. Doesn't your throat get tired singing all those notes?"

"I manage." His laugh was infectious and I found myself chuckling, too. "You must be more careful. There are many in Venice who live by duping the unwary, especially foreigners."

"Yes." He sighed. "I should know better by now. Since my arrival, I've sprung several traps baited for fools. Your Count of Monteverde set one for me."

"Don't call him my Count. I barely know him and have no intention of extending our acquaintance. What happened?"

"In short, the man is a scoundrel. He cheats his own guests at the card table. After losing forty *zecchini* I could ill afford, I saw what he was up to and threw the cards in his face. He ran for his sword, shouting a hundred dire threats, but one of his friends held him around the waist so I could get out of the house."

"Fortunate for you. He is known as an accomplished swordsman."

His blue eyes twinkled. "I don't credit fortune for my escape. The Count had no intention of fighting. If he has a reputation, it must have been made in his youth. Now, he's much too proud of his handsome cheeks to risk a scar."

With a formal bow, I said, "As a citizen of the Republic, I offer my apologics for any Venetian vices you have encountered. Please believe that we are not all thieves, Signor..." I faltered for a moment. "Pray forgive me, I have forgotten your name."

"Augustus Rumbolt, at your service." He pumped my arm in the English fashion and clapped a meaty hand on my shoulder. "But you must call me Gussie. All my friends do."

The Englishman with the funny name insisted on buying me a glass of wine, but first he jerked his head toward the disreputable showman. "Shouldn't we do something to break that up?"

"He won't last long. I don't imagine he obtained a license for his charade." Even as I spoke, the church doors parted and the mountebank turned with a startled look on his dark face. "See, the noise has drawn the attention of the priests. They will soon shut him down."

My new friend steered me toward the nearest tavern. Its painted sign depicted Aeolus blowing spiraling gusts of wind to the four points of the compass. I had found Luca's favorite haunt. Tucked between an apothecary shop and a draper's, it was better than most others in appearance and social degree. The tavern keeper, a sharp-eyed fellow clad in bright yellow breeches, stood outside his door watching the priests reprimand the crowd for letting themselves be taken in by humbug.

The barman stood aside to let us pass. When he noticed the bloody cloth wrapped around my hand, the worthy man insisted on seating us at a table and fetching a balm and clean cloth to dress my wound. I took the opportunity to inquire about the theater's missing painter.

"Luca Cavalieri? He's in here almost every day," the tavern keeper answered. "Where's he been?"

"That is what everyone at the theater is asking. Luca didn't report for work yesterday. Or this morning, either. When did you last see him?"

"Must have been day before yesterday. Yes, I believe it was." He scratched his stubbled chin. "Luca had his dinner here. He ordered a roast capon."

"Did he dine alone?"

"Yes."

"Do you know any particular friends of his who might know where he's gone?"

At Gussie's nod, the barman refilled our glasses and stood pulling a napkin through his hands in a thoughtful manner. Finally, he said, "Luca seems to know a lot of people. He always has a good word for everyone. But the only ones I see him in serious conversation with are other theater folk. You must know them. One is called Aldo."

I nodded. "Anyone else?"

"Luca occasionally drinks with a wellborn gentleman. Don't recall ever hearing his name."

"A patrician?"

"Acts like one." He sniffed. "Won't sit in my chair without wiping the seat with his handkerchief. Always wrinkles his nose like he smells burnt cabbage."

His apt description brought only one individual to mind: Signor Morelli, the Ministro charged with squeezing a profit out of the theater. That fastidious nobleman seemed an unlikely drinking companion for the free-living scene painter.

After the tavern keeper left us to attend to other customers, Gussie questioned me about my small mystery. Notwithstanding his peculiar accent, the Englishman spoke excellent schoolbook Italian. If he failed to comprehend a term exclusive to Venice, I was able to supply the meaning from the language of the mainland or from my meager stock of English. So, with just a few linguistic fits and starts, I explained the mission that Torani had placed on my shoulders. Gussie was immediately intrigued.

"Sounds a deuce more interesting than what I usually do," he said.

"And what is that?"

He wrinkled his brow. "Wander around mostly. I found a café that knows how to cook a good English breakfast, so I go there every morning. Then I take a gondola to see some paintings or a church that someone has recommended. Sometimes I have an invitation to dine. If not, no matter." He grinned and patted his sturdy midsection. "I could stand to lose a stone or two."

"Then, you are making what your countrymen call 'the grand tour.'"

"Well, I was. I seem to have gotten stuck."

I cocked an inquiring eyebrow. At first glance, Gussie Rumbolt had seemed a typical English tourist, the sort of young man who was perpetually prepared to jump on a horse and gallop over his father's fields in pursuit of some unfortunate species of wildlife. But as he told me over another glass of wine, "That's my brother Gerald. I'm the one my family has always despaired of. While Gerald was out with the dogs or down at the stables, I was in the library poring over Father's moldy art books or piddling around with a daub of my own."

"You paint?" I was unprepared for the discomforting shift in mood that my simple question produced.

"I did," he answered in a voice heavy with bitterness. "Father made me give it up before I went up to Cambridge. When I stopped here in Venice, I thought I might get some canvas and oils and give it another try, but..." He shook his head.

"I have no right to ask, but you will find I seldom let that stop me. Why haven't you taken up your brushes again?"

"Sheer cowardice." He sighed. "I'm surrounded by inspiration, but the competition is daunting. Everywhere my eyes light, from the walls of the great houses to the stage of your theater, there are beautiful paintings. Work that I could never aspire to."

I nodded, reminded of my own situation. The challenge of singing on the same stage as the famous Francesco Florio had rekindled the burning ambition of my student days, but not before I had wallowed in a fortnight's worth of paralyzing self-doubt. I had the idea that Gussie might uncover his own burning embers once he became accustomed to the engulfing beauty that is Venice.

We drank in silence for a few moments. The Englishman's smile had vanished; he appeared lost in thought. The interior of the tavern was warm, and the soothing murmur of nearby conversations lulled me into a drowsy state. To forestall a yawn, I asked, "How long have you been in Venice?"

"Three months. Father died last year while I was away at school. The estate was entailed, so Gerald inherited everything. He and my mother expected me to start a career in law. When I refused, they started pushing the church. I think they were surprised when I completely stubbed up on them." A playful smile returned to his lips. "To get me out of the way for a while, Mother induced Gerald to send me around Europe. They arranged for my old tutor to travel with me and gave him instructions to lecture me on my familial duty at every turn. For weeks, I viewed the sights of Paris and the ancient ruins of Rome with his dull voice droning in my ear, draining the joy out of every excursion. Then fate took me in hand."

"How was that?"

"About the time we landed in Venice, my father's oldest sister followed him to the grave. Aunt Maud was a widow, well provided for, and childless. She did not forget her favorite nephew in her bequests." He wiggled his eyebrows over a grin. "When I realized that my good aunt had left me an income sufficient to live in Venice with a modest degree of dignity, I sent my tutor packing. If I spend carefully and do without a servant, I can stay here as long as I like."

I smiled, now fully alert and conscious that the afternoon was wearing on. As pleasant as the Englishman's conversation was, I needed to continue on to Luca's rooms. But before I could take my leave, Gussie continued, "At first being on my own was a great adventure, but lately I've lacked good company and the days have become... well, rather boring."

I looked into his candid blue eyes and made an impromptu decision that I have never had cause to regret. After months of fawning attention from what *my* favorite aunt would have called "dubious company," this cheerful, well-scrubbed, pink-cheeked Englishman was just the sort of companion I needed. "Why don't you come with me to the painter's lodging?" I asked. "We can have a little fun solving Torani's mystery."

Chapter 5

The address that Torani had given me was in one of Venice's more expensive neighborhoods. When our gondola stopped at a flight of well-scrubbed stone steps, several porters sprang to steady the boat so Gussie and I could alight. Their frowns told me they expected this small favor to garner more than the paltry coins I tossed their way. I asked myself how Luca could afford to live in this quarter. Did he have a wealthy patron I had never heard about? Or had he managed to find a distressed widow forced to split her once fine house into apartments to survive?

My second guess struck closer to the mark. A few steps down a nearby *calle* brought us to a peaceful square. Late afternoon sun warmed a central well, concentric circles of paving stones, and house fronts of pale yellow stucco. As Gussie and I searched for the right number, a row of pigeons on a balcony railing furnished the only onlookers. Luca's house turned out to be the neglected stepchild of this neatly kept *campo*. It was a weather-stained, three-story structure with cracked windows and sagging shutters as its only external ornament. I pulled the fraying bell cord.

After a decent interval, I gave a stronger pull.

A female squawk echoed the bells' last jangle. The shuffle of slippered feet approached the door at a snail's pace. At last, we beheld a bent woman with wispy gray hair surrounding her head like a halo of smoke. One eye was nearly shut; the other fixed us with a clouded pupil.

"Eh? Who are you and what do you want?" Her head bobbed from side to side.

"We are looking for Luca Cavalieri," I answered. "Does he live here?"

"I don't want any. Go away and leave a body in peace."

The old woman shuffled back. The door swung toward us. After trading wide-eyed looks, Gussie shot a flat hand against the stout wood and I fumbled for my purse. A few silver coins gained our admittance to a dingy corridor that must have led straight through to the kitchen. The unmistakable smell of over-boiled liver thickened the air. Hangings of dusty fabric concealed doorways leading off the corridor. Halfway to the kitchen, an uncarpeted staircase rose to an empty landing, made a square turn, and continued at a steep angle.

With considerable difficulty, and the transfer of several more coins, we learned the details of the household. We were in the residence of a vineyard owner who preferred to live on his mainland estate and traveled to the city only for occasional business. Our nearly blind and deaf hostess was an old family nurse who'd been lodged in the town house to serve as house-keeper and watchman. It was probably just as well that she couldn't hear Gussie's quaking chuckles when she gave herself that last designation.

We convinced her we were friends of Luca—a practical approach that fell just within the bounds of truth. Our mission was not unfriendly; we definitely had his best interests at heart. Torani would not be able to cover up the painter's absence much longer. Luca might be the best scenic artist in Venice, but if Morelli discovered he'd been shirking his duties, he'd never work in a Venetian theater again.

"Does Signor Cavaliere keep rooms here?" I asked, just a whisker below a shout.

"*Si*, the master rents out the top floor. He says it pays to keep a tenant around. Your friend has been here about a year."

"Is Luca at home now?"

"Don't ask me. He has his own keys and comes and goes as he pleases. I couldn't keep up with that young buck if I tried."

"When did you last see him?"

She shrugged, working toothless gums. "Not today. Not yesterday. Must have been the day before. Yes, it was marketing day. Signor Cavaliere helped me carry my baskets. He does that if he sees me going out. Nice young fellow, even if his paints do stink up the second floor."

When I explained the urgency of our mission, she offered to climb the stairs and let us into Luca's rooms. She seemed relieved when I assured her we could manage by ourselves.

Key in hand, I led the way up two flights and unlocked the door of a large, L-shaped apartment that doubled as studio and living quarters. One end was arranged as a sitting room with a faded Turkey carpet and a few pieces of shabby furniture. The larger space was hung with numerous unframed views of canals and buildings and contained the typical artist's paraphernalia. Light from a long double window fell on lightly dusted surfaces. If the windows had been open, Luca's studio would have been pleasantly airy. As it was, a mixture of pent-up odors hung like an invisible fog: wood smoke, unwashed chamber pot, and an unrecognizable spicy fragrance that competed with the expected paint and turpentine smells.

"What are we looking for?" Gussie asked, eyes roving the simply furnished apartment.

"I'm not sure. Anything amiss, I suppose."

Gussie moved to open a tall wardrobe while I approached an easel that held a cloth-covered canvas. The easel looked down on a low couch overspread with jumbled bedclothes and pillows. Near at hand, an artist's palette dotted with dabs of paint leaned against a jar of turpentine bristling with brushes and paint knives shaped like miniature trowels. A faded blue smock smudged with a rainbow of hues hung from a peg.

I poked at the colorful blobs ringing the palette. Their crusted skins yielded to my forefinger. "Look, Gussie, these paints are still soft. Luca must have been using them recently."

My friend came over to study the palette and the soaking brushes. "Maybe. It's hard to say. Oils can take days to dry out, especially in thick blobs like these. Let's see what the painting can tell us."

He threw the cloth off the rectangular canvas, and we stared at Luca's work for a few seconds of stupefied silence. Finally, Gussie gave a low whistle and said, "I'd like to know where this fellow hired his model."

"I recognize her. She's not a professional model. She's a seamstress who makes costume pieces for the theater. Her name is Liya Del'Vecchio."

"A most attractive woman, painted in loving detail."

"Yes," I answered absently, absorbed by the striking depiction in front of me. The woman I had admired in the heavy skirts and modest bodices of a working seamstress sprawled across Luca's canvas in a state of exuberant undress.

Liya lay on her stomach, left leg hanging off the low couch so that the tip of one pink toe barely touched the floor. The twisted sheets angled across her arched back leaving her smooth, rounded bottom as the focal point of the painting. Her chin rested on her raised left hand. With head slightly turned, she gazed out from the painting with a mischievous, challenging look. The braids piled on top of her head struck an incongruously formal note in this riot of dishabille.

I shook my head slowly. I didn't like the sensation that was rising from my gorge. "I had no idea that Luca and Liya were on these terms," I muttered.

Gussie gave me a sharp look. "You know her well?"

I affected an indifferent tone. "No, not really. She's a Jew. Her family has a workshop in the ghetto. A young man usually comes to the theater with her, some brother or cousin I think."

Using two fingers, Gussie patted around the edges of the canvas, then bent close to take a long whiff. "It's not totally dry. He's been working on the background bits, but not for four or five days I'd say."

As Gussie replaced the cloth, I reluctantly tore my eyes away from the easel to examine the cupboards that lined the lower walls of the studio. Glass phials of oily liquids, tin boxes filled with powders, and twists of paper from a chemist's shop stacked the shelves in chaotic profusion. Most were unmarked, but one ceramic pot was labeled *dragon gum* in faded ink. It contained yellowish granules but gave no clue to their intended use. On top of the cupboard stood a mortar and pestle that contained remnants of reddish-brown powder.

I questioned Gussie. "Are all these substances used to make paint?"

The big Englishman rummaged through Luca's stock of materials. "Most serious artists grind their own pigments, and I do recognize some of these." He rubbed the powder from the mortar between thumb and forefinger. "I'd wager this is cinnabar. It makes a lovely scarlet. But most of these have me stumped."

We explored further. A trunk with a coverlet thrown across it held a number of books on magical lore and occult sciences. I reached for the largest volume and carried it to the long windows. "*The Keys of Solomon*," I read from the gilt letters stamped on its worn leather cover. The book fell open to a page marked with a strip of torn paper. The wording of the passage was flowery and esoteric, but it seemed to be a treatise on how to conjure demons and spirits.

Gussie was flipping through another volume illustrated with pyramids of oriental symbols and fantastic figures labeled with Latin names. "Does the artist also fancy himself a magician?" he asked.

"Who knows? Luca has never mentioned anything of the kind within my hearing. At least he has enough sense to keep these books hidden. A person can get away with quite a bit in Venice, but the State Inquisitors take a dim view of alchemists and freethinkers."

We replaced the books and turned our attention to a chest of drawers. The first two contained a generous quantity of under-clothes, frayed neckbands, and stockings with darned toes and heels. These, together with the coats and breeches hanging in the wardrobe and the traveling cases stacked above, argued against Luca having set out on a planned journey.

I opened the last drawer to find a stack of curious scarves or kerchiefs. "What do you suppose these are?" I asked, handing one to Gussie.

The cloths were fashioned of delicate, age-mottled silk, a rich cream the color of old parchment. They were all rectangles of varying sizes. Hemmed along one long edge, the others lightly fringed, the largest couldn't have measured over fifteen by eighteen inches.

Gussie was holding his up to the window. "There's an image drawn or painted here, but I can't quite make it out."

I picked one out, held it at arm's length, and turned it this way and that. Suddenly, the mingled strokes of faded brown resolved into a recognizable pattern. "Don't look straight at it. Hold it like this, at an angle. See the swelling cheek and the flowing hair. It's the face of a woman."

"I see it now," Gussie cried. "She's done in profile, barely sketched in. Her eyes are closed. Here the lashes lay on her cheek. Are these tears?" He indicated russet flecks tracking down the curved cheek.

I shrugged and began to fold the cloths back into the drawer. Fighting mounting exasperation, I said, "This is all very interesting, but not likely to help us find Luca. What we need are letters, diaries, invitations. Anything that would tell us where he's been spending his time."

"With company like that," said Gussie, jerking his head toward the easel, "why would he want to spend time anywhere else?" The Englishman smiled as he handed me his cloth. On impulse, I slipped it into my waistcoat pocket.

The apartment had little else to tell us. I opened the windows and stepped onto a narrow balcony where a row of flowerpots filled with dirt awaited the blooming of spring flowers. Gussie found a few tradesmen's bills tucked under a blotter on the writing table, but no other personal papers. We both turned our noses up at a pot of mold-skimmed coffee sitting on the corner stove. Feeling a little foolish, like a couple of amateur spies playing at intrigue, we finally decided to give the puzzle of Luca's disappearance a rest and repair to my house for a much delayed dinner.

꼬뮤ꞷ ꬉ뮤ꞷ ꬉ뮤ꞷ

"So Luca has taken a fancy to a Jewess. Doesn't he care what people will say?" My sister Annetta toyed with her empty wine glass.

"Apparently he does. At the theater, I have seen him walk right by Liya without so much as a smile of recognition. I would never have guessed they were in the midst of an amorous dalliance." I poured more wine for Gussie. My sister shook her head as I stretched my arm toward her glass.

I'd invited Gussie home to dine, and we were still at table, picking at some fruit and cheese. The candles in their branched holders were burning low. Their flames illuminated my sister's soft brown eyes and coronet of chestnut hair. Her wide mouth had settled into an uncommonly relaxed smile. Gussie had tucked into her simple meal of risotto and grilled perch with a gusto that had charmed her almost as much as his ready smile and eager, often ingenuous, questions. My new friend showed particular interest in the customs of the city he had made his temporary home.

"What would people say if they knew Luca and Liya were romantically involved?" Gussie asked, nibbling at a cube of blue-veined cheese.

Annetta leaned forward, gripping the arms of her chair. "A Jewess from the ghetto and a Christian man? Such an outrageous relationship simply would not be tolerated. The Jewess' family would disown her in disgrace. Even if she turned her back on her religion and allowed herself to be baptized, the Christian's family would always look on the couple with scorn. Is it not the same in England?"

"I suppose so. I never really gave the matter much thought. I grew up on a manor in the Wiltshire countryside. The nearest Jew was probably in London, well over a hundred miles away."

"You see Jews everywhere in Venice. They live in the ghetto, but have the run of the city during the daylight hours," Annetta said as she cut off a handful of grapes. "One brought his barrow to our *campo* just this morning, crying for old rags to buy."

"Yes, I've seen them. Near the café where I breakfast, a bearded Jew sets up a cart to sell old pots and pans. He has a running war with some boys of that neighborhood. They keep trying to snatch his hat."

"That's a cruel game they are playing." I went on in response to Gussie's questioning look. "The red hat rule is strictly enforced. When venturing out of the ghetto, a Jewish man is required to wear a crimson hat. A woman must wear a red kerchief or scarf. If the *sbirri*, or the constables as you probably call them, catch a Jew without his identifying head cover, they can beat him and extract a heavy fine."

"I see. I'm beginning to understand why Luca's relationship with the lovely seamstress is so fraught with risk," said Gussie thoughtfully. "Are all the Jews of Venice poor?"

Annetta and I both laughed, but I answered. "Not at all. Despite the limiting regulations, there are many wealthy families in the ghetto. The trades allowed the Jews by law are restricted to moneylending, pawnbroking, and dealing in used and wholesale goods. But everyone knows that many of the maritime trading houses have their capital supplied by patricians who are only providing a legal front for Jewish investors."

"And yet, Liya delivers her wares to the theater. Is that not a retail business?"

This time Annetta answered Gussie's question. "Her family buys second-hand clothing. Not rags, but good quality items from Christians who are hard up for some ready cash. Most of the clothing they repair or sell as is. From the finery too tattered to repair, they snip off the intact trims and bits of good fabric and use them in masks and headdresses. In the strictest sense, the theaters are buying used goods."

"Are Christians allowed in this ghetto?"

"Of course," Annetta answered. "The economy of Venice would surely collapse if the ghetto were off limits. I can't think of a single person I know who hasn't gone in to pawn a cloak or some household item at one time or another." She shook her pile of chestnut braids and pointed to the candelabra. "When our father was alive, these candle holders spent more time in the pawnshop than on this table. Father always had notoriously bad luck at the gaming tables."

I sighed theatrically. "Sister, you are letting Gussie in on all our family secrets. What will this good Englishman think of us? I am sure the Rumbolts were never forced to pawn the family plate."

Gussie laughed uproariously at my weak sally, or perhaps at the very thought of the squire of Rumbolt manor hauling his valuables to a Jewish pawnshop. "Well," he finally said, "I'm sure you two have had your fill of this ignorant northerner. It's been a long day and I'm off to my lodging and a soft bed. Will you walk with me a bit, Tito?"

Annetta let us out the door with an open invitation for Gussie to dine whenever he liked, and we strolled across the Campo dei Polli and down the narrow *calle* that led to a gondola mooring. Dusk was well past and the moon had not yet risen. The only light filtered through the curtains and shutters of the houses that lined the way. I could barely see Gussie's face but I sensed his newly somber mood.

"Your city is most pleasing to the eye," he said, "but not so much to the heart."

"I would not attempt to argue with that. Venice has always been a city of contradictions, never more so than in these difficult times."

"Her glory years are fast retreating."

"True. We lost most of our eastern empire at the beginning of this century. It must have been a crushing blow at the time, but the defeat turned out to be of little consequence in the long run. The profitable trade continues to shift to the west, and the English and Dutch ships have always dominated those waterways. People no longer come to Venice to launch armies or conduct business. They come to be entertained."

"Or to escape," whispered my friend.

We walked on in silence for a moment, approaching the mist-laden canal. "You said you had been here three months," I observed. "You must have witnessed the last few weeks of Carnival."

"Oh, yes."

"Did you notice all the masks?"

"How could I miss them? Everyone went about in disguise, even if it was just a simple half-mask that covered the eyes and nose. I bought one myself."

"How did you feel when you first donned your mask?"

Despite the darkness, I knew he was grinning. "Liberated. Boundless," Gussie replied. "It was downright intoxicating."

"You are not alone in that. Disguise is a seductive lure, especially when it seems that everything you have learned to count on is fast disappearing. Venice herself wears a mask these days. If you stay here much longer you will find that nothing is truly as it seems."

"You make Venice sound like a dangerous place."

"She can be. My city dons a mask of grandeur and dances to a gay tune, but snatch her mask away and you will see fear and desperation."

"Does this melancholy line of thought have anything to do with your missing scene painter?"

"I sincerely hope not," I answered quickly. But once I had made plans for Gussie to attend rehearsal the next day and watched the Englishman's gondola slide into the mist, reason forced me to consider Luca's disappearance in a more sinister light than I had at first. Though it was really none of my business, I was decidedly unhappy with Luca's secret relationship with Liya. I had to wonder what other secrets lay behind Luca's mask of careless bonhomie and what difficulties they might have caused.

Chapter 6

The next morning I rose early, made a hasty breakfast of bread and fruit, and started off for the ghetto with my manservant Benito in tow. Luca's artful likeness of the Jewish seamstress had convinced me that the Del'Vecchio establishment was my best hope for obtaining information about the missing painter. I knew Maestro Torani would be expecting some news at rehearsal later that morning, and I was loath to disappoint him.

We didn't stop to hire a gondola; the ghetto lay only a few squares away from my house on the Campo dei Polli. Venice had gathered her Hebrew inhabitants onto several islets in the Cannaregio over two hundred years ago. The site was a former iron foundry, a *geto*, hence the current designation. Several thousand Jews lived behind the stout walls and were shut in by locked gates from sundown to sunup. During the night, two barges manned by archers of the Republic patrolled the canals ringing the walled enclave. My city looked on the Jews not only as foreigners inherently separate from the rest of Venetian society, but also as enemies of her devoutly held Catholic faith. Venice was also suspicious of any outsiders doing business within her territory. Even the Germans, Europeans and Christians all, had their trading activities confined to a compound on the Rialto.

Benito and I soon reached the wooden bridge on the east side of the ghetto. The massive gates had been thrown back and traffic over the bridge was brisk in both directions. We stepped aside to let several handcarts of caged geese trundle by.

"What do you want me to say to the Jewess, Master?" asked Benito, plucking at a snowy feather that had floated onto my sleeve.

"Just apologize. Beg her pardon for causing her extra work."

"But I was only looking after your interests. Signor Florio's costume should not be allowed to outshine yours."

"I know what you were trying to do, and I don't blame you. But I need to get into Liya's workroom. Your apology will be our entrée."

Benito's sharp features danced with curiosity. I forestalled his questions by darting through a break in the crush on the bridge. I crossed a noisy *campo*, then started down a twisting street just wide enough to accommodate two people passing sideways. The buildings around us reached toward the sky. Like trees enclosed in a narrow space, the ghetto dwellings had grown up rather than out. Layer had been added to layer in seemingly aimless fashion. Crooked foundations and oddly slanted rooflines were the order of the day. Above us, jutting balconies blocked the light and kept the walkway damp and musty. When we emerged onto a rambling, untidy square, I saw that Benito was pressing a perfumed handkerchief to his nose.

This brick-paved *campo* was lined with shops disgorging a profusion of goods from open doorways. A bustling crowd intent on morning errands swirled around us. This could have been any neighborhood in Venice—almost. Here the Venetian dialect was spiked with bits of Spanish, Hebrew, and other tongues unfamiliar to me. The expressions on the faces of the shoppers were more mobile, their eyes sharper, and their lips more generous. Bright colors accented the women's dresses, and many of them wore festoons of gold chains that I would never have seen on the neighbors in my own dull *campo*.

I hesitated uncertainly, looking for the Del'Vecchio shop. Benito pointed to another dark alley, really more of a tunnel formed by an addition spanning two tall buildings. One had been washed with a fresh coat of pink plaster, the other presented a less well-kept façade. At its entrance sat two young girls. They were surrounded by large baskets of clothing and had their heads bent to their laps. As we approached, I saw that one was ripping the seams of a damask garment and the other was repairing a cloak. Her needle flew down a seam, working the thread over and under the layers of thick wool. I reached for a handsome waistcoat hanging on a line tacked to the side of the building. The proprietor was instantly upon me.

"A wise choice. Signore shows good taste," said a stooped Jew with a rounded belly and fleshy jowls. He wore a black wig dressed with an oily pomade and a snuff-colored coat adorned with stamped gold buttons. Limp ruffles tickled his chin, and worsted stockings covered his lumpy calves. Officious to a fault, he brushed the hanging waistcoat with a short-handled broom, talking all the while. "An elegant garment, Signor. Fit for any occasion. Shall I wrap it up for you?"

"Is this the Del'Vecchio establishment?" I asked, ignoring the waistcoat.

"The very same," he answered, eyes suddenly wary. "I am Pincas Del'Vecchio and this is my shop. What can I interest you in? The weather is turning warm. Perhaps you have need of a taffeta coat that will withstand the summer heat?"

"No, no. I am not looking for something to wear. I came to speak with your daughter."

Giggles erupted from the girls at their mending. The look in the Jew's eyes turned from wary to puzzled.

"I am Tito Amato, from the Teatro San Marco. I wish to speak with Liya, the one who makes headdresses for the opera. Her workshop is here, is it not?"

The merchant knew who I was. On hearing my name, his eyes darted to my cheeks, my throat, then farther down. It is always so when someone realizes I am a *castrato*. The looks can vary from outright disgust to veiled admiration. The look Pincas gave me was of the curious variety, followed by a slight blush of his loose jowls.

"Is there some problem, Signor Amato?"

"Not at all. My servant wishes to apologize for misleading Liya on the requirements for one of my helmets. That is all."

As Pincas stood in the doorway, chewing at his lip, another face appeared over his shoulder. I recognized the hungry, hollow eyes, elongated jaw, and prominent teeth of the young man who usually accompanied Liya to the theater. He must have been listening from the dim interior of the shop.

"Cousin," he said near Pincas' ear, "I will convey the gentleman's apology upstairs."

Pincas started to smile, but I shook my head and attempted a stern expression. "My servant has overstepped his bounds. I am requiring him to make reparation with a formal apology. Please allow us to speak with your daughter."

The two clothing dealers passed a veiled look, still hesitating.

I reached out to finger the fine cloth of the waistcoat again. "And perhaps I could take a look at the other items you have within."

The young Jew scowled, but Pincas pasted his wide, seller's smile firmly in place and ushered me inside with a low bow. After the morning sun of the *campo*, it took my eyes a few moments to adjust to the gloomy interior. Shelves and counters were piled high with male and female attire. Dresses and coats hung suspended from wires that crisscrossed between the rafters. The small shop was neatly kept but pervaded by the heavy, sour odor of garments worn by a multitude of people and only superficially cleaned. Benito's handkerchief drifted toward his nose, but I pushed his arm down with what I hoped was an unobtrusive motion. I glanced back toward the sunlit doorway. One of the girls had left her mending and was peering around the doorframe with bright, curious eyes.

Pincas frowned, gently chucked the girl under the chin, then softened his expression with an apologetic smile. "Mara, the cloaks must be finished by dinner time. Get back to work with your sister." Leaving the surly cousin on duty below, the clothing dealer passed through a drapery at the rear of the shop and led Benito and me up a short flight of stairs. The slanted ceiling of the enclosed staircase was so low that I had to stoop as I climbed. The hallway upstairs was no taller. It stretched on toward another dark staircase, but we turned to our right to enter a room that seemed palatially spacious by comparison.

I straightened up and immediately met a pair of wide black eyes. We'd clearly taken Liya by surprise. She cocked her head in a questioning manner, running her hand through the fine curls of a tiny girl who clung to her skirts. The child wore a length of colored glass buttons that someone had fashioned into a necklace. She toddled forward a few steps and held out her arms. "Papa," she cried and was immediately scooped up in Pincas' arms.

An old woman occupied a low chair by one of the open casement windows. "Pincas," she chided in a croaking voice, "that child will be the death of us. She won't drink her milk and won't keep her hands out of the pin box. She is into everything."

The miscreant grinned at her father and gave his cheek a noisy kiss. "Ah, my wicked Fortunata," he said. "You must mind Nonna and Liya while Mama is at the market." He returned the child's kiss and smoothed her silken curls. "Where is your doll, my precious one?"

Liya tapped her foot. "Fortunata has thrown her doll out the window. That's the second time this morning."

Pincas puffed out his cheeks. Fortunata squealed with delight and beat her little fists on his swollen jowls, causing his breath to spurt out through pursed lips. Both father and daughter laughed uproariously.

"The doll, Papa." Liya sighed, irritation rising. "I won't be getting any work done until Fortunata has something to play with."

"Ah, yes." He kissed the girl in his arms. "Don't worry, little princess. We'll go down to the courtyard and rescue the fair dolly." The child clapped her hands. More kisses were exchanged. As they headed for the stairs, Pincas called back to Liya, "These gentlemen wish to say something to you, my dear. You know them, I believe."

Liya raised an eyebrow. Without prompting, Benito stepped forward and made his apology with all the grace and considerable charm of which he was capable.

"It's good of you to come up," she replied with a smile, "but you needn't have bothered. I often have to make changes in my creations, for a host of different reasons. So, as I'm working on a mask that must be finished before my mother returns…" She inclined her head toward the doorway.

I couldn't let her dismiss us so easily. Spying my helmet, now shorn of its plumes, on the wide worktable in front of the windows, I walked over and plucked it out from a tangle of ribbons and lace.

A note of irritation crept back into the seamstress' voice. "You can stop fretting over your headgear. You may have lost your feathers, but I'll make sure it is decorated with enough trim to satisfy even the most exalted prince."

I winced inwardly. Is that how she saw me? As vanity obsessed as Il Florino? I set the helmet down quickly. "I'm not concerned about that. While we're here, there is something else I need to ask you."

I looked around the airy workroom. The old woman had closed her eyes. A bit of forgotten piecework had fallen from her limp hands, and her chin had sunk to her chest. In the opposite corner, a trio of slat-backed chairs fenced an unlit stove.

"Perhaps we could sit?" I ventured.

"All right." Liya glanced toward the stove, but gestured to the nearest window instead. "Here. Papa may need me to point out Fortunata's doll."

Benito retreated to the doorway. He affected an air of unconcern, but I knew his ears would be prickling. Liya and I settled ourselves on the wide windowsill, knees almost touching. The sun had risen high over the ghetto buildings and fell directly on the woman who sat so near but seemed determined to distance herself with an air of dignified reserve.

She wore a gown of dusky blue with the sleeves pushed up above the elbows. A light apron wrapped her bodice and covered the front of her skirt. Her back was straight, pressing against the window frame as she looked down to the courtyard behind the shop. A healthy glow suffused her finely textured olive skin, and the sunlight caught highlights in the thick braids entwining her head.

I cleared my throat, and her dark eyes turned to meet mine with a hint of amusement that recalled her expression in Luca's painting. I cursed myself for not planning what to say. Suddenly, the alluring portrait on Luca's easel was the only thought in my head.

"Look, there's Papa." Liya waved and pointed. "He won't be able to reach the doll unless he climbs. He should have sent Isacco."

"Isacco?" I asked, glad for the distraction.

"The son of Papa's cousin in Livorno. Papa produced a family of women, but his cousin's family has sons to spare." Her well-formed mouth worked itself into a sneer. "Papa imported one of them to help with the shop."

"A reasonable solution, surely?"

The black eyes flashed, no longer amused. "Papa has good help right here. I am capable of much more than piecing these scraps together. I could help Papa run the business."

"But daughters usually marry away. Where would that leave your father if you went off with a husband?"

She gave me a withering glance. "I'm sure you didn't come here to talk over our family's business arrangements."

"No, of course not. Maestro Torani has sent me on an errand." Shifting my weight on the window ledge, I took my verbal plunge. "One of the theater staff is missing and he is desperately needed to finish the sets for the new opera. I've come to ask if you know where Luca Cavalieri has disappeared to."

She stiffened almost imperceptibly. "Signor Cavalieri? I'm sure I have no idea. Why on earth do you ask me? I barely know him."

"I've been to his rooms."

The Jewess stared out the window.

"And examined his paintings," I added quietly.

A dull flush formed at the hollow of her throat and crept up to her cheeks. The vessel at the angle of her jaw fluttered. If I had entertained any doubts that the painter and the Jewess were seriously involved, that subtle yet definite display put them to rest.

Liya jumped up and leaned out the window. "There Papa, she's on top of those mattresses." The courtyard must have lain at the end of the tunnel that bounded one side of the Del'Vecchio shop and home. Reconditioning mattresses was one of the traditional ghetto industries, and mounds of old bedding reached to the first floor windows. Several women were hard at work: laying the laundered batting out to dry in the sun, combing, fluffing, and stuffing it into lidded baskets. Pincas borrowed one of their stools to retrieve his daughter's doll.

Liya left the window to pace at the head of her worktable, hugging her arms to her chest. I followed. "If Luca is in trouble, perhaps I can help. He will surely lose his position if he doesn't get back to work or send some word to…"

She shushed me with a quick glance at the woman drowsing across the room. In sharp, jabbing whispers, she said, "Tell Maestro that Luca has gone. He found a better job and he's left Venice. He's sorry… but he had to go. That's all. You can say that without mentioning me."

"Left Venice? Without packing up his things? Where has he gone in such a rush?"

She chewed on a thumbnail, regarding me with eyes as hard as obsidian. "He will send for his things. He had a letter from his mother. She's an actress. Did you know?" I shook my head and Liya went on in a fierce whisper. "Luca's mother has been touring the German courts. She found work for him. A wonderful position, she wrote, but he must drop everything and come at once."

"Are you certain?"

"Yes. Luca must be well over the mountains by now." Her words tumbled from her mouth so quickly, she was almost stammering. "I'm sure he is. He sent me word from the road. I had a message just yesterday. The theater will have to find another painter."

I nodded doubtfully, thoroughly puzzled. What job could be so pressing that a man couldn't take an extra hour to pack his clothing, speak with his housekeeper, and send a note to Maestro Torani?

Squeals of laughter resounded up the stairs and roused the sleeping woman by the window. Liya grabbed my wrist, pressing her fingers into my flesh. I felt her warm breath close to my ear. "Signor Amato, I beg you. Luca has gone to Germany. Tell Maestro Torani, but leave me out of it. You must promise."

Liya's face was just inches from mine. Her mouth trembled; her eyes were pleading. "Please," she breathed.

How could I withstand such a heartfelt request? "I promise," I whispered, just as Pincas came around the doorway carrying Fortunata in one arm and waving a bedraggled cloth doll with the other.

Benito and I took leave of the sunny workroom. Forgetting about the low stairwell, I managed to give my forehead a sharp bump on a crossbeam. I was picking my way through the deserted shop, rubbing my throbbing head, when Benito's high-pitched voice sang out from behind. "Master, you should have let me know that you were looking for Luca Cavalieri. I could have told you a thing or two about that young rake."

We both jumped at the rattling cascade made by hundreds of buttons hitting the flagstone floor. A long face with a clenched jaw and startled eyes popped up from behind a showcase devoted to trays of jewelry and other small items. Cousin Isacco was in for a time-consuming cleanup.

Chapter 7

Instead of the typical exit aria that gives the hero an opportunity to sweep offstage to enthusiastic applause, Maestro Torani decided to end the first act of *Cesare* with an ensemble finale. The tune was an agreeable gavotte, but unfortunately we were all accustomed to the prevailing fashion that favored arias and duets above ensemble singing. I was struggling to modulate the force of my voice to blend with the rest of the company, but no one else was bothering. Emma's clipped, bell-like notes clashed with Rosa's mellow delivery, while Niccolo and the other supporting singers insisted on increasing their volumes to be heard over everyone else. To top it off, Florio was demonstrating his displeasure by producing reedy, wavering tones that were a parody of his authentic, powerful soprano. Our director had tossed his wig aside some time ago and was tearing at his gray frizz in frustration.

Torani had accepted my news of Luca's departure for Germany with more equanimity than I had expected. After an initial exclamation of surprise, he had simply nodded in his staccato fashion and thanked me for my time and trouble. Awkward questions about how I acquired my information never arose. Perhaps Torani had been preoccupied with worry over the finale that his singers were now in process of mangling.

After a few more ragged choruses, Torani signaled the harpsichordist to be silent and stepped back to glower at the lot of us. I expected a tirade, but the director continued to surprise me.

"We will pause for now," he said with a sigh. "Emma and Rosa, you two report to Madame Dumas. She has costumes ready for fitting. I must ask Signor Florio to grant me a few moments. You others may do as you wish."

As Torani and his prize plum of a soprano disappeared into the wings, the stage crew moved in. With so many planned scene changes, Aldo could waste no time. If there was a break in rehearsal, the stage manager directed the crew to run through one of their transformations. The wing flats passed through slits in the stage floor and rested on wheeled trucks which ran in channels below stage. An ingenious series of winches and counterweights allowed one set of flats to be rolled on stage as another receded. When coordinated with the lowering of backdrop and borders, the entire set could be changed in the blink of an eye. Timing was the key; many repetitions were required to make it immaculate. As the stagehands aligned themselves for a drill, I went down to the pit.

Gussie had been watching the rehearsal from a bench with his feet spread wide apart and elbows on his knees. When he saw me come through the door, he jumped up and began to applaud and shout "Bravo," stretching out the last syllable, as the English tend to do.

I shushed him. "Gussie, you shouldn't be clapping. You have just witnessed a shameful disgrace."

"Really?" He sat back down and stretched his legs long, crossing them at the ankles. "It sounded all right to me. But I declare I don't understand the fuss over this Il Florino. He doesn't sound any better than the rest of you. In fact, if you ask me, his voice sounds a bit weak and prissy."

"Florio wasn't doing his best. He prefers to sing alone."

"Oh, I see." Gussie wrinkled his brow, making me think that he most certainly did not. I suspected that the manipulative schemes of temperamental stars were well outside his straightforward way of thinking. "Can you credit it?" he continued. "They are selling things with his likeness painted on them."

"Things?"

"All sorts of trinkets. Snuffboxes for gentlemen, fans and garters for the ladies. I saw some at a shop on the Mercerie."

"It doesn't surprise me. He is the man of the hour as far as Venice is concerned. When we sing at the pageant that will welcome the bridegroom, more people will turn out to hear Florio than to get a glimpse of the bride or her prince."

"The much-heralded groom is a prince of Croatia, is he not?"

"Yes, one of a host. That region seems to produce as many princes as our lagoon does fish."

"What will you be doing in the pageant?"

"Several platforms for musicians will be set up on the Molo near the water's edge. As the bridegroom's ship approaches the quay, we will serenade the spectators and the Doge's court. The Basilica choir is scheduled to sing first. They are to break into a Te Deum as soon as the Croatian ship enters the basin. Then, the singers from this theater will alternate with the girls from the choir of the Pieta."

"Quite a show by the sound of it."

"Oh yes, it will be the sort of spectacle that only Venice can mount, complete with a fireworks display after the sun sets. You will have to get a place near our platform so you won't miss anything. I have an idea—you could take Annetta. I'm sure my sister would appreciate having an escort."

Gussie readily agreed, then added in a lower voice, "Did you manage to speak to the Jewess?"

"I did," I answered, glancing over my shoulder. Even whispers tended to carry in the vast, empty auditorium. "Perhaps we need a walk."

Gussie caught my meaning at once. He swung his legs over the bench and accompanied me into the shadows at the back of the pit. When I judged we were far enough away from idle ears, I told Gussie what I had learned in the ghetto that morning.

"That's an odd way for Luca to behave, just running away without a word to anyone besides his mistress."

"Yes, exceptionally odd."

He swept a few straw-colored locks out of his eyes. "Do you believe her?"

I pictured Liya's proud, almost aristocratic features, pathetic in their pleading. "I would like to believe her." I sighed. "But I don't. Her story just doesn't make much sense."

"And yet you repeated it to your director."

"I told him the Germany trip was only a rumor, yet he chose to take it as gospel. I'm beginning to think that Torani assumed another painter would have to be hired all along."

"Then why send you out to look for Luca?"

"So he could assure Morelli that he'd at least tried to find his missing employee. I suppose that's all Torani really wanted—an excuse to replace Luca." Glancing toward the stage, where one of Luca's delightful creations was rising toward the flies, I grunted softly. "Whatever that blasted painter's been up to, he's out of a job now."

Believing our little adventure concluded, I shrugged my shoulders and started across the pit, but Gussie halted me, not content to let the matter rest. "Is it true that Luca's mother is an actress?" he asked.

"I don't know. I've never heard Luca, or anyone else, talk about his family."

"It seems an easy point to verify."

I grinned. "I think you are beginning to enjoy playing bloodhound."

"It gives me something to do… something to pass the time. And a mystery is always intriguing." A somber frown replaced his usual smile. "I envy you, Tito. You've found your life's true calling. Watching you up on stage… you seem so full of life and passion. It's as if God created you just to sing."

"Someone created my voice," I answered quickly, "but I doubt that the deity had anything to do with that horrible business."

Gussie looked stricken. "By Jove, you must think me very foolish. I didn't mean, I mean I wasn't thinking…"

"That's all right." I placed a hand on his shoulder. "I've come to terms with my condition. The sacrifice that turned my throat to gold was thrust upon me, but now I am paid, even feted, for doing what I love. How many men can say the same?"

Aldo's bellowed call excused me from having to elaborate on my tangled relationship with music. Gussie started back toward his bench, and I mentally girded my loins for the next assault on the finale. I ignored the sounds of stealthy movement that had come from the lowest tier of boxes above us. I decided it must be one of the cleaners or the box office staff sneaking a nap. If someone had been listening, it was really no matter. This time Luca had pushed Torani too far, a new painter would be hired, and that was that.

Emma grimaced when I met her on stage. For the director's inspection, she had donned Madame Dumas' conception of Cleopatra's ceremonial garb. The poor *prima donna* was so tightly corseted that rolls of flesh spilled over her bodice of pleated linen. A robe trimmed with fur painted to resemble spotted leopard was fastened round her neck with a heavy chain, dragging at her shoulders and further spoiling the image of a sensuous Egyptian princess. While we waited for Torani, Emma drew close and put her mouth to my ear. With the instincts of a seasoned performer, the soprano had divined that the scene was about to undergo a major change.

"Will you take a wager, Tito?"

"On what?" I answered in a whisper.

"Five ducats says that our parts are cut even further."

"I wouldn't want to bet against that. If Florio could find a way to sing the entire opera by himself, I'm sure he would."

Emma snorted as she reached up to adjust Cleopatra's cobra-headed tiara. The golden snake sported glinting eyes of ruby glass. I found myself wondering if the headdress was another of Liya's creations.

"Have you heard about his latest foolishness?" Emma asked.

I shook my head and the soprano continued *sotto voce*. "Florio complains of many ailments, but above all, he fears losing his voice. His imagination has persuaded him that the air of Venice is full of poisonous dampness and that his throat is in peril. For days, he's had his poor manager combing the city for charms and talismans to protect his precious pipes."

I chuckled. "What a crazy notion. If the air of Venice is so bad, how has our city managed to produce so many great singers?"

Emma leaned so close I could smell the flowery pomade that kept the curlicues in perfect alignment around her full face. "I'm not sure Florio ever considers other singers. In his mind, Il Florino stands alone."

The subject of her comment was just coming out of the wings, clutching a musical score and looking inordinately pleased with himself. Torani entered from the other side. They met at centerstage and the score changed hands. The director read it through, silently moving his lips and beating time with an outstretched hand. He pondered for a few moments, then wiped his forehead with the trailing end of his shirtsleeve. He finally nodded to Florio and handed the score down to the rehearsal accompanist at the harpsichord.

Torani clapped his hands. "Attention everyone, the gavotte is coming out. Signor Florio has graciously offered to close Act One with an aria that he has performed to great acclaim in other theaters. You will all hold your last places and the curtain will drop as Signor Florio makes his exit."

As we found our marks, Emma sent me a wink and a knowing look. The look Niccolo trained on Florio was much more pointed. The tenor had only a few arias in the entire opera and he obviously resented having any of his songs, even an ensemble, taken away for yet another Il Florino triumph. And it would be a triumph. The aria was challenging, loaded with high F's, and Florio sang it beautifully. There was no denying the purity of his soprano or his command of technique. But despite his performance, the piece had nothing to do with Roman generals or Egyptian royalty. Moreover, the composer's style was at considerable odds with Maestro Torani's work. I knew Emma would not offer any criticism. The roll of her eyes at Florio's last flourish would be the only response she would allow herself. I was debating whether to raise a tactful objection when Niccolo's voice rang out.

"Forgive me, Maestro, but I must speak. How many arias does that make for Caesar in this act? Four?" Niccolo's face was red, and try though he might, he was unable to keep his voice level. "There are other characters in this opera. Devoting so much time to one makes nonsense of the story."

It was a daring comment for a tenor who had little prestige and less following. Niccolo seemed to have lost sight of the rigid vocal hierarchy of the company. His pleasant features were contorted by an angry scowl, and his soulful green eyes were flashing fire.

Florio massaged his temples, then signaled to Ivo Peschi, the manager who seemed to pop up whenever the singer's dignity was threatened. "What does the story matter?" Ivo barked. "No one comes to the opera for the story. This theater will be full of people who have paid to hear Francesco Florio. The more he sings, the happier they will be."

"But this is an opera, not a concert," Niccolo fumed.

Florio puffed out his chest and shook his full, powdered locks. He was ready to enter the fray, but Torani stepped in to prevent further outbursts. "I am still the director of this production, and I have decided that Signor Florio's aria will close the first act. There need be no more discussion on the subject." Torani's commanding presence had resurfaced. The group on the stage stared at him in frozen silence.

"Now, we will go on to the scene that opens Act Two," Torani continued. *Did I detect a note of relief in the director's voice? Had he doubted his ability to bring the company to heel? Carpani's nitpicking and Florio's displays of temperament must be affecting him more than I had thought.*

Niccolo hung his head, but his mouth was still set in an angry line. Florio waved Signor Peschi away and fiddled with a number of scarves that he had wound around his throat. Emma's face had settled back into its usual affable but inscrutable mask.

Torani's eyes ranged over the singers. "Where is Rosa? Madame Dumas should have finished with her by now."

"I'm here, Maestro, if this insolent fool will just turn loose of my arm."

Rosa and Carpani came around a flat of painted marble columns. At first glance, I thought they were dancing, so near was Carpani's shoulder to Rosa's and so closely did their movements harmonize. But I quickly saw that they were locked in a struggle. The more she tried to pull her wrist from his grasp, the more tightly he held on. The combatants made their way across the stage, Rosa hissing like a cornered cat and Carpani keeping his nose firmly in the air.

A bemused Torani took a few steps to meet them. The clerk flung Rosa's arm aside. She tossed her head and shook her skirts in a froth of undisguised rage. "What on earth…?" the director began.

"What we have here," proclaimed a precise, disdainful voice from the wings, "is an outrage."

Signor Morelli, the Ministro del Teatro, strode out of the shadows swathed in his *veste patrizia*, a voluminous robe that all nobles were entitled to wear. Judges in their violet and senators in red were a common sight on the Piazza, but the less exalted aristocrats tended to dispense with their stifling black robes whenever possible. Not Morelli—I'd never known him to miss an opportunity to remind his associates of his station. "As if we were likely to forget," I whispered to myself as everyone on stage gave Morelli the bow or curtsy that was his due.

The Ministro was a bit taller than average and carried himself with dignity. If his shoulders had been wider and less sloping, and if the fingers of one hand had not been nervously drumming against the other, he would have cut an impressive figure. I had often wondered exactly how old he was. His smooth skin showed no wrinkles, but his deep-set brown eyes reflected the doubts and regrets of middle age rather than the optimism of youth. I had heard that his first government post sent him to France when the present King Louis ascended the throne. Morelli had spent several years in Paris as secretary to the Venetian ambassador. That probably placed the Ministro somewhere in my father's generation.

The unhappy Ministro was stalking back and forth, robes dusting the floor. "I come to the theater to see how rehearsals are progressing and look what I find." He gestured toward Rosa and curled his lip into a very patrician sneer.

Maestro Torani scratched his head. "Excellency, has Rosa done something she should not have?"

"It is not what she has done, but what she is wearing."

Hearing a sharp intake of breath, I turned to find Madame Dumas right behind me.

Torani gave Rosa's costume a brief survey. "I'm not sure what you mean," he said carefully.

"Use your eyes, man. This woman is insufficiently clad. You can see straight through her dress. And underneath, it appears that she is barelegged." The nobleman made an impatient gesture. "Carpani, take her over in front of that footlamp."

The clerk reached for Rosa's arm, but the contralto gave him an evil look and flounced to the front of the stage on her own. As another economizing measure, only a few of the footlamps had been lit. Many women would have quailed under the scrutiny of the theater management, fellow singers, and ogling stagehands, but Rosa was a born performer. She bobbed and twirled, causing her flimsy skirts of russet and lemon yellow to billow around her. The warm glow of the footlamp illuminated the lithe form beneath the transparent layers, and her flesh-colored hose did indeed give the appearance of nakedness.

Niccolo was standing near enough for me to hear his murmur of delight and appreciative whisper: "I'd say that's a perfect costume for an Egyptian slave girl." But our *seconda donna* was not posturing for Niccolo. Her performance was aimed at Florio. She need not have made such an effort. Florio was massaging his throat and gazing into the middle distance as if lost in a world of his own thoughts.

Madame Dumas, black-clad figure as upright and unbending as the long sewing shears hanging from her belt, stepped out from behind me. "Maestro, I fashioned the costume that you requested. You asked for an oriental gown that would catch the attention of the young dandies in the boxes."

"Well, yes," Torani admitted. "You've succeeded admirably in that, but perhaps a bit more fabric would not be amiss."

"More than a bit." Signor Morelli swept a wide-sleeved arm toward the now pouting Rosa. "I will not have the females in this production looking like common courtesans. Remember the occasion this opera celebrates. The Doge and his entire family will be in attendance—the bridal couple—senators and their wives." His thundering voice lowered to a petulant complaint. "Licentious living may be shaking the foundations of our Republic, but, by God, it will not overtake the stage of this theater."

Maestro Torani knew he was beaten. He ordered petticoats, white stockings, and several fichus of gold lace (all duly noted in Carpani's notebook). By the time Madame Dumas finished making additions to the female costumes, the audience would see barely a hand's breadth of skin below the ladies' throats.

The rehearsal was further delayed so that Torani could take Signor Morelli to his office to smooth the Ministro's ruffled feathers with whatever beverage he had at hand. The cast began to disperse, some irritated at the interruption, others glad for an opportunity to partake of their own beverage of choice.

Rosa rearranged the sleeves of her costume to emphasize the graceful curves of her white shoulders. She approached Florio and gave one of his neckscarves a playful tug. "Francesco, you have appeared in the finest opera houses of Europe. Surely you can see what a backward attitude Morelli is taking. Can't you tell him what an audience wants to see in a lady's costume?" Smiling seductively, she walked her fingers from the end of the scarf up Florio's chest toward his chin.

Perhaps Rosa was expecting a frank leer, or maybe a bemused grin. She received neither. Florio jumped back more quickly than I had ever seen his bulk move before. He grabbed Rosa's wrist and flung her arm away from his throat. He addressed the contralto in scornful tones, "What you cover yourself with on stage or off holds no interest for me, Signorina. I advise you to wear the clothing you are given and keep your hands off mine."

Rosa's flirtatious charm disintegrated before my eyes. Her smile tightened into a bloodless line while her eyes turned to burning coals. She balled her hands into little fists and stamped her foot like a child in the midst of a tantrum. She practically hissed, "How dare you? You *castrato*, you overgrown boy. Why would I think you know anything about women?"

She would have gone on but for Emma rushing to draw her away. Florio seemed not a bit perturbed by Rosa's outburst. Ivo Peschi arrived with his master's crimson cloak, and the singer made a majestic departure through the wings opposite the way Emma had led Rosa.

I went in search of Gussie, fearing he must be bored beyond measure, but my friend met me with a cheerful grin. "I say, Tito," he practically bubbled, "this opera is turning out to be a lot more interesting than I ever imagined."

Chapter 8

Over the coming days, the atmosphere of tension that had plagued our early rehearsals gradually dissipated. We all reminded ourselves that Florio's reign would not last forever. The celebrated singer might have captured Venice, hoisted his standard over the Teatro San Marco, and proceeded to exercise the privileges of a conquering hero. But after the run of the opera he would be marching out again, ready to seize whatever territory his next contract specified.

As life around the theater fell back into its normal rhythm, Torani gathered the orchestra musicians to begin learning their music, and the dance master brought his troupe around to practice the entr'acte ballets. Work on the sets resumed under the brush of a painter hired away from the Teatro San Benedetto. Carpani grumbled at the expense, and Morelli declared he would see that Luca never worked in Venice again, but all in all, the production was coming together. *Cesare in Egitto* was beginning to look like an opera that would admirably enhance the wedding festivities.

One afternoon while Torani was rehearsing the orchestra, I was lying down on the sofa in my dressing room, trying to rest before a run-through of the pageant program that would greet the Croatian bridegroom. The weather had turned foul again. Outside, sheets of rain transformed Venice into a sodden, gray ghost laced with misty ribbons of deserted canals. Benito had fired up his little stove to heat a goffering iron for my neckbands and ruffles. The warmth from the stove, the drumming of the rain on the windowpanes, and the quiet, familiar movements of my manservant conspired to make my eyelids feel like leaded weights. A heavy, dreamless sleep stole upon me.

I awoke to the sound of hushed conversation. Benito was blocking the crack in the door, one foot acting as a doorstop. Though his back was to me, his lilting voice carried: "It is impossible. My master is resting."

A woman's voice, softer and barely audible, replied, "I must see him. Please."

"But what do you want?"

Silence.

Benito again: "You may give me a message for Signor Amato."

"My business is not with you. It is for your master's ears alone."

I raised up on one elbow and tried to chase the fog from my brain. "Who is it, Benito?"

He opened the door another crack, and I saw the strained face of Liya Del'Vecchio. "It's all right. You may let her in."

Liya entered with small, uncertain steps. As she turned to see that Benito had shut himself on the other side of the door, the unbound hair streaming from her scarlet kerchief made a black curtain dotted with shimmering raindrops. I pressed my fingers to my temples, disoriented from my sudden waking. Time seemed to have bent itself into a confusing coil, and my familiar room had taken on an air of unreality.

The Jewess drew my dressing table bench close by the sofa and sat down. Her cheeks were haggard, eyes red and swollen. How could her lovely face have changed so much in just a few days?

I forced myself to sit up. "What is it, Liya? Are you ill?"

"No, I'm not ill. It's just that you are the only one I could think of to come to." She stared down at her lap. "You were searching for Luca. I must ask… have you found him?"

"You're asking me about Luca? You told me yourself that he had set off for Germany."

"I know. I… may have been mistaken."

"But you said you'd had a letter. You were very sure."

She still refused to meet my eyes. "I can't explain. It's all so complicated. Just tell me, please. Have you found any trace of him?"

"No, I stopped looking when I told Maestro Torani that Luca had taken another job. Are you telling me that I've misled my employer?"

She jumped up, overturning the light bench in her haste. "Oh dear, everything I do goes wrong today. Signor Amato, you must believe I never intended to cause you any trouble. Perhaps I should just go."

"No, don't go." I rose from the sofa and righted the bench, now fully alert. "And please, no more Signor Amato. I am simply Tito, and I am at your service. I can see you are troubled. Let me help you."

"The only way you could help me is to find Luca." She grimaced, making a fist of her hand and bringing it to her mouth.

"I don't understand. In your workshop, you practically begged me to leave Luca's disappearance alone. Now you are asking me to find him?" I shook my head in bewilderment.

"There are many avenues open to you that are closed to me. As a Christian man, you have the liberty to go wherever you like."

"Yes, I see, but why are you so distressed? Do you think Luca is in trouble?"

"Perhaps, I have no way of knowing…" She let her comment trail off with a helpless shrug and placed her hand on my arm. At the same moment the door burst inward.

Liya's cousin Isacco stormed into the room with Benito at his heels. "So here you are." The Jew shook a round, damp box in Liya's face. "You said you were going to deliver these headpieces, but you didn't even bother to take them off our cart. I found them under the portico, about to be ruined by the blowing rain."

Liya's demeanor turned from lamb to lioness. "I thought you had business of your own to attend to, Isacco. What are you doing following me around?"

"You obviously need someone to look after you." The Jew showed his prominent teeth in an unpleasant grin. "You should know better than to be alone with this man in his dressing room. These opera people do nothing but gossip. You wouldn't want to disgrace your reputation, would you?" he finished nastily.

"Just leave me alone," Liya said in a weary tone. "As usual, you have it all wrong. Besides, this is only Signor Amato. No one could possibly object to my speaking with him."

Isacco threw me a brief, contemptuous look. "Even if he is a capon, you shouldn't be here. You're coming with me now." His hand shot out and grabbed her wrist.

"Just a minute." I squeezed the Jew's damp shoulder in a firm grasp. "This is my dressing room and Liya is welcome to speak with me at any time. You are the intruder here, Signore."

Isacco dropped his cousin's arm and turned to me with a pugnacious scowl.

I kept my grip on his shoulder. My jaw tightened. Isacco clenched his right fist, eyes narrowed. The air around us shuddered with tension. I didn't want a fight, but I refused to be the first to back down.

Liya gave an audible sigh and shook her head, sending ripples through the shimmering curtain of jet black hair. She pushed Isacco's fist down, shoved me aside with a flat hand to my chest, and strode to the door. I heard her hoarse whisper as she passed: "Men! You are all useless."

Once Isacco had retreated to the hallway and Benito had locked my door, I sat my manservant down on the bench that Liya had just graced. "Benito, it's time to dip into your store of gossip. I need to know every scrap of talk you have ever heard about Luca Cavalieri."

ᏬᎥᎯᎾ ᏬᎥᎯᎾ ᏬᎥᎯᎾ

The next day brought gray skies, but despite the threat of rain, the entire city turned out to welcome the Croatian bridegroom. Seats for the public ran along the parallel lengths of the Doge's palace and the Broglio. The benches were stacked nearly as high as the tops of the columns and descended to the pavement in shaky stairsteps. Even so, they couldn't accommodate the huge mass of people congregating on the Piazzetta that opened onto the Molo at the water's edge. Before I took my place with the other singers, I searched the mob for Annetta and Gussie. To no avail.

Even during Carnival, I'd never seen this space so crowded. Latecomers shoved their way onto the benches, attempting to displace those who'd already claimed good seats. The inevitable fights broke out, but the dense crowd kept the *sbirri* from intervening. Every bridge and staircase was packed. A few youngsters even tried to climb the flagpoles for a better view.

The Doge, his family, and his closest advisors occupied a canopied platform that had been erected between the columns of Saint Mark and Saint Theodore. These soaring pillars of granite looked out over the basin that the bridegroom's ship would soon traverse. As I followed Torani toward our makeshift stage on the Molo, I spotted the Savio alla Cultura mounting the steps to the Doge's platform. Signor Morelli followed, strutting like a peacock with feathers in full array. They trod a thick red carpet that covered the platform and descended between a double wall of gaily uniformed soldiers to make a crimson path to the stone steps of the jetty.

On the water, the basin presented a spectacular display. Military contingents with full-bellied sails and banners flapping in the breeze were tacking back and forth, narrowly avoiding the barges of the nobility that were decorated with family pennants and flowery garlands. Gondolas, sleek and shabby, hugged the stones of the Molo and clogged the mouth of the Grand Canal. Many of the smaller boats were trailing lengths of velvet or silk. These brightly colored trains carried flowers that spread out across the water as the boats progressed. If the day had been fair, with sunlight burnishing the surface of the water to its most beautiful shade of jade green, the trailing silks and the multitude of flowers would have transformed the basin into a floating garden. But with the lowering clouds hovering over Venice like an inverted bowl, the choppy, gray water swallowed the blooms almost as soon as they were released.

The bridegroom's ship sailed into the basin right on schedule. A battery of cannon on the island of San Giorgio Maggiore boomed a welcoming salute. In between thuds, a great cheer arose. It started with the sailors on the boats, rippled over the water, then was taken up by the crowd on the Piazzetta. I looked across the red carpet to the basilica choir's platform. Their singers' lips were moving, but I couldn't hear a note for the booming cannons and cheering crowd.

By the time it was our turn to perform, the tall-masted Croatian ship was at the mid-point of her slow, stately passage across the basin. The crowd had quieted considerably. As Torani rose and gave the musicians their cue, a thrill of anticipation swirled around our platform. Emma sang first. She executed her arias with sweetness and virtuosity but received only scattered applause and no cries of "brava." Torani shrugged helplessly and motioned for me to step forward.

Barely aware of the murmur sweeping through the Piazzetta, I faced the Doge and his retinue. I had prepared several popular arias from operas that the theater had offered during the last Carnival. Since I'd been making enough time for practice, my voice was nearly back to top form. Even my rival Florio had noticed the change and complemented me in rehearsal. I took a breath, anticipating the opening chord. The sea of listeners swam before my eyes.

I was stopped before uttering so much as one note. Someone in the crowd shouted, "Il Florino! Where is Il Florino?" Others took up the cry and it became a chant: "Il Florino, Il Florino, give us the best, Il Florino."

Torani called for silence, but the frenzied chant drowned him out. The crowd stamped their feet, relentless in their demand for Florio. The fickleness of the public sliced through my heart like a stiletto. Only two months ago, I was the most acclaimed *castrato* in Venice. Every person on the Piazzetta would have been thrilled for the opportunity to hear me sing without having to lay out money for a ticket to the opera.

In one heartbreaking moment I realized that it would be impossible to perform for this mob that had ears only for the imported soprano. With bile rising in my throat, I turned and walked stiffly back to my seat between Emma and Florio. Kind as always, Emma slipped a comforting hand in mine. I steeled myself to meet the eyes of the *castrato* who had stolen my public. Expecting a look of gloating triumph, I was astonished to see a tear trickling down Florio's plump cheek. He sent me a sad smile before moving to strike a majestic posture in the middle of the platform.

How can I describe the intensity of the moment? The nobility under the canopy, the populace crowding the seats and the pavement, even the pigeons lined up on the roof of the palace were absolutely still. It seemed as if the clouds themselves nestled as close to the earth as they dared, just to experience the glory that was Florio.

His first aria was slow and simple, no doubt chosen to demonstrate the quality of Florio's voice in all its purity. He began with a few soft notes interspersed with frequent pauses, but how artfully those notes were sounded. When our ears had been ravished by the pathos of their limpid beauty, Florio soared up the scale, swelling each tone to an amazing volume. His voice was a palpable force, lifting us to the heights of heaven, supporting us on wings of ethereal perfection. Behind me a woman made a sound that was something between a scream and a sigh. I turned my gaze away from the singer just in time to see several ladies swoon into the arms of their escorts.

Then Florio dropped to his low, mellow register and his voice became a whirlpool, drawing us down in dizzying, seductive swirls, drowning us in irresistible waves of song. Even though I knew what the man was doing, I found myself as overcome as anyone else. I had been taught the same techniques, but Florio was performing them so much better than I had ever dreamed of doing. Get hold of yourself, Tito, I thought. Don't let jealousy get the upper hand. Listen and learn.

Another scream sounded, this time filled with horror instead of yearning. The pigeons took flight; their wings whirred frantically over my head. An uproar swept through the boats clustered against the Molo steps. Florio kept producing beautiful music, but his eyes flickered from the Doge's platform toward the water where the banner-draped Croatian vessel was drawing near the jetty. I craned my neck to locate the source of the disturbance.

A swarm of boatmen were poking their oars into a length of scarlet silk trailing one of the larger gondolas. The boat's owner, a florid-faced gentleman waving his tricorne hat in agitated circles, leaned over the gondolier's deck and peered into the water with a look of revulsion. I stepped to the edge of our platform. As the gondola bumped against the Molo, the crowd on the stone steps parted. People twisted this way and that, fairly climbing over each other to get away from whatever was tangled in the coil of scarlet silk.

A pair of hearty boatmen jumped down to make splashing grabs for the fabric that roiled and tumbled in the gray-green water. I glimpsed a swollen, pallid hand flung up by the waves. As one of the gondoliers braced himself against the steps and gave the length of red a mighty tug, the body of a man wrapped in a heavy cloth or sack bobbed into view. They rolled him onto the pavement just beneath our platform. The poor creature had drowned, but not during that afternoon's festivities. He had been in the water more than a few hours. His skin was bloated and bloodless, as white and slick as a porcelain dinner plate. The fish had nibbled at him here and there, but enough of the man's features remained for me to recognize him. I was staring down into the lifeless face of our missing scene painter, Luca Cavalieri.

Part Two
Fiamma: Flame

Chapter 9

"No, not a drowning." The doctor sank his chin into the white neckcloth that topped his severe black coat and pursed his lips thoughtfully. "This man had the life choked out of him by human hands." He poked at Luca's neck with long, sure fingers. "Here, you see? The cartilage of the larynx is broken and, even with this amount of lividity, the deep bruising around the throat is evident."

We were gathered around a makeshift bier in a storeroom at the back of the Doge's palace: the Savio alla Cultura, his Ministro del'Teatro, Messer Grande, Maestro Torani, and I. Doctor Gozzi, the Doge's personal physician, had been summoned to examine the body. When the discovery of Luca's corpse had threatened to ruin the bridegroom's reception, the theater's performance had been swiftly curtailed. To draw attention away from the gruesome sight beneath our platform, the Basilica choir had been ordered back into song while the *sbirri* and the soldiers and a gaggle of minor officials scurried to restore order.

Torani had slipped a hand under my arm as I had pushed through the crowded Piazzetta, so consumed with hurt and shame that I even forgot to look for Annetta and Gussie. I was surprised that the director found me. I was trying to slip away unseen, keeping my chin down and my tricorne low on my forehead. Luca's corpse had provided a shock, but the more painful blow was the crowd's refusal to hear me sing. I had been ready to offer them every pleasure my voice could bestow, yet they dismissed me like a clumsy footman who had dropped a tray loaded with the master's best china. My one thought was to leave the capricious mob to its revelry and get home to my refuge in the Cannaregio, but when Torani begged me to accompany him in his sorrowful duty, I found myself unable to refuse.

They had laid poor Luca out on a rough table. His bloated corpse had been stripped, then covered to the waist with a piece of well-worn canvas. The few dark, curling hairs sprouting from his blanched chest put me in mind of the pin feathers on the carcasses hanging in the window of the poultry shop. Luca's clothing and a length of dark cloth that had been wound around his legs and entwined with the gondola's scarlet train made a soggy pile on a barrel next to me at the foot of the table. Wanting to look anywhere but at the wreck of the man who had been so cheerful and charming in life, I squeezed a rivulet of water from a ragged edge of the heavy cloth and spread it out over my palm. It was velvet of a deep purple hue, a finely figured cloth that would once have been high quality.

The Ministro, Signor Morelli, stood at my other side, covering his nose and mouth with a handkerchief. Cold water had delayed the body's decay, but the smell was distinctly unpleasant nevertheless. The two palace servants holding lanterns for the doctor were turning a sickly shade of green that I feared mirrored my own color.

The doctor noted Morelli's squeamishness with a scornful glance. "Once they come out of the water, they do start to stink almost immediately. At least we don't have maggots to deal with when the lagoon delivers them to us," the medical man observed with a hint of amused superiority.

Beside me, Morelli swayed slightly and I reached out to steady him. The muscles of his arm could have been tightly coiled springs. I thought he might bolt, but the nobleman kept his place at the table.

"Come, come." The Savio directed his remark to Messer Grande, that being the title accorded to the chief of Venice's constabulary. "Let's get this over with."

Messer Grande had not been long in his position. The gazettes had reported his appointment only a month or so ago. I couldn't recall ever laying eyes on him, but then, his was not a memorable face. He was a youngish man of average height, neither fat nor thin, with a narrow, guarded countenance. That day he seemed to wear his red robe of office uneasily. I wondered: could this be his first violent death? His eyes kept flicking from the Savio to the body on the table. As if he had suddenly remembered what his role in the proceedings should be, he asked, "Doctor Gozzi, are you sure this man wasn't alive when he went in the water?"

"Yes. I've been unable to expel any foam or fluid from the lungs. If he were still drawing breath when he went under, he would have inhaled a copious amount of water."

The new Messer Grande bit his lip and pointed in the general direction of Luca's head. "And that other wound?"

Turning Luca's head with difficulty, the doctor motioned with his chin to one of the servants. "Bring the lantern closer." The man complied with a shaking hand. "Hold the light still, you fool," the doctor growled, "this one is long past doing damage to anyone."

Doctor Gozzi's long fingers ranged over Luca's matted hair and pressed into the prominence where forehead met temple. The bruising there was very dark and the flesh had been torn; one ragged edge extended across the flattened cheekbone. I had to look away when the doctor began to wiggle the flap of bluish skin back and forth. He said, "The damage to the skull is serious but probably not deadly. It could even have happened in the water... the body being struck by a boat or some debris."

The doctor paused, considered, then added, "A head wound in a living man bleeds a great deal, but if he was struck before he was strangled, the water's had ample time to wash any blood away. It's hard to say whether this injury occurred before or after death."

With an air of bright finality, Doctor Gozzi put both hands on the table and leaned on his spread fingertips. "Those are my findings as to the cause of death. You will have them in writing tomorrow. Will there be anything else, Excellencies?"

While Messer Grande dredged up a few more questions about the possibility of infectious disease and threats to public health, the Savio drew the rest of us into the hallway outside the storeroom. He directed the servants to hang their lanterns from hooks on the wall and dismissed them back to their regular duties. The Savio was not a young man; he defied his years with the erect bearing of the military commander he had once been. A neat pair of powdered curls sat above each of his tufted ears and a long, leather-wrapped plait of the sort found on campaign wigs hung down his back. He drilled me with hard black eyes dusted by shaggy, trailing eyebrows. I almost wondered if I was expected to salute.

"Torani," the Savio barked. "What is your capon doing here?"

The director shuffled his feet and replied uneasily, "I thought Signor Amato might be of use. He has a gift for seeing details that others miss."

"His presence is unnecessary. A waste of his time, in fact. He should be warbling scales somewhere. You have an opera to bring to the stage in one week, I believe."

"Yes, Excellency. We're expecting great things from Signor Florio. He's in particularly good voice. You would have heard one of his arias from *Cesare* if not for the... interruption." Torani gave the storeroom door an uncomfortable glance.

The Savio ran disparaging eyes over both of us but spoke directly to Torani. "This wedding opera had better be a triumph, Maestro. With its budget swallowing ducats like sweets, your opera house is fast becoming a liability. No one has forgotten the tragedy of La Belluna. Now another murder connected with the theater occurs and that disgusting corpse washes up to embarrass the government on a day that should have found Venice in her glory."

Torani stared at his shoe buckles. I wanted him to defend us, to remind the Savio that the murder of former *prima donna* Adelina Belluna happened three years ago, before the state appropriated the theater for its own use. The degenerate nobleman who had owned the theater then was long gone; not one of the current company was in any way to blame for that old business. And what about the many evenings of pleasure and distraction the theater provided for the city and its visitors? Why choke at a few ducats when Venice was bent on ending her days as an empire in a protracted, all-consuming carnival whirl?

The Savio again turned his gaze to me. "Besides, Messer Grande will need no assistance in finding the murderer of Luca Cavalieri. I'm sure he will have a man to take before the Tribunal within days. Perhaps within hours. Eh, Morelli?" He clapped the Ministro on the back, but received only a brief nod from behind the linen handkerchief.

Torani took a hard gulp. I had never seen him so full of humble submissiveness. "Surely, Excellency, Messer Grande must concentrate on handling the crowds at the wedding festivities. His *sbirri* must be spread very thin. If we might be allowed to look into this unfortunate matter, I'm sure we could be helpful. Luca was, after all, one of the theater's own."

Morelli finally removed the square of linen from his mouth and nose. His aristocratic features bore the stamp of recent shock, but they were rapidly regaining their usual haughty cast. He spat out, "Oh, Torani, do be quiet. You are digging into matters quite beyond your scope."

"You misunderstand. I am not trying to usurp Messer Grande's duties." Torani bowed his head. "I am merely offering the theater's resources. We could make a thorough inquiry that could relieve…"

"Humph." The Savio cut Torani's plea short. "Ottavio—I mean Messer Grande—will direct the investigation. He does not have a great deal of experience, but he knows how to delegate his men and he displays a sharp mind. Always has. Very clever at games, too. Ottavio is my wife's cousin, you know." The Savio favored us all with a satisfied smile.

Morelli responded with a dignified nod and addressed Torani. "As Luca's employer, you were called in only to identify the body for the official record and to contact his next of kin. Does he have any?"

Torani answered after a brief pause. "His mother and father were both actors. The father died some years ago."

"Is the mother in Venice?"

"No. She has not appeared in Italy for several years. I gather she is much admired in certain German states. I have no idea where she is playing now, but Luca has a brother in Padua. I will send for him."

The Savio reached into the folds of his robe and brought out several objects. "These belong to him then."

Gold glinted in the flickering lantern light. Torani held out his hands, glanced at the objects, then passed each one to me. I examined a waterlogged watch that was attached to a beautifully embroidered fob ribbon, several small iron keys, a small case chased with gold filigree that held an ivory pocket comb, and a purse that contained a few coins. There was no snuffbox, but that didn't surprise me. I had never seen Luca indulge in the weed.

I looked up from the painter's small legacy to meet the Savio's stern face. "You two may go," he said, a commander dismissing his troops. "But Maestro, hear me well, let Signor Morelli be your guide in bringing this opera to completion. If you go over the budget for *Cesare*, it may be your last."

⚬⚬⚬ ⚬⚬⚬ ⚬⚬⚬

A footman was summoned to guide Torani and me through the maze of storerooms, pantries, and kitchens that supplied the Doge's table. The bare stone walls and soot-stained ceilings were a world away from the lavish banquet hall where hundreds of guests would soon gather to view the bridegroom and sup off plates of gold and silver.

The servant hurried us through the palace's main entrance at the Porta Della Carta. The rain that had held off long enough to complete the ceremonial reception of the Croatian delegation had started falling in sheets. The clock on the north side of the Piazza struck seven, but the sky was as black as midnight. A phalanx of footmen stood by with torches, ready to greet the noble guests. The light from the torches and the lamps that hung from the arched colonnade illuminated the walls of pink Verona marble with a rosy glow. The palace was a refuge of warmth and light, but I wasn't sorry to leave it behind and plunge onto the rain-drenched Piazza.

Torani and I passed under the clock tower and through the archway that leads to the Mercerie. Most of the shops on this mercantile byway had closed for the evening. The director quickened his steps when he spied a lighted portico that displayed a sign bearing a bunch of faded purple grapes.

"I need a drink, Tito. And some company." He steered me into the tavern's gloomy interior.

The interconnecting rooms reeked with the smoke of cheap tobacco and the stench of old cooking grease. A pitiful orchestra of several violins and cornets was attempting an off-key dance tune that only heightened the misery of the place. I followed Torani to an alcove well away from the ears of the other patrons, mostly sailors and shop workers eyeing the harlots laughing unconvincingly around a smoldering stove.

The day's events had unnerved me, and I worried that Gussie and Annetta had been searching for me—just a quick drink to appease my director and I intended to be off. I threw myself down on a backless bench and slumped against the wall. A sticky sensation persuaded me to lean forward on my elbows instead. A girl brought our wine; Torani fell on his glass as if it had come from a cask in one of the Doge's storerooms.

"The Savio means to shut us down, Tito," he said after a series of hearty gulps.

"How can he? The Teatro San Marco is Venice's theater. It's a source of pride, a boon to the city."

Torani shook his head. "The Savio doesn't see it that way. He only sees the figures in the account books. There are other theaters in the city that can keep the populace and the tourists amused. And we are not the only opera house among them. The San Moise has a good company, and the San Cassiano has improved in recent years."

"So Venice can entertain all she wants as long as a private investor funds the enterprise?"

"Just so. The public wants to see a comedy one night and an opera the next. They don't care who owns the theater as long as their eyes and ears are satisfied. The government is weary of shouldering the burden."

Torani ordered more wine and regarded me wryly. "If the San Marco closes, we will all be out of work."

I nodded, thinking of the multitude of people that earned their bread at the theater. It was not just the musicians, but countless copyists, stagehands, seamstresses, hairdressers, and more. Every task required so many hands. There were even men employed solely to light the candles in the great chandeliers and raise them to the ceiling before performances. All these, and their families, would be hurting if the Savio had his way.

Torani swirled the wine in his glass. Was he mulling over past triumphs or an uncertain future?

"Something occurs to me, Tito," he said eventually.

"What is it, Maestro?"

The director glanced around the dimly lit tavern, then scratched the scalp under his wig, leaving it distinctly askew. He leaned forward and whispered, "What if we beat the Savio to the punch?"

I eyed him quizzically.

Torani put his glass down. His hands sketched a scene in the air as they did when he was blocking the singers' movements on the stage. "What if we were able to find Luca's murderer before Messer Grande? We could approach the Tribunal ourselves. Such a coup would override any of the Savio's complaints about mismanagement."

"I don't know. The Savio is a powerful man… well respected, with many influential connections. He is accustomed to getting what he wants."

"Even so, it would certainly buy us some time. It would reflect badly on the Tribunal and the Senate if they were to shut us down after we uncovered a murderer in our midst and publicly delivered him up to justice."

"You are getting ahead of yourself, Maestro. These are unwarranted assumptions. We don't know that Luca's killer was a theater person or even if the deed was committed by a man."

"What? Oh yes, of course you're right."

The director leaned toward me and clamped a hand on my shoulder. He smiled for the first time since Luca's body had been dragged onto the Molo steps. "You see, Tito, you are the only one with a brain for such matters. You ferret out truth almost as well as you sing. I am hereby placing you in charge of the theater's umm… unofficial investigation."

He saw the look on my face and forestalled my objections with a squeeze of his hand. "This may be the only chance for the theater's continued existence. I know you wouldn't lack for work, but what about the rest of us? I'm ashamed to say that I haven't set much aside for my old age. I suppose I thought time would never catch up with me. I need my position at the San Marco. So does Emma, and many others."

I remained silent. Torani's crooked wig gave him the look of a tipsy buffoon, but I knew he was in deadly earnest.

He continued heatedly, "I give you leave to do whatever you must. Question any employee, search the theater high and low. If anyone objects, you may invoke my authority."

"What about Messer Grande? He may not appreciate my treading on his toes."

"No matter how highly the Savio regards him, the young Messer Grande is unseasoned. The numerous public celebrations planned for the upcoming week would overwhelm a man of much greater experience. The city is full of foreigners eager to amuse themselves in any and all ways. Can you imagine the number of pickpockets, imposters, and card cheats that will be operating?

"No," he continued. "Messer Grande will find time to come to the theater to make his inquiries, but his other duties will distract him. Meanwhile, you will be at the theater every day and already know Luca's habits."

"Hardly, Maestro. If I have discovered anything about our unfortunate friend, it is that Luca was much more than he seemed to be."

"Then you will uncover his secrets. I know you can do this for us, Tito. I have faith in you. Say you will find Luca's killer."

Torani's eyes sparkled with enthusiasm, but the lines around his mouth deepened and his lips stretched into a taut, bloodless smile. I considered refusing his request but found the recent memory of the crowd booing me and shouting for Florio as compelling as any of the director's arguments. I was no longer the most popular singer in Venice, but I could still prove my worth by saving the theater from the Savio's misguided inclinations. I swallowed a gulp of sour wine, then slowly nodded my head.

Chapter 10

Our stage manager was a busy man. If Aldo didn't have a task to occupy his time and energy, he quickly created one, gathering up any stagehands who looked like they might have a free moment on their hands. The distinctive clop of his heavy-soled work boots coming down the corridor was a signal for all the men to either make themselves scarce or jump to their work with renewed vigor.

On the morning after the ill-fated welcoming ceremony, I located Aldo the moment I reached the theater. He was in the corridor outside Luca's studio. I hailed him, but he blew past me like a gust of alpine wind, muttering, "Later, Amato." That afternoon, after our first rehearsal with full orchestra, I thought I had Aldo cornered, but one of the machinist's winches froze and the stage manager rushed to help. I followed him into the wings. He pushed up his sleeves and added his strength to that of the other stagehands. Straining at the handle, his thick neck and muscular arms were soon covered with a sheen of perspiration. When a rope snapped and gears went flying, I knew our conversation would have to wait.

I had better luck in the scene painter's studio that afternoon. The high windows filled the workroom with golden light, illuminating the backdrop covering one long wall. Six days earlier, I had admired a half-finished depiction of the banks of the Nile. That canvas now hung in the flies above the stage, and an interior of Ptolemy's palace had taken its place. No one was about, so I strolled over to the slant board that held the designer's original sketch. The pen and ink drawing pinned to the board had been divided by a checkerboard grid. A similar grid had been ruled onto the canvas backdrop. By enlarging each square, the scene painter produced an enormous copy faithful to the designer's small rendering. The new artist tempted away from one of our rival theaters had painted the Egyptian columns and monumental stairs in realistic detail right down to the weathering of the stone, but his work did not have the same elegance that had characterized Luca's.

"Good morning, Signor Amato." It was one of Luca's assistants, the tall one. He was carrying a bucket of varnish along with an unwieldy armload of long-handled brushes. Racking my brain for the man's name, I hastened to take the bucket from him.

"*Grazie*, Signore. Just sit it over there."

"We had a terrible shock yesterday... Matteo." The name popped into my head at the last moment.

"*Si*, poor Master Luca. Who would have thought he would end his days beaten, robbed, and tossed into the lagoon?"

"Is that the story that is going around?"

The man looked startled. "Is it not true?"

"Luca was not robbed. His purse and his valuables were still on him when the body was examined."

Matteo gave a low whistle. "That's a very different kettle of fish then."

"Most certainly. Tell me, Matteo, during that last evening, did your master speak of a later engagement?"

"No, Signore. If he had, we would have informed Maestro Torani when he asked about our master's disappearance. Tonio and I worked late that night, until the light failed and beyond. Master Luca wanted us to finish the grids on some flats. When he sent us home, he said he was going to stay and study the sketches for the next day."

"Did he seem worried or vexed about anything?"

"No, not at all. He was just… Master Luca. Laughing, joking, not a care in his head."

"What time did you and Tonio leave?"

"A quarter past nine, give or take a few minutes," Matteo answered cautiously. He gave me a suspicious look. "I should go, Signor Amato. This is our dinner break. Tonio will be wondering where I am."

He began to back out of the studio, but I stopped him with a hand on his arm and what I hoped was a reassuring smile. "Just one more question. It may prove important. Can you picture the studio the first morning Luca failed to show up for work?"

"I suppose so." His words came slowly.

"Was anything out of place? Anything broken or pushed over?"

"You think Master Luca was killed here?" Matteo's eyes widened and he pulled his arm from my grasp. He was ready to bolt.

It was time to invoke the director's authority. "Maestro Torani has asked me to look into the possibility. If violence occurred in the theater he wants to know what happened."

Matteo ran his hand over his mouth and chin, took a few steps forward, and turned slowly in a full circle. His eyes darted from pots of pigment to rungs of scaffolding. "No, everything was in order. At least it seemed so. We weren't looking for anything in particular." The painter spread his hands helplessly.

"Was anything missing?"

He made another tour of the studio with his eyes and shook his head.

I sighed. After all, it had been almost a week. What could I expect the man to remember about a day that had started like any other?

"Wait," he said, one finger in the air. "There is something. Master Luca's Venus."

"Venus? The goddess of love?"

"Yes, Master Luca kept a bronze statue of Venus right here." Matteo smacked his hand on a crowded shelf near the door. "She was a beauty, about so high." The painter put his hands together and raised one about a foot and a half above the other. "He brought her in a few months ago and took to calling her his guardian angel. We kept telling him she was a heathen goddess, not an angel. But he would just laugh and say, 'When Venus is here, my angel is with me.'"

"How long has she been missing?"

"I don't know." He shrugged. "The shelves in here are so full, I probably wouldn't have noticed she was gone now if you hadn't made me look around."

Matteo was glad to scurry away to his dinner. I knew it would be only minutes before he told Tonio about my visit to the studio. Soon the entire company would know I was asking questions about Luca's murder. I would have to be quick if I wanted to search the studio without curious faces appearing at the door.

The doctor said that a head wound bleeds profusely. If Luca had been attacked in the studio, with the missing statue or some other bludgeon, there might be some traces remaining. I reached toward the shelf Matteo had indicated and picked up an imaginary statue. Arm above my head, I whirled and tried to picture the scene. Luca had been struck from the front, so the blow had not been a sneak attack. Had he been arguing with someone? I brought my arm down as hard as I could. In my mind's eye, Luca staggered and fell to his knees. I did the same.

The floor was fashioned of tiles, large hexagons smoothly abutted, their grimy surface pitted and cracked by years of use. Dots and smudges of every imaginable hue filled the imperfections. Had that smear of rusty red once coursed through Luca's veins, or had it splashed out of a paint pot on its way to becoming a fiery sunset on a backdrop? I would never be able to tell. I sat back on my heels and looked around. There was not a surface in the studio that did not carry the colorful remnants of the scene painters' activities.

I explored further, but the rest of the studio offered nothing else of interest. The shelves held no tomes of magical lore or jars of exotic powders. Luca had wisely confined the evidence of his interest in the occult sciences to his lodging. I also failed to find any small paintings or decorated cloths in any way similar to the ones Gussie and I had found tucked in Luca's drawers at home.

Footsteps sounded in the corridor and I stepped quickly to the door. A leg in a black stocking and the tail of a faded black coat were disappearing around the corner that led to the dressing rooms. Carpani, I presumed. Would my inspection of Luca's studio soon become an entry in his black notebook? From the other direction, a pair of seamstresses with their heads bent together giggling over some shared secret approached the door opposite Luca's studio. Madame Dumas, the company's costumer, followed a few paces behind. She took a small key from her waistband, unlocked the door, and let the women into the costumer's workroom.

"Madame, you are just the person I wanted to see. Can you spare me a moment?"

The Frenchwoman crossed her spare arms and raised her eyebrows. "You have questions about Monsieur Cavalieri?"

"News travels on swift wings."

"You may be sure of that. Everyone is asking why Maestro has you poking your nose into Luca's death. Are we not to have an official visit?"

"I'm sure Messer Grande will be conducting an investigation, but…" I hesitated.

"You don't have to explain it to me." The costumer's wrinkled face broke into a brief, slanted grin. " I've known Rinaldo Torani lo these many years. He cannot abide being left in ignorance. *Zut!* I've not forgotten that you found La Belluna's murderer and neither has he." Her expression settled into its usual sober state. "I will help you if I can, but I was as surprised as anyone that someone hated the painter enough to kill him."

Madame Dumas' unbending manner along with her tight coil of graying hair and icy blue eyes intimidated many in the company, but I knew her for an honest, well-meaning woman. If she offered her help, I knew I could depend on it. I asked, "How late did you work on the last night Luca was here at the theater?"

"I dismissed my girls and closed the workroom at seven o'clock. If you come in on time and keep your mind on your work, there is no need to keep the late hours that some do." The delicate sniff and roll of her eyes clearly expressed her opinion of Luca's work habits.

"Had you noticed any arguments in his studio?"

"With Matteo and Tonio?"

"Well, yes. We can start with them. Any raised voices or signs of upset?"

"Luca Cavalieri struck me as a man very slow to anger. If you ask me, he was too soft on those two assistants of his. He left them on their own a good deal—of course, they took full advantage—but Luca never complained if they wasted time or got something wrong. They would have been foolish to quarrel with such a lenient master."

"What about anyone else from the theater, or even a stranger?"

Before she could answer, a group of dancers rounded the corner from the dressing rooms and headed to the stage. The girls were full of childlike vivacity and gamboled down the corridor like a herd of young ponies, but their breasts bulged enticingly above their laced bodices and their cheeks were rouged and patched like seasoned courtesans. If Morelli got a good look at their gauzy skirts, Signor Carpani would have to find funds to purchase sturdier coverings for their shapely legs. The costumer shook her head as the heels of their delicate slippers clattered past. "They seem to get younger every year," she whispered.

Madame stared at the backs of the retreating dancers so long that I almost concluded she'd forgotten my question. Then she spoke in a low voice. "There was one who wasn't so happy with Luca."

"Yes?"

She hesitated, fingering the scissors that always dangled from her belt. "It probably means nothing."

"Madame, I pledge to use discretion in this matter. If your information has no bearing on Luca's death, it will go no further."

"Rosa," she said shortly, "our calculating little contralto. She usually picks her suitors from the third tier boxes, but a while back she developed an appetite for Luca's good looks."

I thought of all the wealthy fops who continually besieged Rosa's dressing room with flowers and gifts. I would expect a scene painter with a modest income to hold little attraction for her, but I had to admit Luca had a way about him that appealed to both women and men. "Did Luca return Rosa's interest?"

"Not that I could see. It was all sighs and tender glances on her side, but nothing from his. Luca had no feeling for her, and Rosa couldn't quite get over it. The shameless coquette kept finding excuses to visit the studio and throw herself at him. Luca asked her to leave him in peace more than once."

"How long ago was this?"

"Several months ago. It didn't take the girl long to come to her senses." She cocked an eyebrow and gave me a cool look. "I believe a young son of the Gritti family is currently keeping Rosa supplied with gowns and trinkets."

I nodded, then posed my most important question: "Did Signor Carpani ever find that lost bolt of cloth?"

Flames flared behind the seamstress' icy gaze and I was treated to a tirade of her native language. Eventually she slowed to the point that I could understand her. "*Ce cochon!* He is almost beyond bearing, this little man with the notebook. I am not careless and I am most certainly not a thief. He had no right to accuse me."

"So the bolt is still missing?"

"It is gone, yes. It simply vanished. One evening it was leaning here against the wall, right inside the workroom door. The next morning... gone!"

"Was that after Luca's last evening here?"

She thought for a moment, then nodded. "Yes, it was. I am sure of it."

"Was the door locked?"

"I always lock up at night, Monsieur," she answered starchly. "When I unlocked the door the next morning, the fabric was gone."

"What sort of fabric was on the bolt?"

"Why, it was a figured velvet. *Tres cher*. It was meant for Monsieur Florio. I believe you are aware of his exacting standards."

Agreeable as it would have been to find fault with my rival's extravagant demands, I pressed on. "What color was your missing cloth?"

"Purple." The costumer eyed me questioningly. "Have you found it?"

I took her gnarled hands in mine. "Madame, you will never retrieve this fabric, but it may prove more valuable in its absence than on Signor Florio's back. I must ask that you not speak of the velvet again until I am able to tell you more about its fate."

The Frenchwoman compressed her lips, eyes frosted sapphires once more. When she spoke, it was with vehemence. "I will do as you ask, Monsieur Amato, but for God's sake, keep that *cochon* of a Carpani away from my workroom."

Chapter 11

Leaving Madame Dumas to her damasks and silks, I went to my dressing room to find Gussie sprawling on my sofa with eyes closed and chin nodding into his chest. I was glad to see the big Englishman. In only a few days his cheerful company had filled a hole in my life that I'd been but dimly aware of. Since I wouldn't be needed on stage until evening, I invited my sleepy friend home to dine.

We hadn't had an opportunity for a good talk since the discovery of the body. Gussie was brimming with questions, but confined himself to pleasantries until we sat across from each other in a gondola bound for the Cannaregio. "So, Tito, your instincts were right. Luca never made the journey to Germany. All the while we were hunting for him, his body was bobbing around the lagoon."

I squinted up into the warm, blue sky. "Liya admitted as much when she came to my dressing room the other day."

"Do you think she suspected that her lover had been murdered?"

"I don't know." I thought back to the scene that had occurred in my dressing room the day before the pageant. "But after she'd abandoned the fairy tale that started with his mother's letter, Liya did seem quite genuine in her plea for news of Luca."

"Why the sudden change of heart?" Gussie posed the question that had kept me worrying my pillow half the previous night.

I shook my head.

We were approaching the Rialto Bridge, the imposing span that connects the two halves of the city and provides the only means of crossing the Grand Canal on foot. As we neared this busy marketplace, the boat traffic picked up and the surface of the canal leapt with tiny, sun-kissed waves. Under the bridge and around the bend, we'd find the canal that led to the ghetto. One brief detour and I could pose Gussie's question to Liya herself.

A tingle of excitement drove thoughts of Annetta's waiting dinner from my head. It must be the lure of a mystery, the beguiling opportunity to cut through a tangled skein of secrets, that made my blood run hot. Surely, it had nothing to do with sitting on the wide window ledge, the Jewess' skirts nearly touching my knees, my eyes following the curve of her throat as it disappeared beneath her apron. No, I told myself sternly. To remain objective, I would have to keep my distance and banish fantasies about the beautiful Liya to some point in the future when the unhappy details of Luca's life and death had been fully revealed.

I sat forward, hands on my knees. "Gussie, you have need of a new waistcoat."

He looked down and smoothed the brocade over his wide midriff. "I thought I had put those gravy stains to rout," he said impatiently. "Sometimes it is deuced awkward not having a valet. I've learned to dress my hair without help, but keeping my waistcoats and my linen clean is a never-ending chore."

By the time I had given the gondolier new instructions and turned back to face my friend, Gussie was grinning broadly. "Oh, I see. We are visiting the Del'Vecchio establishment."

"The perfect place to look for a new waistcoat, is it not?"

The *campo* in front of the Del'Vecchio shop was empty except for a few idlers around the steps and one mongrel dog trotting across the bricks with the purposeful air of an urgent canine errand. Most of the ghetto inhabitants were still at table, or perhaps enjoying the little nap that often follows the midday meal.

I pulled the bell outside the shop's latched door. One of Liya's young sisters answered the ring. She kept her eyes tightly glued to the floor, giving Gussie and me a perfect view of her shining hair covered by a white cap. While I stated our business, she giggled and fidgeted with her fingers, sneaking several anxious looks toward the curtain at the rear of the shop. It took Gussie's teasing charm to convince her to escort us up to the family living quarters.

Instead of entering the workroom at the top of the stairs, the girl led us farther down the hall and turned into a cramped chamber that served as both sitting room and dining room.

I met the grandmother's eyes first. She was sitting in a low chair by the cold stove, wrapped in a flannel coverlet. The old woman was not drowsing that day. Under the wispy topknot held fast by ebony combs, her lined face was alert and intelligent. I've been expecting you, her bright eyes seemed to say.

Liya was clearing dirty dishes from the table onto a wooden utility tray. Her eyes also held an easily readable message. If looks could wield palpable force, Gussie and I would have been blown through the back wall of the house into the mattress makers' courtyard beyond.

Another woman with a tray under her arm appeared at a passage behind the table. I didn't know her, but she could only be Liya's mother. Proud and straight, complexion of a more Eastern hue than her daughter's, she possessed Liya's firmly chiseled nose and determined chin. Lines surrounded her eyes and fissures cut from her nostrils to the tips of her downturned mouth, but the mother was still a striking woman. And a formidable one.

She eyed us coldly. "Can't you dandies wait until the shops reopen? We've just had our meal and my husband is lying down."

Liya clapped the crockery on the tray with a sharp clatter. "They are not here to shop, Mother. They are from the theater."

The older woman approached us. Over her shoulder, she flung at Liya: "Mind the plates, daughter. When you have your own house you may break as many as you please. Until then, you will treat my things with respect."

To me she aimed a tight, straight smile. "And pray, Signore, what do you do at the theater?"

I made a formal bow, tricorne under my arm. "Forgive me, Signora Del'Vecchio. I am Tito Amato and this is my friend, Augustus Rumbolt. We beg only a few brief moments of Liya's time."

"That pretty bow doesn't answer my question."

"Oh, Mother. You know that Signor Amato is a singer. You have heard me read his name from the gazettes often enough." Liya read my reviews? I hadn't realized that she cared enough to bother.

I suppressed a smile.

Her mother eyed me appraisingly, no blushes on those cheeks. "One of their performing capons, I presume."

I shrugged. "That is what some say. I call myself a singer, nothing more or less."

"If you ask me," she said, hands on hips, "capons are for eating, not for singing."

Liya groaned, put her tray on the table, and grabbed a shawl from the back of a chair. "Come, Signori. We will walk in the *campo*."

I heard a soft rustle by the stove. The grandmother was leaning forward in her nest of blankets, intent on absorbing every moment of this unexpected after-dinner drama.

Liya's mother threw her hands in the air. "Oh, of course. Walk with the fancy gentlemen. Leave the rest of us with the washing up. Anything to get out of chores." Signora Del'Vecchio's grating voice carried down the stairwell. She called for her other daughters, drawing out the last syllable of each name. "Mara, Sara. You have work here."

When we reached the pavement I offered Liya my arm, but she shook her head and kept her arms firmly wrapped in her shawl. She didn't seem to notice the idlers at the well observing our trio with narrowed eyes. The three of us walked in silence until we reached the opposite side of the square and stopped before a pawnbroker's shop. The window was a haphazard jumble of goods. Behind the panes of wavy glass, a shiny pair of tall riding boots stood beside a porcelain inkstand that would have been quite elegant if it had not been missing its quill holder. To its side, a silver-handled looking glass leaned against a tower of snuffboxes, while tangled strands of bright beads snaked around the lot. Given pride of place on its own stand was a dress sword in a gadrooned scabbard that had probably graced the costume of some patrician captain until a run of bad luck had sent him to the pawn shop. Liya gazed at the ceremonial weapon as if it were her fondest desire.

"Luca bought a statue here," she said in a dull, faraway voice, "not long after he had first declared his love."

Gussie and I shared a quick glance over Liya's head. I had told my friend about the search of the studio and the rest of my day's activities during the gondola ride to the ghetto.

"A statue of Venus?" I asked quietly.

Liya's jaw tightened, but her gaze never wavered from the sword in the window. "Yes, it was a bronze, done in an old-fashioned style and covered with tarnish and grime. Luca said it reminded him of me. I didn't see the resemblance, but Luca saw with an artist's eye and he seemed quite taken with it. It was a lovely thing after he had cleaned and polished it." She sighed heavily. "I was a secret, you see. He would never acknowledge our love to others."

I said, "At the theater, Luca mostly ignored you."

"Exactly. It was a sore point between us, the source of many arguments. He kept the Venus in his studio to placate me. He told me, 'How can my angel of love be far from my thoughts when her likeness watches me work?'"

She swallowed hard, turning to face me. "Have you seen the statue?"

"I'm told it has disappeared."

She turned back to the shop window and murmured, "Along with everything else."

I kept quiet, thinking that Liya's own sorrows might lead her to disclose more than probing questions. But I hadn't reckoned with her unshakable equanimity. The Jewess' eyes of liquid jet stared at the sword but silently beheld something far beyond the cast-off valuables on display. The minutes stretched to an uncomfortable length.

Gussie could stand it no longer. His low baritone rumbled, "Perhaps your lover was just trying to protect you. I am only a visitor to your city, but I have been in Venice long enough to realize that a romance between a Christian and a descendant of Abraham would cause great difficulties for both of you."

Liya tossed her head. "It has happened before."

"Yes, Signorina," Gussie said sadly, "but how does it end?"

"Oh, what do you know?" Liya clutched savagely at the ends of her shawl and tipped her chin back to look Gussie in the eye. "You big ox of an *Inglese*. I see your brothers come here and fall in love with the Venetian beauties, but do you marry them? No! When your money runs out, you can't wait to run home to the rosy-cheeked blondes you left behind. Luca was different. He was an artist, a creator. He had vision and courage. My family's objections would mean nothing to him."

I raised an eyebrow, wondering how the carefree Luca would have faced all the difficulties such a union would bring. Liya caught sight of my reflection in the window. She whirled, now gulping back tears. "It's true, Tito. My Luca laughed at tradition, Hebrew or Christian. Venice and all its strangling rules and regulations didn't suit him any more than it suits me." At that moment there was something so tragic in her voice that I reached involuntarily for her hand. I pulled back as her tone became flinty again. "Luca wanted us to marry and promised to take me as his wife. He just needed time to overcome some..." difficulties. To get enough money for us to go away. If only..." Liya choked on her words, composure dented at last. She whirled and rushed blindly across the *campo*.

We caught up with her outside a barbering establishment a few doors down from her family's business. The proprietor was just opening his door, putting out a sign that advertised inexpensive but miraculous drops for the cure of toothache. The *campo* was coming back to life after its midday break. The barber and a wandering boy with a basket of lemons on his head were both regarding Liya's tear-stained cheeks with curiosity. This time she let me slip my hand under her elbow and lead her into a quiet shadow cast by a jutting balcony.

"Liya, at Maestro Torani's behest, I am searching for Luca's murderer. Surely, you also want your lover's killer to face justice. Tell me of these difficulties Luca mentioned and tell me of any enemies he may have had."

The Jewess bit her lip and searched my eyes with her own. I moved as close to her as I dared. She voiced no objection, in word or gesture. Did I detect a spark of yearning, an impulse to share her anger and grief? The moment passed in the space of a heartbeat. She said, "I'm here because agreeing to walk with you seemed the easiest way to get you out of my house. I'm sorry, Tito, but Luca's problems are no business of yours and neither are mine."

"That wasn't how you felt the last time we spoke."

"Things are different now," she replied in a whisper so low I had to strain my ears to hear. "You can't help me. No one can… so stop trying to bring trouble to my house and don't come here again unless you intend to buy something," she finished abruptly and fled for the door of her father's shop.

Her path led her straight into the arms of her slack-jawed cousin, who had draped himself against the doorjamb. Isacco staggered when she gave him a rough shove. Since Gussie hadn't noted Isacco's presence any more than I had, I was left to wonder how long his inquiring face had been peering out of the shop.

⌒⌒⌒ ⌒⌒⌒ ⌒⌒⌒

Back at the Campo dei Polli, the front door of our house swung open before I could fish my key from my pocket. Lupo, our elderly house servant whose bent back and crabbed hands confined him to the duties of minding the door and chasing fluffs of dust with a straw broom, blinked in the bright sunlight. He greeted Gussie and me with a cautionary shake of his wizened head.

"You'd best tread lightly, Signor Tito. Signorina Annetta has been holding your dinner an hour or more. She has already kicked the cat out the back door and yelled at Lucia in the kitchen."

I groaned. Just what we needed, another unhappy female.

The object of Lupo's warning came around the corner of the dining room with the sort of look that Medusa must have used to turn her enemies to stone. My sister squared her shoulders and put her hands on her hips.

"So, is the famous singer too busy to come home to dinner on time? Did a throng of your admirers keep you in your dressing room for just one more story, one more pleasantry? Surely, Il Florino has not stolen *all* your following?"

I winced. Annetta certainly knew how to wound me. During the lonely years at my *conservatorio* in Naples, Annetta was the only member of my family who had bothered to keep in contact. My sister and I must have exchanged hundreds of letters full of our dreams, hopes, and youthful secrets. When my training was complete and the tug of remembered people and places—and perhaps the need to impress those who had sent me away—drew me back to Venice, the sister who was so close to me in age and temperament quickly became my most loyal supporter and intimate confidant. Then no woman could match her in charm and generosity, and her delicate diplomacy curtailed many a family argument.

When had I first noticed the bitter twist in her smile, the dejected slump as she sat staring into the flames of the sitting room stove? At twenty-five, Annetta was considered a spinster by Venetian standards, and it had been a long time since she'd mentioned the romances and courtships of her friends. Did Annetta despair of finding her own eternal love? Did she blame my brother and me for monopolizing her time and talents? She used to wait up for me until I got home from the theater. We would talk until the embers in the stove grew cold, but I could barely remember our last heart-to-heart conversation. While I had been gallivanting with frivolous friends, my sister had become nearly as distant as a stranger.

"*Beh*, you might as well come and eat, though the polenta is burnt and the meat has simmered 'til it's dry."

Annetta's arms remained at a sharp angle on her hips.

We filed into the dining room and took our seats at the table. The drapes had been thrown back to admit the late-afternoon sunshine that warmed the cloth neatly set with a few pieces of blue and white Chinese porcelain, my long-dead mother's pride. My father's portrait above the sideboard gathered a bit of the prevailing light and reflected his austere gaze down upon us. I tried to make amends with my sister by recounting our visit to the ghetto, but Gussie's smiles and courteous attentions were far more successful at wiping the frown from Annetta's face.

Benito served our dinner. Since Berta, Lupo's female counterpart, had succumbed to a fever during the winter, Annetta made do with Lucia, a young girl from the neighborhood who came in for day work of scrubbing and cooking. Benito's primary duties were to look after my wardrobe and organize my affairs, but he was often pressed into service to perform tasks that were beyond Lupo or Lucia. My mouth watered when my manservant brought in a heavy platter of mutton that had been marinated in wine and simmered in milk laced with ginger and cloves, then followed that with several other dishes. Annetta had exaggerated the dinner's destruction. The mutton, the creamy polenta, and the leeks that surrounded the meat were all delicious.

Appropriately enough, the principal topic of conversation at table was food. Annetta attributed the flavor of the dishes to the excellent spices procured by our brother Alessandro in foreign ports and told Gussie about Venice's justly extolled salt marshes that provided a seasoning of unmatched quality. The Englishman countered with tales of his family's holiday feasts: roast sides of beef dripping with juices, rabbits and wild fowl from his father's estate, endless kegs of ale, and a curious sounding pudding made with suet, bread crumbs, and fruit. By the time we had moved to the sitting room and Benito had deposited the coffee tray on the round table, my sister had shaken off her annoyance.

"Well, it's obvious, isn't it?" Annetta was responding to my musings about Liya's contradictory behavior concerning her missing lover.

Gussie drew his eyebrows up to meet his tousled locks. "Is it?"

"Of course. The girl is pregnant." Gussie's blank look prodded Annetta to tick her points off on her fingers. "First Tito shows up at her workroom asking about Luca's disappearance, but Liya seems more worried about her family overhearing Luca's name than about where her lover might have got to. So… to stop Tito's prying questions, she puts him off with a hastily constructed, far-fetched story."

Gussie and I both nodded.

"Then," Annetta continued, holding up a second finger, "sometime before she makes her desperate visit to Tito's dressing room, Liya discovers her condition. That changes everything. Suddenly, finding the artist so that their plans to marry can go forward becomes her prime consideration. Imagine her disgrace if she turned up pregnant and unmarried, especially in the ghetto. There could be no packing her off to country cousins for Liya's family. She might have come to you as her last hope, Tito."

"Something was certainly bothering her that day, and she seemed eager for my help," I answered. "But why has she pushed me away again?"

"Now that Luca is dead and marriage is out of the question, Liya must find another way out of her dilemma. If I were her, I would try to keep the child a secret as long as possible. That would make your questions more of a hindrance than a help."

"Bloody Hell, but you Italians are clever," said Gussie, wide-eyed. "I could have thought all day without hitting on that. Makes Liya's position a damned sight more ticklish, doesn't it?" A hangdog look quickly crossed his face. "Oh, forgive my curse, Signorina, I meant no disrespect."   ·

Annetta snorted with laughter, and I had a glimpse of the old, comfortable days. "You forget that our brother is a sailor. Express yourself any way you wish, dear Augustus. Alessandro has accustomed me to plain speaking and I find I prefer it."

Gussie continued with a hint of a smile. "I wonder why Liya bothered to invent the story of the trip to Germany in the first place? When Tito starting asking questions about Luca, why not just order him out of her home?"

I took a few sips of Benito's smooth, sugary brew, then set my coffee down. "I think she was protecting someone, and still is."

Annetta rose to refill Gussie's cup. "Someone other than herself, you mean?"

"That has occurred to me. Her cousin Isacco generally accompanies her to the theater, wheeling their cart piled with deliveries. Sometimes he stays outside, but usually he comes in. I've seen him all over the theater. He may have gotten wind of her relationship with Luca and taken steps to stop it."

Gussie narrowed his eyes. "Then Liya thought that Isacco was responsible for Luca's disappearance? What we now know as his murder?"

"Perhaps, but I see little love lost between Liya and her cousin. If she is shielding anyone, I wager it would be Pincas, her father. He seems like a mild man, but he obviously dotes on his daughters. The fear of losing Liya to a Christian might provoke him to violence."

Gussie nodded and leaned forward, eyes glittering. "I'm beginning to understand. One of the Jews must have killed Luca—Isacco, Pincas, or someone they hired to scare the artist away from Liya. Perhaps they only set out to threaten him, but Luca refused to give the Jewess up. Or perhaps he fought back so strongly that the violence got out of hand."

I shook my head. "One piece of the puzzle doesn't fit, though. Luca's body was wrapped in a length of cloth that had been stored in a locked workroom across from Luca's studio. The murderer must have used the cloth to drag the body from the studio, to a waiting boat. None of the Jews would have had access to that bolt of cloth."

Gussie sat back with a sigh. "I should have known that solution would be too easy."

I stood up to stretch my back. "The obvious solutions usually are. Besides, this is all idle conjecture. We have no proof that Annetta's speculations are correct and that Liya is pregnant. Or that anyone besides you and me had discovered her affair with Luca."

Annetta was tapping a foot on the stool in front of her chair. "Who could have gotten at that cloth, Tito?"

"Besides Madame Dumas, I'm sure that Maestro Torani and Aldo both have keys to the workroom."

"What about that man with the notebook?" Gussie chimed in. "He seems to have made himself an authority on everything that goes on at the theater."

"That is certainly true. I wouldn't be surprised if Carpani didn't have keys to every door and drawer in the building."

"And then there is this." I took a folded scarf from my jacket pocket.

"You kept one of the painted veils we found in Luca's lodging," said Gussie.

"Yes. I can't think why, but I am glad I did. If we are to discover who killed the painter, we must learn more about his projects and associations. This is a curious thing. I'd like to know its purpose."

Annetta rose and took the delicate scarf from me. She squinted at the image, then carried it to the fading light at the window and held it close to her eyes. "This is silk, rather old, but the decoration is not painted on the fabric. There are no brushstrokes and these lines are visible on the backside. What does it represent?"

"Hold it at an angle," Gussie and I responded in unison.

"Oh yes, it becomes clear. It's a woman's face. Whose, I wonder?"

Neither Gussie nor I could hazard a guess. We remained silent, sipping our coffees and pondering the mystery in our own ways. Annetta stared at the scarf thoughtfully. "Let me keep this, Tito. I want to have a better look at it in the morning light."

I nodded, and, mindful of the gathering shadows, I consulted my watch. "Important as they are, I must put these questions on the shelf for now. Tonight is the first *prova generale*. We will rehearse the opera from start to finish with full costume and scenery changes. It's likely to be a long night, but you are both welcome to come and watch if you like."

Annetta begged off. She had sat through a *prova* before and preferred to wait until opening night when the opera would have most of the kinks worked out of it. Gussie was keen, however, and we were searching for our hats when the bell at the front door sounded. Benito had already left for the theater to see to my costumes and Lupo was in the kitchen. Rather than wait for the old man to shuffle to the door, I opened it myself. I saw the back of a young man, a porter by my brief glimpse of his loose linen shirt and rough trousers, running down the *calle*. An envelope of cheap paper lay on the threshold. I carried it back to the sitting room. Annetta was opening the tinderbox to light the lamp.

The three of us bent over the table and examined the envelope's contents in the circle of yellow lamplight. Venice had numerous gazettes at that time. Most were published weekly, but a few came out daily. All were penned by anonymous scribes. New ones seemed to blossom on every street corner whenever there were rumors that the curious public would pay to peruse and rehash. I had already seen the column that had been neatly cut from one of the dailies. It detailed the recovery of Luca's body in the most lurid and speculative terms. The information that was new to me had been scrawled across the newsprint in red ink. *Look to the Jews* it exhorted in bold, block style lettering. My friend Gussie had not been the only one to spring to the obvious conclusion.

Chapter 12

Gussie and I made our way back to the Teatro San Marco in the gathering dusk. All about us, Venice bristled with restless energy. Any other year, the lengthening days and warming weather of early June would have signaled the patrician families to move to their mainland villas for the summer. During this *villegiatura*, the Venetian *palazzi* were shut up tight and amusements shifted to rural pursuits. The theaters were forced to close down; not enough paying society remained in the mosquito-ridden city to make an opera or play profitable. Those noblemen who could not afford a country home stayed in Venice, keeping to themselves and, in their shame, wearing masks when they ventured into the streets with the rabble. During previous summers I had been in demand to sing serenades on the terraces of the splendid villas up the river Brenta or on the Terraglio, the highway that led north to Treviso. This summer was starting out differently. The rapidly approaching marriage of the Doge's daughter had delayed the annual pilgrimage to the mainland and swelled the city's population with visitors.

It was almost as if it were Carnival, with the dull days of Lent still to come. As our gondolier propelled us down the canals with easy, graceful swings of his oar, I saw messenger boys running about the *calli* delivering notes and parcels, stalls set up to sell trinkets and refreshments, and maskers made anonymous by the all-concealing *bautta* prowling in search of their varied pleasures. Amusement was not the only topic on the citizens' minds. Passing a *campo* near the heart of the city, I saw a knot of soldiers gathered with torches and placards declaring that they had not been paid for months. Despite their grievance, the men appeared more convivial than angry. With smiling faces, they were slapping each other on the back and raising their bottles in spontaneous toasts. Even so, I expected the *sbirri* would soon be moving in to break up their display.

On the last turn before the theater, a parish church swung into view. It was not the usual time for a service, but the doors were thrown back revealing the yellow glow of wax tapers deep within. The altar candle nesting in its red shade glowed like a flaming ruby, and the pungent smell of incense wafted across the water. A thin stream of petitioners mounted the steps to the church. Were they going to pray, or did they intend to confess their transgressions so that they might begin another evening of debauchery with shriven souls?

In a moment the water-lapped steps of the theater were before us. A flock of gondolas bobbed and creaked at their moorings. I paid our boatman, then hustled Gussie through the brightly lit lobby. There was always a crowd invited to a *prova*, and I didn't want to be delayed by fawning admirers or self-appointed critics. Once the Englishman was installed in a second tier box with a good view of the stage, I headed for my dressing room.

I stopped at my door but didn't go in. Across the way, several young dandies garbed in the latest French fashion clustered at Rosa's open doorway. They appeared supremely interested in whatever transpired within.

"I could have been the next victim!" shrieked a female voice in a dudgeon of high drama.

I approached and peered over the dandies' shoulders. They declined to spare me more than a brief glance. Rosa sat before her mirror in a dressing gown of green paisley. Its emerald tones set off the golden tips of her brown curls and amplified the sparkle of the diamond necklace adrift on her fleshy bosom. Her maid was attempting to arrange the singer's hair for the powder, a task made all the more difficult by Rosa's frequent expansive gestures. Every few moments she twisted to clutch the knee of the gentleman who sat by her dressing table. His wardrobe eclipsed even that of his friends: he was pomaded, powdered, laced, and beribboned like a king's mistress. I recognized his smooth, heavy-jowled face. His father maintained a box at all of Venice's popular theaters. Rosa's admirer was Signor Bassano Gritti, the scion of one of Venice's foremost families.

Rosa had begun to repeat herself. "I could have become the killer's next victim. I tell you, Bassano, I could be dead right now." She grasped her throat at a sudden thought. "What if the murderer returns. I may yet be bludgeoned to death." Her widened eyes glittered almost as brightly as her diamonds.

One sleeve of Rosa's dressing gown had slithered down to the elbow, revealing a naked, pink shoulder. Her doting cavalier gave it a clumsy pat and said, "*Carissima*, don't distress yourself. No harm has come to you and the villain is well away."

"But we were right here in my dressing room that night—Emma and I. She went to get something and heard an argument coming from the studio corridor. What if she had gone to investigate? What if she had surprised the murderer in the act? What if he finds out we were in the theater and comes back for us?"

Signor Gritti gazed wearily about the room and treated himself to a pinch of snuff. Finally, he drawled, "If he has good sense, he is miles from Venice. Besides, no sane man could harm a vision as lovely as yourself."

"Ah, but what if he wasn't a sane man. He might be a madman escaped from the lunatic hospital, or a Turk addled by the fumes of his strange pipe." She put a small hand to her chest; her breath came in shallow gasps. "Or one of those devilish Jewish beggars bent on Christian slaughter."

As the overwrought singer threw herself into Signor Gritti's arms, I looked away to meet another's eyes. Emma was hovering in the next doorway, twisting a thumbnail between her teeth. She darted back into her dressing room, but I got there before she had time to turn the latch. With no attempt at ceremony, I launched myself through her door and posed my question. "Is

Rosa speaking the truth? Did you overhear an argument the night of Luca's murder?"

The soprano sank down on a backless sofa and covered her eyes with her hand. On a stand behind her, Cleopatra's cobra-headed crown seemed to menace me with malevolent red eyes. Emma whispered in a heavy voice, "Please, Tito, go away. I have a terrible headache. I've sent my maid for some drops."

I replied gently, "It's a simple question, old friend. I'll be glad to go once you've answered it."

Emma sneaked a look at me through spread fingers. "You're not going to let this rest, are you?" she asked in a more natural tone.

"Not until Luca's murderer is found."

Emma dropped her hand to her lap. "It's bad enough having Messer Grande popping in and out and quizzing everyone. Why do you have to upset us further? You are one of us. You know how difficult it is to keep your nerves in line before a *prova*. You should be encouraging your fellow singers, not harassing us."

"I wasn't aware that I was harassing anyone."

"Well, you're harassing me. I need to rest and get rid of this headache before I have to sing."

I tried another tack. "I would rather hear the truth from you than the ravings of an ingénue who fancies herself the queen of the stage."

Emma's lips curved in a reluctant smile. "Conceited little trollop, isn't she. There's no situation Rosa wouldn't take advantage of to be the center of attention." The singer's hand flew to her mouth. "Oh, you didn't hear me say that, Tito."

I nodded and waited expectantly.

"All right, you may as well know. Rosa is telling the truth. We were talking in her dressing room that night. Rehearsal was long over and we had both discharged our maids. I was more than ready for my supper and kept trying to take my leave, but Rosa was upset. She just wouldn't be comforted."

"What had upset her?"

"The usual tale. Her current lover is rumored to have an eye for a ballerina at another theater."

"Signor Gritti seems attentive enough."

"Yes, he is dancing his attendance this evening, but he has yet to make arrangements for Rosa to follow him to the country for the summer and has ignored all her hints that he should do so."

Emma moved to her dressing table and began to apply a thin layer of cream to her cheeks and forehead. She continued, "Rosa was sobbing and moaning. She couldn't seem to stop crying. I couldn't leave her like that. Then I remembered the flask of brandy I keep in my trunk, just for emergencies you know. I nipped down the hall to get it and heard voices. I thought everyone had gone so I stepped to the corner where this hallway joins the workroom corridor and listened for a few seconds. Someone was arguing with Luca in his studio."

"You are sure the voices came from the studio?"

"Yes. That corridor was dark. I suppose Aldo had already extinguished the lamps. The only light came from beneath Luca's door."

"Did you hear any of the words?"

"No. Just angry voices."

I moved behind Emma and studied her expression in the mirror. The flickering oil lamps on either side gave her greased face a look of sickly pallor. "You recognized Luca's voice?"

"Yes." The loose skin under her chin quavered.

"And the other voice?"

"I don't know."

"Could it have been Aldo's?"

"I really couldn't say, Tito." She dropped her eyes to the sticks of grease paint and pots of lotion on her dressing table. Snatching up a scent bottle, she flicked the amber liquid in the direction of her chest and throat. "I'd like to help you, Tito. I truly would. But all I can say is that the other voice was... muffled."

I took a shallow breath. The air in the room had suddenly become oppressively sweet. Unless I missed my guess, my friend Emma had just told me her first lie.

The *prova* proceeded in the way of all such ordeals. The opera was coming together one moment, falling apart the next. I opened Act One with a lovely aria of sweet running passages accentuated by glances and gestures that perfectly expressed the feeling of the song. It was applauded by all and brought a grin to Torani's face. But my next performance was flawed with failed high notes and awkward phrasing that Torani's increasingly strident instructions from the harpsichord in the orchestra pit could not help me correct. Thus it went, scene after scene. Once, after Emma had extended herself to the utmost and exacted more from her aging voice than any director could hope for, Torani left his harpsichord and ascended to the stage with open arms. The flamboyant embrace he bestowed on his perspiring Cleopatra may have been calculated to chide Il Florino.

The unpredictable star was "saving himself," which meant dawdling in his dressing room, missing cues, and singing half-strength. Florio had once cautioned me: "Don't let them spoil your voice with overwork, Tito. Never forget that your throat is your most valuable asset and every note chips away at your stock of vocal capital. Once you learn your part, what are these rehearsals good for? For the crew to practice a scene change? For the machinist to time his cues? For us, a *prova* is singing for nothing—a monumental waste of time and voice."

I didn't share Florio's sentiments about rehearsals. I was willing to admit that my part still needed work, but I confess that Torani had less than my full attention. As I waited in the wings or struck a pose on the stage, my mind was on murder—not the staged slaying of Egyptian royalty, but the authentic, grisly death of one of our own company. I was trying to imagine what could have motivated someone to kill the genial scene painter.

While Luca had not exactly been soaked with holy water, his reputation was superior to that of many Venetians. Despite the books Gussie and I had found at his lodging, he had never aroused the ire of the State Inquisitors for dabbling in magical operations. In fact, I'd hardly heard an evil word spoken against the man. He was known as an honest gambler: he didn't cheat at cards or press friends for loans, and he paid his debts on time. He did sometimes drink to excess but kept his good humor even deep in his cups. The only vice that had ever caused Luca trouble was women. Jealous lovers had set their bravos on him several times, but Luca had survived the beatings with only minor wounds. Could it be that he had run afoul of a man whose honor demanded more than a bloody nose?

I thought back to the information that my manservant had given me. According to Benito, who somehow felt it was his duty to keep abreast of all the shifting relationships within our little world, Luca had dallied with a number of ladies. There had been some ugly talk about a young ballet girl whose mama had put a sudden halt to the budding romance. Though the good woman was bent on saving the girl's unsoiled treasure for a man with a heavier purse than Luca's (Benito reckoned that the mother had already lost that battle), I doubted that this affair had anything to do with the painter's death. The little dancer and her mother were long gone. Since then there had been several singers and a maid or two, but those affairs had all ended amicably.

And then there was Rosa. On that score, Benito agreed with Madame Dumas. They both believed that Luca had never succumbed to Rosa's charms. By the time the painter had aroused Rosa's interest, he seemed to have sworn off theater romances. Benito theorized that a secret liaison with a high-placed, married woman was monopolizing Luca's passions. I knew better. It was an alluring Jewess, not a fashionable *signora* that fascinated the painter. It surprised me that for all his prodigious stock of gossip, my manservant had not known about Luca and Liya. The painter and the Jewess must have been very cautious indeed.

I glanced toward the stage where Florio was serenading Emma's Cleopatra as a distinctly half-hearted Caesar. The act was almost over, so I set my brain to working out how Liya had managed to get out of the ghetto to visit Luca's lodging without attracting attention. I was trying to calculate how much it might take to bribe the ghetto guards when an angry snort sounded behind me. The curtain was coming down, and Aldo was looking at his watch in consternation.

"Almost eleven o'clock and two acts to go," the stage manager complained to no one in particular.

"When do you think we will get out of here?" I asked.

"Do I look like a fortune teller?" he answered, rubbing the back of his thick neck.

I cocked my head and pretended to ponder the question. "Perhaps. Who knows what hidden knowledge lurks behind those bright eyes of yours? If you wore a caftan and carried a witch's ball, you would quite convince me."

A slow smile transformed the stage manager's face. Without his usual scowl, Aldo appeared surprisingly amiable, friendly almost. He said, "If I were a magician, I would keep the ropes on the pulley for the last backdrop from tangling, add a few more notes to Niccolo's top register, and blast the delicate songbird who loves to wallow in imaginary ailments out of his dressing room on time. Then we might all be home and abed before the sun rises."

"Is it Florio that's been holding us up?"

"He offered a temporary dyspepsia as the excuse for the last delay, but it was not his stomach that kept him offstage."

"What was it then?"

"Florio and his manager are organizing a claque. They were closeted in his dressing room with one of the leaders, giving him instructions on positioning his men and timing their applause. They were offering ten *soldi* apiece for general clapping with enthusiastic bravos and a *zecchino* for cheering sufficiently insistent to interrupt the performance."

"Why does Florio bother with that nonsense? Venice can hardly wait to hear him. When *Cesare* opens, he will receive tumultuous applause for simply walking out on stage."

"Ivo Peschi explained it for me. No matter where he appears, Florio always demands insurance."

"Insurance?"

"Signor Peschi likens Florio to the shipholder who sends his fleet out on waters swept by storms and infested with pirates. The prudent merchant purchases insurance to offset the threats to his goods. The claque is Florio's insurance. Even if he comes up with a sore throat or swollen tonsils, his singing will not fail to garner a wild display of admiration."

I shook my head, wondering if Florio was also paying the claque to hinder his fellow singers with boos and hisses. "Who will lead the applause?" I asked Aldo.

"Giacomo Croce, one of those threadbare nobles from San Barnaba."

Aldo was speaking of the Barnabotti, impoverished noblemen so called because they clustered their lodgings in a poor neighborhood near the church of San Barnaba. With family fortunes swallowed up by the vicissitudes of the day or ruined by personal extravagance, the Barnabotti existed on tiny allowances provided by the Senate. Like all the heads of families listed in the Golden Book of the nobility, they fulfilled their duties as members of the Great Council. But after they had deliberated cheek by jowl with their more affluent brethren, the Barnabotti could only return to their squalid rooms for a glass of cheap wine and a dish of plain polenta. These paupered aristocrats were notorious for wasting their allowances at the gaming tables, selling their votes on the Council, or launching schemes designed to regain the luxurious life they fancied their exalted pedigrees deserved. If he was a typical Barnabotti scoundrel, Signor Croce wouldn't stick at booing one of Venice's own to enhance the vanity of a visiting star—not if there was money to be had.

"Perhaps I should also have a talk with Signor Croce," I said to myself as much as to Aldo. "And, by the by, I need to talk with you about…"

The stage manager's friendly smile had been replaced by his more familiar harried scowl, but Aldo was no longer attending to me. He was regarding the delegation fumbling its way through the folds of the curtain and coming onto the stage.

Chapter 13

"*Dio mio*," Aldo muttered, as Carpani found a velvet handhold and pulled the curtain aside for the Ministro del Teatro and his followers. "We'll never get to Act Three if Morelli starts his usual harangue."

The Ministro had dispensed with his patrician robe for the night. He was clad in a coat of sky blue silk figured with twining vines of a darker hue that exactly matched his breeches. The garments were beautifully tailored, but for another man's frame. Morelli's narrow shoulders failed to fill the coat, and though the buckles on the breeches were drawn tight, the dark blue silk bagged about his knees like the hide of an African elephant. Several other gentlemen, including Messer Grande, who had not abandoned his red robe for less official garb, attended Morelli. All the men were frowning.

Morelli bore down on Torani as the director was correcting the phrasing of Niccolo's last aria. I mentally saluted Torani's bravado as he made his bow to Morelli and invited the Ministro to congratulate the performers on an outstanding performance.

Morelli answered in a snappish tone, "Outstanding, Maestro? I suppose that term is accurate, if you want to describe something that stands squarely outside the boundaries of excellence and convention."

"You are not satisfied with our opera, Excellency? I admit it needs a few more days of polishing, but everyone has been working day and night to make *Cesare* a success."

The Ministro narrowed his eyes. "The Senate particularly wishes an entertainment that will spur patriotic fever and glorify our distinguished ruler. You were to draw parallels between Caesar and the Doge. Instead, you have served up a nauseating stew of squabbling pharaohs, superstitious infidels, and a Roman general besotted with an Egyptian harlot. The Savio will not be pleased. If so much money had not already been wasted, I'm not sure I wouldn't simply advise him to cancel the opera."

Signor Morelli's words precipitated a collective paralysis. The crew that had been scurrying to change the scene halted in their tracks. A seamstress who was bent over Rosa's bodice stitching a torn seam froze in the act of biting off a thread. The singers all stared at Morelli in incredulity. Even Florio was shocked into silence.

After a strained moment, Torani took up the challenge. He reminded Morelli that the Savio had approved the opera's libretto before the first rehearsal ever took place. The Ministro countered with more recriminations. The obsequious Carpani stood at his master's elbow, ready with nods of agreement for every criticism Morelli raised. To my mind, the Ministro was spouting nonsense. In my short career, I had learned a thing or two about audiences. *Cesare* was destined to be a crowd pleaser. Even without the excitement engendered by Il Florino's first appearance in Venice, the opera's stirring arias and spectacular effects would keep the entire theater entranced.

Only one person appeared oblivious to the battle of words between the director and the Ministro. Messer Grande was striding around the stage with a brusque energy that made the sleeves of his red robe swirl around him like the wings of a blood-drenched bird of prey. After stirring up a good deal of dust and peering up into the grid like he expected Luca's murderer to descend on a wire from the cotton wool clouds, he came to rest beside me. Aldo had been edging unobtrusively toward the wings, but he backtracked a few steps when Messer Grande addressed me in a gravelly whisper.

"Signor Amato, you have been asking questions about the murder of Luca Cavalieri. Why?"

"I am trying to be of some small assistance to Maestro Torani."

The chief of Venice's peacekeeping force eyed me disparagingly. "Yours is bound to be a trifling inquiry. You spend your time singing amusing ditties at supper parties and traipsing around the stage as some dead prince or pagan god. What would a creature like you know about the kind of brute who committed this crime? You and Torani should leave this task to those who are capable of handling it."

"That would be you and your *sbirri*."

"Exactly." Messer Grande squared his shoulders and raised his sloping chin. "I am the authority entrusted with this investigation."

I forced a humble smile to my lips. "And how does your investigation proceed? Are you near to finding the... brute?"

As Messer Grande hesitated, I sensed Aldo stretching to lean as close as he dared. The movement caught the chief's eye as well. "You there—you seem very interested in this conversation. You're the stage manager, I believe. Don't you have some business to attend to?"

Aldo was not intimidated. "Everything that affects this opera is my business, Excellency. Right now, my crew is spending more time speculating about the murder than doing their jobs. This show won't go smoothly until Luca's killer is put under the Leads."

"Don't worry. We will deliver him to prison soon enough," Messer Grande replied. "He's a violent man, a raging beast that couldn't stop at bashing his victim's head but also had to strangle him. He does not have the wit to evade us much longer."

"I'm curious, Messer Grande," I said. "Why do you think this violent beast attacked Luca?"

"I'm told a valuable statue is missing. The killer must have slipped into the theater to steal whatever he could lay his hands on. The painter caught him in the act and was killed for his trouble."

I spread my hands. "The statue of Venus was not so very valuable—Luca kept it in the studio as more of a keepsake than an ornament. Is anything else missing from the theater? Money from the box office perhaps?"

Messer Grande suddenly took a great interest in adjusting the folds of his robe. "No, but that doesn't signify. The killer didn't have time to take anything else. He was surprised by the painter and then had a dead body to dispose of."

"But if the killer was a simple thief," I mused, "why take the time to convey Luca's body to the lagoon. Why not just run away?"

Messer Grande's thin cheeks were flushing as scarlet as his robe. "What a ridiculous question! Only a frivolous dabbler would try to complicate the matter with such foolishness. I'll get at the meat of the details once the killer is found—I have a man able to get the truth out of anybody in less time than it takes for me to have my dinner." He punctuated his comments with several grunting snorts, then lifted one long finger and poked me in the chest. "Look you, just leave the investigating to me. Keep your mind on your singing—while you still have a theater to sing in."

The angry voices of the Ministro and the director had died down, but the looks on their faces told me that no accord had been reached. The arrival of the Ministro's wife had only deferred their dispute. I could see why: Signora Isabella Morelli could be quite distracting. Though no one would mistake her for a bride fresh from the convent, she was younger than her husband and still an uncommonly attractive woman. Her upswept curls had been coaxed to a sumptuous shade of golden red, and her heart-shaped face turned to porcelain by a dewing of white paint tinged with a faint rosy blush. A gummed patch in the shape of a star nestled near the corner of one lively, black eye. It would be hard to say where the *signora's* chief attraction resided—her curious, playful intellect or the full-blown loveliness of her face and figure.

I had heard the whispered stories of her history: how adept she had been at slipping away from the watchful nuns at the convent where she had been schooled, how she had later held her own in the company of Venice's literary philosophers and wits, then still later been publicly ruined by a handsome, but fickle Spanish count. The dashing Spaniard had been followed by a Venetian naval officer and, most scandalous of all, a Sicilian prizefighter. Her family had been forced to offer a generous dowry to be rid of her. Her marriage to Morelli could not have been a happy match. While the nobleman distanced himself from the world with his air of scrupulous superiority, his lady embraced the delights of Venetian society with as much gusto as her position would allow. After I sang the next act, I had the opportunity to observe Isabella's amorous strategies in action.

Gussie had been watching the *prova* from the luxurious heights. From the stage, I'd had no trouble picking out his box. The *prova* was meant to duplicate the conditions of opening night in every respect, so all the candles in the great chandeliers above the pit and in the sconces along the walls had been lit. During my arias, my friend had fixed his elbows on the box railing and regarded me with an intense expression, intermittently transferring his attention to something in his lap. When Torani called the last break, I ascended the stairs to see how Gussie was faring.

On opera nights the wide, curving corridors behind the boxes were always crowded with footmen running errands and elegant ladies and gentlemen mingling with acquaintances, but that night the second-tier corridor was nearly deserted. Only the few who had been invited to the *prova* by someone connected to the company were in attendance. I had almost reached the door of Gussie's box when a lilting voice called my name.

"Signor Amato, what incredible music you are making tonight. Your last aria left me quite overcome—you sang with such fervor. How on earth is a *castrato* able to raise such a passion?"

I bowed and acknowledged Signora Morelli's left-handed compliment with a murmur of thanks, but didn't waste my

time attempting to answer her question. A woman so infatuated with audacious masculinity could never understand the
passions of a eunuch. There were some women who found our
physical charms as fascinating as our voices—I admit to having
dallied with several myself—but the *signora* was not one of our
admirers. In fact, I suspect she had only approached me to lead
her to her preferred quarry.

As I turned back to Gussie's box, Signora Morelli snapped
her fan shut and tapped me on the shoulder. "Oh, no, my
pretty nightingale, I can't allow you to fly away so easily. I'm
told the Englishman in this box is a friend of yours—I wish to
be introduced."

There was no refusing her. Signora Morelli and I entered the
box and startled Gussie from his chair. The mellow candlelight
flattered my female companion; it erased the lines at her eyes
and throat and gave her painted complexion a radiant glow.
Surprised as he was, Gussie was unable to take his eyes off her.
The lady seemed no less transfixed.

After the Englishman had been formally presented, Signora
Morelli gave the interior of the box a pert, inquiring look. "Have
you no refreshment? Is it possible you have survived this endless
rehearsal without a drop of wine?" Gussie threw me a stricken
look, but the *signora* had the situation well in hand. She seated
herself on an empty chair, spread her damask skirts, and opened
her fan. Over its fluttering folds, she tossed a command disguised
as a request. "Be a dear, delicious songbird and tell Fabrizio to
fetch us some wine. I imagine you'll find him right outside the
door, in the blue livery."

Thus Isabella Morelli demoted me still further, from the
company's *secondo uomo* to her messenger boy. I stuck my head
out the door, but Fabrizio was lax in the performance of his
duties. I had to search the length of the corridor before I finally
found the surly footman gossiping on the back stairs with some
other servants. When I returned, the *signora* was teasing Gussie
to show her something he obviously wanted to keep hidden.

"I pray you, Signora, these are poor scribbles, not worthy of the time it would take for you to peruse them." Gussie sat in a chair that had been turned away from the railing to face the interior of the small but beautifully decorated box. Signora Morelli bent so low over his shoulder that I could have counted the stays on the corset that defined her shapely waist and supported her upthrust breasts. As she whispered in Gussie's ear, she was tickling his midriff, coaxing him to release a small, leather-bound portfolio that he was shielding under his coat. When my friend appealed to me with an outstretched arms, the aristocratic minx plucked the portfolio from its hiding place and danced a few gamboling steps around the box.

Giggling like a schoolgirl, she waved the book in the air. "I've been watching you sketch all night—bent over the papers, your pen flying, your tongue between your teeth. I've been dying to see what you find so inspiring."

I smiled at my friend. "You've started drawing again? Have you taken up your brushes as well?"

Gussie shook his head, eyes trained on the pages that Signora Morelli was leafing through. "I just wanted to see if I still had the knack. I thought I'd try a few sketches, but... they're not... very good." The Englishman's voice trailed off to a miserable whisper as Signora Morelli positioned herself under a lamp bracket and began to study Gussie's drawings in earnest.

With the candlelight burnishing her ringlets to copper coils, the noblewoman held the first page at arm's length. In a moment, her eyes slid away from the page to give my features a brief inspection. She turned a page and repeated the procedure—a second time and a third.

"Did none of the singers besides Signor Amato interest you tonight?" she asked.

Gussie remained silent but gave his head a tiny shake. Intrigued, I moved to her side and peered down at the pages she was slowly turning. Gussie had sketched me in my Egyptian tunic and crown, in my battle armor, and in the loose robe I wore in my love scene with Rosa. He had undervalued his work. The sketches were brimming with grace and energy. My form looked as if it could spring right off the page.

Signora Morelli shook her head as her beringed finger paused at the next page. My image was still in the flowing robe, but Gussie had drawn my hair loose around my shoulders, not in the tightly curled wig I wore in the scene. The next drawing changed my form even more. I was reclining on a low divan, my head thrown back, my chest thrust forward in a decidedly sensual manner. It was not a pose I struck on stage.

"I'm beginning to see what inspires your art, Signor Rumbolt." The noblewoman closed the portfolio with an impatient snap and handed it to me. "Perhaps you are not quite the man I imagined you to be."

I ran my hand over the pebbled texture of the leather binding. Did I want to look at the rest of Gussie's drawings? I didn't think so, yet I found my thumb slipping between the pages. I drew a few quick breaths, my back pressed into the gilded moldings on the wall. With the candles hissing softly at my ear, I flipped the book open to Gussie's last sketch. The figure was drawn with graceful legs and swelling breasts peeking through the flowing robe, wanton tresses tumbling to a trim waist, and a wide, welcoming smile. There was no mistaking what this drawing represented.

"Gussie!" I cried. "You've drawn Annetta." It was my sister as I had never seen her, but it was most definitely Annetta. My friend fancied my sister!

Gussie sprang from his chair and joined me under the light. He looked down at the drawing with the besotted pride of a mother cat for her litter. "By Jove, Tito, isn't she lovely? That's exactly how I imagine Annetta's hair would look if she would just take it down from that tight braid she wears."

Signora Morelli halted in the act of gathering her things. In just a few minutes she had infused the box with her presence by strewing fan, scent bottle, sweetmeat tin, and se;eral handkerchiefs in various corners. She cocked her head. "Annetta? Who is Annetta?"

I showed her the drawing. "My sister, Signora. Anna-Maria Amato. We call her Annetta."

"This sister of yours. Is she on the stage as well?"

"No, Signora. She is neither singer nor actress. She keeps house for me and my brother in the Campo dei Polli."

"Umm… now I understand." She chuckled deep in her throat. "For a moment I thought my judgment had deserted me. I rarely make a mistake about men's tastes, but I suppose even I can't be right all the time." She pulled a copper ringlet across her cheek and regarded Gussie through half-lidded eyes. "Signor Rumbolt, an artist requires more than one muse lest his work turn boring and stale. I know just the thing to inspire your pen and convince you that you still have… what did you call it? The knack. I am receiving guests at the Palazzo Morelli on Sunday afternoon. I will expect both of you."

Gussie started to refuse, but I put a cautionary hand to his back. I had my own reasons for wanting to learn more about Morelli and his household. I was tolerably confident that the Ministro was feeding the Savio damning reports about the theater, and I wanted to know why. I also had not forgotten that Morelli had been Luca's drinking companion on several occasions. As Signora Morelli adjusted her skirts to pass through the narrow doorway, I bowed and said, "You are too kind, Signora. We accept with pleasure."

Chapter 14

"Look here, the chief magistrate of the Piovega reports another well gone bad." A melancholy-looking man with pockmarked cheeks raised his voice above the din of the coffeehouse. His finger coursed a line of the latest gazette and he continued to speak as it moved back and forth across the page. "The well is in the parish of San Rocco. Yesterday morn, a housewife went to fetch water for her washtub and found it foul and brackish. The magistrate has put a guard on the well."

"Fat lot of good that will do," drawled a bedraggled dandy with coffee stains down his front. "Why post the guard on a ruined well? Dispatch the soldiers to protect the other wells, or Venice will end up as dry as a bone."

His neighbor slurping coffee from a shallow dish chuckled and spoke up. "Who needs water when we can drink Peretti's coffeehouse dry?"

The dandy was quick with a reply. "Ass! How do you think coffee is made? They steep the roasted beans in boiling water. The purer the water, the sweeter the beverage."

The noisy coffee drinker was affable if not particularly keen-witted. He simply smiled and replied, "We could always switch to wine."

I was listening to their conversation from a table under the arcade in front of Peretti's, a favorite gathering place of musicians. Earlier that morning I had followed Luca's funeral gondola to the cemetery island of San Michele. Only two attendants rode in the gondola that bore the black coffin draped in tasseled red velvet: a priest displaying a disconcertingly jolly countenance and Silvio, Luca's brother from Padua. As I stood at the open grave with Torani, Emma, and a handful of others from the theater, I searched the field of iron crosses and budding plane trees for a red-kerchiefed figure. I knew Liya would be barred from the service within the church, but I expected she would find a way to witness her lover's final reunion with the earth. I was wrong. Perhaps the rituals of mumbled Latin, flickering candles, and sprinklings of holy water insulted her Hebrew beliefs and she preferred to avoid them and honor his memory in her own way.

The funeral had put me in a somber mood that boded ill for my performance in the second *prova* that would take place that evening, so I headed for the lively atmosphere of Peretti's in an attempt to lighten my melancholy. There, for the price of a steaming cup and a pastry, a fellow could spend the afternoon dissecting the latest opera, gossiping about other singers, or catching the attention of impresarios looking for new talent. The décor of the place was shabby, but comfortable, with tables spilling out under the arcade and onto the Piazza when weather permitted. The billowing, gray clouds had given the priest a respite to bury our murdered painter but, around noon, the showers that had been soaking Venice resumed to cause Peretti's waiters much scurrying back and forth with chairs and tables.

Well-covered by the vaulted ceiling of the arcade, I was watching the raindrops splash into tiny fountains out on the pavement and fielding various acquaintances' questions about *Cesare*. As the opera's opening was set for three days hence, interest was running high. Most of the questions concerned Florio, of course. What was his highest note? How many bars could he sing without taking a breath? How had he developed his excellent trill? I soon wearied of the inquisition and sent a waiter for fresh coffee and more gazettes. When the fragrant cup was set before me, I pulled it to the table's edge and unfolded the first gazette. Encircled by a wall of paper, I could avoid questions about my rival and catch up on the news of the day.

The situation with the wells topped the columns of grimy newsprint. The San Rocco well was the fifth to go bad within the past week. The others had been scattered throughout the city, and the many households and shops that depended on their pure water had been greatly inconvenienced. The gazettes were rife with speculation about what might be causing this unprecedented occurrence. By far the most sensible theory was that the unusual amount of rain had caused a shift in the water level beneath the city and was allowing waste and sea water to seep into the cisterns. The officials of the Piovega, whose job it was to keep the canals free of accumulated rubbish and ensure a reliable supply of fresh water, were said to be taking measurements.

Unfortunately, many more columns of print were devoted to fantastical or preposterous theories. *L'Osservatore* blamed the phases of the moon allied with a hostile instability of planetary influences and called for the Senate to employ a renowned French astrologer to give advice on protecting the rest of Venice's wells. A daring stance indeed. I shook out the folds of the second gazette, a paper known for its close association with the Bishop of San Marco. Rather predictably, it warned that further calamities would surely follow unless the populace attended daily Mass and mended their lascivious ways. My third paper laid the blame at the feet of an earthly agent. Without naming names, the popular *Mondo Morale* suggested that noxious substances were being introduced into the wells for unexplained but clearly malicious purposes. The Jews and the Turks were both hinted at as possible culprits. My perusal of the hysterical rhetoric was interrupted when the tip of a walking stick crumpled the top edge of my paper.

"Maestro! You surprise me. I don't think I've ever seen you here at Peretti's."

"*Ciao*, Tito. I intended to nap before tonight's *prova*, but I was much too restless for sleep. I thought a turn around the Piazza might do me good, but the rain drove me under the arcades."

Without waiting for an invitation, Torani seated himself at my table and beckoned a waiter. "Watching Luca's box go into the ground reminded me of that eternity of solitude we all face. I found I couldn't just lie on my bed wondering how close my time might be."

"An eternity of solitude? Don't you believe in what the church teaches—that the angels carry the righteous up to heaven after death?"

Torani sucked in his cheeks, then declaimed in a flat voice, "The church is full of fairy tales for fools, my boy. If they would pay attention to the words you sing, people could learn more truth from our operas than from any churchman's rant."

I looked around uneasily. I saw no one that I did not recognize as being connected with Venice's musical world, but anyone could be a government informer. My city, that mercantile oligarchy that called herself a Republic, reveled in her role as Christian defender. She discouraged unorthodoxy with a number of unpleasant procedures that usually began with denunciation by an anonymous, but well-paid informer.

To my relief, Torani did not continue with that line of talk but instead turned to extolling the young man we had helped to bury that morning.

"What a waste, Tito. Luca's talent was superb. No theater artist could best him in creating illusion. He could transform any surface—canvas, plaster, wood—into anything he wished. If he had lived he could have been another Tiepolo."

"Artistry must run in the Cavalieri family. Luca's brother designs illustrations for a printer in Padua. Did you speak with him?"

"Silvio, younger than Luca by two years," the director observed, staring into space as if he was remembering events that had occurred long before that morning's funeral. "Yes, I spoke with him. The poor man was overcome with remorse. He told me that as boys he and Luca had been as close as two brothers could be. After their father died, their mother returned to the stage to earn their keep. She found work with a troupe that plays Italian comedy all over Europe, and though the boys were very young, she found a printer who took them on as apprentices. She sent money regularly but rarely visited. As the brothers reached manhood, they went their separate ways. Silvio was content to stay in Padua, but Luca wanted to expand his artistic talents and craved the excitement of Venice. Tears streamed down Silvio's cheeks as he told me the tale. Only thirty miles separate Padua from Venice, yet he had not seen his brother for almost two years."

"What a shame," I murmured, thinking of my own brother abroad in distant lands, then continued, "Silvio looks very like Luca. It gave me a moment's shock when I saw him in the funeral gondola. It was almost as if Luca's ghost had materialized to shepherd his own coffin to San Michele."

Torani nodded in agreement. "I saw you talking with Silvio, too. Did he tell you anything that could help find Luca's killer?"

"No, we spoke mainly of his mother, Theresa Cavalieri. She is currently appearing in Bremen, too far away to have returned to Venice for the funeral…" I hesitated, remembering Silvio's bitter comments about his mother's long absences, then added, "even if she had wished to."

Torani regarded his coffee cup with a pensive stare. He ran one finger around the rim, pausing in each circle at a chipped depression in the china. There would be no better time to ask a question which had been on my mind.

"Maestro, where were you on the night Luca was murdered?"

The director slowly looked up from his cup. The skin around his eyes was wrinkled and puffy. "Why do you ask, Tito?"

I met his gaze squarely. "On the night he disappeared, Luca was overheard having an argument with someone in his studio. I only wondered—if you were in the theater, you might have heard or seen something of it."

Torani arranged his lips into a casual smile, but his eyes watched mine carefully. "I wasn't there. I left the theater directly after rehearsal. I had other business to attend to."

"Oh. I see, other business."

"Yes." His voice sounded unnaturally thick in the damp air. "Who told you about the argument?"

"At present, it doesn't matter who."

"Must I remind you that you are working under my auspices?" His smile didn't waver. "I have a right to know whatever you have discovered."

I inclined my head toward the older man. "And so you shall, Maestro. When I have woven my slender strands of information into a recognizable pattern, you will be the first to examine it."

I knew that Torani was not pleased with my answer, but he didn't press me. The director simply nodded, then collected his walking stick and tricorne as he bade me be on time and in good voice for the *prova*.

⁂ ⁂ ⁂

The rain had settled into a light, but steady drizzle that showed every sign of continuing throughout the afternoon, but I had the good fortune to find a covered gondola to carry me home. I was mounting the slick steps at the bottom of the *calle* that led to the Campo dei Polli when a cloaked figure darted toward me from under the awning of a nearby shop. My hand sprang to the pocket that had housed my small stiletto ever since I had first interested myself in murderous doings. Unnecessarily. I relaxed when the figure lowered her hood.

"Please, Signore, my grandmother said I must find you. I've been waiting for hours. I thought you would never come."

"Mara," I exclaimed. "You are soaking wet. Come with me to my house. My sister will find something dry for you to put on."

The girl could have wrung water from the hood of her cloak and her dark hair clung to her cheeks in wet tendrils, but she managed a shy smile. "You know my name?"

"Of course, I heard your father call you by name the first time I visited your shop." I reached for her hand. "Come, my house is on the *campo* down this alley."

"No, no." Her eyes widened in distress. "You must come with me."

"Why?"

"My grandmother has something to tell you." Mara pulled anxiously at my hand. "Mama took my sisters to visit Aunt

Esther and the men are at synagogue. We have to get home before they return."

The gondola with the protective covering had departed, so I followed Liya's sister down the pavement that ran along the canal to the ghetto. It was Saturday, the Jew's Sabbath. All the shops within the walls were shut up tight, and the twisting alleys that led to the Del'Vecchio's *campo* were deserted. Even so, Mara rushed me past her family's clothing shop and into the shadowy tunnel by its side. She stopped at a recessed door, pressing her ear to the crack. Apparently satisfied, she drew me inside with her finger to her lips. In silence, we navigated stairways, halls, and storerooms that were as dark as the inside of my pocket. Finally, she led me into a corridor that I recognized from my previous visits to the Del'Vecchio home. The door to the sitting room stood open. I hesitated, but Mara resolutely hustled me into the room made overly warm by the crackling stove.

"At last! You certainly took your time, child. When I was your age, my legs could have outrun yours by a mile, especially if I'd been given an errand of trust." Despite the smothering heat, Liya's grandmother was nesting in layers of blankets and shawls. She flicked a long, bony finger in Mara's direction. "Close the door. You know what to do. I don't want your mother surprising us."

To me, the old woman croaked a more pleasant welcome. "Take your coat off, boy. Hang it there. It will dry. And sit, sit. Warm yourself at the stove." She reached forward in painfully slow jerks and took up a thin bamboo cane that leaned against the wall. She tapped at a three-legged stool before the stove. "Sit, warm yourself. I don't want you catching a chill when you have important work ahead of you."

"Right before the premiere of the new opera would be the worst possible time for a head cold," I agreed, moving the stool a few feet back from the stove's fire.

She shook her head, eyes bright and black within a frame of wrinkled skin that seemed as fragile as old parchment. "I am not speaking of your opera. I am speaking of what you are going to do for me, and for my granddaughter."

Intrigued, I held those bold, bright eyes with my own. "Why have you called me here, Signora Del'Vecchio?"

My question disturbed her. Her thin shoulders trembled beneath the shawls, and her cane tapped peevishly on the floor tiles. "Never call me Del'Vecchio. My name is Filomena Gallico. My daughter may please herself to ally with the Del'Vecchio clan but I am not one of *them*."

"*Scusi*, Signora Gallico, I meant no disrespect. I didn't know."

"There is much you don't know, you Venetians. You look to this ghetto, this pen where you have herded us, and see only a mass of Hebrews. You have no idea, the differences among us." She sighed wearily. "Tell me, do you know where my family, the Gallicos, hail from?"

I shook my head.

"Barcelona, the most cultured city in Spain. My people were scholars and physicians in the crown's service. For years of loyalty, my ancestor was made a cavalier with his own coat of arms. We had land, wealth. The Gallicos were a family of note." As she spoke, Liya's grandmother slowly uncurled her spine and sat very straight with the bony sweep of her aquiline nose high in the air.

I decided to hazard another question. "Why did your family leave Spain?"

"Leave? As if we were given a choice! We were banished, driven out. Thrown to the wolves by those we served." The bamboo stick rattled on the tiles. Spittle whitened the corners of her mouth. "It was the Devil's consort, Queen Isabella, and her Cardinal henchmen. First she banned the Hebrews from our trades, then stole our estates to enrich the royal treasury. When we were nearly starved she gave us all two months to get out of the country or be forcibly baptized into Spain's accursed religion. My grandfather's grandfather sold our last possessions for a mulecart and a few provisions, but the bandits on the highway took even those. We were forced to walk, walk through the countryside on bare feet like peasants, all the way to Italy."

"You amaze me, Signora. Queen Isabella ruled Spain over two hundred years ago, yet you speak as if you witnessed these events."

The old woman sank back into her nest of shawls and blankets. She answered in a voice heavy with the sorrows of centuries. "In my family, memories live a long time."

"And the Del'Vecchios—are they also from Spain?"

She barely shook her head. With her chin resting on her chest, she stared into the grate of the stove until I wondered if I should speak again or just creep away. Then she whispered fiercely, "The Del'Vecchios are rag-pickers from Livorno. Before they reached Italy, who knows where they wandered? Germany? Poland? What does it matter? It only matters that my granddaughter is not sacrificed to another Del'Vecchio."

I leaned forward. "Is that where I come in?"

She withdrew her gaze from the fiery grate and gave me a coy, almost flirtatious smile. "Just so, your cue I believe you call it at your opera. Pincas has it in mind to marry Liya to the son of his cousin. Before that can happen, Isacco Del'Vecchio must be persuaded to leave Venice. You are the man to persuade him."

I shook my head in bewilderment. Was the old woman more addled than she appeared? What would make Liya's cousin listen to me?

Signora Gallico had her argument on the tip of her tongue. "You have taken a decided interest in the painter who was killed at the theater."

"Yes," I answered cautiously.

"Would it interest you to know that Isacco had made a business partner of him?"

"What sort of business?"

"The details I cannot say, but I do know that Isacco and the painter had joined forces to make money off certain items that the painter provided and Isacco offered to interested customers."

I must have looked dubious, for she nodded vigorously and tapped my shin with her cane for emphasis. "Yes, it is so. I know what I'm talking about. People forget that I'm here, you see. They are so accustomed to Nonna drowsing by the stove that they look right through me. But I am not always asleep. My body is failing but my ears and eyes are not. Several times, Pincas warned Isacco away from this scheme, whatever it was. Pincas called it a dangerous game, but Isacco wouldn't listen. The boy just bragged on his cleverness and shook his heavy purse in my son-in-law's face."

"Did the painter—Luca Cavalieri—ever come here?"

"No, I never laid eyes on the man, but I heard Isacco speak of him more than once."

"They were friends?"

She snorted. "Not those two jackals. They needed each other for something, but there was no love lost between them. I knew they would fall out eventually."

"Are you telling me you think Isacco could have killed Luca?"

She narrowed her eyes and thought for a moment. "I doubt that. Isacco is a physical coward. He would run from violence as fast as his legs could carry him. Greed is that boy's vice—it will be the death of him one day."

"Then I don't understand. How is it that you propose I convince Isacco to leave the city?"

"Isacco and the painter were cheating their customers. They had to be. Isacco knows no other way of doing business, and besides, if the business had been aboveboard, he wouldn't have extracted a solemn promise of secrecy from Pincas." She pursed her lips, rocking back and forth from the waist, then continued, "I believe that Isacco and Luca ran afoul of someone who refused to be bilked, and the painter paid the price. Find out what they were up to. If you can convince Isacco that he is also in danger, he'll run back to Livorno like someone lit a fire under his tail."

I thought furiously. Luca and Isacco working together, selling something, the old woman said—who would have thought it? I wiped a hand over my forehead, now damp with sweat. Unable to bear the heat of the stove a moment longer, I stood up, paced the room, and found cooler air by the windows. As I watched the rain snake down the glass panes I thought back to that other wet day when Liya had come to my dressing room to beg for my help. She had needed me then. All pride and stiffness thrown aside, she had spoken right to my heart. Now her grandmother was asking for my help.

I turned back to the old woman. "What you have told me is one possible explanation for Luca's murder, but I can think of several others. It may take some time to discover the truth of the matter."

"There is no time." The *signora* worked her mouth anxiously. "I expect Pincas to approach the rabbi about Liya's marriage before the month is out. If Isacco is still in Venice, he will surely become her husband."

"And if he flees?"

She smiled broadly over toothless gums. "There is a medical student at Padua. Not a Gallico, but a young man of a good family connected to us by marriage."

"Your granddaughter does not seem particularly anxious to marry anyone. Why rush her to the altar?"

"Liya has made her choice—whether she realizes it or not."

I raised my eyebrows in a questioning look but Signora Gallico trained her gaze on the stove. Her voice became weak again. "You must leave an old woman some secrets, my boy. Use your wits to discover what devilment Isacco and the painter were up to. That way, you can find your murderer and chase Isacco away from Venice at the same time."

Despite Signora Gallico's reluctance, I wanted to ask more questions about Liya's situation. After all, the woman was requesting a favor; she should be willing to do me a service in return. But Mara, damp hair now covered by a white cap, emerged from the hallway with the breathless news that her mama was halfway across the *campo* and hurrying toward the shop. Instead of more information, Liya's grandmother gave me only a quick handclasp and a pleading look before Mara again led me stumbling through the labyrinth of stairs and corridors. Before I knew it, the girl was giving me a playful, conspiratorial wink and shoving me out yet another doorway onto the *campo*. The dripping, dreary walk home provided the perfect setting for moping over the possibility of Liya's marriage to either of her Hebrew suitors.

Chapter 15

The second *prova* proceeded more smoothly than the first. I was particularly pleased with my performance. If anything, the damp weather had limbered up my vocal cords, allowing me to execute all of my intricate embellishments with ease. There was only one bad moment. Florio must have been feeling bored, or perhaps my voice had improved enough to provoke his jealousy. During my final aria, with our characters of Caesar and Ptolemy facing each other at center stage, Florio sighed with exasperation, rolled his eyes, and turned a petulant face toward the pit, as if to ask the gondoliers who would be sitting there in three nights' time how much incompetence he could be expected to stand. When he began beating time with his forefingers in the air, suggesting that my rhythm was faulty, I strangled on my notes and erupted with a torrent of angry curses.

Florio met my outburst with a self-satisfied smile and a toss of his powdered curls. Too late I realized that the unpredictable *castrato* had provoked me deliberately, hoping that my anger would ruin my performance. He tricked me that time, but I vowed not to let him unsettle me again. More and more I was convinced that fate had supplied me with this challenger for a reason. Florio was meant to test my mettle. Would I continue to coast along on the natural splendor of my voice, settling for a flashy, crowd-pleasing display that ignored the composer's intent? Or would I delve into the beauty that could be achieved when the words and music were perfectly matched, when heartfelt sentiment was not overwhelmed by empty ornamentation? I was coming to understand that following Florio's path meant denying my very soul, at least the part of it that gloried in using the voice that the knife had bestowed on me.

With all the discipline I could muster, I calmed myself and approached the edge of the stage. Torani sat at the harpsichord, mopping his perspiring forehead with the end of his neck scarf. When I asked if we could repeat the scene, the director agreed with a preoccupied air that made me wonder if he had even attended to my fit of irritation.

I pondered Torani's attitude from the snug warmth of my bed the next morning. It puzzled me that the director had not intervened when Florio's foolery had commenced; Torani did not usually put up with such offensive behavior. Throughout the *prova*, our director had seemed curiously disconnected. He had guided the orchestra through the recitatives and arias but had addressed few corrections to the singers. The scene changes and other backstage business he had left totally in Aldo's hands. Was he worrying about with the future of the San Marco company? Had the Savio threatened him with closing the theater again?

With a lazy yawn, I put my questions about Torani aside and thought ahead to the rest of the day. It was Sunday, so there would be no *prova* that night—the final rehearsal was scheduled for tomorrow—but Gussie and I were expected at the Palazzo Morelli in the afternoon. I felt surprisingly fresh for having endured two lengthy rehearsals in as many nights, but I wasn't at all sure I was ready to face Isabella Morelli's overripe coquetry.

Benito entered and set a roll and a steaming cup of chocolate at my bedside. With graceful gestures he unfurled a cloth on top of the bedclothes and rearranged my pillows. As I reclined at an angle and bit into the buttery pastry, my manservant flipped through the coats hanging in my wardrobe.

"Which suit will you wear today, Master?"

"Nothing fancy. Just pick out something I would wear to a rehearsal."

"Master? A plain suit for the *palazzo*? Why not the peach taffeta with the embroidered waistcoat? I have it ready—clean and pressed." Benito's lilting voice held a wheedling note.

I smiled, but answered firmly, "No. I don't want to call attention to myself today. I plan to fade into the background and let Signor Rumbolt take center stage. Get out the green broadcloth."

Benito retrieved the dark jacket and breeches with unconcealed disdain. As he checked the buttonholes and seams for stray threads, he observed sulkily, "There is no way you could fade into the background—even if you donned a tradesman's smock."

"You exaggerate as usual. There are some who find Signor Rumbolt much more interesting than myself. Signora Morelli for one."

Benito rolled his eyes and shook his head.

"Oh, yes. The *signora* has an eye for a robust male, and her tastes suit my needs admirably. While our English friend amuses the lovely Isabella with sketching and flattering conversation, I will be prowling the *palazzo*."

"What are you looking for now?"

"Anything that could tell me why an arrogant patrician like Morelli would be drinking in a tavern with a painter of little social standing." I thought for a moment, sipping the warm chocolate. "Signora Morelli seems quite taken with Gussie as he is, but perhaps I should send you around to his lodging just in case. His mop could benefit from your talented curling wand."

"Too late, my friend," Gussie's voice boomed out as he bounded through my door, all smiles and good humor. "As you requested, I am here and turned out in my best."

Gussie had outdone himself. The coat that covered his broad shoulders, though cut in the English fashion, was the bright blue of the lagoon on a sunny day, a color that also precisely matched my friend's eyes. He had polished the coat's gold buttons to a high luster and found a new pair of stockings to cover the muscular calves that should hold Signora Morelli's attention for at least a few minutes. Unfortunately, my friend's unruly yellow hair was springing from his forehead at an odd angle.

"Good, well done," I told him. "You have me beat this morning. Make yourself comfortable. When Benito is finished with me, perhaps he could give you a few minutes. His combs and brushes can work magic."

Gussie glanced in the mirror, shrugged, and threw himself in a deep chair by the window. "Why not? I have schooled myself to be the soul of agreeability the whole day through. Just don't leave me alone with our hostess at the *palazzo* for too long, Tito."

"You speak as if you were afraid of Signora Morelli."

"I suppose I am a bit. I fear that she is cleverer than I… at least in the banter of romance." He gave a mock shudder and continued, "You will owe me an enormous favor for spending the afternoon with such an odious woman."

I smiled as I had a quick wash at the basin that Benito had filled with hot water. "I wouldn't call her odious. She is not the first Venetian wife to be a little naughty. Can you really blame her? What must her life be like with Morelli as a husband? That man is trying to single-handedly preserve the atrophied society of our grandfathers' time."

As Gussie shook his head in reply, Benito studied something he had removed from the pocket of my broadcloth coat. "Do you need this, Master?"

He handed me a folded slip of paper. The piece had been torn from a larger sheet; the diagonal edge was ragged and uneven. Was it a name and address? The top line read There-, a torn space, then -ieri. On the next line: H-, Bremen. I turned the paper over. The written address on the other side was easily readable. "Oh, yes. This is the address Torani gave me. Remember, Gussie, when we went to Luca's lodging? I have no further need of it."

I handed the paper to Benito, who reached to feed it to the flames in the little stove he used to heat his curling wand. The manservant squealed when I whirled around, grabbed his wrist, and ran to the window blowing on the smoking paper.

"What is it?" Benito's soprano and Gussie's baritone sounded in a spontaneous duet.

I studied the scorched paper in the patch of sunlight streaming through the narrow panes. The first line could represent Theresa Ballieri, or Dottieri, or any number of other names. But who was the Theresa whose son had just told me that she had a two-month contract to appear in Bremen? Only Theresa Cavalieri, mother of Luca and Silvio.

⁂

"What does this mean, Tito?" Gussie and I were leaning on the railing of a small wooden bridge that spanned a canal near the Campo dei Polli. The day was mild and the sound of church bells carried on the light breeze. The sun, arching toward its zenith, would soon dry the puddles left by yesterday's rainstorm. The birds washing their feathers would be the only ones disappointed to see the puddles' demise. All the people crossing the bridge and strolling the pavement had their faces raised to the clear blue sky, doubtless hoping that we had seen the last of gray days.

I frowned down at the slowly moving green water under the bridge. "It means that Torani, the director I have worked with and trusted for most of the past four years, has something to hide."

"Because…"

"Because Torani wrote Luca's address on a corner torn from a larger sheet of paper on his desk. Yet when the Savio asked him how to contact Luca's family, Torani said he had no idea where the mother was. He acted as if he barely knew who she was."

"You didn't notice the back of the paper before?"

"It wouldn't have meant anything to me if I had. I just learned Luca's mother's Christian name and whereabouts at the funeral yesterday morning."

Gussie regarded me bleakly but didn't speak.

I drummed my fingers on the smooth wood of the railing. "We need to find out more about everyone's movements on the night Luca was murdered. Torani said that he left the theater after rehearsal, but Emma heard someone arguing with Luca."

"I thought she was unable to recognize the voice?"

"So she says, but I wouldn't be surprised if she weren't protecting someone."

"Torani?"

"That would make sense. What would happen to Emma if Torani were arrested? Her voice is beginning to decline and her face is no longer fresh. She and Torani share a comfortable working relationship, but a new director would likely hire a new soprano."

"But Tito, if Torani had a hand in Luca's death, why would he ask you to investigate his disappearance in the first place?"

I turned my back to the railing and let the sun warm my face. "I don't know. I'm still wrestling with the idea that Torani could be capable of bashing Luca's skull, strangling the life out of him, then dumping his body in the lagoon like a bag of refuse. No matter how hard I try, I just can't picture it.

"Come on, Gussie, I can't just stand here. Let's walk." I started down the descending arc of the bridge at a fast pace.

Gussie tapped me on the shoulder. "Tito, the Palazzo Morelli is on the Grand Canal. Aren't we going the wrong way?"

"If we want some answers about who was in the theater during the last hour of Luca's life, we are going in the right direction." I paused to bring my friend's steps in line with my own. "We are going to Aldo's house. He lives on a *campo* just on the other side of the ghetto."

"But… the *palazzo*."

"It's early yet. There is still plenty of time for you to amuse Signora Morelli. You didn't forget your sketchbook, did you?"

He patted a pocket, shook his head, and once again fell in behind me as a pair of porters wheeling carts full of crockery and covered dishes nestled in straw took up most of the pavement. A large family followed: a smiling, prosperous papa with a silver-headed walking stick, a mama rigged out in a *zendale* edged with fine lace, and six children in perfect stairsteps whispering and giggling in a train behind them. It was a lovely day for a picnic. I wondered if they would hire a boat to carry them to the public gardens on the Giudecca. With the state wedding close at hand, they would find the park filled with booths selling treats and makeshift stages with clowns and marionette shows to delight the children.

Not everyone milling about in the sunshine shared the family's holiday spirit. When Gussie and I rounded the tip of the ghetto, we found a crowd gathered at the foot of the north bridge. Most were men who appeared to be shopkeepers or craftsmen, but there were also quite a few women dressed in the modest skirts and shawls of housewives. An air of crisis hung over the group. Angry words floated up from knots of sullen-looking men and a few fists were raised. The Christian guards at the open gates seemed more entertained than threatened by the display.

I approached a slight fellow in a coarse waistcoat and shirt-sleeves who was hovering around the edge of the crowd. "What goes on, friend?"

"Haven't you heard? The Doge's own well has been poisoned. Someone got to the inner courtyard of the palace. Crept in right under the soldiers' noses."

"Then why are people gathering here?"

The man grabbed at the chance to enlighten someone who had not heard the news. "They say the Jews are behind it all. The old people remember when such things happened before. Now the villains are at it again."

I kept my tone as affable as I could. "Surely not. I thought it was the wet weather that was playing havoc with the wells."

The man's lip curled up in disdain. "If you believe that story, you should be listening to fairy tales in the nursery with the other children."

A red-faced woman with heavy breasts straining at her tightly lapped shawl elbowed the little man aside. "Marcello knows what he says. Already the ghetto pawnshops rob the poor of their heirlooms and make beggars of honest citizens. Now the Hebrews want to steal our water to ruin us entirely."

"No one is forced to visit the pawnshops," I countered. "If we didn't pauper ourselves at the gaming tables, the pawnshops would have no business."

My adversary rolled up her sleeves and began to move her head from side to side in a show of blowzy belligerence. I shook my head, unsure of what to say to calm her agitation. The man took my silence as an invitation to pipe up again in self-important tones. "Next thing we know, the infidel dogs will be trying to sell us water. You're not taking their side, are you?"

Gussie tugged at my sleeve. He leaned close. Distress, or perhaps an instinct for self-preservation, moved him to speak in his own tongue. "Tito, I am at your service, but two cannot fight a mob. I suggest we retreat. Now."

The meaning of half his English words escaped me, but the looks on the faces around us did not. My conversation with Marcello had attracted attention. The crowd was taut with anger, like a drawn bow searching for a target. Gussie was right. A strategic retreat was called for. I made a series of quick half-bows, murmured apologies for my thick head, and soon Gussie and I were hurrying down a side-street, concerned but unharmed.

Aldo lived on a little *campo* to the right of a rambling church owned by an order of barefoot friars. His square was treeless and only partially paved. At midsummer it would be uncomfortably hot and dusty. A woman packing an oil jar directed us to the right house, and a few loafing boys gathered to watch me pull the bell cord. The door was opened by a wide-eyed girl of perhaps six years. Her siblings were making a racket in the room behind her.

"Is your papa at home?" I asked.

She eyed us warily, sucked at two of her fingers, and looked as if she might slam the door at any moment.

Gussie smiled and squatted to her level. "Please, *cara* Signorina, your papa?"

Without changing her expression, the girl disappeared into the depths of the house. The door slowly swung shut; our audience of idlers laughed derisively. My eye caught a flurry of movement from a window on an upper story.

"Should we ring again, or go on to the *palazzo*?" Gussie asked.

I reached for the cord. Aldo had avoided me long enough.

Before I could ring, the door opened again. A delicate woman with a pile of untidy hair and shy, downcast eyes met us at the threshold. She balanced a chubby baby surrounded by a sour odor on her aproned hip. "I'm sorry, my husband is not at home."

"When do you expect him, Signora?"

"I don't know." She smiled and looked up at us through thick, coal-black lashes. "Aldo went to Mass early this morning. After that, he had business to take care of… people to see. He will probably be quite late," she finished softly.

There was no use questioning her further. Gussie and I strolled back across the *campo* with the boys straggling behind us. When we reached the corner of the church, I turned and asked, "Who knows the café under the red awning on the other side of the canal?"

Four voices competed to assure me they knew the very place.

"I will be waiting there for the next two hours. I have a *zecchino* for the first to bring me word that the master of the house which I just visited has stepped over his threshold."

With whoops of excitement, the boys scurried back to the *campo*.

Gussie grinned. "What luck! I'm glad Aldo wasn't at home. Taking a glass at a café with you is a much more pleasant prospect than dodging Isabella Morelli's amorous volleys."

"I'm sorry to disappoint you, my friend, but I'll be drinking alone. You are going to the *palazzo*."

The Englishman's stricken face was a sight to see. "Oh no, Tito. I can't distract Isabella and look around the *palazzo* at the same time."

"You won't have to. Put your creative powers to work. Ask Isabella to give you a tour of the place. I'm sure she will if you find the right way to ask her."

"I don't even know what to look for."

"Use your artist's eyes. Observe everything as if you were going to draw it later. Pay close attention to the unexpected or anything that doesn't seem to make sense. And try to get

Isabella talking about the theater. Luca's death still has tongues wagging—ask her if she knew him."

After a few more minutes of persuasion, Gussie trudged off on what he termed his "loathsome errand" and I settled in at the café. I refused to believe that Aldo had roused himself for an early morning Mass. I had not left the theater until an hour after midnight, and the stage manager's duties would have kept Aldo busy long after the cast had been released. Before long, I fully expected one of the boys to fly around the corner with the news that Aldo had left the house. My intent was to follow the stage manager and learn whatever I could. If I was wrong and Aldo was away from home, at least I would be alerted when he returned. And I would not allow myself to be turned away again.

Chapter 16

There is a blessed sense of release that comes with the completion of a challenging task. Mastering a tricky aria always makes me feel as if I am walking on the clouds, as free ranging as a bird. So does fashioning a clever plan that comes to fruition with every detail realized. Unfortunately, that does not describe my frame of mind as we dined on our roof terrace that Sunday evening. I couldn't even remember the last time I'd felt the elation of an unqualified success. It was beginning to seem as if everything I touched was doomed to frustration and failure.

"Our day a failure? I wouldn't call it that." Gussie interrupted himself to take a bite of cold chicken, then continued. "We both found out something of interest. Now we know that Morelli is presenting Venice with a sham of a *palazzo*."

Annetta left the table and wandered over to the stone parapet that enclosed the open end of our garden terrace and gave a fine view of the neighboring squares. Ever since I had returned home, she had been fussing and driving Benito to distraction over supper preparations, yet her plate of food sat at the end of the table, barely touched. She asked, "Did Signor Morelli attend his wife's gathering?"

Gussie shot me a quick look before he answered, "No."

My sister leaned against the railing with arms crossed over her simple dress of russet red, hair wound around her head in the thick braids that Gussie would rather see flowing free. She plucked a blossom from a terra-cotta urn overflowing with pink geraniums. Picking nervously at the petals, she posed another question: "How ever did you manage to get away from Signora Morelli and her guests to explore the *palazzo*?"

"The other guests were all female. I think Signora Morelli wanted to display me to her friends like I was an exotic pet—a trained monkey or something of the sort. When I excused myself to find the water closet, they could hardly follow."

"Oh, I see. Isabella Morelli thinks she owns you now."

Gussie pretended not to hear the pique in Annetta's tone and went on to describe what he'd found. "The sitting room where we were received was set up well enough. It was part of our hostess' private suite. The furniture was of excellent quality, and the ceiling was frescoed with some lovely clouds that looked as if they'd been freshly painted. But when I looked behind the hangings that hid other rooms outside her suite, all I saw were bare floors, walls discolored by damp, and fallen moldings crumbling into powder."

"Any furniture or paintings in those rooms?" I asked.

"No. I went through one chamber that opened onto a balcony overlooking the main reception hall on the first level. The hall below was in decent shape, but the chamber leading to the balcony was completely bare. Its walls showed light-colored patches where paintings and mirrors would have once hung, but now... nothing. Mind you, I didn't have time to look everywhere—the *palazzo* is a sprawling old pile—but the whole place had a musty air of disuse about it."

"Did any footmen pop up to direct you?"

"The only servant I saw was an ancient crone who brought in a tray of lemonade."

I rubbed my chin, ignoring the cold fowl and fruit laid out before me. "So Morelli is deceiving Venice with a few showy rooms. He plays the affluent aristocrat, excessively proud of his long pedigree and always careful to echo the dictates of the supreme Tribunal, but he must be nearing the end of his family's fortune."

Gussie nodded. "Unless he has a chest of gold ducats hidden away, it looks like there's not much left."

From behind me, Annetta asked, "And what of Isabella? Was she wearing jewels? A fine gown?"

I sent Gussie a warning wink, but I needn't have bothered. For all his naïve charm, Gussie knew a thing or two about the matters that take precedence in the female brain. He affected a disinterested look and said, "She may have worn a small necklace of pearls. I'm not sure. I didn't notice her gown. I stayed as far away from my hostess as possible. I don't care for her ways—her smiles have evil designs behind them."

Though she was out of my sight, I knew Annetta had relaxed. I wasn't surprised when she returned to the table and began to nibble at a slice of watermelon. "What was the interesting thing you found, Tito?" she asked with a bright smile.

I sighed, "I hardly like to say. I watched Aldo set off for a private meeting with Torani."

Annetta drew her eyebrows up and spit a watermelon seed into her napkin. "Is that unusual? After all, they work together."

"I can't think why they would meet outside the theater. Torani rarely socializes with anyone from the company, certainly not Aldo, and any opera business could be addressed during the long hours we've all been putting in at rehearsals."

"Perhaps it was a chance meeting."

"No, I'm certain it was prearranged."

"What happened?"

"I hadn't been at the café long when the swiftest of the boys came to claim his *zecchino*. I had no problem following Aldo down the wide Fondamenta della Misericordia and over to the Strada Nova. He was not trying to hide his movements… seemed quite full of himself, in fact, calling greetings to acquaintances and swaggering like a man who'd just broken the bank at the Ridotto."

"Did you mean to overtake him?" That was Gussie, waving a pesky fly away from the melon.

"I did, but I was hanging back to see where he was going. When we neared the Rialto, I thought I should make my move." I paused, remembering how Aldo had consulted his watch, then increased his pace through the network of mazelike *calli* around the markets. That area is thick with shops and taverns that line some of the narrowest, crookedest streets in the city. Aldo lost me several times, but each time I managed to spot him again as he crossed a square before one of the innumerable churches that also pack the neighborhood.

"Where was he going, Tito?" Annetta asked.

"The quay between the bridge and the German warehouse. When he stepped onto the open pavement, I was just a few steps behind and ready to tap him on the shoulder, but he didn't hesitate for even an instant. He'd found what he came for."

Benito chose that moment to come onto the roof and offer us a plate of lemon biscuits and a pot of coffee. He gave a discontented shrug as Gussie and Annetta shook their heads. "Go on, Tito," Annetta cried. "Was Torani waiting for him?"

"A solitary gondola was bobbing at the quay. Aldo made straight for it and I drew back behind a group of countrywomen arguing about the quickest way to the Piazza. The gondola's passenger was masked, but he raised his mask for a moment when Aldo stumbled and had to be steadied into the boat."

"You're sure it was Torani?"

I nodded ruefully. "Oh yes, I have no doubt that it was Maestro Torani in the gondola. He clearly had business with Aldo that he wanted to discuss in private. But what they talked about—I have no clue."

Annetta had wandered back to the parapet. "Did you try to follow the boat?"

"Of course, they headed south. I ran along the canal, hoping to pick up an empty gondola, but on such a beautiful day every boat was engaged. I finally lost them near the Palazzo Grimani."

Gussie shook his head and took his cup to the railing to join Annetta. The sound of their low voices provided a background for my thoughts. Something had just occurred to me—perhaps I had reversed the true situation. Torani's status led me to assume that the director had called for the meeting, but Aldo could just as well have arranged it for reasons of his own.

Annetta raised her voice. "Tito, leave your gloomy face over there and come look at this amazing sunset."

We had not had such a celestial display for a long time. Above the slanting rooftops and church spires, a ragged bank of clouds glowed like a crescent of flame. With each passing second, its crimson glory deepened and intensified. Just as it seemed the shining arc would burst and run with molten gold, a cascade of bells rang out across the city and was answered by a murmur from the bell towers on the lagoon islands. The sobbing of the bells sounded a dirge for the flaming cloud. It abruptly grayed and shredded away to the west, leaving us wondering if the sunset we had just witnessed could possibly have been as beautiful as we remembered.

Benito had been hovering around the table, brushing up crumbs and stacking dishes onto a tray. After folding the table-cloth into a neat square, he threw something down on the bare tabletop. "Master, have you seen what is being distributed on the Piazza?"

I crossed the tiles and picked up a slim pamphlet entitled *The Truth of the Villainous Crimes Recently Perpetrated on Our Most Serene and Christian Republic*. It was the type of partisan booklet often printed by those with more money than reason. A quick leaf through the pages made this pamphlet's intent perfectly clear. In flagrant language that made the article I had read in the gazette seem like a model of subtlety, the anonymous author accused the Jews of a plot to corrupt all the island's wells and cisterns.

"Where did you get this?"

Benito's eyes lacked their usual twinkle and his voice was solemn. "On the Mercerie. At a coffeehouse I often visit. Hundreds must have been printed. By the end of the afternoon, everyone in the vicinity of the Piazza seemed to have one in their hands."

"What were people saying?"

My little manservant shrugged. "All manner of things. Most people laughed and tossed the pamphlet aside, but some discussed it with others and seemed concerned. A few cursed and looked angry enough to throttle the next Hebrew they saw."

Gussie and Annetta had their heads together, examining the booklet more carefully than I had. My friend gave a low whistle. "Here, Tito, you had better take a look at this." He handed me the pamphlet with his finger pointing to a long passage.

After exhausting his malicious invective concerning the water supply, the writer turned his attention to another recent crime. The murder of Luca Cavalieri was rehashed and presented as another strategy in the Jews' scheme to terrorize the city and enslave the Republic to the nation of Abraham. As the writer strove to connect the ruined wells and the painter's death, he asked: "Will those who crucified our Lord be allowed to murder good citizens one by one as we go about our daily business?" With a duplicitous show of discretion, the writer even alluded to one "I____o D__'V____ o, a thieving infidel lately arrived from the free port of Livorno" as the murderous agent. No evidence was given to convince the reader of Isacco's guilt, but then, there was not one true, undistorted fact in the entire vile publication.

I threw the pamphlet on the table. Disgust and anger gave my voice a sharp edge. "Benito, you should have given me this at once."

My manservant assumed his most pained, affronted expression. "I didn't think it would be proper to ruin your supper. After all, what can you do about it? The book is all over Venice by now."

"Still…" I muttered, trying to find the right words to sooth Benito's ruffled feathers and explain the sickening uneasiness that was stirring within me.

"Oh, no," Annetta whispered behind me. She rushed to the railing. "Something has caught fire."

Beyond the rooftops of the neighboring *campi*, wisps of gray smoke were barely visible against the darkening sky. "Perhaps someone is burning a pile of trash," Gussie said hopefully. We all nodded, praying the Englishman was correct. But presently, the breeze wafted small pieces of ash to our terrace and the air over a cluster of taller buildings to the west took on a subtle yellow-orange glow. Annetta clutched my arm.

"Oh, Tito," she said, telling me what I already knew, "it must be in the ghetto."

Chapter 17

"I have to get to Liya." That was all I had to say to start our rush to the ghetto. With Gussie's bright blue shoulders parting the way and Annetta and Benito directly on my heels, we hurried along the crowded pavements. A few people were running the other way, driven by some animal instinct that warned them away from danger, but most were hurrying our direction, unable to resist the lure of an exciting blaze.

The fire was definitely within the ghetto walls. The smoke had thickened into a black column above the tightly packed buildings. Each time I passed a man carrying a torch, I thought of the heaps of cotton wool in the mattress maker's courtyard behind Liya's building and urged Gussie to quicken his steps. We had headed for the nearest bridge over the encircling waters, but soon saw that passage across it would be impossible. We were on the fringes of a growing riot.

Violent mobs are not common in Venice. When a crowd gathers, it is usually to frolic, not brawl. But the scurrilous pamphlet, building on the groundwork laid by the gazettes and who knows how many rumormongers, had raised citywide tension to an unprecedented height. That night, Venice's mask of grandeur and gaiety fell away and all that remained was a hideous face filled with hate and fear.

The four of us were quickly hemmed in by angry rioters carrying sacks of rotten fruit or more substantial missiles—stones.

Dodging fists and elbows, I turned and yelled to Benito, "Get Annetta out of here. Take her back home."

My sister shook her head and cried above the din, "What about you and Augustus? We can't leave you here in this mob."

"We'll take care of each other. You go with Benito." Annetta had a determined set to her jaw so I went on, "You can't be of any help here. Please, Annetta, do as I say for once." To my great relief, she nodded, and with a last worried look, let Benito draw her away from the hectic, roiling crowd.

"Come on! This way!" Gussie dove into a narrow alley that led in the general direction of the north bridge. By the time we reached the pavement beside that span, my heart was pounding and my side was burning. Luckily, the crowd was thinner there, and its tone was more curious than angry. For the first time that night, I caught sight of an official presence. A small barge of Venetian archers floated on the canal, but the men appeared leaderless and at a loss as to what they should be doing or whom they should be arresting. The gates in the stout walls were still open. No one tried to stop us as Gussie and I crossed the bridge and followed the smoke to the fire.

At first, Liya's *campo* seemed like a swirling mass of pure confusion. People were pounding past us, running aimlessly, tripping over furniture and merchandise that had been tossed from endangered homes and shops. Women wailed, children sobbed, and dogs barked. Gradually I saw that efforts to fight the blaze were underway. The fire must have started in the Del'Vecchio shop. The front windows had been broken out and tongues of flame were shooting through the openings. The tunnel-like passage that Mara had led me through only yesterday afternoon was belching smoke at an alarming rate.

Some men and boys in shirtsleeves were working at a pile of sandbags, emptying them around the foundation of the pink-plastered building on the other side of the tunnel from the Del'Vecchio establishment. Another group had formed a tight line that snaked out from the well in the center of the *campo*.

They were passing buckets in a well-drilled formation and throwing water on the pink walls.

We found the Del'Vecchio women huddled in front of their burning house. Pincas and Isacco were nowhere to be seen. The grandmother was propped up on a pile of clothing and bedding, her head bent nearly to her knees, her eyes covered by one skeletal hand. Signora Del'Vecchio was shaking Mara by the shoulders. "Where is the baby? You and Liya were supposed to get her while Sara and I carried Nonna down the back stairs."

"Mama, stop." The girl's teeth were rattling. "Liya has Fortunata, they were right behind us."

Her mother's sweaty, soot-streaked face showed livid in the fire's glow. "But where are they? Where is Liya? Where is Fortunata?" She released Mara and began to shake her younger sister, shouting the same questions.

I turned my attention to the Del'Vecchio building. The shop had become a furnace of solid orange, and the growing heat forced us all to shuffle backward. Gussie and I carried the grandmother, her weight no heavier than a bundle of dry sticks. As we set her down, the fire found new strength, leaping along the outside walls toward the upper floors. A white face appeared in the dark rectangle of a third-story window. Liya. In that instant, my blood chilled and my ears reverberated with Signora Del'Vecchio's wailing scream.

Liya leaned over the casement, but a stream of orange flame shooting out of the window of the second story drove her back. The heat must have been intense, but she didn't panic, just peered around the window frame more carefully, twisting from side to side with a calculating look. Anguished moans and feverish curses rose from the crowd. I yelled up to her, not even sure what I was saying.

Liya didn't seem to hear any of it. The fire had shut her into an isolated, nightmare world where only the next few moments' survival mattered. Suddenly, a huge crack sounded, and a cloud of black smoke rolled up the front of the building, obscuring my view of the woman I then realized had taken full possession of my heart. Dimly, I felt Gussie squeezing my shoulder so hard I thought he might splinter my bones.

The light breeze soon sucked the smoke away in writhing wisps. I spotted the window, but Liya had vanished.

"Gussie, we've got to do something." I whirled in a tight circle, desperate, searching, then ran toward the cordon of men passing buckets. Stumbling down the line, I begged them to turn from the pink building, to throw their water on the Del'Vecchio house, but they continued to douse their target with dogged precision. I shoved and pulled, grabbing at their buckets. "Can't you see that someone is still in there. She's trapped for God's sake."

A tall, bearded man in the garb of a rabbi grabbed my shoulders and spun me around. "Leave them alone, my son. The fire brigade is doing what needs to be done. The Del'Vecchio house is lost, but if this building catches, the fire will burn right around the *campo*."

I swayed on my feet, not sure whether I had tears or sweat running down my cheeks. "What about that building?" I pointed to the taller edifice on the opposite side of Liya's house.

The rabbi had to raise his voice to be heard over the terrible clash of roaring flames and shouting people. "Its roof is tile and its walls are brick. Triple-thick masonry between it and Pincas' place. With God's mercy, that house will withstand the blaze." Sure enough, there was no sign of fire in the neighboring house.

Gussie ran up, gesticulating wildly. "Look, Tito. She's still there."

My gaze followed his pointing arm. Liya had found her way to the house's top story. She stepped onto a balcony that embraced a tall, narrow window just under the eaves, then pulled a wiggling bundle through the window behind her. It was Fortunata. Both girls were coughing and grimed with soot, but Liya still had her presence of mind. She pushed the window casement closed and knelt on the balcony to tend to her sister.

On the pavement below, several men made a cradle of their arms and urged Liya to throw Fortunata down to them. Others fetched a canvas tarpaulin, stretched it into a taut square, and shouted for Liya to jump with Fortunata in her arms. Nearby, Signora Del'Vecchio covered her face with her hands. The woman was near collapse, held up only by her other two daughters pressing to her sides.

Still kneeling, Liya looked down through the bars of the iron railing. I imagined the thoughts that must be fleeting through her mind: were the excited men capable of catching the child that would drop like a thirty-pound cannonball, could that canvas hold their combined weights or would it rip apart to dash them both on the hard paving stones? From her fourth-floor perch, the ground must have seemed very far away. Groaning, my hands balled to fists, I watched Liya place Fortunata's hands firmly around the railing bars and put her mouth next to her ear. Was she instructing the little girl to jump if the flames broke through the window? I shook my head as Liya stood up, patted her stomach, and climbed nimbly onto the balcony railing. Balancing carefully, she began to inch her hands along the window frame toward the lower edge of the roof. It wouldn't work. Liya wasn't tall enough to reach the roof. Even if she could, there was no way she could pull them both over and around the projecting overhang.

"Come on, Gussie." I pulled my friend toward the brick building to the right of Liya's. "I have an idea… if we can just get up to them." The brick house topped Liya's by a story and, so far, its façade was free of flames. Its inhabitants had fled the building, but were standing in a protective knot in front of it. They howled as we barged through and Gussie applied his shoulder and then his foot to their door.

Though the inside was smoky and dim, enough light filtered through the large shop windows to see the stairs at the back. I looked furiously for a length of rope or wire that could help us get to Liya's roof, but we were in a bookshop—not much useful there. I finally charged the stairs, somehow believing that we would find a way to rescue Liya and Fortunata if we could just make it to the roof.

Above the first floor, the smoke thinned and breathing was easier, but the thickening darkness made for a treacherous enemy.

We banged into closed doors, smashed heads on low crossbeams, and tripped over crates of books. Clumsily feeling my way to the top of the staircase, I found the arrangement much the same as at my own home. A door opened onto a flat roof area surrounded by sloping, tiled surfaces dotted with chimney pots. Only the bookshop family did not use their roof as a garden. Soot-flecked laundry was strung on a line that ran from corner to corner.

Gussie had the rope down in an instant. He wound it several times around a stone drain spout and grasped the end with his feet firmly braced against the parapet. "Can you get down by yourself? I'll have to stay up here to catch the rope and pull you and the girls back up."

I didn't stop to discuss the plan, just grabbed the rope and threw a leg over the parapet. As boys, Alessandro and I had climbed every tree and bridge support within a mile of the Campo dei Polli, but those energetic days were long past. I had forgotten how much strength it took to hang by arms alone and found I had no idea how to make my feet find the wall and start backing my way down to the lower roof. I simply slid, burning the skin from my palms and meeting the roof tiles with a hard thump on my backside. Dazed, I struggled to my feet and explored Liya's flat roof on rubbery legs.

The smoke was thicker there, making it difficult to get my bearings. Cautiously, I peered over one edge, hot breath catching in my throat. I was staring down into the gateway to hell. Individual fires like dancing haystacks of flame dotted the courtyard, and the very air shimmered with the terrible heat. A roar more like the crashing waves of the sea filled my ears. It was the mattress maker's courtyard. I was on the wrong side of the building.

In a blind panic, I ran straight across the roof. I don't know which angels kept me from tripping over loose tiles or crashing into chimney pots, but I reached the opposite edge and threw myself down at full length. Clutching the edge of the tiles, I extended my head and shoulders out into smoky space. Liya was crouching in the corner of the balcony with Fortunata in her arms. Black, grasping tendrils swirled around them. I only had to cry her name once.

"Tito! Where did you come from?" She jumped up, face blackened by smoke but brightened by new hope.

"I'm going to pull you up."

Her eyes searched the roof overhang in desperate confusion. "How?"

My heart sank. In my haste, I'd left the rope back where I'd slid down. I looked into Liya's huge dark eyes. How could I have been so stupid? A glowing strand of flame started up the wooden frame of the balcony's window. Fortunata screamed in terror. Liya called up, "Hurry, Tito. Do something or we'll have to jump."

Would there be time to go back for the rope? Sobbing in fear and frustration, I bounced to one knee for the dash back across the roof. But no, I didn't need to run. The rope was suddenly in my hand, and Gussie was materializing out of the billowing smoke like a stage god lowered magically to the rescue.

"We have help," he shouted as he made the rope fast and threw one end over the edge. Through gaps in the smoke, I saw several young men positioning a ladder against the wall of the bookshop building that connected the two roofs. After I'd raised Fortunata from the balcony, a muscular Jew about Mara's age took the shrieking child and ferried her to others who passed her up the ladder in short order. Together Gussie and I hauled at the rope until Liya was also pulled from danger.

Finally I held my beloved in my arms. She was coughing and sputtering, sweat-soaked, and soot-streaked, but she was alive. I caressed her hair and cried with joy.

Liya clung to me for a few moments, then pushed me away. She tilted her chin back and looked deeply into my eyes. She shook her head. "You don't know what you've done, do you?"

"I saved you and Fortunata," I answered, surprised by her accusing tone.

"Yes, you saved us." Her blackened face was a study in warring emotions. "From a fire that would never have started except for your meddling."

Part Three

Terra: Earth

Chapter 18

The ghetto finally slept. The riot had been quelled by the arrival of Messer Grande and his constables. The *cittadini* had gone more than a little mad that night, but it had taken only the sight of Messer Grande's red robe to restore their sanity. No man wanted to face Venice's dreaded prisons if he could avoid them. After the rioters had slunk back to their own neighborhoods, many no doubt bewildered by the uncommon violence they had wrought, the ghetto had licked its wounds, shuttered its windows, and locked its gates.

The Del'Vecchio family had taken refuge at the house of Pincas' brother, Baruch. A few alleys away, the ruins of their household and shop were smoldering under the steady patter of a light drizzle. The skies had eventually answered the Jews' prayers with yet more rain, a bit late but welcome nevertheless. Gussie and I were sitting with Pincas at his brother's dining table. The clothing dealer stared into an untouched glass of wine, blood crusted along a gash that blazoned his forehead. His bruised jowls hung slackly and his face seemed drained of all emotion. Fortunata nestled fast asleep on her father's lap, one cheek buried in his shoulder. Someone had wiped the little girl's face and hands, but she was still wearing her reeking, smoke-stained dress.

"Pincas, if you won't drink your wine, take a little brandy." Baruch, a stocky graybeard several years older than his brother, poured some amber liquid from an exquisite Murano glass decanter. "Here, just a thimbleful. You have need of a restorative."

Pincas barely shook his head. I glanced across the table at Gussie. Was he feeling like as much of an interloper as I was? My friend looked as exhausted as I felt, and since we had both inhaled a copious amount of smoke, I suspected his throat must be burning as fiercely as mine. We had made several attempts to leave, but each time I stood and reached for my jacket, Pincas placed a restraining hand on my arm and murmured, "No. Don't go. Not yet."

Across the room, a door opened with a soft click and Liya emerged from the shadows surrounding the table. She had bathed and changed into a clean but over-sized gown that she'd hitched up with a man's belt. She reached toward Pincas. "Papa, let me take Fortunata. The others are finally asleep. She needs to get in bed, too."

Pincas' eyes glinted with a wary but unfocused light. His arms tightened protectively around the sleeping child.

"Papa, please. She's safe now. We all are." Liya stroked her father's cheek with the back of her hand. He inclined his head in Liya's direction and relaxed his grip on Fortunata but wouldn't allow Liya to remove the child.

"Isacco isn't safe," Pincas said in a low, monotone rumble. "I let them take him and now he's dead."

Baruch shook his head sadly. "Pincas, Pincas, you mustn't blame yourself. You did everything a man could do."

Gussie and I had heard the story along with Baruch and his family. How a jeering crowd had invaded the square, stormed the Del'Vecchio home, and demanded Isacco, the murderer of Christians. How the terrified Jew had scrambled to escape through the maze of passages that connect all the ghetto dwellings only to be brought down as he called attention to himself by running across the *campo* like a hunted rabbit.

Pincas and some of the other men of the *campo* had followed along, remonstrating with the crowd, pleading that Isacco be released or at least given up to the authorities. Their brave efforts had come to naught. With the fury of a storm at sea, the mob rained violence on everyone in its path. They strung a rope around Isacco's neck and threw him from the bridge on the eastern side of the ghetto. Anyone who resisted was threatened with the same treatment.

No one was quite sure how the fire had started. Signora Del'Vecchio ranted and swore that the blaze had been deliberately set, but Pincas and Liya blamed a lamp that had been accidentally overturned in the melee.

I felt Liya's black eyes drilling through me. It was definitely time to leave. I put my hand on Pincas' unencumbered shoulder. "Signor Rumbolt and I must go. Believe me, we are both sorry for the fire and the loss of your cousin."

"Yes, Signore. Tonight I was ashamed of my adopted city," Gussie added uncomfortably.

Pincas nodded slowly and shifted Fortunata so he could place his hand on mine, but Liya sprang forth with a snappish reply. "You should be sorry, Tito. Since it was the scheme you and my grandmother concocted that put the mob onto Isacco's scent in the first place."

Gussie rose to my defense. "That's an absurd idea. Tito knows Isacco didn't kill Luca. He would never accuse an innocent man."

Pincas shook himself out of his gloomy contemplation. "You should bite off your tongue, daughter. Is this a way to speak to the man who saved the lives of you and your sister?"

Liya would not let her father's words shame her. She stood before us, straight and proud in her borrowed, ill-fitting clothing. "I'm grateful for what you did tonight, Tito. And you, too, Signor Rumbolt. But your heroics would not have been necessary if the rumor had not gone round that Isacco murdered Luca over a business deal gone sour."

For the second time since we fled the fiery rooftop I denied having spread such a tale, but Liya was not to be convinced. She had decided I was out for Isacco's blood after Mara had bragged about the secret errand she had carried out for Nonna. Under

Liya's pecking questions, perhaps spurred by a girlish craving for attention and self-importance, Mara had added considerable embroidery to the fabric of my conversation with Signora Gallico. Liya might be silent for her father's sake, but the look on her face made her feelings quite clear.

I thought of a few more things I could say, then bit my tongue, sighed and shrugged. Perhaps I could explain in the future, but just now, Liya was ill-disposed to hear me out. Gussie also started to speak again, but Baruch interrupted. The man had been rummaging through the contents of a basket on a nearby shelf. He handed a pamphlet to Liya. "My dear, I also think you accuse unjustly. Many of the intruders were waving one of these. I plucked this one out of the gutter after they'd passed by. This little book is what inflamed the mob against Isacco."

Liya quickly flipped through the pages of the same pamphlet that Benito had presented to me. I let her read in silence for a few moments, then asked, "Do you really think me capable of expressing the opinions contained in those vile papers?"

She grimaced and drew a shuddering breath. "No, of course not. You are not the man who penned these lies, but I would very much like to know who did."

I remained silent, watching the blood drain from her face.

"What you must think of me, Tito," she finally whispered. "Forgive me. I didn't realize…" Her words trailed off as her chin sank to her chest.

"That's better, daughter." Pincas nodded. "It's the author of the pamphlet that's behind all this. He has much to answer for."

"We should live to see the day." Baruch sighed, shoulders bowed. "A Jew dies. A Jew's home is burned to the ground. Who cares besides his fellow Jews?"

Pincas did not seem to share his brother's pessimism. He was studying me with a practiced smile, as if he were measuring my frame for a new suit of clothing. "Things might be different this time. The authorities don't want to waste their time investigating ghetto crimes, but Messer Grande is interested in apprehending the murderer of Luca Cavalieri, is he not?"

"What are you saying?" I asked.

"Yes, Papa. What are you hinting at?" Liya sank into a chair at the table, propping her chin up on her hand.

Fortunata moaned in her sleep. Pincas smoothed her hair with loving fingers. To me he said, "You and your friend are partially right. Isacco did not kill the painter, but the son of my cousin was not blameless." He patted my chair. "Sit down, my friend, I will tell you all. Since you've been pestering everyone with questions about the painter, you should find this of great interest.

"Isacco was a good boy, serious and hard working like his father, but he was never satisfied. Scraps... that is what he called my profits from the shop... scraps from the Christians' table. Isacco aspired to greater things than the lot our God bestowed on him. So did this painter, Luca Cavalieri."

"Father." Liya scowled and shook her head.

"It's all right, Liya. Isacco and Luca are no longer with us. They have gone on, and nothing on earth can hurt them now. I don't know how their association began—men who value the same things seem to find each other no matter what barriers of religion or nationality separate them—but this was the sum of their business. Luca produced relics that your fellow Christians believe to have great powers, and Isacco sold the counterfeits for handsome sums. The latest was a veil that the woman you call the Blessed Virgin wore at her son's crucifixion."

I nodded slowly, realization dawning. "A cloth with the Virgin's face magically transferred to the fabric."

"Yes, I don't understand it. It seems like a ridiculous idea, but when Isacco was selling something, his tongue turned to gold. He was able to convince a number of people that these veils were genuine."

"All very hush-hush, I'd imagine," Gussie put in. "Wouldn't do to have more than one Madonna's veil floating around."

"Exactly." Pincas nodded. "The boys had the scheme well planned. Part of Isacco's role was to convince the buyers that the veil's powers depended on absolute secrecy."

I looked at Liya. "Did you know about this?"

She shrugged uncomfortably. "What if I did? This is the ghetto, Tito. You may live just down the canal, but you have no idea of how we are forced to exist."

"I think I'm beginning to understand the obstacles that Isacco faced, but what was Luca's excuse?"

"That I couldn't say. Remember, I barely knew the man." Liya wouldn't look me in the eye. She turned her face away so that the lamp on the wall behind her outlined her profile with a glowing nimbus of light. As I regarded her just-washed hair that had dried in soft, curling tendrils surrounding her strong nose and cheekbones, several thoughts washed over me in a tumbling cascade.

Liya had posed for the veil. Whatever ingenious science Luca had employed to create the relic, he had modeled the subtle image of the weeping Virgin after Liya's striking profile. And Pincas didn't know it. Somehow, Liya had evaded the protective family net and kept her trysts with Luca a secret. Only her grandmother, whose wise, old eyes missed very little, might have a hint of Liya's love for the painter. Liya was a clever girl, no doubt about it, but I found myself dismayed that her cleverness had more of cunning than wisdom about it.

Gussie was questioning Pincas. "Is that why you say Isacco didn't kill Luca, because their deception was so successful?"

The clothing dealer gave his head a decisive shake. "No, not at all. It was because of the argument and... what happened after."

"What argument?" Liya asked quickly.

Pincas was silent for a moment. When he spoke, his voice was tremulous. "It was a dilemma such as I had never faced. I've never courted trouble. You know that, daughter. I've told you and your sisters a thousand times—outside these walls, a Jew should be invisible. It is the only way to keep safe. So I cautioned Isacco, but he refused to listen." The Jew's jowls quivered with emotion as he looked around the table. "Wealth is a blessing if fairly got, but Isacco was pirating on men's weaknesses, exploiting the gullible. I knew the scheme with the veils would come to ruin."

Baruch sighed with frustration. "You never could tell a coherent story, Pincas. Just get back to this argument and tell us what happened."

"I'm trying, I'm trying." Pincas handed Fortunata to Liya and began to pace the floor, running his hand over his shorn pate. "It must have been almost two weeks ago. I was playing cards with Signor Cardoza from across the *campo*. He had acquired a cask of Cyprus wine. Excellent wine it was, so smooth and mellow. What? Oh, yes, the argument. Well, we were at our cards and Isacco burst in. We invited him to join us but he prowled the room, as nervous as a cat, and finally insisted I come away with him. It took me a moment to understand it all, to realize what a terrible pass Isacco had come to. He had quarreled with Luca over those damned veils. The painter accused Isacco of breaking their bargain and skimming the profits. They argued, horribly. I think there was more to it, but after I'd learned the worst, I didn't want to hear any more."

Pincas covered his face with his hands and rocked on his bowed legs. He seemed about to collapse. Baruch hurried to his side with the brandy. This time Pincas drank a bit and allowed himself to be supported back to the table. He continued in a grim voice.

"Those two didn't stop at angry words. They pummeled each other and yelled odious names. At one point, Luca had Isacco pinned against the wall and was beating his head against the plaster. The boy thought Luca was angry enough to kill him so he grabbed something off a shelf and brought it down on Luca's head."

I heard an odd hissing noise. It was Liya, ramrod straight with Fortunata on her lap, shaking her head and expelling her breath through clenched lips.

As Pincas paused to take another sip of brandy, I spoke up. "This object. Was it a statue by any chance?"

"Why, yes." Pincas gave me a vague look. "Some sort of bronze, Isacco said."

"Did Isacco take it away with him?" Liya asked, staring at her father intently.

"No, my dear. Our cousin panicked. When Luca fell back, blood streaming from his head, Isacco bolted. He ran straight back to the ghetto as fast as his legs would carry him. By the time he got to me, he was in a terrible state. He didn't know if Luca was alive or dead or what should be done about either eventuality. He wanted me to go back to the theater with him."

Gussie wrinkled his brow. "But, how could you get through the gates and over the bridge? Wasn't it after dark by then?"

The Jews traded uneasy glances among themselves. Baruch finally answered, "There are ways. Boats can be hidden. Guards can be bribed."

Pincas quickly resumed his tale. "I didn't know what to do, but I had pledged to Isacco's father that I would look after him as my own son. Isacco was determined to go back, that meant I had to go with him. We approached the Teatro San Marco with care, but there was no one about. The place was dark and shut up tight. It was then that Isacco showed me another secret he'd been keeping. At a back door covered by a portico, he pulled a wicked-looking dagger out of his waistcoat. I didn't even know he carried a weapon! He forced the door latch as if he had been breaking into buildings all his life." Tears started down the Jew's cheeks. "Oh, how will I ever tell his father about all of this? He will never understand how I let this happen."

"Papa! We'll worry about that later." Liya's jaw was shaking but her voice was steady. "Tell us what happened next. Did you find Luca?"

Pincas took a long, deep breath. "No, we found nothing. No Luca, no statue, nothing."

"Did you search the studio?" I asked.

"Most certainly. I was shaking in my boots, but Isacco had regained his courage. After we had ascertained that the theater was empty, he lit a few lamps and we went over the studio inch by inch. There was blood where Luca had fallen. Someone had tried to clean it up but had left a damp smear. And there were other drops of fresh blood scattered around the studio. Isacco was heartened by that. He said it meant Luca had been alive when he'd run away." Pincas fumbled for more brandy. "'A dead man doesn't bleed,' he told me."

I thought back to Luca's body on the table in the Doge's storeroom. "Pincas, could Isacco have set on Luca after he fell. Strangled him perhaps, and not remembered in his rage and fear?"

"I don't see how. If Isacco had strangled Luca, he would have had blood all over his hands and cuffs. I didn't see a drop on him. Why?"

Liya sat as still and silent as a statue while I briefly described the head wound and the unmistakable signs of strangulation on Luca's corpse. Baruch appeared puzzled, but Pincas and Gussie were nodding their heads.

"Don't you see, brother?" The clothing dealer smacked the palm of his hand on the table, startling Fortunata into a wailing cry. "That's our man," he said as he gathered his squalling daughter into his arms. "The man who choked the life out of Luca after Isacco left him on the floor of the studio."

I leaned forward. "Do you mean to say that whoever finished Luca and tossed his body in the lagoon also penned the pamphlet that incited tonight's riot?"

"I do say it." The Jew's voice rose in his excitement. "It's as plain as day. Luca must have been dazed from Isacco's blow, but he was still conscious. There is no need to strangle an unconscious man. Luca must have been able to tell his second attacker about the fight with Isacco. Perhaps Luca was begging for help or expected someone to give chase or… I don't know. The important thing is that the actual killer must have known that it was Isacco who'd bashed Luca over the head."

"I say, Tito," Gussie said. "Pincas' theory makes a good deal of sense. It would take a wicked mind, but what better way to focus public inquiry than to blame someone with half-truths—someone from a group that people already suspect of something else?"

I pictured a faceless devil: strong hands locked around Luca's throat while the bloodied painter gasped for breath, frantic feet running to find something to cover his hideous deed, back bent to the task of dragging Luca's lifeless body swathed in royal purple through the theater corridors. A man who could do all that would surely not lack the villainy to manufacture a scapegoat, but a new wrinkle occurred to me. "No matter how cunning the pamphlet's accusation of Isacco was, it would not have provoked a riot and a mob hanging unless the populace had already been worked up about the wells going bad. I can't see the murderer running around Venice poisoning wells. It's too far-fetched."

Pincas shook his head. "He didn't have to. Our man is clever and knows how to turn events to his advantage. He would hardly be the first to blame the Jews for Venice's ills. The situation with the wells simply provided an opportunity."

"As did the half-dead painter," whispered Gussie.

"None of which tells us why this clever someone strangled Luca," I answered.

"Perhaps Isacco wasn't Luca's only business partner," ventured Pincas.

I nodded, giving the pensive and unusually restrained Liya a long look. "Yes. Our painter friend wore many masks. I see that I will have to give all of Luca's associates a harder look."

Chapter 19

The longer I pondered Pincas' argument, the unhappier I became. Luca was killed, or at least rendered helpless, in my own theater. The faceless devil of my imagination might very well be someone I worked with every day. Like fireworks exploding against the night sky, the faces of possible killers sprang to my mind. Towering over them was my old colleague, Maestro Torani. The director had lied about knowing Luca's mother. What other connection to Luca might he be concealing? Was his original request for me to find the missing painter, and later Luca's killer, just an elaborate charade to deflect suspicion should the need ever arise? At the time, I thought that Torani had accepted my report of Luca's departure from Venice far too readily. Now I wondered if the director had been expecting his amateur sleuth to fall for the rumors blaming a Jew and hand the authorities a murderer whom no one of influence would rise to defend.

And what about the Ministro, Signor Morelli? His tavern meetings with Luca had not occurred to discuss stage settings for the next opera. The nobleman who took such pains to present himself as a leading patrician was, in reality, barely hanging on to his ancestral *palazzo*. Thanks to Gussie's keen observation, I knew that Leonardo Morelli was staring an impoverished Barnabotti existence straight in the face. He and the lovely Isabella could be just one onerous tax away from pure ruin. How Morelli's financial difficulties might tie in with Luca's murder, I knew not, but I thought it worthwhile to investigate.

My thoughts grew grimmer and grimmer. I remembered Rosa's fit of pique at being rebuffed by Florio. Could her wounded vanity have led her to take revenge on another potential lover who had rejected her advances? I found Rosa's hysterical fear of the murderer's return roughly as believable as the simpering persona she often used on the stage. I realized that the delicate singer could not have lugged Luca's body to the lagoon, and besides she was with Emma during the argument in Luca's studio, but Rosa would not have committed the deed herself. The contralto had a captivating way about her, and Bassano Gritti was only the latest in a long line of *amorosi* ready to do her bidding.

And Aldo—why was he turning handsprings to avoid my questions? I'd worked with the man for years. I knew him for a hotheaded taskmaster, but he was reliable in his work and could be surprisingly gentle when the demands of a production were not hard upon him. What was he hiding and why the discreet gondola ride with Torani?

Even the nattering clerk Carpani and his disparaging remarks about Jews popped into my head. Ever since the Ministro had installed Carpani as his general factotum around the theater, I had suspected that the clerk reported on a number of points besides expenditures. Was he simply Morelli's tool, or had his snooping uncovered traces of Luca's scheming—traces that he decided to confront the scene painter about on his own?

Unfortunately, the demands of the opera did not leave me many free hours to ponder these questions or to trace the scurrilous pamphlet to its source. Gussie, more at liberty than I, took on the chore.

The day after the fire, I slept the morning and afternoon away and awoke with an aching, swollen throat that would barely give passage to a reedy whisper. Annetta supplied warm cloths to wrap around my neck, and Benito brewed endless pots of his famous tea, a soothing concoction laced with brandy, honey, and more esoteric ingredients that he had always refused to reveal. When I reached the theater for the last *prova*, my throat had opened a bit, but I was still incapable of projecting a song past the footlamps. Torani was furious.

"*Cesare* opens tomorrow night," Torani barked as he paced a small cleared circle in the downstage wing. "You know how important this opera is—the company's entire future rests on it. You shouldn't be risking so much as a chill and yet you go charging into a smoky fire as if your lungs are made of leather."

I swallowed painfully, not a little disconcerted by the numerous pairs of eyes staring at me. Stagehands and singers alike had interrupted their routines to watch Torani upbraid his former *primo uomo*. Emma tossed her head and swept her leopard cape across her shoulder. "I think Tito acted bravely. He should be applauded, not criticized." The soprano started to do just that, but when no one else followed her lead and Rosa gave her a withering stare, Emma turned her clapping into hand wringing and tried to blend back into the ring of onlookers. I was only glad that Florio wasn't around to witness my disgrace. As usual, the pampered star was secluded in his dressing room, nursing his own precious throat.

Torani wasn't finished with me. By the time he came to the end of his tirade, I was feeling much the same as when my father had beaten me for putting a toad in the choirmaster's organ when I was eight years old. There was no one who could step in and sing the part of Ptolemy. Opera companies of the day spent money on cloud machines and flying chariots, not extra singers to cover emergencies. Thus, Maestro Torani could only allow me to rest my voice by miming my way through the *prova* and hope that I would recover sufficiently to sing on opening night.

After the curtain went up, Florio reacted to my indisposition much as I expected. He swanned around the stage, delivering his arias with many a mocking glance sent my way, but somewhere during the third act, he took a more kindly tone. We exited together and, as we waited in the wings for our next cue, he asked, "You really can't sing?"

Surprised, I whispered, "No. If I were able, I would be singing my part. I certainly wouldn't inconvenience everyone like
this if I could help it."

A puzzled look settled on Florio's round face. He swept the
plumes of his headdress off his forehead. "Then this is not a
trick? A stratagem?"

"A trick? Whatever for?"

He shrugged. "To obtain an eleventh hour salary increase.
Or to snatch a bit of my glory." His plump lips stretched into
a smile. "I've known singers to employ any number of tricks to
draw attention away from me and back to themselves. I can't
really blame them. It must be frustrating to be upstaged by the
world's greatest singer. But faking a sore throat—I would expect
a clever fellow like you to show more ingenuity. So I've been
thinking—poor Tito must actually be in pain."

I'm afraid I must have opened and closed my mouth like
a wooden character in a marionette show. Florio was just too
much! What a sad, lonely life he must lead. I answered with all
the offended dignity my injured windpipe would allow, "Yes,
Francesco. My throat is burned raw and it hurts even to whisper,
but I will try my best to sing tomorrow night. I owe my colleagues and the audience that has paid to see us no less."

Florio cocked his head from side to side like a dog who hears
a sound beyond human capacity. The singer regarded me so long
that he almost missed his next entrance.

I wasn't alone in the wings very long. While I was absorbed
in the intricacies of a duet between Niccolo and Rosa, Carpani
drifted up behind me. He started to lean against a board and
canvas flat whose front represented a tent in Caesar's camp, but
a gruff warning from an alert stagehand changed his mind.

"You know His Excellency the Ministro is very angry with
you." The clerk's tone was severe but his mouth held the hint of
a smirk.

"You may assure Signor Morelli that my voice will improve
by tomorrow night."

"How can you be so sure?"

"I've had years to get to know my voice and its constitution. It won't be my finest performance, but I will be able to sing."

Carpani clutched his notebook to his chest and pursed his thin lips. "I confess I don't understand you, Signor Amato. They say you risked your life to save that woman who makes the masks and headpieces."

"I suppose I did, but I wasn't the only one. I had a lot of help rescuing Liya and her sister from the fire."

"But you put this opera in jeopardy for the sake of a worthless Jew, a person of low degree and lower consequence. I'm amazed that Signor Morelli didn't order Torani to kick your backside right out the door."

His callous comment filled me with disgust, but before I could form a reply, a taller figure rounded the flat to loom over the scornful clerk. The Ministro was definitely angry, but his rebuke was not aimed at me. "Signor Carpani," he said, "you take excessive liberties. It displeases me to hear myself discussed by underlings behind my back. Those who do so will not remain long in my employ."

The clerk's face went white and he bowed over his notebook, but Morelli did not stop to hear his stammered apology. The Ministro was touring the backstage area with the Savio and an attractive woman who seemed vaguely familiar. She was tall, dark haired, and so white of complexion that her cheeks could have been sculpted from marble. Her large blue eyes rarely left the Savio's face though he was obviously trying to show her the finer points of the Teatro San Marco. Strolling arm in arm as if they were promenading on the Riva instead of walking over cables and dodging sandbags, the Savio and his companion disappeared around a tower of machinery followed by a very stiff, upright Morelli.

Carpani, still with his head hanging low, muttered something about needing to see the box office manager, but I forestalled him with a hand on his sleeve and asked, "Who is that woman with the Savio alla Cultura?"

The clerk gave me a mirthless smile and jerked his arm away. "Don't worry. You will be introduced soon enough," he whispered before scurrying toward the front of the theater.

The last *prova* finally concluded after an amazingly smooth performance. The orchestra had provided an inspired accompaniment, the River Nile had behaved itself and carried Caesar's barge to perfection, and I was the only member of the company not in good voice. Still, Maestro Torani wasn't happy. With the entire company and crew assembled onstage to receive last words of criticism and advice, Torani prowled the boards like a caged lion. The director subscribed to the old theater adage: bad dress rehearsal, good performance. In this case, it was the reverse that worried him. The opening of *Cesare in Egitto* would fill the Teatro San Marco with every Venetian of note and all of the foreign dignitaries who had been invited to attend the wedding. From the royal box, the Doge and his advisors would be watching our every move and expecting a triumph worthy of Venice at the height of her past magnificence. If anything went amiss or the box office takings fell short of expectations, we might all be given the boot.

While Torani gave us our instructions in increasingly vehement language, the Savio, his raven-haired companion, and Signor Morelli made a strikingly complacent tableau as they surveyed the company from a sweeping staircase constructed for one of Cleopatra's grand entrances. Torani's anxiety seemed to have no effect on the Savio. The old military man turned government minister nodded his head in agreement at many of the director's points, favored the company with a benign smile, and finally suggested that Torani dismiss us all to a well-deserved rest. As the musicians dispersed, Torani and the Savio were head to head in intense conversation. The mysterious woman and Morelli listened silently. I approached them, still racking my brain for where I might have encountered the Savio's companion, but Torani gave me a slight shake of his head and led the group offstage toward his office. Balked of my prey, I set out to find Aldo but wasn't surprised that the stage manager had contrived to be on the highest reach of the catwalk surrounded by his crew.

There was nothing else to do but repair to my dressing room. There I found Gussie passing time by sketching my manservant. Benito had taken a coquettish pose on my dressing table bench. He made to jump up as I came through the door, but Gussie begged for one more moment to finish his drawing. At my nod, Benito settled back into his pose, obviously relishing the opportunity to play artist's model. I threw Ptolemy's wig on a trunk in the corner and wearily began to undo the fastenings of my brilliantly sequined costume armor.

"There, I have it. You can move now," Gussie said, putting a finishing touch on the sketch. Benito sprang up to assist me, conscientious manservant once more. He asked, "How is your throat, Master?"

"No better." I sighed. "I'll need some more of your medicinal brew if I'm to produce any tunes tomorrow night."

Benito nodded with a worried expression as he carried my costume to the wardrobe. I continued, "It is not just the performance. There are questions I must put to certain people. How can I find out what I need to know if I have to save my voice for singing?"

"What people, Master?"

"Aldo for one. His presence in the theater near the time of Luca's murder is crucial. He spoke to Luca before Isacco first arrived, and he locked up before Isacco and Pincas returned. He's been dodging me for days. By all the gods in heaven, I'd wager my voice that he knows something."

On the sofa, Gussie groaned and said, "By Jove, Tito, don't tempt fate. You never know what old gods might be listening in."

Benito had become very busy with the repair of some loose sequins, but he suddenly looked up from his needle. "Aldo wouldn't hurt anyone, Master."

"I don't say that he did, but I need to question him about his movements that night." I swallowed hard. It felt like a piece of tissue had dislodged itself from the back of my throat. I poured a splash of wine from the decanter on my dressing table but immediately regretted the first swallow. A fit of coughing brought Gussie and Benito to my side.

Seeing that Gussie's broad hands were more suited to pounding me on the back, Benito stood back and twisted his own delicate fingers in an anguished gesture. He said, "Is it so very important that Aldo speak with you?"

Under Gussie's ministrations, I recovered sufficiently to answer in a breathless whisper, "Yes, very important."

A pensive Benito returned to his mending, and Gussie spun me around to face him. "Come, Tito, sit on the sofa for a moment. I have some interesting news that might make you feel better."

"I'd welcome anything that might make my mind rest easier."

Gussie tossed his sketchbook aside, sat down, and leaned forward with elbows on his knees. "I've spent the day getting to know the Venetian press. Quite a fanciful lot these journalists are—much more interested in ridiculous diversion than useful information. When I started inquiring about having a pamphlet authored, I was besieged by a flurry of would-be essayists and poets who assured me they could turn out any number of words, in any style, on any topic that I cared to name. Veracity never entered the discussion."

"We agreed that the first step must be to determine who printed the pamphlet."

"Yes, that was the most troublesome part of the business. In Venice, it seems that every man with an opinion on anything has access to a printing press. But I had a stroke of luck at a coffeehouse that caters to literary men. A playwright scribbling a tragedy among the coffee cups gave me a lead. The ghetto riot had fired his imagination at a time when he had despaired of finding the necessary inspiration to complete his opus. When he heard that I had been in the thick of the event, he questioned me at length and wasn't loath to share information in return."

"What did this playwright have to say?"

"More than you want to hear about right now. Sipping coffee all day long had left the man quite talkative. The important thing is that the printer who publishes his plays also printed up the pamphlet."

"You found him?"

Gussie nodded. "He keeps a little shop off the Mercerie. Not near as helpful as our playwright, though. The printer declined to give me any information about who supplied the manuscript and arranged for the pamphlet's publication and distribution."

"He wanted a bribe. I should have warned you. It takes a bit of silver for a foreigner to get anything out of a Venetian. They think all Englishmen are rich." I gestured to Benito to fetch my purse. "Here," I croaked, "I'll give you enough to loosen his tongue."

Gussie chuckled a bit, holding up his palm to show me the coins were unnecessary. "You are not telling me anything I don't know. My purse may be light, but I was able to provide the printer with something else of value."

Benito and I both regarded the big Englishman with undisguised curiosity. Gussie reached for his sketchbook and began to doodle on a blank page. He appeared to be enjoying keeping us in suspense. In a moment, he turned the book toward us. "Who is it?" he asked with a grin.

Benito shook his head in puzzlement, but I recognized the figure at once. With a few quick strokes, Gussie's pen had exaggerated the haughty smile and all the man's other identifiable characteristics. The beaklike nose, skinny calves, and ultra-fashionable high heels of his shoes were unmistakable.

"It's the Croatian bridegroom! What a wicked caricature," I said in admiration. "How did you catch him so completely?"

"It was the day Luca's body surfaced. I had plenty of time to observe the prince's peculiarities as his retinue was detained on the red carpet by the removal of the corpse. Of course, the drawing I did for the printer was more complete."

"What is the printer going to do with it?"

"Some wit has written a satire on why the daughter of the Doge failed to find a suitable bridegroom among the Venetian aristocracy. The printer was setting the type for the article while we talked. When I offered to barter a drawing of the prince for information, he jumped at the chance to have a free illustration for the piece."

Gussie turned the sketchbook around. He gave his work a brief, private smile, but then his face darkened. He looked up at me. "Tito, I know who wrote the pamphlet against the Jews. The printer gave me a name. And an address. It's in the parish of San Barnaba."

Chapter 20

It was washday at the Amato household. By the time Benito rolled me out of bed, Annetta had been up and about for hours and Lucia was at my door demanding my bed linen. In the kitchen, copper pots rattled and bubbled on the cookstove, and corsets and petticoats hung from dripping clotheslines. Annetta had put old Lupo to work stirring the contents of the largest pot with a long wooden paddle. When I appeared at the door, hoping for some breakfast, he gave me a miserable shake of his head through the coiling mist. There was only one thing for me to do: grab my hat and hurry over to Gussie's lodging.

Gussie lived a brisk walk away. To stretch his funds, my friend had avoided the houses near the Grand Canal that had been broken up into elegant suites of furnished rooms. He had instead settled on a narrow alley in the Castello where native bachelors who worked at that quarter's huge shipyard could let rooms at reasonable rates. He had his own entrance from the street, and while the walls of his two meager rooms were unpainted and his shutters were missing half their slats, he possessed a charming little balcony that overlooked a canal and made his lodging pleasantly habitable.

Though the morning was waning, I found my friend in the midst of dressing. "Tito," he said, throwing the door open with one hand and gathering his hair back with the other. "I trust you slept well. I certainly did. I'm fine as a fiddle and ready to chase down the author of that pamphlet."

I returned his broad smile and answered in a measured whisper, "I swallowed more smoke than you did, but the night's rest gave me some relief. If I'm careful, I'll be able to sing tonight. Have you eaten?"

Gussie answered negatively, intent on restraining his unruly locks long enough to bind them into a black ribbon.

"Then introduce me to the delicacies of this English breakfast that you can't start the day without. My own kitchen has been turned into a laundry, and I don't think I can storm San Barnaba on an empty stomach."

Gussie readily agreed and reached for a waistcoat of canary yellow. He topped that garment with a dark brown coat lined with yellow shaloon that turned back on the sleeves to form deep cuffs dotted with gold buttons. My stomach rumbled while he tarried with his neckcloth, a linen band edged with expensive Alcenon lace if my eyes judged correctly. Not for the first time, I wondered how long the prosperous English family that Gussie was avoiding would allow their son and brother to bide his time in the decadent pleasure capital of Europe. How would my friend react when his family ratcheted up the pressure for him to come home?

Finally pleased with the lay of his neckwear, Gussie ushered me out into the alley and we hurried toward the nearest canal. The day was fine, blessedly warm and dry with stacks of snow-white clouds hanging above the lagoon, but time was at a premium so we took a gondola to the Englishmen's café.

I was not prepared for the quiet of the place. At any café where Venetians meet, an animated din of talk and laughter engulfs you the moment you step over the threshold. But these English—so restrained, so dour, so unmelodic with their clipped phrases.

Gussie ordered a full breakfast for both of us, then chattered away on inconsequential topics. He pointed out a few men he knew and told an amusing story about a young English lord who had become enamored with a lovely woman he had encountered at the theater. Fascinated by her coquettish charm and longing to see the face that she had kept hidden by a velvet mask, he canvassed his Venetian acquaintances, only to be told that she was a nun of the Santa Clara escaping the confines of the convent for an evening of frivolity.

In deference to my throat, Gussie did not expect more than a nod or low chuckle in response. I found my friend's company as congenial as always, but confess that my mind began to wander when he launched into a story I had heard once or twice before. My fingers strayed to an inside pocket. I had taken to carrying the Madonna's veil, the counterfeit that Luca had fashioned after Liya's profile, as a kind of talisman. Once I had identified his model, I saw that the artist had pictured the details extraordinarily well: the soft hollow of Liya's neck, the sweep of her cheek, the curve of her lips. To Benito's great amusement, I made sure that the veil was housed in a pocket over my heart no matter which jacket I wore.

Even as I touched the cloth, I realized the futility of my gesture. When we'd left her uncle's home, early on the morning after the fire, Liya had seen us to the door with a heartfelt apology for her misplaced accusation and even placed a kiss on my cheek. Still, I knew that the painter owned her heart. Liya had loved Luca enough to deceive her family and defy the age-old prejudices that divide the races. What could I offer to inspire such devotion? Since the *castrati* are unable to father children, the church has denied us the sacrament of marriage. I did know of one fellow *castrato* who had renounced his Catholic faith and married in a Protestant country only to have his wife isolated by scandal and malicious gossip. And then there were other singers who kept their beloveds near them in a state of unsanctioned union, but my brave Liya deserved better.

A waiter appeared and arranged heaping plates before us, but Gussie ignored the steaming eggs and sausages. He was telling me something that had put a serious expression on his usually cheerful face. I immediately banished my unrewarding line of thought and attended to his words.

"I would marry her if she'd have me," he said, "but there are obstacles to be dealt with."

"What?" I was momentarily bewildered. Gussie mirrored my thoughts exactly. Had I spoken my reverie aloud? Could the Englishman peer into my soul? Then I noticed the special sparkle that seemed to appear in Gussie's eyes only when my sister was near.

"Annetta," I whispered.

"Of course. Who else have we been talking about?"

A glad smile sprang to my lips. "Nothing would give me greater pleasure than to see my sister settled and happy."

"But would a thick-headed Briton with a negligible income and few prospects make her happy?"

"My dear friend, Annetta enjoys your good humor and common sense as much as I do. She also glows when you walk in the room, a trait I cannot claim. No one I know has ever had such a marked effect on her. I am convinced she would welcome a declaration from you."

"Do you really think so?" Gussie's blue eyes were growing misty.

"I know my sister very well. She tries overhard to please those she loves. She will attempt to turn herself into the perfect country squire's wife if that is what you want." I chuckled at the thought of Annetta even sitting on a horse, much less riding over fields and jumping streams.

He sat back, drawing a long breath. "That is not what I want at all. Annetta is a Venetian—as full of warmth and beauty as the city itself. I would no sooner have her change as I would leave Italy."

"Then you do not intend to someday return to England?"

"I do not—at least not to live." Gussie glanced at his countrymen around us, then spoke slowly and quietly. "In my home, there was so little joy. I think my family and their neighbors must have invented dullness and boredom. They have a cell prepared for me there, in a prison of convention and social obligation. They expect that when I've indulged my taste for the Continent, I'll come docilely home and let them slam the door on my cage. But I will surprise them all. I'm staying on in Venice."

"Will your income extend to making a home and raising a family?"

He grinned. "I knew the protective brother would show his face soon enough. Actually, I do have a few notions about that. In addition to my aunt's generosity, my pens and brushes can earn our living. My daubs are not near ready to qualify me for the painter's academy, but I can always sell drawings and small oils to chaps who want to take a few views of Venice home for the ancestral walls."

I knew the sort of work he had in mind. "Faded *campi* with picturesque wells. The Basilica and Campanile against a sunset."

"Exactly. Perhaps I could even sell some caricatures to the gazettes. That printer fellow seemed very pleased with my sketch of the bridegroom. I can toss that sort of thing off before breakfast."

We applied ourselves to our plates. Gussie tucked into the fried medley with relish, but I couldn't finish my portion. I was accustomed to much lighter morning fare, and my mind was still more on the veil in my pocket than on the food. We were finishing with sweet tea lightened with heavy cream when Gussie returned to the subject of romance. "I think I am not the only one that Cupid holds in his snare," he said with the exaggerated wink of a stage Arlecchino.

"Oh, Gussie. I am more than snared—Cupid has made me his slave." I couldn't stop the words tumbling from my lips. "The painting of Liya that we saw in Luca's room haunts my dreams and I can barely spend five minutes without imagining the bliss of joining her on that couch. When I'm dressing for the stage, I think I hear her voice in the hall and run to the door only to end up feeling like a fool when it is someone else. At the last *prova*, I peered past the footlamps into every box and the darkest recesses of the pit, hoping against reason that she had crept in to watch me."

"She wasn't there?"

"No, I haven't set eyes on Liya since the aftermath of the fire."

Gussie fiddled with a crust of bread, dipping it in and out of a pool of melted butter and orange marmalade. He asked hesitantly, "Suppose Liya would come to return your feelings, how could you turn your dreams into reality? I mean, besides the difficulties of religion, what kind of husband could you be for her?"

I smiled. "You may speak plainly. You wonder if I am useless where the act of love is concerned."

He shrugged uncomfortably. "This practice of putting boys to the knife—it is one Italian custom that troubles me greatly. Your voice is sublime, but at what cost?"

"Love does present certain problems for a *castrato*," I answered wistfully.

He raised his eyebrows. "I would think so, since the knife struck at the very seat of your manhood."

I contemplated Gussie in silence. Over the years, I had convinced myself that the true seat of my manhood resided in my head and that my lost flesh was not so very important after all, but I had a eunuch's reluctance to try explaining this to a whole man. Did Gussie see me as some did—an eternal boy poised on the brink of a boundary I could never cross? Or perhaps as a freakish amalgam of masculine and feminine attributes? No, I knew that wasn't true. However Gussie saw me, he had treated me with nothing less than the most sincere friendliness and respect since the day I had rescued his purse from the pickpocket. Unlike so many others, Gussie had never regarded me as a mere oddity created to fill opera houses with spectacular song.

I answered softly, surprising myself by loosening sentiments I thought I had chained up long ago. "The surgeon's knife came nowhere near my heart—that organ craves love and companionship as much as any man's. Though I may one day be as celebrated as Il Florino, my life will be a tragedy if my heart has no one to cherish."

"But your bed has not always been empty. I've heard a few stories about ladies who have indulged their enthusiasm for Venice's favorite *castrato*."

I dismissed whatever gossip he had heard with a wave of my hand. "There are always women who are beguiled by the voice and seduced by the glamour of the stage. They throw flowers and send their footmen to my door with gifts and invitations, but when we meet, they are more curious about the imperfections of my anatomy than what is in my heart. I have learned to bring them physical pleasure, but so far, true love has stayed just beyond my reach."

"And now you are pining for a peppery Jewess who is in love with a murdered painter and may even be carrying his child," Gussie observed with concern.

My throat tightened. Suddenly, I wished he had never raised the subject. I took a gulp of tea that had cooled to an unpleasantly tepid state and said, "The refuge of impoverished patricians awaits us, my friend. I think we would do better to spend our time visiting San Barnaba than discussing these vexatious women."

Gussie and I crossed the city's main canal at the Volta, the bend where the waterway curves sharply back on itself, and had our boatman set us down at the canalside square dominated by the uninspiring façade of the church dedicated to San Barnaba. At the quay, a barge of vegetables wilted in the sun, and a few mongrel dogs sought shade under the portico of a run-down inn.

The address the printer had supplied was down a wretched alley lined with ill-kept houses. The way was narrow and littered with broken roof tiles and moldering refuse. Near the end of the cul-de-sac, we came to the building said to house the author of the pamphlet, one Bernardo Nevi. I was glad Gussie had come with me. It wasn't physical violence I feared. I simply wanted his earnest goodness at my side when I confronted the foul scoundrel whose words had sparked the fatal riot.

There was no bell cord. We knocked but were acknowledged only by a frowsy-headed woman who peeked curiously from a window in the next house. We knocked a second and third time, increasing the force of our blows. At last the door was opened by a rope pulled from above, and a reedy voice invited us to climb to the second floor.

Awaiting us at the top of the staircase was an old gentleman of venerable countenance and carriage leaning on a simple stick of polished wood. His stringy white hair was rolled onto curling papers and his shirt was covered with a stained, tattered robe of apple-green silk. He said, "Forgive my not coming down, Signori. A few days hence, I will begin my seventy-fifth year. My legs don't navigate the stairs nearly as well as they used to."

He led us into a chamber that he had rigged out as a pathetic little drawing room. Gussie and I were directed to two thread-bare armchairs while our host settled himself on a wooden stool consisting of a broken-backed chair with the legs cut down. The blinds were closed, throwing everything into a shadowy gloom. At first I thought the old man was trying to keep out the heat but soon saw that the blinds concealed the fact that the windows had no panes. Flies were buzzing around a sticky platter set on a table covered with a patchwork counterpane.

Signor Nevi received us with the open delight of a child, never once inquiring as to the purpose of our visit. When his polite compliments ascertained that I sang at the Teatro San Marco, he regaled us with meandering tales about the operas he had attended forty years ago. His aspect was one of exquisite gentleness, and the appalling conditions of his lodging filled me with pity. Faced with this frail gentleman in place of the vicious rogue I had expected, I hardly knew how to proceed. When I finally worked up the courage to ask about the pamphlet, Signor Nevi began beating his fist on his breast like a penitent at Mass.

"Woe to my household—I have nothing to offer you. Not a grain of rice or a crust of bread. The pittance the government allows me wouldn't keep a cat alive."

"We require nothing, Signore. Only tell us what you know of this pamphlet accusing the Jews."

Signor Nevi sucked his lower lip in a pout. "In the old days my guests and I would talk for hours over the cups."

I sent Gussie a pointed look. Perhaps this disgraced Barna-botti nobleman was more cunning than he appeared. Gussie had also taken Signor Nevi's meaning. The Englishman excused himself, clattered down the stairs, and soon returned with a jug of *refosco* and an armload of bread and cheese.

The food and wine made Signor Nevi as pliant as a kitten. He drew his stool up to the table, cut off a hunk of cheese, and declared himself entirely at our service to speak of any topic we wished.

I asked, "Three days ago, a pamphlet appeared on the Piazza— *The Truth of the Villainous Crimes Recently Perpetrated on Our Most Serene and Christian Republic*. What can you tell us about it?"

"I remember it well—quite a lengthy ramble. It took me nearly three hours to copy."

"Copy?"

"I write a fine hand. Before my family's ruin, I was drilled in letters at the best boarding school in Padua. I earn an occasional *zecchino* copying letters and bits of verse for men who lack an artistic script or have a reason to conceal their own hand."

"So you did not compose the piece?"

The old man gave a musical laugh. "Me? I never fancied myself an author—haven't the wit. But if I should ever dabble with the notion of being a literary man, I would turn to poetry, not political diatribe."

I regarded him steadily, rearranging the pieces of the puzzle I had begun to construct in my mind. "Someone brought you the manuscript of the pamphlet and hired you to copy it. Were you also paid to deliver your copy to the printer?"

"Yes, and to arrange for its distribution." His mouth twisted into a rueful scowl. "It was a full day's work for these tired old eyes and legs, and the compensation not overgenerous. But it gave me something to keep the landlady quiet for another month or so."

It was time to strike at the heart of the matter. "Who was this tightpurse who bought your services?" I asked.

"Now that is an interesting question. I'm not sure I should try to answer it. If I tell you what I know, you will think I am only playing a foolish game."

Gussie hastened to fill Signor Nevi's winecup. "Let us judge the folly of your response."

"Well… the man calls himself Dr. Palantinus."

"Palantinus. Dr. Palantinus." I slid the vaguely Latin name around my tongue. "It sounds like the title of a charlatan."

"That's a fair assessment of my benefactor." The nobleman gave the last word an ironic twist. "Only he would probably call himself a Grand Magister. In this quarter, he is known for hiring people to sell his herbal concoctions. I'm told his aphrodisiac elixir fetches a good price. It is supposed to come from a recipe handed down from King Solomon himself." Signor Nevi thought a moment, then added, "Of course, his tablets and elixirs are just trifles for Palantinus. He is the head man at the Mystical Temple of the Brotherhood of the Golden Seraphim."

"The golden what?" I asked.

"The Golden Seraphim. Palantinus claims he has these celestial beings at his command. For a price, the members of the Brotherhood can partake of the rituals and ask the spirits questions."

Gussie threw me a bemused look. I told him, "Venice has several such societies devoted to separating superstitious fools from their money, but I've never heard of this one."

Signor Nevi chuckled. "Palantinus shrouds the Seraphim in great secrecy. The *brothers* may be fools, but their leader is not. The more obscure and mysterious the society, the more he can charge for admission. He specializes in recruiting wealthy foreigners but does not turn away Venetians who are able to pay. I don't suppose you boys would be interested?" He gazed at us hopefully.

"How much does Dr. Palantinus require?" Gussie asked.

The nobleman named a sum that was more than the total I had received for all my engagements during the past year.

We both gulped and shook our heads.

Signor Nevi shrugged. "Forgive me. My lot of poverty compelled me to ask. Palantinus offers five *zecchini* for a successful referral."

"What result did Dr. Palantinus hope to achieve with the publication of the pamphlet?" I asked.

"That I cannot say. He did not deign to share his thoughts with me, though he was most particular that I copy his words exactly and hung over my shoulder to assure himself that I executed my task faithfully. Several times I invited him to sit, but I fear my humble furnishings did not suit him." Here Signor Nevi broke off and used a blue-veined finger to poke an escaping wad of stuffing back into the arm of Gussie's chair.

"What does this Dr. Palantinus look like?"

"Ah, have I not said? He always wears a dark *bauta* over his head and covers his face with a white mask—a bird-beaked mask like the old plague doctors used to wear. Trying to work with that disquieting spectacle stalking round my chamber was something I won't soon forget."

"Has no one seen his face?" asked Gussie.

"No one that I know of."

I sighed in frustration. "Was he tall or short? Fat or lean?"

Signor Nevi screwed up his wrinkled face in thought. He answered slowly. "Not so tall as either of you, but not so very short either. As to his constitution, it's so difficult to say. Palantinus kept a light cloak wrapped close around him, and with the folds of the *bauta* about his shoulders..." The nobleman trailed off and shook his head.

Try as we might, we were not able to gather any identifying characteristics of the personality behind the vile pamphlet. The harder we pressed Signor Nevi for specific details, the fuzzier the old man's memory became. He appeared relieved when we ran out of questions, and though he overwhelmed us with courtesies as he hobbled out on the landing to see us on our way, his strained face told me that he was glad to see our backsides headed down the stairs. I expected that the coins I had left on the corner of his table would lighten his mood.

Halfway down to the street door, I felt compelled to look back up at the affable aristocrat who had sunk so low. "Signor Nevi, did you read the contents of Dr. Palantinus' manuscript?"

"Of course, how could I transpose the words to a new sheet if I did not read them?"

"Do you agree with the sentiments he expressed?"

He shook his head. "I can't say that I do. I thought it was all rubbish concocted by a bitter mind."

"Then, have you heard that the words you copied incited a riot that left one Hebrew dead and burned an entire family out of their home?"

His smile faded and he sank lower on his stick. "Do not mock me, young *signore*. I pray that you are never in my unhappy situation, but if fortune does desert you, ask yourself how quickly you would abandon your principles to put food in your belly."

Chapter 21

Gussie and I traversed the alley in silence and quitted the miserable parish of San Barnaba as fast as our feet would carry us. When we reached the other side of the canal, we went our separate ways to learn what we could about the mysterious figure that Signor Nevi had described. I stopped in at my coffeehouse, made the rounds of taverns, and even went down to the wharf to inquire of a few of my brother's seagoing associates. I kept my questions as discreet as possible. If my suspicions were correct, the man who posed as Dr. Palantinus had already murdered one man and accused another to cover his tracks.

Only a few men, and no women, had even heard of Palantinus. That few connected his name with alchemy and conjuring but had no idea of where he might be found. After wearing the soles of my boots thin, I knew no more than I had when I'd left San Barnaba and still had several long-postponed errands to perform. In quick succession, I made a purchase at a chemist's shop, did the same at a draper's, and looked in on a housewife of my *campo* who kept a small press to squeeze the juice from apples and other fruit. There, I sought a favor that was readily granted and was also cajoled into accepting several bottles of blackberry cordial. I handed these to Annetta as I stepped over our threshold.

"Where have you been?" she wailed. "Benito is beside himself. He's commandeered my stove to brew your tea and keep your bath water warm, and here you drag in like a foot soldier at the end of a forced march. You're exhausted."

I yawned and stretched in agreement. My whisper came out like a dry croak. "I could do with a nap before the opera."

"Tito, look." She pointed to the clock on the dining room sideboard. "It's almost time for you to leave for the theater."

Annetta was right. After wandering in so many useless circles in pursuit of Luca's murderer, I believed that Signor Nevi had finally set my feet on the right path. In my zeal to follow the old Barnabotti's lead to Dr. Palantinus, I had neglected my responsibilities to the opera. When I had to perform, I usually rested during the afternoon and arrived at the theater with plenty of time to warm up my voice and prepare for my role. But here I was, on the evening of Venice's most anticipated premiere, rushing around like a nervous neophyte before his first student concert. Benito fussed and poured tea while Annetta played some scales on the harpsichord in the sitting room. I followed her lead, bathing my throat with the warm liquid, controlling my breathing, and deploying every trick I'd ever learned for singing with an ailing throat. Little by little, the tightness and pain receded and our little house rang with the light, clear notes of my authentic soprano. All too soon, Annetta embraced me with a whispered reminder that she and Gussie would be watching from a fourth tier box, and Benito bundled me out the door to race to the theater.

I wish I could remember that night as an unmitigated triumph, but it was not to be. As expected, the house was bursting to capacity. All the noble boxes were filled, and for once, none of their curtains were drawn to facilitate gaming or romancing. The gondoliers had taken possession of the first few rows of the pit. Behind them, the rest of the populace was wedged in so tightly that even the fruit and *grappa* sellers were unable to squeeze through. Despite the presence of the Doge and his family in the royal box, the crowd showed no more decorum than it ever did. Each time Florio came on stage, such a din of exclamation and applause greeted him that he could hardly be heard. The men of his claque were certainly earning their pay, but they weren't the only ones clapping. The noise didn't seem to bother Florio. He absorbed the adulation like it was the breath of life, and when the audience's enthusiasm drowned out his magnificent arias, he simply repeated them until there was enough silence for his voice to carry throughout the auditorium.

I made it through the first act, but at an excruciating price. My throat was on fire. After every passage, I had to fight a compelling urge to cough and swallow. It was an ordeal to keep to the melodic line, impossible to add ornamentation. At first the audience didn't seem to notice. They were so intent on Florio that we other singers went largely unheeded. It was during the second act that the booing began.

Florio and I were the only singers on stage. My character of Ptolemy was called upon to mount Cleopatra's curving staircase, deliver a short recitative, then sing a cantabile aria with Caesar listening in from a hiding place behind a pillar. It was a slow, sweet melody, the kind of thing I usually excelled at. I did manage to form perfect notes, but my voice had lost its strength. The crowd grew restless; they wanted more of Florio's vocal acrobatics. The gondoliers began to stamp their feet, and the rest of the house, from the highest boxes to the grimy recesses of the pit, followed suit.

I strained my lungs to the utmost and beseeched the crowd with my gestures, but it did no good. My position on the staircase gave me a clear line of sight out into the auditorium. Faces full of derision and ridicule swam in the rippling air above the heat of the footlamps. Ugly, gaping mouths booed and called for me to quit the stage. I couldn't believe what was happening. I, Tito Amato, the *castrato* whose voice had charmed thousands, was being hissed. Suddenly, the staircase no longer provided a firm footing. My legs went as limp as strands of spaghetti, my voice faltered to a halt, and I grasped the handrail for support. I had descended a few, shaky steps, intent on reaching the dark sanctuary of the wings, when a marvelous thing occurred.

Florio abandoned his character of Caesar, stepped from behind the pillar, and mounted the stairs. Throwing all dramatic credibility to the winds, he encircled me with his long arms and embraced me for a full minute. I was amazed to feel the dampness of his tears on my cheek. With one hand on my shoulder, he steered me down the stairs to the front of the stage. In the orchestra, the musicians were scratching their heads and fumbling with their music. Torani had his hands poised over the keyboard, his eyes questioning Florio with an anxious gaze. So unprecedented was the star's behavior that the crowd was stunned into absolute silence. Florio's womanish speaking voice washed over the now puzzled faces. He chided the audience for their cruelty, praising me as a hero and demanding that they attend to my song.

Torani took the cue. He returned to the opening chords of my aria and I struck a graceful pose. Softly, half-afraid of being booed again, I sounded a few notes, ethereal in the stillness. Unable to attempt throat-scorching embellishments, I strove to move my listeners' hearts with simple beauty. When it was time for the repeat, Florio joined in. For once, he did not try to outshine me. He gauged his voice to mine and fashioned impromptu harmonies that spurred me to even greater efforts. Together we wove a braid of melodious delight that bound us by song as surely as brothers are bound by blood.

As the last incomparable notes drifted up to the theater's domed ceiling, the Doge rose from his seat in the royal box. Swathed in a flowing scarlet robe glittering with gold embroidery, his neat wig topped by his single-horned ducal cap, he stared down on the stage like some remote god. When the god smiled and began clapping, the fickle audience followed with more applause and cheers of "bravo" and "bravissimo." Their admiration barely registered with me; I was caught up in amazement at what Florio and I had achieved. By blending my crippled voice with that of my rival-turned-savior, I had just made some of the most beautiful music of my life.

I tried to hold on to that heartening feeling during the remainder of my increasingly weak performance and needed its warm glow more than ever during the Savio's obligatory review. After the curtain had come down for the last time, Torani directed the principal singers to line up at the center of the flower-strewn stage. Florio at the head, then Emma, me, Rosa, Niccolo and, lowest in rank, the bass who had sung the part of Caesar's second-in-command. Then Torani moved aside and awaited the Savio's comments in a poorly concealed sweat of anticipation.

The Savio had a woman on his arm. Not the statuesque beauty he had squired at the last *prova*, but an older, narrow-shouldered woman with a vacuous smile. From the deference paid to her by Messer Grande and Signor Morelli, I took her to be the Savio's wife. Morelli's wife, Isabella, her expansive bosom roped in pearls and her lips decorated with a mischievous smile, brought up the rear of the group.

As the Savio and his party were showering Florio with well-deserved praise, Emma reached for my hand and threw me a pitiful glance. At first I thought she meant to bolster my spirits, then realized that she was seeking comfort from me. Emma had sung well that night, but the soprano was not enjoying the mellow, self-congratulatory exhilaration that should follow a successful performance. Her jaws were clenched tight and the pupils of her eyes resembled hard, black discs. Emma was afraid, close to panic if her vise-like grip on my hand was any indication.

I sought to calm her with a silly quip. "Steady, Cleopatra, there are no asps around here."

Emma's eyes widened even further. "Oh, Tito, how I wish it were so."

The Savio moved down the line and stopped in front of Emma. "A pleasure, as always, dear Signora Albani. You have been so generous to Venice—delighting us with your inimitable song for so many years."

She dropped into a low curtsey. "As I hope to for many more, Excellency."

The Savio twisted one of the medals on his jacket and traded sharp glances with Torani over the soprano's bowed head. He made a sound that was something between a mutter and a clearing of his throat, then abruptly shifted his attention to me.

"You must have been born under a lucky star, Signor Amato."

"Excellency?"

The Savio smiled with one side of his mouth while Messer Grande glowered darkly at his side. The old military commander continued, "If Signor Florio had not seen fit to intervene on your behalf, your fine costume would be carrying the stains of rotten fruit."

Messer Grande chimed in. "I hope you have properly thanked Il Florino for pulling your chestnuts out of the fire."

The remark he had intended as a sanctimonious rebuke must have struck Isabella as irresistibly funny. She erupted into a peal of giggles. Holding her sides, she squealed, "His chestnuts! How amusing. He doesn't even have any."

Morelli grimaced and pulled his wife's arm in a rough grasp. She winced as his long fingers tightened around her elbow. "Excellency, I beg your pardon for my wife's unbecoming outburst." He hesitated, shooting Isabella a venomous look. "She is apt to let her high spirits get the better of her."

The Savio gave Morelli a dignified nod but his eyes were twinkling. He turned back to me. "I'm sure Signor Amato will soon be back to playing the nightingale at full strength. Since the unfortunate business with the painter has been resolved, he'll have no more distractions standing in the way of his recovery."

I cleared my throat. "The *business* you refer to was more than just unfortunate, Excellency. It was murder. And no one has been brought to trial for it."

The twinkle in the Savio's eyes narrowed to a gimlet gaze that must have once had his subordinates squirming in their boots. "Nevertheless, Signor Cavalieri's killer was dealt his punishment and the matter is closed."

"Since when does a frenzied mob take the place of the judicial court?" I sensed my fellow singers drawing away, even

Emma. Not one of them wanted to seem to be in support of a troublemaker.

Messer Grande stepped around the Savio and put his weasel-thin face only a few inches from mine. "What are you saying? I am satisfied that the Jew murdered Luca Cavalieri and so is the Tribunal."

I strove to keep my voice level and my expression benign. "Based on what facts?"

Messer Grande snorted. "Based on the fact that this Jew was known as one of the worst of his whole grasping, thieving tribe. He had been hanging around the theater, obviously making observations toward his personal gain. When he returned under cover of darkness, the painter simply got in the way."

"Did anyone see Isacco Del'Vecchio here the night of the murder?" Thanks to Pincas, I knew all about Isacco's activities on the night Luca was murdered, but I doubted that Messer Grande had uncovered that information.

Indeed, my simple question seemed to confound the constabulary chief. He chewed his lip and tapped his opera libretto on his thigh. I glanced at Signor Morelli. He appeared calm—detached, even. It was Torani whose forehead was covered with a sheen of sweat.

The Savio had had enough. With a last irritated "Harumph," he turned the talk back to arias and roulades. Torani shook his head and wiped his forehead as the remaining members of the cast accepted the Savio's congratulations with grateful humility. I was sorry to distress the director on his important night, but I couldn't accept the sorry, speedy solution that Messer Grande had convinced the Tribunal should close the case on Luca's murder.

Sometimes I wished I were the sort of man who could close his eyes to injustice and just walk away, but I was not. Perhaps I identified with Venice's victims and discards because the knife had doomed me to live as an outcast of sorts. Or perhaps I was just too fond of truth, as one of my old mentors used to say. But I knew I couldn't let Isacco continue to take the blame for a murder he didn't commit. That would dishonor the memories of both Luca and Isacco, and allow a callous killer to roam free. Somewhere the mask of a plague doctor was twisted into a cruel grin, laughing at all of us. I was determined to find the owner of the mask and silence his laughter for good.

I headed for my dressing room with leaden feet. I was tired and discouraged, but at least Annetta and Gussie would greet me with smiles. When I opened my door, I was surprised to see only Benito, laying out a stack of fresh towels.

"Where is my sister? I thought Annetta and Gussie would be waiting for me."

My manservant fiddled with the jars and tubes on my dressing table. "They would have, Master, but I sent them home."

"What? You take far too many liberties, Benito." I would have gone on, but the pleading look in the little manservant's eyes stopped me. With an almost motherly tenderness, he pressed his forefinger to my lips. "Please don't be angry, Master. Just come with me and ask no questions. I have something to show you, something of importance."

Curious then, I let Benito dress me for the street and followed him out the stage door, where he turned right to proceed in the general direction of the Piazza. We met only one other fellow on the pavement by the dark canal—a drunken, pleasure-wasted soldier who muttered a vague apology after lurching into us on a narrow bridge. Before we reached the great Piazza, Benito stopped at the entrance to a modest square and pointed to a church. I knew the place. The church was dedicated to an obscure saint but much visited for its Madonna who was credited with miraculous cures for hopeless illnesses.

My patience was wearing thin. "Benito, I say my prayers where and when I see fit. I don't need to beg for intercession at this altar."

He raised his chin and headed toward the church. "Trust me, Master."

The stoutly paneled door refused to budge under Benito's delicate hand but yielded when I added my own strength. The interior was much like that of my own parish—not an opulent cavern like the Basilica, but a cozy, columned shelter that welcomed the worshipper with the warm glow of altar lamps and the lingering smell of incense. Benito indicated the Madonna's shrine down the nearest shadowed aisle.

A man kneeled before a bank of candles illuminating a life-size statue. His face was hidden, but I would have recognized that bullet-shaped head anywhere. "Benito, you've arranged a meeting with Aldo."

My manservant's lips curled in one of his saucy smiles. "You said it was important that he answer your questions. Aldo has promised to indulge your curiosity as long as you stay on the topic of Luca's murder."

"But… how?" I was forming a theory about the strategy that Benito must have used to bring Aldo to me but could barely believe my own suspicions.

"It was simple," he whispered. "Aldo fancies me. He's been after me for months. I finally granted his desire."

"Benito! The man has a wife and a houseful of children."

The manservant shrugged and tossed his head. "Aldo's little hen is a tasty dish, but sometimes the man requires a bit more spice. Go on, he's waiting for you."

My feet stayed rooted to the worn carpet runner covering the flagstones. "I don't like this. I won't have you playing the whore—even in a good cause."

"Don't worry. I had already decided to indulge him. It was just the timing that I adjusted to suit your needs." Benito made a mock bow. "You know that I am ever in your service, Master. Now, go talk to Aldo. I'll wait at the door."

The stage manager was aware of our presence. He had risen and awaited me with an unreadable look on his robust features. I entered the shrine. The plaster Madonna towered over us with a benevolent smile. "I've been wanting to talk to you for a great while."

"I know that, Amato."

"Then why have you taken such pains to avoid me?"

"I like to keep my own counsel. Life is much safer that way."

"But Luca was your friend. Don't you want to see his murderer punished?"

Aldo rolled his eyes toward the ceiling. "You have it wrong. Luca was no friend of mine."

What kind of game was Benito's new lover playing? I had seen him and Luca leave the theater together many times. I told him so.

Aldo shrugged his thick shoulders. "What you saw was one man preying on another's purse. Luca insisted that I keep his glass and his belly full. Believe me, when we drank together, it had nothing to do with friendship."

"Why would you submit to such an arrangement?"

His eyes flicked to the door that Benito had just passed through. "Your manservant is not my first such companion. Luca found out about... several others. If I didn't do as he asked, he threatened to go to Morelli."

I saw Aldo's plight. Morelli, that self-styled guardian of vanishing moral standards, would have ordered Torani to give Aldo his wages and kick him out of the theater in the blink of an eye. So Luca was a blackmailer as well as a forger—what a thorough scoundrel Liya had become involved with. Luca's charm must have totally deluded her. And what a compelling motive Aldo had for dispatching the blackmailing painter.

The stage manager had been watching me closely. "I know what you're thinking," he said. "Just put it right out of your head. I wanted rid of Luca, but I didn't kill him. He's not worth facing the executioner for."

"Why should I believe you?"

"I'm here, aren't I? If I had something to hide, even Benito wouldn't have been able to persuade me to talk to you."

"Then enlighten me on one point. Last Sunday afternoon, the day of the ghetto fire, you met Torani on the quay by the Rialto Bridge. What was the purpose of your meeting?"

Aldo whistled softly. "You've really been at this game, haven't you? What makes you care so much? Luca was no more friend to you than he was to me. Did you know that he used to amuse his assistants by imitating your voice and your gestures behind your back?"

"Never mind that. I asked you about your meeting with Torani."

"I suppose there's no harm in telling you. You'd have to be a dolt not to have heard the rumors about the theater closing."

I nodded cautiously.

"I can't be left without a job when the bigwigs finally make up their minds. I've been asking around. I have a friend at the opera house in Verona. He says there may be a place for me there, but only if I can bring Torani with me."

"So you asked Torani to meet you at the quay?"

"Anywhere but at the opera house. Verona needs a new director, not a bunch of lackeys. If I approached Torani at the theater, word would get out. The stagehands would be all over me."

"Was Maestro interested in your proposal?"

"He didn't seem particularly keen, but he said he'd consider it."

"Did you discuss anything else?"

"Not really, he had the boatman set me down after just a few minutes. He seemed very tired."

I didn't pause to consider this information. With Aldo in an unexpectedly cooperative mood, I was anxious to press him with as many questions as he would allow. "Let's talk about the night Luca was killed."

The stage manager gave a huge sigh. "Make it quick, Amato. I won't get home before dawn as it is."

"Torani told me that you left the theater to have a drink before you locked up for good."

"He's right. Emma and Rosa were back in the dressing rooms. Rosa was having a fine fit of hysterics. All that afternoon, she'd kept one of the boys busy carrying messages to Bassano Gritti. Every time the boy returned with a response, she'd torn the envelope to bits and stamped on the pieces. Emma was trying to calm her down. Who knew how long that would take? And then Luca was still at his canvas, said he had a bit of work to finish. Why should I wait around with a dry throat?"

"Was anyone else in the theater when you left?"

"Maestro Torani. He was at his writing desk in his office. He was reading a letter. I could see the red sealing wax from across the room."

"Was he still there when you returned?"

"Yes, still there, writing a letter of his own. I told him I was locking up and he said he'd be ready in a quarter hour. He was true to his word. I finished putting the theater to bed, and we went out through the stage door together."

"How did he seem to you?"

"Don't know." He thought a moment. "About like always, I suppose. Looked like he had a lot on his mind."

"How long had you stayed at the tavern."

"About an hour, or perhaps a bit more."

"Was Torani the only one at the theater when you returned?"

"Yes, the others had gone on. Well… I didn't look behind every piece of scenery or open every wardrobe. I suppose there are plenty of places someone could have been hiding. But I go over the theater every night. I know its nooks and crannies as well as I know my wife's. If someone besides Maestro had been there, I'm sure I would have known it somehow."

"Did you go into Luca's studio?"

"Not all the way in. The lamps were out, everything was quiet. I just pulled the door shut. I couldn't lock it. That lock has been broken for some time, I just haven't gotten around to getting it fixed."

"Was Madame Dumas' workroom locked?"

"Oh, yes. The old girl likes to take care of that herself. The sewing room was locked up tight as a drum."

"Who else has keys to the workrooms?"

Aldo rubbed his neck and looked up at the Madonna's painted face as if he needed her permission to continue. He asked, "What are you getting at?"

I told him about the purple fabric that had been wrapped around Luca's corpse.

"So that's what happened to the bolt of cloth that Carpani was in such a rage about." The stage manager considered a moment. "That means Luca's murderer is almost certainly a theater person. Only someone familiar with the backstage area would know which room could provide a handy length of fabric and how to get to it."

I nodded slowly. Aldo and I had come to the same conclusion.

He scratched his chin. "Not a pretty thought, is it? Almost any one of the company could have got at that cloth. Carpani has his own set of keys he demanded those the first day he came to work. And of course, Madame Dumas has had her own workroom key for years, but everyone else uses my set. They hang on a ring by my door. The only theater keys I keep in my pocket are the ones to the outside doors."

I nodded again, this time with a sigh. For the moment, I had run out of questions.

Aldo reached for his tricorne and put the hat under his arm. He gave me a nod, and said, "I don't usually like singers, Amato, but I have to say, you're not half bad. If I can help you again, just ask, I promise not to run." He gave me one of his rare charming smiles and swaggered down the aisle. I was left alone with the smiling Madonna, wishing she could tell me which of Aldo's answers had contained the truth.

Chapter 22

"He's gone to ground. He must know that we're hunting him, so he's found a burrow and pulled the earth in over him." Standing at the railing of our rooftop garden, Gussie brushed a lock of hair out of his eyes and regarded me over his chocolate cup.

"All right," I said. "I take your meaning. Palantinus is the fox and we're the hounds who must flush him out. But how?"

Despite the light breeze and the early morning hour, our rooftop was growing uncomfortably warm. It was June, after all, and the humid, mosquito-ridden days of midsummer were not far off. It could have been a day of leisure for me. My voice was gradually regaining its strength, and after several well-received performances of *Cesare in Egitto*, the opera house would be dark until the much-heralded royal wedding had taken place. Then we would complete *Cesare's* run and Florio would be on his way. But I would not be resting or partaking of the celebrations around the city. Gussie and I were on the trail of the charlatan Palantinus.

Studying the pamphlet that Signor Nevi had so painstakingly copied had already consumed many of my free hours. I had formed the opinion that those words must carry some clue to the man behind the mask. Much like a footprint left in a pool of mud that hardens in the midday sun, a man's written words could not help but form an enduring account of his opinions and personality. I cannot say that the writer's verbal abuses against the Jews shocked me. His sentiments were not universal, but they were widely held and often heard. The main thing that struck me about the pamphlet was the clever manner in which Palantinus linked the tainted wells and Luca's murder to create an all-pervading sense of crisis. The man was clearly adept at influencing people. He had orchestrated a panic out of nothing more than random events and age-old prejudices.

While I had been deep in the pamphlet, Gussie had been asking around the English community for anyone who had been approached to join the Brotherhood of the Golden Seraphim. It seemed that Palantinus had attempted to recruit several of his wealthier countrymen, but these gentlemen must have proved less gullible than he had hoped. They declined his invitation and thus knew nothing about where Palantinus or his temple could be found. I repeated my question, "How are we to flush this fox from his lair?"

Annetta looked up from some sewing she held in her lap. "Instead of chasing after him, why don't you let Dr. Palantinus come to you?"

"How could we arrange that?" I asked. "By now, everyone knows I am determined to find the truth about Luca's murder. Palantinus would be a fool to deliver himself to me."

"A fox gets hungry," my sister replied. "Offer something tempting and he may wiggle out of his burrow and draw near to investigate. Think, what does this man crave?"

"That's easy," said Gussie. "He wants converts to the Brotherhood. Palantinus has a nose for gentlemen who are addicted to magic and have purses generous enough to accommodate his initiation fees. If we could serve up a rich foreigner who has a yearning to be amazed by the impossible, but who...? We know that Palantinus has ties to the opera house. He surely knows Tito and has probably seen me. I don't know anyone I could ask to play such a role. Do you?" He looked from Annetta to me.

"If only our brother Alessandro were in Venice—he would relish this hunt. I can think of no one else." Annetta sighed and shook her head, as did I.

I set my chocolate down and opened one of the morning gazettes that Lupo had stacked on the table before me. An announcement in *L'Osservatore* jumped out at me. "Wait a minute. Tonight is the masked ball at the Teatro San Benedetto. While the court is dining in state at the Doge's palace, the rest of Venice will be pursuing pleasure at the ball. People have been talking about it for weeks. Everyone will be there, all masked and costumed in anonymity. What better conditions for recruiting could Palantinus ask for?"

"What do we do?" Gussie hurried to the table to scan the gazette.

"We disguise ourselves. Why not? We can play this game as well as anyone, only it will be more than idle adventure that we are after."

Gussie got into the spirit of the enterprise immediately. "I must have a fantastic costume—a Moor or a turbaned dervish. But I'll be sure to show my own gold-braided coat beneath the robes and flash my purse at all the stalls."

"There will be faro tables, too." Annetta's eyes glittered with excitement. "You must play a bit, rashly enough to convince everyone that you have more money than sense."

"And are on the lookout for a soothsayer or a cabalist to help you spend it," I added.

We made our plans as the sun climbed its arc into the cloudless azure sky. Annetta agreed to take charge of finding our disguises. We had one bad moment when we realized that she intended to accompany us. Gussie disapproved. He didn't want Annetta exposed to any danger. Perhaps knowing his beloved would be mixing in a crowd where all social barriers were down and license was the order of the day also bothered him. I left them to their disagreement and went on an errand of my own—I needed to pay a visit to my neighbor who owned the fruit press.

⟡⟡⟡

That night at the Teatro San Benedetto, the giddy atmosphere was heightened by the intoxicating effects that disguise never fails to create. Behind the masks, reality retreated and make-believe reigned; tongues were loosened and actions emboldened. We arrived to find the festivities in full swing. From somewhere, Annetta had produced the costume that Gussie had requested— authentic Turkish robes of royal blue silk and a towering turban embellished with glass gems and a rakish egret feather. Thanks to Benito's artistry, Gussie's pale skin had taken on a nut-brown tint and his blond hair had been transformed into dark locks straggling from beneath the folds of his turban. A half-mask with a bulbous nose and a spray of black chin whiskers completed his costume. Only Gussie's commanding height and confident bearing kept him from looking totally ridiculous.

While my friend prowled the theater's brightly lit auditorium, weaving his way through the dancers and making a great show of wanting his fortune told, I played the role of the slightly tipsy friend urging his English visitor to leave no delight untried. In a tricorne hat with flowing black veil, leather half-mask, and long *tabarro*, I hoped that I passed for a typical Venetian more interested in seeking amusement than in fussing with an elaborate costume. My sister looked fetching in the ankle-revealing skirts and laced bodice of a rural shepherdess. Masked in the velvet oval of a lady's *moretta*, Annetta went about the hall asking everyone who this rich, daft, turbaned *Inglese* could possibly be.

Gussie and I eventually moved away from the couples flowing through the graceful footwork of galliard and minuet and concentrated on the hucksters plying their wares and services along the corridors of the huge theater. We found a gypsy, or at least a young woman dressed like one of that wandering race, sitting before a silver vessel filled with water covered by a thin film of oil. For a handful of coins the gypsy would light a candle and describe the visions she saw in the swirling, flickering liquid. To cultivate a further air of mystery, she instructed her customer to ask his question through a tin speaking tube that she held to her ear. To answer, she breathed her prophetic message into the same tube and seemed to gauge the length of her response by the look on her customer's face.

Gussie confounded the young gypsy with one rapid question after another. Remonstrating with her in vile Italian delivered in a booming drawl that I had heard many of his countrymen use, the big Englishman in the fantastical costume managed to draw quite a crowd. "What can you mean?" he asked in a sneering tone. "My father, the old earl, lived to be ninety-two. All my family are long-lived, unless we manage to break our necks on a horse. Ha! What does your bowl tell you about that?"

The soothsayer passed her hands over the shimmering bowl, concentrating as if it were about to reveal next week's winning lottery numbers. She gave Gussie a pathetic smile and tried to sweeten her response by arranging the scarves over her shoulders in even more wanton disarray. Gussie held the speaking tube to his ear, then shook his head vigorously. "Nonsense, I can't see anything in that soup kettle and I don't think you can either." He whirled away from the table, bright blue sleeves billowing out around him. "Does no one know how to conjure the future?" he cried. "I'm searching for genuine mysteries, not some silly miss playing at gypsy tricks."

I surveyed the crowd. People nudged each other and dropped their masks to get a better look at the unruly Englishman. Perhaps Gussie was overplaying his part. I was stepping to his side when I felt a tug on my sleeve.

"Don't run away so fast. I know who you are. Come dance with me."

I turned to face a woodland nymph draped in a flowing tunic. A garland of tinsel leaves contained her brown curls and a narrow strip of satin with oval holes for the eyes formed her mask. The flimsy satin wasn't sufficient to conceal her identity. It was Rosa, smiling an invitation and pulling on my arm.

"Tito, the orchestra is wonderful. They are beginning a quadrille. My partner hasn't arrived and I want to dance. Please?"

Alarmed, I deepened my voice as much as I could. "You mistake me, Signora. I do not know you."

Rosa snorted with laughter. "Now you disguise your voice! Too late, my soprano friend. I've already figured out who you are. Why won't you dance?" She glanced up and down the corridor filled with exotically dressed merrymakers and elegantly turned out courtesans. "Tell me, are you waiting for a certain someone? Does our *castrato* have a secret lover?"

Curious eyes turned from Gussie toward me. I couldn't let the brazen contralto ruin our plans. I shook my head emphatically, bowed, and backed away as quickly as I could. Rosa narrowed her eyes behind the satin mask, fists on her hips in a pose more typical of a fishwife than a leafy sprite.

I caught up with Gussie in a relatively quiet corner of the lobby. He grinned over the scraggly whiskers that Benito had gummed onto his chin. "How am I doing?" he asked in a whisper.

"You have definitely been noticed."

"By the right person?"

"That remains to be seen. This gathering is a perfect recruiting ground for Dr. Palantinus, but whether he is here or not…?" Deep in thought, I let my words trail off for a moment. "Gussie, we need to make you a more attractive decoy. Palantinus would not be likely to approach you and expound on the secrets of the Seraphim where he is likely to be overheard. Let's take a turn in the garden."

Open space is at a premium in our compact island city, but the San Benedetto was lucky enough to possess a long, grassy strip wedged between its east wall and a canal. Gussie and I went out through a side door and started down the meandering gravel path that wound between boxwood hedges studded with potted flowers. The first turning took us to a bench that was already in use. By the light of a few widely spaced torches, we beheld an amorous couple. The man had turned his mask to the side of his head and was fumbling with the fastenings of his lady's bodice. We decided to walk the other way. The garden was pleasantly cool after the warm stuffiness of the packed theater and would doubtless be filled with other couples later in the evening. For now, the sprightly strains of the musicians, the tables laden with exquisite dishes, and the never-ending fountain of wine that had been set up on the stage were keeping the revelers entertained inside.

We paused by an olive tree at the center of the garden, trying to project an image of outward calm. Presently, a boy painted and dressed as an Ethiopian slave ran up to hand Gussie a note. Without even holding out his hand for a coin, the boy was gone as quickly as he had come. I watched as my friend unfolded the missive and squinted in the dim light.

He read, "Take the little-trod path. At the bottom of the garden, by the lilac trees, a master of mystery and magic awaits you." Gussie's jaw tightened. "Is this it? Did Palantinus send this message?"

"There's only one way to find out. Let's go."

We trotted down the path leading to an ancient stand of lilacs. The trees badly needed pruning. Their branches pressed heavily on the stone wall separating the garden from the canal and reached out onto the path with clusters of cone-shaped flowers that brushed our shoulders as we passed. Near the end of their season, the lilacs littered the path with spent flowers and filled the air with a sickeningly sweet odor.

We passed the last glowing torch and were straining to see through the gloom when the outlines of a dark figure became visible at the edge of the little grove. Like me, the figure was draped in black from the brim of his tricorne to the tips of his dress slippers. The space where his face should have been was completely covered by a white mask molded into the form of a beaked monstrosity. The mask's eyeholes had even been netted to conceal the color of the wearer's eyes.

My heart raced. I could hear its frantic beat in the recesses of my ears. We might well be standing in the presence of Luca's murderer. I imagined the masked figure rowing a small boat to the middle of the lagoon and dumping his purple-swathed cargo under the trembling stars. While Gussie cleared his throat and looked the silent apparition up and down, I moved my dagger to my waistband and touched my fingers to Liya's painted image on the scarf I carried over my heart. For luck, I told myself.

"Well, Signore," Gussie finally huffed in the manner of a country squire confronting the local poacher. "You have summoned my friend and me with this cryptic billet-doux. What do you have to say for yourself?"

The voice that issued from under the mask was strange and unnerving—low, sibilant, hissing, yet fascinating in a dreadful way. "You are searching for mysteries conducted in the sphere of the celestial," the shadowy figure intoned.

"Er, well. Yes, I suppose I am."

"What blessing do you seek? Cure of physical ills, spiritual enlightenment, protection from harm, wealth?"

My friend swallowed and shuffled his feet. The immobile, yet compelling figure was taking the edge off Gussie's bluster.

"Speak man, my time is not to be wasted."

Gussie drew a deep breath. "I desire all that and more."

"Then you are in luck, Signore. I can introduce you to a temple where God's highest servants submit to the commands of ordinary mortals, where your every wish can be fulfilled."

"What beings are able to grant such favors?"

The eerie voice deepened, turning from hissing to hollow. "The Holy Seraphim."

"Seraphim? Angels, do you mean?"

For the first time, the figure showed some movement. His shoulders twisted in what I took to be a hint of irritation, and I had the sense of an ordinary man behind the hideous white mask.

"The Seraphim look on mere angels as men do on ants on the pavement. The Golden Seraphim guard the throne of God. They stand at his right and left hands. In days of old they carried coals burning with celestial fire to the lips of the prophets. After years of wandering the East and devoting myself to the study of mystical texts, I have discovered the rites that command the Seraphim to quit their airy abode and heed my will."

Gussie let his mouth go slack. He feigned a perfect picture of reverent amazement before voicing the question that should provoke our agreed-upon signal to forcibly unmask our quarry. "And whom do we have the honor of addressing, learned Signore?"

The figure drew himself up. The beaked nose pointed first at Gussie, then swiveled in my direction, lingering there for a long moment. The eyeholes above the beak could have been tiny pools of gray fog. Gussie's feet made a scraping sound on the gravel pathway. I tensed every muscle.

The mask spoke. "I am the Magister of the Temple of the Golden Seraphim. You may call me Dr. Palantinus."

That was it. I made to spring on the scoundrel in the lilacs and expected Gussie to do the same, but feet were crunching on the path behind me and a feminine voice cried, "There he is, Bassano. There's Tito. Hold him." Before I could move, a pair of strong arms pinned me in an encircling grasp from behind. I writhed and struggled, succeeding in merely pushing my mask askew. Blackness surrounded me as I gasped at the air drenched with the stink of rotting flowers. The din of a furious struggle sounded a few paces in front of me, but I could not free myself to help Gussie. In answer to my bellow of rage and frustration, my captor bent backward, lifting my feet off the path, then set me down hard, buckling my knees but somehow righting my mask. I saw a flash of white drapery and Rosa, unmasked and triumphant, stood before me.

"We found you at last, Tito Amato. You'll learn you can't ignore me and get away with it." With a determined flourish, she bobbed to her tiptoes and tore off my tricorne and mask. "Try enjoying the rest of the ball without these." A rumbling laugh came from her companion applying the bear hug.

I sputtered in fury, frantically trying to look around her into the shadows where Palantinus had been standing. "Rosa! *Santo Dio*, woman. You don't know what you've done."

She gave me a coy look as she tucked my hat and mask under her arm. "Surely, a lady is entitled to a little revenge. Just remember this the next time I do you the favor of asking for a dance."

My arms suddenly freed, I turned to confront the heavy, unmasked face of Bassano Gritti. That patrician stripling simply chuckled and offered Rosa his arm. They strolled back down the pathway leaving me unhurt but seething with anger.

I had no time to deal that pair their just retribution. Where had Gussie and Palantinus got to? I plunged into the thicket of lilacs. In the deep gloom, I could discern nothing but twisted trunks and leafy branches crowding against a wall of blackness where I knew a stone wall existed. Sweeping leaves and flowers away from my face, I fumbled forward. Then, a flash of a glass bauble and a patch of muted blue appeared at a rectangle that seemed somewhat less black than its surroundings. Gussie parted the branches and lumbered toward me.

"He got away, Tito. I had my hands on him, but I couldn't hold him. He's not overly strong, but he's wiry as an eel. There's an old gate in the wall over there. He had it off the latch and a boat waiting on the canal."

The unsuccessful hunt concluded, Gussie pulled the whiskers off his chin and removed the turban that was unwinding down his back. He sighed. "I say, feels good to get those off." He must have had a good look at my face then, for he placed his hand on my shoulder and said, "Save your wrath, Tito. It can't help us now. We'll get our fox. We'll run him down and I'll personally rip that long-nosed mask off his face."

Chapter 23

For the next two days, I went out but little. I flopped around the house, fretting over our failure to unmask Palantinus and hatching useless plans to corner him again. When I tired of those futile fantasies, I read his pamphlet over and over until I could stomach his inflammatory accusations no longer. One particular phrase hung in my mind and refused to be forgotten. Palantinus aimed his most emotional invective at "the Hebrew swindlers who would make capons of us all." Why capons? Was Palantinus referring to the general weakening of the shrinking Venetian Empire? Or was this a more personal issue? Did the man who wrote those words feel that his masculine role had somehow been threatened by a Jew? I stared at the page until the print blurred before my eyes, but no answers were forthcoming. In the end, I threw the pamphlet across the room and myself down on the bench at the harpsichord where I sang furious scales until the cat begged to be let out on the *campo* and the humans retreated to the farthermost reaches of the house.

On the day of the grand wedding, Annetta begged me to come to the Piazza. Gussie was taking her to view the procession of the bridal party from the palace to the Basilica. I knew that the huge square would be decked with golden hangings and miles of flowered garlands, and I could picture the splendid entourage. Musicians with long trumpets supported by children dressed as cherubs were set to herald the start of the procession. Waves of councilors, guild dignitaries, military commanders, and Savii would march by in dazzling robes and uniforms. Finally, the Doge and his daughter would be borne along the route in separate chairs covered with cloth of gold and canopied by gem-encrusted Burano lace. It would be a magnificent sight, but I wasn't in the mood for such a display. I bid Annetta and Gussie *addio* and settled down to examine the project that my neighbor's fruit press had helped me complete.

My decision to forgo the wedding was fortuitous. About noon, the bell at our front door jangled. I had given Benito leave to go to the Piazza, and I knew that Lupo was drowsing in the kitchen. Opening the door myself, I was surprised to find Liya standing on the threshold. She was carrying a basket that contained a wide-mouthed jar covered with a bit of cheesecloth.

"I brought you something," she announced with a hint of a nervous laugh. She wore a day dress the color of yellow corn and had a pretty white shawl crossed over her shoulders. I couldn't take my eyes off her.

I showed her into the sitting room and relieved her of her basket.

"It's *garata*," she told me. "I made it from Nonna's recipe, with special herbs and spices."

"Thank you. It smells wonderful," I replied as I bent my nose to the cheesecloth. "I don't think I'm familiar with the dish."

"It's pickled whiting steeped in olive oil and lemon. In the ghetto it's considered a delicacy."

"I'm sure I will find it so." Wondering what else Liya had on her mind, but mostly just wanting to continue gazing at her, I indicated the most comfortable armchair. "Will you sit? My sister has gone down to the Piazza, but I can have our servant make us some tea. Or lemonade, if you prefer."

Liya consented to sit but declined refreshment.

"Did you have any trouble getting here?" I asked.

"No. No one bothered me. Since the fire, Venice has slipped back to her regular habits. It's helped that no more wells have turned foul. Besides, the whole city is down on the Piazza."

We passed a few more comments on the improved weather, then Liya took a deep breath and cleared her throat. "Tito, I came to apologize again. You and Signor Rumbolt did a very brave thing on the night of the fire. Fortunata and I might not be alive today if you had not climbed to our roof. Instead of thanking you, I accused you. I can't believe how thoughtless and stupid I was."

"Your anger was understandable. You thought I was somehow responsible for the rumor that Isacco murdered Luca."

"Yes, but Nonna and Uncle Baruch have set me straight on that. I'm just sorry that my grandmother drew you into her meddling."

I hesitated for a moment, then replied, "Your grandmother seems like a wise woman. And a good judge of character."

"She certainly had poor Isacco pegged. Nonna knew him for an underhanded huckster the minute he walked in our door." Liya's nimble fingers plucked at the fringe of her shawl, and she raised her chin. "I know I shouldn't speak ill of the dead, but it's the simple truth that Isacco won't be missed, not in my household anyway. He was bossy to me, rude to my mother, and argued with my father almost every day. Papa should have packed him back to Livorno weeks ago."

I thought back to the conversation that Signora Gallico and I had shared before the disastrous fire. Liya's grandmother believed that Pincas meant to marry Liya to his young cousin. "Perhaps your father thought Isacco could be of some use to your family."

The Jewess waved her hand dismissively. "I can't think in what capacity. I certainly had no use for him."

So much for Signora Gallico's fear that her exalted blood would be further mixed with what she called the Del'Vecchio rag pickers. It was difficult to imagine anyone forcing my determined Liya into a marriage she wouldn't agree to. I asked my next question cautiously, striving to keep my manner free from rebuke or jealousy. "What would your grandmother have made of Luca if she had known him?"

Liya's eyes locked on mine; her lips were pressed in a straight line. I feared I had risked too much, but she began answering in a dry voice. "I think you have formed a bad impression of Luca, but if you had known him as I did, you might understand."

I cocked an eyebrow and she went on. "Luca was an orphan. His father died young and his mother Theresa might as well have been dead for all he saw of her. The printer that Luca and Silvio were apprenticed to took a liking to Silvio. To this brother, their master was kind and generous. But to Luca, just the opposite. The printer blamed Luca for everything that went wrong in the shop, ripped up his drawings, and never missed an opportunity to belittle him. He beat Luca almost every day. Through all those unhappy years, Luca lived on dreams of coming to Venice and making his fortune. He knew that his artistic talent was his most precious commodity, and he set about learning to put it to his advantage."

"But Liya, Luca was a master of illusion. He could have had an outstanding career creating sets for the theaters or painting frescoes on the walls of great houses. He didn't have to go into the business of fake relics."

She lowered her eyes. "Luca was impatient. He couldn't wait for a good life to come his way bit by bit. And…" She seemed to be searching for words and continued awkwardly. "Perhaps I was impatient, too. Perhaps I pushed him too hard. I wanted him to take me away from Venice."

"Away from Venice… where? How?" I asked quietly.

"We were going to run away. My family would never have consented to our marriage—they would disown me for marrying a Christian under any circumstances. Luca and I were going to a place where it doesn't matter who is Christian or who is Hebrew."

"Does such a place exist?"

"I have longed to find one all my life. The rabbis and the priests both think they own the truth and teach their followers to hate anyone who doesn't believe as they do. What foolishness—I am sick to death of their arrogance, sick to death of this simmering battle between Christians and Jews. Luca and I had talked of crossing the ocean, going to the American colonies."

"Do you think it would really be different there?"

"Perhaps not, but at least no one would know us, and we could be anyone and anything that we pleased."

"Rather like putting on new masks for Carnival."

"What is wrong with that, Tito? Why not join all those who are making new lives in that new land?"

"Liya, you astonish me. America is a wilderness populated by savages. Besides, your father would be devastated if you ran away."

She shook her head firmly. "It was the only way. I refuse to spend the rest of my life making costume frippery from castoff rags. And I wasn't going to give up the only man who has ever made me happy because he chanced to be born into a different religion." She sighed and her voice softened. "Besides, Papa would still have my sisters. Fortunata has always been his favorite anyway."

I didn't want Liya to see the emotion that her intimate words about Luca engendered in me, so I turned the conversation to practical matters. "Passage for two on a decent ship costs a great deal of money—not to mention the funds it would take to start over in a strange land."

She bit her lip, dark eyes searching mine. Was she seeking for understanding, forgiveness? "Luca was expecting a large sum of money. He told me to be ready to leave at a moment's notice."

My heart quickened. Here was useful information. "Where was this money to come from?"

"I don't know. Luca enjoyed being mysterious sometimes."

"You weren't curious?"

"Oh, yes. I was burningly curious. The more secretive Luca became, the more determined I was to worm his secrets out of him. I was usually successful, but not in this. Perhaps if I'd had more time." A spasm passed over her face and she looked around the room as if searching for a new topic of conversation. She found one lying on the round table in front of the window.

"What is this, Tito?" she asked, crossing the floor to inspect the project I had been working on that morning.

I followed her to the table and unfurled the topmost silk rectangle that represented the most successful of my experiments. "I've been trying to discover how Luca produced the Madonna's image on the veils Isacco sold." My finger traced the crude face I had managed to apply to the fabric. "My work is not nearly so elegant as Luca's but I think I have the process fairly well figured out."

She looked askance at me with a funny crooked smile. "How did you make these?"

"The easiest part was buying some short remnants of old silk that the draper had been keeping in his storeroom. For the pigment, it was trial and error. My friend Gussie is a painter. He identified ground cinnabar in Luca's room. We also found a jar labeled *dragon gum* on Luca's shelves. The chemist told me that is an old name for gum tragacanthe, a powder that mixes with water to form a paste that can be pigmented with cinnabar or any number of substances. I kept trying different combinations of the gum and the cinnabar until I got a brownish hue that seemed to match the image of Luca's Madonna."

"You have one of Luca's veils?"

"Ah, yes. I took one from his lodging. I didn't know what it was then, but I thought it might become important in some way." She was definitely smiling then, so I felt emboldened to go on. "The Madonna's face is not a painted image—there are no visible brushstrokes. It almost appears to have been burned into the cloth. It puzzled me, but then I remembered that Luca was a printer before he was a painter. One of the carpenters at the theater gave me a block of soft wood and I carved a face on it as best I could. Gussie could have done a better job, but this was something I was determined to do myself. I applied the pigment to the raised areas of the block—it took much less than I thought—my first efforts were just messy blobs. I pressed the cloth over the carved block in my neighbor's fruit press." I held my veil up to the window's light. "Not bad for a singer who knows nothing about art. Now it's the background that needs work. This veil looks too new. Luca's seems positively ancient."

She chuckled. "Luca had developed a system. He boiled the veils in coffee, then buried them in the flowerpots on his balcony. A month in the dirt and they could fool almost anyone."

"You know all about this then?"

"Yes. I often helped him finish his work so we could… have time for other things. You have the process nearly correct, only Luca didn't use a fruit press. He just applied the cloth to the wood-cut, stacked heavy books on top, and had me sit on them."

"The woodcut that you modeled for, I think."

She nodded, regarding me with a look I fancied held more respect than she had accorded me in the past. "You have gone to a great deal of trouble, Tito. I've heard that Messer Grande has no intention of reopening his inquiry and that he and the Savio are not pleased with your efforts to find out the truth about Luca's murder. Why do you keep trying?"

I refolded the cloth. "It is just simple decency. Luca's killer is out there somewhere. He cannot be allowed to go free."

She opened her mouth to reply, but I forestalled her. "I haven't seen you at the theater since the fire. How do you know what I've been doing?"

She cocked her head and smiled again. "Someone has kept me abreast of your activities."

Genuinely mystified, I asked a bit gruffly, "Who is it that interests himself in my affairs?"

"Not him, but her." I was getting annoyed, but Liya decided to stop teasing me. "It was your sister Annetta. Where do you think she got your costumes for the masked ball?"

"The Del'Vecchios are back in business?"

"We are indeed. Uncle Baruch is helping Papa get the shop going again. We have rented a little place just down from his house. Annetta visited us several days ago. Since then, I've been trying to work up enough courage to come apologize and ask how your investigation progresses." She moved closer and touched my arm. "Please, Tito. If you have any idea who took Luca from me, you must tell me."

I was in my shirtsleeves with the lace cuffs pushed back to the elbows. Liya's fingers were cool, but my bare skin burned under her touch. I asked, "Is it revenge you want?"

Her eyes widened. "Revenge? What good is that? Can it bring Luca back? No, I have had enough of hate and violence." Her face took on a melancholy expression as her hand left my arm and came to rest on her belly. "I simply want to know what happened—who killed Luca and why. When I know that I can go forward and do what I have to do."

I longed to pull her to me, bury my face in her dark braids wound up with the red kerchief, and assure her that everything would be all right, that I would trample on any prejudice to see that she was safe and happy. I resisted the urge. It was too soon after Luca's death to burden her with a eunuch's declaration of love. Even so, I might have succumbed to temptation if Gussie and Annetta had not chosen that moment to return from the Piazza. My sister's face was glowing with excitement, and she was full of tales about the beauty of the bride and the magnificence of her dress. Liya quickly left me and crossed the room to Annetta to discuss the details that so consume women when a wedding occurs.

♔♔♔

Later that evening, well after Liya's departure had pervaded my heart with a longing emptiness that I was doing my best to ignore, I reported to the theater. *Cesare* would not resume performance until the following night, but Maestro Torani had called a few of us in for an extra rehearsal to perfect a piece of stage business that had not been thrilling the audience as it should.

A scene in the second act found Cleopatra's scheming brother Ptolemy imprisoning her in his palace. Defeated, and desolate because she believed her lover Caesar had drowned, Cleopatra prostrated herself before the statue of a falcon-headed Egyptian deity. With mist rolling in through the grated prison windows, Cleopatra prayed for divine intervention. The heavens answered her prayers as the life-sized statue disappeared downward through one of the stage's five trap doors and Niccolo, costumed as the god, crawled through a slit in the drapery at the back of the statue's alcove. Once in place, he slowly uncurled himself to full height and sang to the queen cowering at his feet.

The illusion of the statue coming to life was one of Torani's more ingenious effects, but the scene involved too many different components. The counterweighted platform to lower the statue, the fog machines behind the grates, the backstage lanterns that heightened the eerie atmosphere, Niccolo's entrance, and more besides—all had to be aligned in perfect timing for the magic to succeed. Aldo had drilled the crew and repositioned the lights and the mechanisms several times but, so far, the living statue had drawn more laughter than amazement. Morelli wanted the scene cut, but Torani wouldn't hear of it. The dogged director was determined to perfect the illusion before the next performance.

Rosa and Florio had not been called in, and I really shouldn't have been needed for this session either. My character of Ptolemy had a duet with Cleopatra, affixed chains to her wrists, then exited before the transformation began. But Torani had insisted that my presence was required, so there I was, standing on stage between Emma and the black square of the open trap door listening to Niccolo's litany of complaints.

"The passage from the wings is too narrow and there are some nails down at the end that keep catching on my costume. But that's not all. My last entrance was late because my spear got tangled up in the drapery." The tenor carried a falcon mask with a long curving beak. Though black in color, the mask was an unsettling reminder of the menacing face that Dr. Palantinus had chosen to present to the world. "Besides," Niccolo continued, "I can hardly breathe in this thing."

Torani reached for the mask and examined it while he called—the third time—for the stage manager. "Aldo, where the devil are you?"

Aldo's round head popped up from the open trap. "Below stage, Maestro. One of the gear wheels has sprung some teeth. We're putting on a new one, but we need some time."

"How long?"

"Half an hour should do it." Aldo didn't wait for Torani's response, just ducked his head back into the gaping hole. I leaned over to take a look at the apparatus. The platform and its statue were resting on the floor of the understage about eight feet below. Luca's successor had painted the papier-mâché figure to resemble highly polished basalt. Its falcon head was turned sideways like the paintings on Egyptian tombs, and it carried an upright spear as tall as itself.

Torani was unhappy about the delay. While we awaited his instructions, he made a circuit of the stage, pausing here and there to visualize some effect that must be going through his mind. Carpani had been hovering downstage, making the inevitable entries in his notebook. When our distracted director backed right over him, the clerk squealed and his notebook went flying. For once, Carpani wisely fastened his lips and made a quick retreat. Niccolo failed to profit from his example. The tenor resumed his complaints in a whining tone.

"Maestro, do I have to carry this spear? It must weigh a ton."

Torani whirled and barked from halfway across the stage, "Are you supposed to be an exact replica of the statue?"

"Well, yes."

"Does the statue carry a spear?"

Sulky now, Niccolo again answered, "Yes."

Torani bore down on our group. "Then show some professional discipline and quit bothering me with nonsense." The director ran a hand through his frizz of gray hair. "Perhaps we can salvage some of this time. Niccolo, take your mask to Madame Dumas' workroom. She didn't make the mask, but she can surely make the breathing holes a little larger. Emma, stay in position. We'll work on the fog and the lighting, but I'll need a word with the backstage crew."

Torani strode offstage. He had not given me any specific instructions, so I stayed where I was to chat with Emma until the scene recommenced. Only a few footlamps glowed to illuminate the murky prison scene. The shadowy surroundings and the relatively small number of cast and crew spread throughout the theater created an air of intimacy. Emma gave me a subdued smile. "Have you heard of any companies that are hiring, Tito?"

"What? Has Florio decided to stay on? Should I be looking for another job?"

"Not for you, silly. For me." She lowered her voice. "*Cesare* will be my last opera at San Marco."

I shook my head. "What are you talking about?"

"Come next season, Maria Banti will be *prima donna*."

An elusive memory finally dropped into place. "Maria Banti is the woman that the Savio has been squiring around. I heard her sing at a local festival in Pistoia a year or two ago. I knew I had seen her before, but couldn't place where. She will be joining the company?"

Emma nodded. "Torani came to see me yesterday. The Savio's new mistress is in and I am out."

"But that's not possible. Unless her voice is substantially improved, La Banti is not up to top roles. Her embellishments are labored and her top notes not at all reliable. Besides, this company may not survive for another season."

Emma removed a handkerchief from her sleeve and touched it to her nose. Behind the backdrop there was a clang of metal and a few muffled oaths. She sighed. "That's the point, you see. I believe that Torani agrees with your assessment of La Banti, but he must bow to the Savio's dictates. As long as Maria Banti is *prima donna*, the Savio will make sure there are many seasons to come. Maestro is just thrilled that the Teatro San Marco is no longer under threat of closure and that he will still have a job. It's almost laughable. After all the fuss about the theater not paying its way and all the work we've done to make *Cesare* a runaway success, in the end it took only a quiver of the Savio's manhood to save the day."

Thin wisps of fog began to snake through the grated windows. Torani would be coming back to check the effect any minute. "Emma," I began, but stopped when I realized that the soprano had turned away from me. Her maid was signaling her from the downstage wing.

"Now what does she want? Will you stand in my place for a minute, Tito?" Emma murmured before hurrying into the wings.

I don't know why I didn't sense the next disaster brewing. Perhaps because I felt as much at home in the theater as I did in my house on the Campo dei Polli, I was not on the alert for a violent attack. As the stage filled with mist, someone called my name, softly, in hardly more than a whisper. Once more, urgent and pleading, the summons came from behind the drapery that formed the statue's alcove. Had Niccolo finished with Madame Dumas and gotten himself hung up in the narrow passage again? Carefully skirting the open trap, I stepped up to the pleated fabric.

"Niccolo?" I called.

A sharp blow struck me squarely in the abdomen and knocked me off balance. Doubling in pain, arms flailing, I sailed backward, straight into the black hole that housed the Egyptian deity on is movable platform.

My plummeting fall allowed time for two fleeting thoughts: "Tito, you are a prize fool" and "Is that damned spear on the right or the left?"

Chapter 24

"He's coming to," announced Emma's voice.

I had a panicky moment when I opened my eyes and saw nothing but blackness, then realized that Emma was bathing my face with a large, damp cloth. I pushed her hand out of the way and tried to sit up. Waves of dizziness engulfed me as twin shafts of pain pierced the left side of my head and my right ribcage.

"Here, get that rag out of his face." Benito, clearly itching to tend to me himself, inserted himself between Emma and me. "Master, are you all right? Do you know where you are?"

I looked up at the semicircle of concerned faces. Benito knelt at my side, hands fluttering from the bloodied cloth wound around my head to the soft cover that someone had thrown over my body. Emma stood behind him clutching a handkerchief and twisting a thumbnail between her teeth. Torani and Aldo looked on from the foot of my dressing room sofa with Niccolo hovering in the background.

My side ached when I drew breath, but I spoke anyway. "I think I'm all right. How long was I unconscious?"

Aldo answered. "Only a few minutes. The boys and I moved you from under the stage once the worst of the bleeding stopped. The statue's spear grazed your temple. Luck was with you. If you'd fallen more to the right, it could have pierced your heart."

Emma and Benito began chattering at once, but Torani broke in with his authoritative tones. "How did you happen to fall, Tito?"

"I didn't fall. I was pushed. Someone was hiding behind the drapery in the alcove."

"Impossible," Torani countered quickly.

I gingerly raised up to one elbow. "I may be mistaken in many things, Maestro, but not in this. I was pushed by unseen hands."

Torani's face was pale and grave. "I can't believe it. You hit your head. You must be more confused than you realize." He peered into the others' faces. "Emma, did you see what happened?"

"No, Maestro. I was in my dressing room. My maid called me to change to a different headpiece. She was helping me pin it on. She said you sent her to fetch me so you could see how the larger crown would look in the transformation scene."

"Ah, yes. So I did. Niccolo?"

"I wasn't anywhere near the stage. I was still in Madame Dumas' workroom getting my mask fixed."

"Aldo? You always know what is going on backstage."

"Not this time, Maestro. I was below, helping the boys with the gear wheel. I didn't know anything was amiss until Tito came crashing through the trap."

I spoke quietly, firmly. "There are only two ways to get behind those draperies. No one entered from the stage, so whoever attacked me had to pass through the tunnel passage from the wings."

Torani gazed at me as if I were an exotic species of animal on display during Carnival. He ran his tongue over his thin lips. "Of course. I'll make inquires among the crew. I had stopped in my office to retrieve some notes, but perhaps one of them can shed some light on this."

Aldo had another idea. "Let's see where Carpani's got to. He was fussing around backstage."

Emma nodded vigorously. "His prying eyes might prove valuable for once."

Torani pursed his lips thoughtfully. The light from the oil lamps on my dressing table threw his profile into a distorted shadow on the wall. The black outline held a menacing air, but the director's manner was all concern. "I'll question Carpani, too. Don't worry, Tito. I'll get to the bottom of this. I won't stand for anyone else getting hurt at this theater."

His eyes held mine for a strained moment, then turned back toward the doorway as Madame Dumas' accented voice announced the arrival of the doctor. Torani grabbed at the opportunity to head back to the business of rehearsal. He hustled Aldo, Emma, and Niccolo out of my dressing room before the doctor could even get his spectacles onto his nose. As Torani passed the length of my sofa, I couldn't help but notice that the seat of his breeches had developed a hole. The fabric had been torn into a small triangular flap—as if it had been caught on an errant nail.

☙☙☙

The doctor's diagnosis was plain enough: a bruised rib, a shallow laceration to the temple, and a mild shock to my system. If I stayed in bed and did as I was told, I should be able to sing the next night. I don't suffer inactivity well, but by the time I had limped in my front door, been clucked over by Annetta, and endured Benito's application of a poultice to my ribs, I was more than ready for my bed.

The next day brought another surprise, of a more pleasant variety. I was propped up in bed, drinking my second chocolate of the morning, when Benito ushered in an unexpected visitor. The manservant drew the room's only comfortable chair close to my bedside and asked my visitor if he would also take some chocolate.

Francesco Florio acquiesced with a short nod. He inspected my lumpy armchair, then perched on the edge of the cushion with his plump legs spread before him and both hands poised at the top of his silver-headed walking stick.

"I've already been to the theater," he said with a timid smile very unlike his regal stage persona. "I heard about your accident. You seem to be having more than your share of bad luck."

"I believe we make our own luck, Francesco. I've been attracting misfortune because I'm engaged in a protracted duel with a devilish scoundrel."

Florio cocked his head questioningly, but Benito distracted him by fetching a small table and pouring a cup of fragrant chocolate. While the singer sipped at the sweet beverage, his eyes roamed my chamber. He watched Benito tidy the room and took in all my mementos: books, opera playbills, a statue of an exotic Persian deity that Alessandro had smuggled past the pashas, even a battered toy boat that I had saved from my boyhood years. He pointed to a miniature of my mother surrounded by an oval frame set with tiny pearls.

"That is a pretty thing. Who is the woman?"

"My mother. She died when I was a young boy."

He gazed at the portrait for another moment. "I have nothing like these things," he said with a slight shake to his voice. "I possess only what my man can pack in my trunks."

"You must receive a number of gifts. I heard that when the Prince of Wales heard you sing in London, he removed his diamond shoe buckles on the spot and had them sent down to the stage."

Florio rolled his eyes. "Thank the good Lord for such generous gestures. People think I must be wealthy, but they don't understand how much it takes to travel all the time. I don't keep the gifts, you see. All the rings and buckles and snuffboxes must be sold to cover expenses. Ivo, my manager, takes care of all of that. He seems to think I rack up an uncommon amount of expenses."

"Don't you have a family home, somewhere that you could send the things you'd like to keep?"

He shook his head so violently that his chocolate cup rattled in its saucer. "I don't go home. When my father delivered me to the music lover who guaranteed to perfect my voice, he thought he was sealing his fortune with my future income." He snorted. "Today, my father is fortunate in only one respect. He still lives. I could cheerfully strangle him for having me butchered. And my mother, too, for encouraging him. But I haven't. I just... don't go back."

I nodded slowly, inching farther up on my pillows. "I've always envied you, Francesco… sailing high above us on a cloud of glory. But I'm beginning to think those elevated realms must be terribly cold and lonely."

"You are very wise for such a young man." He smiled bleakly. "You say you envy me. I could say the same about you. You have everything that makes a man truly happy. A real home, loving family, friends, even the admiration of your fellow singers. You can sing your colleagues at the San Marco right into the ground, yet you retain their goodwill. How do you manage it?"

"I don't know. I just go from day to day, doing the best I can."

He raised a dubious eyebrow and chuckled a bit. "I expect there's more to it than that. But I won't press you, not in your present state."

"I'm all right." I sat forward, suppressing a wince of pain. "I must rest today, but I'll be on stage tonight."

"I was afraid you'd take that attitude. That is precisely the reason I'm paying you this visit. I hate to see you punishing your voice. If you take care, your vocal instrument could someday be the equal of mine, but if you push too hard, you will find yourself in the back row of the choir in some country church. So I decided to share something with you—a talisman that will speed the healing of this latest injury. It has certainly kept my throat in top form during my stay on this low-lying, pestilential island." He began to unwind the yellow scarf around his neck.

"Francesco, did you ever think that your throat remains vigorous because you have the constitution of a coach horse?"

He put his hand to his heart. "My dear Tito, you have no idea. I have always been inclined to a malign concoction of humors that leaves me susceptible to all manner of ills. It is only this wondrous artifact that has allowed me to sing *Cesare* without falling victim to Venice's noxious airs."

As Florio gently shook his long yellow scarf, a square of silk fell out of its folds. "Here it is, Tito, a true miracle." He held up an imprint of Liya as the Blessed Virgin. "This treasure is the actual veil that the mother of our Lord wore at his crucifixion.

By divine intervention, the marks of her terrible grief were transferred onto the silk. See here, how her tears fall over the swell of her cheek. I keep it around my throat at all times." The singer's voice was soft and reverent as he draped the fabric over one hand and extended it to me. "It is my most precious possession, but you may touch it if you say a prayer first."

Benito had come to the foot of my bed and looked as if he might burst into giggles at any moment. I gave him a small shake of my head. To Florio, I asked, "How did you come by this veil?"

"Can you imagine it? The precious thing had come into the hands of a filthy Jew, a dealer in rarities and relics. It didn't come cheap, I assure you. But I would have given my last ducat for such a worthy treasure."

"What makes you think the cloth is genuine?"

"The Jew provided a certificate which gives its history and proves its authenticity. It is written in Latin, but he told me what it says. The Madonna kept the kerchief with her until she rose to meet her heavenly son. It was then entrusted to an apostle who soon divined its miraculous properties. Down the centuries, the veil was worshiped under close guard at a monastery high in the Vogelsberg Mountains. Some years ago it was stolen by a lay servant who needed money to get his old father out of prison. Since then, the veil has changed hands many times, always bringing good health and prolonged life to everyone who reveres it and keeps its secrets."

"Francesco, I hardly know how to tell you." I sighed, then plunged ahead. "This veil is a fake. You have been duped."

Florio gazed at me in horror. When he spoke, there was an edge of anger to his voice. "Are you one of those modern men who reject the notion of miracles?"

"Not at all. God has graced me with several over the years, but this veil is not one of them. I know it for a false relic, a cloth crafted to deceive."

"You don't know what you're talking about," he said brusquely. "I should have known better than to offer to share my treasure with anyone."

Benito had guessed my intent. He had already retrieved the veil I had found in Luca's lodging. He handed the folded cloth to me and I unfurled it on top of my bedcover.

Florio's face was a study in loss and disillusionment. He rose from the deep armchair and laid his veil beside mine, then bent to examine both closely. To give him more light, Benito opened the window draperies as far as they would go.

Florio's voice quavered. "I don't understand. I paid the Jew a king's ransom. He had a certificate." A hopeful light sprang to his eyes. "Perhaps yours is a copy. Mine is the true veil and yours is a fake."

I shook my head. "I knew the man who sold you the veil. He and the painter who was murdered at the theater had devised quite a scheme." As I recounted the ingenious process that Luca had used to make the relics, Florio sank back into his chair. A dull film covered his eyes and his cheeks seemed to deflate. He said, "So the Jew who spun such a convincing tale wasn't a dealer in antiquities at all."

"I'm afraid not. Besides forged relics, Isacco Del'Vecchio dealt in used clothing."

Florio's eyebrows shot up. "He was not the Jew who was mobbed and hanged for the painter's murder?"

"The very same. His cousin makes the headdresses and masks for the theater."

"I hadn't realized. Ivo told me he'd found a dealer in rarities. I thought… oh, never mind. What a fool I've been." Florio's voice trailed off and he gave the twin veils a vacant stare.

I smiled gently. "If you would come out of your dressing room now and again, and mix with the company a bit, you might know more about what is going on."

Florio returned my smile and nodded. He seemed to be contemplating my words as if they had come from the lips of a learned philosopher instead of a singer who lacked the sense to stay away from open trap doors.

He finally said, "Perhaps I do need to change my ways. People really don't like me very much, do they?"

I shrugged apologetically. "I know you can be kind. You should try showing that kindness more often."

Florio gathered his Madonna veil in one plump fist. With a sigh, he pushed the fabric deep into his coat pocket, then sank back into his chair and remarked, "Suppose I begin by asking about this violent duel that landed you in a tangle with the Egyptian statue?"

"It is a duel of wits, actually." Before I could elaborate, my door resounded with a cadence of sharp raps. Benito attempted to admit Florio's manager, but the man insisted on hovering at the doorway. "Signori, you must pardon my intrusion. Signor Florio is expected at the residence of the French ambassador. We should be getting down to the boat."

Florio frowned and said, "I've changed my mind, Ivo. I won't be dining with the ambassador. I'm going to spend the rest of the day with my friend Tito. Make my excuses. You know how to invent something."

Ivo Peschi hesitated, a puzzled look on his thin, wrinkled face.

"Well, what are you waiting for? I've spoken, man," said Florio with a sharp nod.

His manager retreated with a small bow and Benito clicked my door shut.

Not certain whether to be flattered or annoyed, I asked, "Are you sure you want to hear about my doings? They comprise the longest of long stories."

My self-designated friend spread his hands and settled back into the cozy armchair. "We aren't due at the theater for hours. Perhaps your man could find a bite to keep our stomachs occupied while I hear your tale?"

I nodded at Benito and beat at my pillows to make a more tolerable resting spot for my tender ribs. I thought a moment, then began, "It all revolves around this masked scoundrel called Palantinus."

A stricken gasp from Florio stopped me short. He asked, "Dr. Palantinus? From the Temple of the Golden Seraphim?"

I nodded.

"Ah, what a wretched day this has become," he said in a strangled groan. "Are you going to tell me that Magister Palantinus is a fraud, too?"

Part Four

Aria: Air

Chapter 25

"We must disembark here and walk over a few squares," Florio said as he signaled the gondolier to stop at a deserted quay.

"Why?" I asked.

"It is one of the rules that Dr. Palantinus insists on. He doesn't want to attract attention to the temple by a number of gondolas arriving at a building that is supposed to be empty."

"I see," I said, trading uneasy glances with Gussie. "What other rules does Palantinus require of the Brethren?"

"No masking. He says the Seraphim must be able to see each man's naked face to judge his sincerity and worthiness."

The ever-practical Gussie countered that one. "Shouldn't a spirit as powerful as a Seraph know what is in a man's heart without looking at his face?"

Florio shrugged. "I know it sounds like nonsense. After hearing Tito's story, I can't think how Dr. Palantinus ever took me in. It's just that I worry so about my throat. If I were voiceless, I would sink into decrepitude while my fame dwindled away to nothing. I might as well be dead. When the masked stranger approached me and told me that he held power over beings who could guarantee my continued health, well… He was very convincing, you see. Even knowing he's all humbug, I'm shaking with fear at the thought of incurring his displeasure."

"When Palantinus requested such a liberal initiation fee," Gussie continued, "did that not raise your suspicions?"

"Not so much. You see, Dr. Palantinus is no pavement char-latan hawking cheap talismans to guard against the evil eye. He is a man of intelligence who reads ancient languages and has knowledge of the most abstruse sciences."

During the intermissions of that night's performance, Gussie and I had discussed every nuance of Florio's childlike belief in the Seraphim and their earthly Magister, but my friend was still curi-ous. "I don't suppose Palantinus ever takes off his disguise?"

"No," replied Florio, stumbling a bit as he started down a short flight of stairs that dumped us into a narrow alley. "He always remains masked and cloaked, but he has good reason. If his true identity were known, he would be besieged with supplicants. Everyone from the poorest fisherman to the Doge himself would be after him to call on the Seraphim. The man wouldn't have a minute's peace."

We fell silent, minding our footing on the rough stones. I was not particularly familiar with this district. Florio had ordered the boatman to set us down to the east of the Arsenale, Venice's huge shipyard, in an area crowded with old foundries, docks, and ware-houses. A hundred years ago, the Arsenale had employed thousands of men to construct and repair the mighty fleet that maintained a millennium's worth of maritime superiority. But by my time, the dockyard had dwindled to a pale relic of its former self, and many of the surrounding buildings were rotting on their piles.

Florio seemed sure of his way despite the midnight gloom. A bright quarter moon enveloped in a misty halo lit the sky above, but its rays barely penetrated the maze of massive structures. The fetid odor of the docks permeated the damp alley. A bead of sweat trickled down my face. Wiping my forehead on the edge of my sleeve, I glanced at Gussie. He was following Florio with a buccaneering glint of adventure in his eyes. Before we had set out, he had tucked a pistol into his waistband and recounted the story of a wellborn highwayman famous in his home county. My aching ribs wouldn't let me forget that the hunt for Palantinus had become a matter of great personal risk, but Gussie was still fascinated with the larking excitement of it all.

Florio paused and pointed across the juncture of several alleys. Gussie and I drew back under the cover of a top-heavy, timberframed structure and inspected our destination. It was an enormous warehouse with a lower level of thick stone blocks and upper levels of masonry punctuated by a few recessed, shuttered windows. Its foreboding façade was totally devoid of life, and its arched entryway was littered with pieces of a broken packing case and other, less identifiable, debris. I questioned Florio with my eyes.

"This is it," he whispered. "We enter by a side door. You can't see it from here, but you go down the length of the building, turn the corner, and proceed about twenty paces. See, someone is turning in there now."

We leaned forward, straining our eyes. Two darkly clad men stood out from the shadows by virtue of their white stockings below and the light ovals of their faces above. They hesitated at the opposite end of the warehouse, peered this way and that, then disappeared into the passage that Florio had described.

Our guide continued. "This is where I must leave you. When Dr. Palantinus calls a meeting of the Temple Brotherhood, a boy delivers a triangular token inscribed with the time and the day. No Brother is admitted without his token. Don't doubt it, I know. I forgot mine once, and the doorman would make no exception, even for me."

"How are we to get in?" I asked in a low whisper.

"When it is time for the ceremonies to begin, the guard bars the door with a stout plank and goes to attend Dr. Palantinus. Wait here about twenty minutes. That should give me plenty of time to sneak out of the temple chamber and lift the bar."

"Where do we go from there? We can't mix with the Brethren unmasked."

"I've been thinking about that. The temple chamber is in the very center of the building. It's a large room that rises three or four stories. A gallery runs around three sides and looks down on the floor where we gather. Once in the door, you'll be in a corridor that ends in a winding flight of stone steps. Those stairs must lead up to the vicinity of the gallery, but the exact route I cannot tell you. Once you've passed the first turn of the steps, you two are on your own." Florio finished his instructions with a quaver to his voice. In the luminous moonlight, his face looked as if his manservant had applied a thick layer of white greasepaint.

"Are you all right, Francesco?" I asked. "Are you going to be able to slip away and unbar the door?"

He nodded resolutely. "We mingle for a bit before we take our places—that will be my chance. Thanks to your friendship, I have been cured of superstition and reclaimed my good sense. I don't know if Dr. Palantinus is the murderer that you suspect him to be, but I do know that he is a perfidious rascal who preys on trusting innocents. It is my duty and pleasure to help you."

With that, Florio launched himself down the alley, leaving Gussie and me to hug the shadows.

I whispered, "What do you think, my friend? Is tonight the night we corner our fox?"

"With luck…" he began, then pressed a quick hand to his lips. Another dark figure was picking its way down one of the intersecting alleys. We waited in silence as several others gathered from different directions, and finally it was time for us also to creep down the alley toward the secluded entrance. Florio was as good as his word. The door opened easily, with nary a creak, and we found ourselves in a dimly lit hallway with the dark mouth of the curving stairway before us.

No one hampered our anxious flight to the upper stories. Gussie and I didn't stop climbing until the stone stairs ran out and we were in a bare passage illuminated by a hint of moonlight filtering through the shutter slats. The sound of muffled chanting wafted down the deserted hall. Feeling our way in the gloom, we followed the droning cascades. The passage turned a corner to take us into the heart of the structure, and I paused to set the turns we had already made firmly in my mind. Getting lost in the rambling warehouse was definitely not on my program for the night's activities.

As the chanting rose in intensity, a pool of yellow light bisected the passage ahead. Gussie and I crept forward and peered carefully around the open doorway. We had located the gallery above the temple chamber.

I put my finger to my lips and pointed downward. Wincing inwardly over the ruin of a good pair of breeches, I sank to my knees and crawled forward. Gussie did the same. Years of accumulated dust, bits of plaster, and the remnants of insects and rodents crunched beneath us. Beside me, Gussie pinched his nose to ward off a sneeze.

We soon reached the railing that defined the gallery's perimeter. It was constructed of smooth planks roughly the width of my outstretched hand topped by a rounded cap molding. If we turned our heads just so, we could view Dr. Palantinus and his converts through the slits between the planks. The cavernous space must have once stored the raw materials of the shipbuilding trade. I could imagine the warehouse owner standing at this gallery railing to inspect his lengths of raw wood, pallets of oakum, and casks of caulking tar. The rafters above soared high enough to accommodate the mast of even the largest vessel. Across the space, the opposite wall was bare except for a small balcony jutting out one level below our gallery. I had no idea of its original purpose, but I instantly recognized what a perfect stage for a magical apparition it could make.

On the floor of the chamber, Palantinus had assembled enough esoteric paraphernalia to serve as a stage set for a wizard's den. Thick tallow candles and glowing braziers surrounded the Brethren in a circle of smoky, yellow light. At the cross quarter points of the circle stood tall lamps fashioned with glazed, wrought iron covers that transformed them into pyramidal flames of blue, red, green, and yellow. Hangings with Egyptian or Assyrian symbols worked in metallic thread shimmered in the shadows.

The Brethren occupied a semicircle of low benches arranged around a raised dais. About forty men were standing before their benches, swaying back and forth to a monotonous chant of wordless tones. Besides Florio, I recognized no one. Most of the younger men possessed the sleek, well-bred blondness of the Northerners who came south to make Italy their personal pleasure ground. The older men were Venetian, their faces harder to read. They presented a range of aspects: tentative hope, fearful longing, wry amusement, unshakable devotion. Here and there, the bright eyes of the genuine fanatic burned.

The figure on the dais needed no introduction. Dr. Palantinus wore the same beaked mask, veiled tricorne, and trailing cloak that I had seen in the garden at the San Benedetto. He was standing silent, completely motionless, yet he drew every eye and radiated a palpable energy like the waves of heat rising off a distant plain baking under the summer sun. Another masked man that I had not yet noticed banged an oriental gong. The chanting ceased immediately. Not a sound escaped the lips of the assembly, but I was conscious of a building sense of anticipation.

When Palantinus did speak, he used the familiar hissing tones, but these were not the soft, seductive raspings of the garden. For the temple, the Magister heightened the power of his voice. If the dragons of old fairy tales could speak, this would surely be their monstrous voice. I wondered if the cavities within his grotesque mask contributed to this strange effect or whether the man who played Palantinus was someone who had a professional command of vocal technique.

The Magister's first words were uttered in a language that I was sure was pure gibberish but seemed to impress his followers. At the close of each thundering phrase, the flames in the pyramidal lamps shot upward and the gong sounded a brazen rumble. Eventually, his words became recognizable.

"You who revere the celestial guardians. You who worship the attendants of the heavenly shrine, perfect from their moment of creation. You who beg assistance from God's highest messengers. Bow down."

To a man, the onlookers crumpled to the floor and prostrated themselves like a bevy of Turkish slaves. I saw Florio sneak a peek up toward the gallery. "Have a care, Francesco," I intoned softly. With darkness behind us and the spectacle of Palantinus focusing the attention of the Brethren to the fore, I doubted that Gussie and I would be noticed, but there was no sense in taking chances.

Palantinus kept his flock in this submissive posture while he lectured them on chastity and obedience and promised that the Seraphim would deliver longevity, splendid health, and a prolonged state of happiness to those who followed their tenets. As his hissing voice droned on, my right foot prickled with the pins and needles of my constricted position. Gingerly, I rearranged my arms and legs and stretched my neck. Now that my eyes had adjusted to the hazy illumination, I noticed something I had not seen before. There was a definite path cutting through the detritus on the floor of the gallery.

I signaled Gussie to stay where he was, rubbed my aching side, and followed the trail in a painful, duck-like crouch. At several notches along the gallery railing, I encountered a familiar object—a pot of the pyrotechnical substance that produces the semblance of flame. At the theater, these were used in bunches to simulate the conflagration of a palace or city, or singly to shoot through a trap door that supposedly led to the underworld. I turned the last of the terra cotta pots over in my hands. Stenciled in block letters on its side were words that didn't surprise me very much: *Property of Teatro San Marco.*

As I made my way back to Gussie, he pointed downward and shook his head. There was trouble in the mystical realms. The Magister had withdrawn. The dais was empty and the room so silent that I could hear the quiet crackling of the braziers below. The seemingly unaccountable pause stretched from seconds to minutes. The men of the temple began to murmur and lumber clumsily to their feet.

Gussie whispered, "I think it's time for the Seraphim's appearance, but something has gone wrong."

Several of the Brothers sat down heavily and crossed their arms with decided frowns on their faces. One of the men I had guessed might be particularly anxious for a boon from the

Seraphim raised his voice in whining complaint. "It has been over three weeks since we've had a full manifestation. The Seraph Azadabel promised to return and bless me at this meeting. I've bathed in holy water and fasted for days. What more must I do to be worthy?"

Another, younger man declared in a mincing French accent, "I don't understand. We've all paid our money, but we've barely seen the Seraphim. Palantinus can start delivering the spirits or be damned."

At that moment, Dr. Palantinus emerged from the shadows behind the dais. His absurdly beaked mask was as inscrutable as ever, but a new note of uncertainty underscored his sibilant tones. "The spirits of light are angry, Signori. The solemn acts of adoration have not been fulfilled."

Disparaging murmurs echoed up from the semicircle of benches. I sensed rebellion in the ranks.

Palantinus froze for one long moment, then raised his arms in a commanding gesture and thundered words of reproach that made all present cringe. I had to hand it to him: the man certainly knew how to control a crowd. His rant finished on a gentler note. "If you return to your knees and beg forgiveness, your guiding spirits may yet favor you." Palantinus threw his head back and implored the empty air, "Oh, Seraph exalted, pity these foolish mortals and give form to your invisible reality."

The kneeling Brethren scanned the dark space above, but nothing happened. Palantinus raised his voice another notch. "Oh, Seraph, give form to your invisible reality."

There was movement on the little balcony opposite. Gussie and I adjusted our positions to afford the best view. A golden figure seemed to float to the edge of the balcony and look down on the gathering. From somewhere, the harp-like tones of a lyre sounded. The hovering figure was covered with a shining suit of gold that fitted like a second skin. Was it male or female? I really couldn't tell. Its body was slender, almost elfin, with no discernable breasts, but a curving swell to the hip region lent a hint of the feminine.

Feathered wings tipped with more glittering gold arched over the Seraph's shoulders, spanning the narrow balcony. Following the strum of the lyre, the golden figure began a rhythmic series of arm movements, as if it was going to break into a dance, or flight. At one point I clearly saw the creature's face—a molded visage of gold stretching from chin to crown-like headpiece, eyes painted in a wide-open stare. I could have sworn that I'd worn the very same mask as an operatic Apollo several seasons ago.

At the start of the Seraph's manifestation, the Brethren had gasped in a mixture of relief and wonder, but when the golden figure vanished after only a few short moments, the audience turned angry again. I gazed up into the shadowy rafters and imagined the dazzling spectacle that Luca must have made of the Seraph soaring in space accompanied by shooting flames and other illusions.

For I had no doubt that Luca had directed the temple displays. The Brethren complained that the Seraph's display had been lacking for three weeks. Exactly the length of time that Luca had been missing. Difficult to put on a show when your illusionist is at the bottom of the lagoon.

Gussie nudged me with an elbow. "It's getting ugly down there. Perhaps we should go."

Palantinus had disappeared again, and some of the younger men had jumped onto the dais. One even produced a sword and brandished the blade above his head, calling for "that cowardly blackguard." I was wondering if Gussie and I could possibly find Palantinus in the vast warehouse when the Magister's masked attendant returned to the dais, gave the gong a resounding blow, and attempted to calm the crowd.

His strained cry held a note of panic. "Everyone just go home. Dr. Palantinus is ashamed of all of you. He has left the temple to meditate and propitiate the Seraphim for your undisciplined display."

His words only set the Brethren clamoring all the louder, but the masked man on the dais stood his ground. "Go on," he shouted, "just get out."

Gussie and I didn't need to be told twice.

Chapter 26

Emma lived on the Calle Bernardo, not far from the Campo San Barnaba where Gussie and I had first learned of Dr. Palantinus. Her lodging far surpassed the rooms of the impoverished Barnabotti copyist, but it was still a modest residence. The neat, yellow house faced onto a quiet street and, at the back, overlooked a square shaded by several spreading trees.

It was ten the next morning when I rang at the street door, but Emma was still asleep. I told her maid I would wait. The girl conducted me to a charming sitting room done up in rose and yellow striped silk and chased a lazy, fluffy dog off the sofa so I could sit. The sun streaming through lace curtains made a cheerful pattern of light and shadow on the Persian carpet and cushion-laden armchairs. Over the trinkets on the mantelpiece hung a portrait of Emma as a young woman. The artist had painted her in profile, chin raised and lips parted to greet the brilliant adventures that life must surely hold in store for her.

When the subject of the youthful portrait entered the room in a thick dressing gown, it was almost a shock. I was used to seeing my friend after her maid had completed a thorough *toilette*. Emma's uncorseted flesh, undressed hair, and blotchy, unpowdered cheeks made her look more like a washerwoman than a *prima donna*.

"What a surprise, Tito," she said after sending the maid for chocolate and rolls. "You are always welcome, but you would have found me in a better state if I had known you were coming."

"It is of no consequence, *carissima*," I answered. "We have been friends long enough that we don't have to stand on ceremony. Besides, I want to talk with you in private, away from the flapping ears at the theater."

"Go on, then." She encouraged me with a smile as she installed a wiggling ball of canine fluff on her lap. "Here, the only ears that are flapping are mine. And my precious, sweet Bebe's, of course." She applied pecking kisses to Bebe's pointed ears and was rewarded by the swipe of an enthusiastic pink tongue.

"I was distressed to hear that Maria Banti will replace you for the next season."

Emma nodded slowly but remained silent.

"I wonder if you have made any plans?"

She frowned, absently running her fingers through Bebe's yellow fur. "I'm nearing the end of a long road, one I've been traveling for many miles. It's hard to see over the last rise, but I feel sure there will be other paths to take."

"Do you mean to stop singing, then?"

"Soon, soon. I'm trying to find an impresario to arrange a farewell tour. I envision a series of benefit concerts all over Italy, even Germany perhaps. Then I'll return to Venice and... do something else. Perhaps I'll take on a few students."

I studied her soft, amiable countenance. "You seem remarkably calm about all this. I don't think I could so easily resign myself to leaving the stage."

Emma nodded again. She consigned Bebe to the floor and made an eager grab for the chocolate that her maid was delivering on a wheeled cart. "You are only twenty-two, Tito. I'm considerably on the wrong side of forty. I've realized that my career has been on borrowed time for several years. I thought I might squeak through another few seasons, but La Banti's charms have put an end to that. I was disappointed when Torani delivered the news, but I can't say I was surprised."

"How did he tell you?"

"Maestro?"

I nodded.

"He tried to be kind, to spare my feelings, but he was adamant. La Banti will star in every opera next season. He didn't seem happy about it, but…" She finished her sentence with a shrug.

"Did Torani take your part with the Savio? Point out what a splendid run you've had in *Cesare*?"

"I don't know, but I doubt it. Maestro Torani has not been as frugal as I have over the years. He is probably not in a position to challenge the Savio."

"Did Maestro have no roles to offer you?"

"No, but that is for the best. I would never consent to go out as *seconda donna*." Emma flashed a brave smile and called for more pastries. She chuckled. "One good thing about retirement—I will no longer have to starve myself to get into the costumes."

I leaned back into the commodious sofa, wrapped in thought. "You're not eating," Emma said, pressing a plate of rolls on me. Bebe immediately jumped on the sofa and focused his beady black eyes on the pastries on my lap.

"I'm considering how to ask my next question."

"Out with it, Tito." She paused to lick some sticky icing off her thumb. "I'll probably tell you what you want to know. At my age, I have no naughty secrets."

"All right, then. Are you ready to tell me whose voice you heard arguing with Luca the night he was killed?"

She froze with her thumb to her lips. As her hand slowly descended to her lap, she answered stiffly. "I told you that I was too far away to hear plainly. The voice was muffled."

"I remember what you said. At the time, I was sure that you were shielding someone. We both know who I'm talking about. What reason do you have to protect him now?"

She exhaled wearily. "Tito, you are just like Bebe when he's found a bone. You worry things to distraction. Luca's death distressed us all, but it is part of the past. Even Messer Grande has put the matter to rest. Why can't you be content with that?"

"Messer Grande has been deceived by a master strategist. To cover his guilt, the man who murdered Luca set a mob on an innocent Jew, and now he's after me."

"Tito, no."

"I didn't imagine the voice that called me to the trap door or the shove that sent me through it. I can't help but wonder—what would the blackguard do with someone who actually heard his voice?"

Emma bit her lip. Her eyes darted around her comfortable sitting room, then stopped to give me a piercing look. I was an unwelcome whirlwind stirring up dust on her placid road of life. I thought she might ask me to leave, but instead, she composed herself with a long drink of chocolate and called Bebe back to her lap. With her face half buried in his fur, she said, "You think I heard Maestro Torani arguing with Luca."

I nodded.

"You are right. Their voices were raised. Luca's sounded angry and defensive. Torani's less angry but quite severe. Maestro was remonstrating with Luca over something." She held up a quick hand. "Don't even ask. I don't know what it was about. I'm not that much of an eavesdropper."

Before I could respond, Emma sat up very straight, rearranged her dressing gown and ran her hands through her loose hair. Somehow, the frumpy washerwoman was metamorphosed into the haughtiest of sopranos. "I've answered your question, Tito, but I still know something you don't."

"What do you mean?"

"I know that Rinaldo Torani is no killer. He could never bash Luca's skull in. Or try to pitch you to your death on that spear. I know that as surely as I know I'm sitting here having chocolate with you and Bebe."

"People wear many masks, Emma, especially in these uncertain times. Torani has always kept to himself. How can you be so sure that the man we see at the theater doesn't have another persona we have not even imagined?"

"Because." She shrugged and seemed to be struggling to find the right words. "He is... the maestro."

❧ ❧ ❧

I knew what Emma meant. Though Maestro Torani's singers knew little about his personal life, we all shared a special bond with our director. In his less pleasant moods, Torani could be sharp with his tongue and exasperating with his demands—a dogged perfectionist, a temperamental tyrant, a songmaster so intent on his unique vision of an aria that his corrections felt like personal attacks. But was it not so with every creative genius?

There were also the wondrous times when he and I had been in perfect accord, when pleasing the maestro meant searching within myself to find a degree of perfection I didn't know I was capable of. On these occasions, I loved Maestro Torani as I had never been able to love my own father. Could this determined director, by turns severe or inspiring, possibly be the murderous Palantinus? That is what I had resolved to search his office to find out.

It was early in the long, hot afternoon that would end with the next to last staging of *Cesare*. The initial momentum of the production had flagged. It had been at least a week since any of the performers had come to the theater to soothe their jitters with a little extra rehearsal, and Maestro Torani wasn't expected until two hours before curtain. Like Aldo drowsing in his cubbyhole near the stage door, the few crew members that were around the theater were relaxing on a long dinner break. Avoiding the backstage area, I slipped along the curving walls of the dark auditorium and crossed to the warren of passages that led to Torani's office. The director's door was shut tight, but I took a page from Isacco Del'Vecchio's book and coaxed the lock open with my small stiletto.

I had no doubt that Maestro Torani was capable of playing the role of Dr. Palantinus. After all, the business at the Temple of the Golden Seraphim was nothing more than a staged performance employing the sort of illusions that he had perfected during his years at the opera house. But even the maestro couldn't pull the shows off by himself. If he had killed Luca, he would be searching for another experienced hand. I didn't find Aldo nearly as trustworthy as Benito obviously did. I suspected that Torani's gondola ride with the stage manager had seen more discussion of flying Seraphim than openings at the Verona opera house.

All things being equal, I wouldn't have begrudged Torani his Seraphim scheme. The Senate had never paid its artists according to their true worth, and we all knew of countless times when the director had opened his own purse to help a musician who met with illness or misfortune. If Torani chose to replenish his funds with a bit of mystical tomfoolery that harmed no one, I would not condemn him. But murder, scapegoating, the attack on me—these were monstrous acts that couldn't be forgiven.

So I was looking for something to explain what could have driven the director I respected so much to strangle Luca with his bare hands and heave his body into the lagoon. Given desperate enough circumstances, I believed that anyone was capable of murder. But what were the circumstances in this case? Torani had more than a merely professional connection to Luca and his family. The torn paper with Theresa Cavalieri's Bremen address on it told me that. More than any other thing, I needed to find the rest of that letter.

I started with the chaos of his desk. I thought it unlikely that Torani would leave any document pertaining to Luca in plain sight, but I couldn't leave any papers unexamined. After quickly reviewing a portion of a mawkish libretto, a list of operas in consideration for the future repertoire, and what looked like instructions for the tailor concerning a new silk coat, I turned my attention elsewhere.

Glass-fronted cabinets lined the walls, full of scores, bound and unbound. A letter could be tucked in any of these, but one touch sent the dust flying and made me think they hadn't been disturbed for months. I surveyed the rest of the office. A small chest of drawers under the window behind the desk looked promising. I tried the top drawer. It was unlocked.

I found a worn leather portfolio bulging with documents and spread the pages out on top of the sun-dappled chest. The portfolio failed to yield the letter I sought but did contain a number of other letters that warmed my heart. On sheet after sheet, Torani's precise hand praised "Emma Albani's pleasant voice, amiable nature, and accuracy of intonation." I recognized most of the names on the salutations. They were the most influential impresarios and theater managers from Lisbon to Vienna.

I was bending over, rattling the drawer and rooting for a roll of papers that was caught at the back, when a sudden intake of breath made my own catch in my throat. I whirled quickly, but it was too late to hide. Maestro Torani stood in the half-open doorway, gripping the edge of the door with whitened knuckles.

His mouth was slack with surprise, but his sharp eyes took in the recommendation letters spread out on the chest. He spoke with rigid control. "Emma's voice is not what it used to be, but conscience and honor oblige me to see that she is looked after."

Receiving no response from my paralyzed throat, he entered and made a leisurely circuit of the room, straightening a few of his possessions here and there. He stopped at the end of his desk, squarely between the door and my position at the window. He continued with his forebodingly calm tone. "What are you doing here, Tito? Surely you did not break into my office out of concern for our unfortunate *prima donna*."

My heart was pounding, but from exhilaration, not fear. Whatever was about to happen, I sensed that the mystery consuming me like a relapsing fever would finally be solved. If I got out of Torani's office with my skin intact, I would be able to tell Liya who murdered Luca.

"I am doing as you asked, Maestro. I am uncovering Luca's killer."

Torani gave me a long, searching look. He said, "I relieve you of that charge, Tito. We no longer need to impress the Savio or anyone else. Maria Banti's vaulting ambition and mediocre talent will keep the Teatro San Marco open until I'm either in my grave or driven to the madhouse."

"Then at least allow me to give you a report. I promised that you would be the first to hear what I discovered."

He slid his wig from his head, tossed it on the desk, and mopped his head with the palm of his hand. "I sincerely wish that I had never involved you in this, Tito. But I suppose there's no stopping you. Go on. Give me your whole clever theory. Explain what suspicious secret your fancies have convinced you I'm hiding in here."

"You lied about your whereabouts on the night Luca was killed. You didn't leave the theater directly after rehearsal. You stayed behind and argued with Luca in his studio. Do you deny it?"

Torani shook his head slightly, his eyes trained intently on mine. I suddenly felt as if we had exchanged roles. For once, I was directing the tune and the maestro had become my songbird. "What was the argument about?" I demanded.

My nightingale refused to warble.

"You might as well tell me. Gussie knows where I am and why I came. You won't be able to toss me down a hole or into the lagoon without someone being the wiser."

Torani's face lost its composure. I watched as his features melted into the suffering rictus portrayed by the traditional mask of tragedy. "My God, boy, you can't think I did it." He took a small step toward me and extended a hand. His voice dropped to a wounded whisper. "But you do. You think I killed Luca and pushed you through the trap. How can you possibly have come to that conclusion?"

I retrieved my purse and took out the corner of paper that had Luca's address written on one side and the remains of Theresa Cavalieri's on the other. I handed it to him. "Do you remember giving me this?"

He examined both sides closely, then gave me an incredulous look. "You think that because I had a letter from Theresa, I must have killed her son?"

"That was only one of your lies. You said you knew nothing about where Luca's mother was appearing, then you lied about leaving the theater before Luca was strangled. You were arguing with him. Less than an hour later he was dead."

The man was weeping now, but I plunged on relentlessly. "The night I was pushed through the trap, you had Emma's maid call her away so that I would be alone on the stage. You tore your breeches when you squeezed through the tunnel to get behind the draperies to push me."

Torani was leaning heavily on his desk. He stumbled back a few paces to sink into the chair that faced it. "Tito, you have it all wrong." He wiped his eyes and stared at me with naked anguish. "How could you think that I would harm you? You, of all people. I treasure you more than any singer I've ever had. I couldn't love you more if you were my own son. You don't know the whole story."

I gazed into the eyes that seemed to have aged ten years in the last few moments. I remembered all those times when Torani and I had been connected by the magic of music, thinking with one mind and singing with one voice. I spoke very gently: "Then explain it to me, Maestro."

Chapter 27

The director bowed his head and covered his eyes with a limp hand. It took several glasses of wine from the decanter on the sideboard before his spate of melancholy retreated. Then, sitting in Torani's chair and facing him across his desk in the sunny office that I had so rudely invaded, I heard his story.

"It was all so long ago," he began, "before you were even born. I was an actor playing comedies on a makeshift stage in market squares. Can you imagine me as an Arlecchino hitting my enemies over the head with a wooden sword? No, I thought not. I can hardly believe it myself." He raised a weak grin. "The boisterous farces of our little company did not suit me at all. I was searching for another position when our manager hired a new Brighella. A more beautiful, vivacious soubrette never graced a stage. Just to look at her took my breath away. It was Theresa, of course."

Torani fell silent, gazing at the quavering patches of sunlight reflecting off the canal outside his window.

I prompted him. "You fell in love."

"Oh yes," he replied in a far-off voice, "for the one and only time in my life. Madly, irrevocably, passionately in love. At first, Theresa seemed to return my feelings. She moved her trunks to my rooms and we were together constantly. I gave no further thought to leaving the company. Then Flavio Cavalieri joined us—he was tall, handsome, the perfect leading man. Theresa was smitten at once. The rest of the story is as big a farce as any we ever played. Within a month, the love of my life married Flavio, and I turned my talents from comedy to opera."

The gears in my brain were spinning. "Then Luca, could he have been your son?"

Torani shook his head. "Both Luca and his brother Silvio are the very image of Flavio Cavalieri. But I could see Theresa in Luca as well. That smile that made you think of so many delicious opportunities, the graceful way he held his head when he was at his canvas, so many of his ways reminded me of her."

"What did you and Luca argue about?"

Torani slid his hand under his coat and let it rest on his heart in just the same way that I so often touched my image of Liya. After a moment, the director drew out a folded letter and flattened it on his desk. The letter was missing one corner. He fitted my bit of scorched paper along the jagged edge and invited me to take a closer look. The edges met in a perfect match.

He said, "Theresa and I have kept in contact over the years. When she is hard up or in trouble, she always lets me know. I may be an old fool, but I continue to help her. My heart would never allow me to do otherwise. Apparently, Luca's heart was made of sterner stuff. Theresa wrote him faithfully, but his replies had dwindled to nothing. It was a great sorrow to her. Luca knew that I was an old friend of Theresa's—he had asked me for a job on the strength of that association. When I hired him, I told him that I expected him to make a better effort where she was concerned. He promised, but in true Luca fashion, he continued to go his merry way without a thought for his mother. In this letter, Theresa begs me to intercede with Luca on her behalf. Would you like to read it?"

Torani stood up and proffered the letter. I hesitated, then took the worn missive from his hand. The paper was thin and wrinkled from being carried in his pocket for weeks. It was as he said. After reporting a bit of theater gossip, Theresa implored her old lover to encourage her son to mend his relationship with her.

The director continued. "Luca never could stand criticism. I didn't go to his studio with the idea of starting a fight. I was just trying to make him understand how much his rebuffs hurt his mother, but Luca bridled the minute I mentioned her. I defended Theresa and, before I knew it, we were both shouting. I made a quick retreat—nothing of substance could be accomplished with Luca taking that tone. I went back to my office to write a response to Theresa. I wanted to let her know that I'd tried and would keep trying."

"You didn't return to Luca's studio later that night?"

"No. Why would I?"

"I've discovered that Luca was not above blackmailing colleagues, and I know that he was expecting a large sum of money. I thought you might be one of his victims."

Torani looked at me blankly.

"You are not a man to be bullied, Maestro."

"That is true. I would never surrender to blackmail, but then, I have no secrets worthy of extortion. My pathetic tale of unrequited love might as well be ancient history. I don't enjoy talking about the embarrassing shambles of my life, but I can't imagine Luca thinking I would pay him to keep quiet about Theresa."

He punctuated his statement with a look that made me shift uneasily in my chair. "You must believe me, Tito," he went on. "There is no great mystery in my life. And besides, there is no power in earth or heaven that could make me harm Theresa's child."

I did believe him. When confronted with such bare, unvarnished emotion, I found it easy to tell the difference between a mask and Torani's true face. I left the director's office feeling ashamed and relieved—ashamed that I had doubted the man who had guided me through so many feats of vocal wonder and relieved that I would not be forced to give him up to Messer Grande's cruel justice.

⁂

I determined my next course of action after an hour of furious thought over a cup of Peretti's stimulating brew. I had always known that Luca's murderer would turn out to be someone who could not simply slip away from our island republic like an anonymous villain of the back streets. The killer had to be a man whose absence would have caused inconvenient speculation. He had tossed Luca's body in the lagoon and gone about his business, hoping the corpse would never surface. But when the swollen body displayed itself so prominently during the bridegroom's reception ceremony, the killer's way of life, his very existence, was threatened. He scrambled to cast suspicion as far away from himself as possible, blaming the Jew who had fought with Luca only moments before his arrival at the studio. How irritating he must have found my refusal to accept Isacco as the real killer. After I'd made the connection between the killer and Dr. Palantinus, irritation turned to murderous rage.

I'd made no progress in identifying my assailant at the theater. Besides Maestro Torani, the clerk Carpani was the only person not accounted for when I'd tumbled into the trap. Small-minded and waspish he might be, but could Carpani possibly possess the arrogance and gall needed to pull off the role of Palantinus? No, it was ridiculous even to consider.

And so, my head wreathed in puzzles, I boarded a gondola for the Grand Canal and was soon installed in the second lady's sitting room of the day, facing a second charming hostess. This time I was offered lemonade, and a striped tabby draped itself across the mistress' lap.

Isabella Morelli fluttered a large, painted fan that depicted the mythological coupling of Eros and Psyche in salaciously vivid detail. Tiny beads of sweat gathered above her generous lips. "How hot the afternoons are becoming, Signor Amato. I am inclined to skip tonight's performance. The opera house will be stifling and I can't abide the thought of being shut up in that stuffy box for four hours."

"That would be a pity, Signora. The entire company would miss your gracious presence. I hope you will reconsider. I'm told there will be ices in the refreshment room to provide for a cooling interlude."

Her fan fluttered violently. "My husband prefers that I stay in our box. He is very conscientious in observing the proprieties."

"Surely there is nothing improper about enjoying an ice on a warm summer evening."

"It is not so much the ice that he objects to, though he would not care for one. My husband has schooled himself to keep his natural appetites at bay."

"What is it, then?" I asked, keeping my voice as casual as possible.

She narrowed her eyes. "He objects to who I might talk to, what I might say. If I'm kept in our box I'll have fewer opportunities to embarrass him and his illustrious lineage."

Could it really be this easy? I had presented myself at the Palazzo Morelli, uninvited and fresh from my enlightening session with Maestro Torani, intent on engaging Isabella in conversation about her husband. The lady had just handed me a beautiful opening, but she snatched it away with her next words. "I really don't wish to speak of Leonardo Morelli. Why bore ourselves to death?"

She changed her tone with a pert smile. "Tell me why your handsome English friend has not paid another call. When you were announced, I hoped that Signor Rumbolt would be with you But no, here we are—a lonely woman pining for a bit of harmless flirtation and a *castrato* who is immune to such dalliance."

I shook my head in deliberate fashion. "I doubt very much that Signor Rumbolt will make a return visit. He has asked my sister Annetta to marry him."

"I see. Your friend must have an independent streak. Not many *Inglese* venture beyond their borders where matrimony is concerned. I truly wish your sister and Signor Rumbolt the best. Marriage can be a blessing if the parties are united by love." She touched the rim of her fan to her cheeks. To hide her disappointment? If so, any sorrowful expression had been replaced by a mischievous smile when the fan was lowered. "And what of you, Signor Amato. I find your condition most curious. Tell me, how does a eunuch endure, cut off as you are from the bliss of romance?"

I pondered my response as Isabella grasped the unintended double meaning of her question and tried to drown her bubbling laughter in a gulp of lemonade. Her boldness surprised me. I knew she took delight in overstepping the bounds of polite society, but such a direct inquiry was impudent indeed. Perhaps her upbringing in a privileged caste had left her with the notion that we musicians were little more than amusing servants and thus fair game for any request. Ah well, I thought, if discussing my private life will keep her talking, so be it.

"My surgery did not leave me entirely immune to the desires of the flesh."

Her cheeks colored and she snapped her fan shut. "Explain this to me," she commanded abruptly.

"When I am in the presence of a woman whose nature pleases me, I feel the tug of desire much as any man would." Isabella had pushed the cat off her lap and leaned forward to catch every word. I found myself searching for an explanation sufficiently vague to leave myself some sense of modesty. "But I must harbor my desires carefully or risk not being able to carry them out."

"Ah," she breathed, "so the rumors are true. Despite all appearances, your potency was not entirely destroyed."

It was my turn to ask for an explanation. "Signora?"

She sat back, regarding me appraisingly, tapping the closed fan on her breast. "Is it possible that you don't realize what a strange effect you create?"

I shrugged dumbly, so she began to instruct me.

"You are beautiful, of course, but powerful, too. Not with the strength of brawn and sinew. Yours is a soft, subtle force. Honey, not beef."

"Are you talking about my voice?"

"I'm talking about all of you. Your amazing voice is just the most obvious characteristic that sets you apart from the normal run of men. When I watch you move across the stage with those impossibly long strides, then stop and captivate the audience with one of your graceful poses, I fancy you are not of this world. You are intriguing, disturbing almost. You seem to belong to another race of beings altogether."

"I assure you that I am quite human."

"Yes, now that we are having this intimate chat, I can see that you are." Isabella opened her fan and fluttered the bodies of Eros and Psyche into motion. Her manner had changed. Her smile was beginning to resemble the jaws of a hungry tigress. She continued, "Let me satisfy myself on one more point. You are not able to father children, are you?"

"That is true," I answered slowly, unnerved by her question and by the willful fire that had sprung into her eyes.

She rose with a crisp swish of her satin skirts and moved to the window to draw the drapes. As she returned, she bent over the back of my chair, caressing my ear with her breath. "The sun has moved around to this side of the *palazzo*. It makes the room so hot. Would you not like to move to someplace cooler and more comfortable?" She swept her fan toward a door that could only lead from her private sitting room to her bedchamber. Her sudden desire threw me off balance. I had not foreseen this eventuality at all.

I was saved from my dilemma by the arrival of the footman who had attended Isabella at the theater. He entered the room without a shred of the deference expected in a servant.

Isabella jerked up straight. "Fabrizio, what are you doing here? I didn't send for you. Withdraw at once."

Barely sketching a bow, he replied, "Signor Morelli has sent a messenger, my lady. Senator Paolo Rossi is hosting an assembly before tonight's opera. The master has instructed me to convey you to the Ca' Rossi in good time. He will meet you there."

My hostess scowled and balled her hands into fists. "I have not yet decided if I am going out tonight. I have a guest."

"So I see." The man's reply was sharp and cool. "The gondola will be waiting at the front in twenty minutes." He turned on his heel, then paused at the threshold. "Ah, one more thing.

The master directs you to wear your dark gray gown with the high lace collar."

I expected a scene replete with tears and breakable objects shattering on the walls, but Isabella surprised me again. The color drained from her face and she sank to the floor in a froth of satin. I rushed to her side.

She hadn't fainted, but some overwhelming emotion robbed her of speech. She simply clutched my arms, shaking, trying to master herself. We must have made a strange sight, clinging to each other like frightened children on the carpet of her white and gold sitting room. When the unhappy noblewoman did speak, her voice was taut and tired. "*Che bastardo*, a more arrogant fool never blighted this earth."

"Your footman?"

"No, my husband. Fabrizio is just a blockhead that Leonardo hired to run his errands and spy on me. I don't conform to his standards of wifely behavior, you see. He got me at a bargain, thinking gratitude would bend me to his will. We've been at daggers drawn ever since."

The strain between Morelli and his wife was no revelation. If I was to solve the mystery of Luca's murder, I needed to know if Morelli had assumed the persona of Dr. Palantinus. I decided on an oblique approach. "I fear you are outmatched. Unless you have an income of your own, your husband is bound to prevail. In a struggle of this type, the heavier purse always wins."

She sighed. "My purse is as light as air. Leonardo's only slightly heavier."

"But the Morelli family has been in the Golden Book since the founding of the Republic."

"My husband is rich in titled ancestors, but they don't pay the bills. If truth be told, we would do better without his pedigree. The Morelli name requires responsibilities that end up costing more than they bring in. The wedding present for the Doge's daughter cost the earth, but what of it? Leonardo marched in the procession with the other heads of noble families, so we had to give the same as they did. We'll be dining on nothing more than watermelon and polenta for weeks."

I gestured to the gilded walls surrounding us. "I would have guessed that your husband possessed a considerable fortune. Otherwise, how would all this be possible?"

Isabella leaned back on one arm, calmer now, face pale but composed. "It's all a sham. We use our private suites and a few receiving rooms. The rest of the *palazzo* is a moldering wreck. Still Leonardo insists on continuing with opulent pretense. My foolish husband will pawn his own clothing to lay a table to entertain a few senators, then send Fabrizio to buy him a suit from a ragshop in the ghetto. Somehow he always contrives to keep some cash flowing."

"Signor Morelli doesn't strike me as the merchanting type. I wonder how he does it."

"I'm really not sure. He doesn't discuss his activities with me. I've always thought that he scraped along by begging loans from associates and finding a few windfalls at the gaming tables. The man certainly has no head for business. None of the Morelli family ever did. We wouldn't be in this fix if his father Stefano hadn't lost the family fortune."

I let my eyes question her, but even that was unnecessary. Isabella was overflowing with contempt for Morelli and his entire clan and was determined to express it.

"Oh, yes. Stefano was Leonardo's father, an only son of an only son, just as my husband is. Unlike my husband, Stefano was a wastrel, a good-for-nothing addicted to wine and gambling. Do you know how quickly a fortune can be lost at the Ridotto?"

"I have an idea," I replied, remembering my own father's misadventures in that state-sponsored gambling hell.

She continued, "Leonardo grew up with every privilege, including the expectation of inheriting a comfortable estate. He excelled at scholarship—even now he always has his nose in a book of some ancient lore. But thanks to his father's extravagance, Leonardo was forced to give up his dreams of studying at

Padua and take a position of secretary with the Venetian delegation to King Louis' court. He's been bitter ever since."

"The entire fortune was lost to gambling?"

"No, there was more to it, but it's a mystery to me." She shook her head. "Leonardo has always refused to speak of it, except to rail against the Jews, of course."

I caught my breath. "Jews? How did they figure into the family's downfall?"

Her eyes narrowed at the vehemence of my question. "I don't really know, Tito, only that Leonardo has always blamed them."

Springing from the floor, I offered my arm to help my hostess rise. Isabella had recovered from her spate of anger. "Surely you're not going?" she asked in a husky tone.

I hated to disappoint her, but time was of the essence. After kissing her hand, I left the *palazzo* and headed for the theater as quickly as possible.

Chapter 28

By the time I arrived at the San Marco's gondola landing, dark clouds had delivered an early twilight. I lifted my nose. The sharp Adriatic wind blowing down the narrow canals carried the scent of rain. I took the steps up to the theater two at a time, nerves tingling with anticipation. The hunt for Palantinus was nearing its end—I could feel it.

Most of the cast were in their dressing rooms, beginning the transformation to the larger-than-life characters they played, but I went below stage, to the green room that contained a table and chairs and a few dilapidated sofas. After watching one performance of *Cesare*, Carpani had declared that he didn't really care for singing and installed himself in the green room for the duration of the opera's run. I found the clerk making notes in his huge black book.

He gave me a sidelong glance. "Shouldn't you be dressing?"

"I will, in a moment. After you tell me how your master's father lost the Morelli fortune."

"What?" The clerk whipped his glasses off his nose and half rose from his chair.

"You heard me." I forced him down with a heavy hand to his shoulder. "Stefano Morelli had dealings with a Jew that paupered the family."

"Really, this is inexcusable." His bony shoulders were shaking. "What makes you think I would know anything about my master's personal business?"

With a burst of energy, I jerked his chair around to face me. "Before Morelli hired you, you worked for the court of probate and estates. I know you for a careful man, a man who relishes detail like no other. You would never have accepted Morelli's offer without checking up on your prospective employer." Placing both hands on the arms of his chair, I leaned over and put my nose two inches from his. "Now, out with it. Tell me what you know."

Carpani answered with a reedy tremor, eyes darting toward the door. "My master won't tolerate discussion of such private matters."

I sighed, suddenly exhausted by the rigors of the day. The first strains of violins drifted down from the orchestra pit. I moved my hands to Carpani's coat lapels and gave the little man a rough shake. Surprised at my own violence, I said grimly, "I'm due on stage in twenty minutes. Speak now or I'll make sure this turkey neck of yours never makes another sound."

"All right, all right." Fixing me with bulging eyes, Carpani drew a black rectangle from an inside pocket. It was a notebook, a miniature twin to the thick book on the table.

"Go on," I growled.

Nodding, he cleared his throat and turned the little book's pages with a hook-like finger. "It's all in here," he commenced. "For decades the Morelli family entrusted their fortune to a shipping house that traded in the Levant and paid a regular interest of six percent. Stefano's father drew a good income from the investment and owned some warehouses besides. He sent Stefano to the University at Padua and expected him to eventually take his seat on the Great Council and apply himself to the art of government, but Stefano's wayward passions destroyed his father's hopes."

He bent his head and turned a page. Upstairs, the brass and woodwinds joined the violins. I had no time for a leisurely recounting of Morelli's family history. I grabbed the book, only to find it scrawled with meaningless signs.

"My own cipher," he said apologetically.

I shoved the book back in his hands. "Go on. Hurry!"

"Stefano inherited the family estate when Leonardo was sixteen. By the time my master reached his majority, his father had lost the family's warehouses and was barely covering his gaming debts with the interest from the shipping investments. In 1718, while my master was still away in France, Stefano needed a large sum of money. Quickly. A clever Hebrew had been keeping an eye on the reckless fool and was ready with an offer—the money Stefano needed in trade for the inheritance of the Morelli shares in the shipping house."

"But that's illegal," I broke in. "The Senate banned the practice of selling inheritances so they wouldn't be burdened with the upkeep of more impoverished aristocrats."

Carpani nodded. "That is so, but not before Stefano concluded his deal. That unusually perspicacious law was passed at a later date. Stefano collected three thousand ducats from the Jew. But instead of paying his creditors, he lost it all in one wild night at the Ridotto, then went straight home and hung himself from the canopy rails of his own bed. The Jew received the shares in the shipping firm. My master inherited a decaying *palazzo* and a stack of tradesmen's notes."

I shook my head. "No wonder Morelli has such a bilious nature, he was done a great injustice. To sell his son's birthright, Stefano must have been exceedingly greedy and shortsighted."

Carpani snorted in disgust. "Apparently. But my master refuses to blame his father. In his eyes, a Morelli can do no wrong, whatever sort of blackguard he is. No, my master has always blamed the Jew who dangled an attractive prospect before a heedless, drink-addled fool."

"Who was this Jew?"

"I have a name, but the man is long gone. The Jew took his newly won riches and immediately set out for England. Unable to take revenge on his foe, my master transferred his anger onto the entire race. To him, the ghetto is no more than a nest of vipers. He rails against the Hebrews constantly. If I've heard it once, I've heard it hundreds of times: 'Swindling thieves who make capons of us all, they should all be thrown into the waves.'"

My blood ran cold. Carpani had just repeated a phrase from Palantinus' pamphlet. I had to be sure. I asked quickly, "Did you say capons?"

He gave an embarrassed little nod. "My master's words, not mine."

Of course they were. The puzzling phrase from Dr. Palantinus' pamphlet that had repeated itself endlessly in my head: "Hebrew swindlers who make capons of us all."

While the shifty Magister went to great lengths to hide his face, his very words revealed him. Morelli must be Palantinus—he had to be. That he had killed Luca and authored the pamphlet I had no doubt, but how was I going to convince Messer Grande?

ᕮᗡᕮᗡᕮᗡ

Maestro Torani was furious, but he held the curtain until Benito made me presentable for the stage. Instead of singing, I wanted to shriek Morelli's crime to the audience that filled the boxes and the pit, but I realized what a foolhardy course of action that would be. Messer Grande was fixed in his belief that Isacco killed Luca. That unseasoned official was not about to back down and arrest a member of the aristocracy because a singer playing detective had noticed a few matching words. What I needed was a plan, a foolproof plan that would convince Messer Grande of Morelli's guilt before the nobleman had another opportunity to be rid of me.

It helped that *Cesare* was so far along in its run that I could perform my part without much thought. As I sang my way through that next to last performance, keeping a wary eye out for open trap doors and plummeting sandbags, I worked out the details of my scheme to snare Morelli. Early the next morning, I put Gussie on the boat to Padua, set Liya and Annetta to work at the Del'Vecchios' new shop in the ghetto, and gave Benito a long list of needed ingredients. At my heartfelt pleading, even Aldo and Maestro Torani agreed to help.

Later that evening, *Cesare in Egitto* went out in a blaze of glory. My voice was back in top form and my side barely hurt at all. For his part, Florio kept his pompous airs in check and made an earnest attempt to be part of the company. Our final duet had always been a sore point; Florio had never cared for my timing or ornamentation. But this time, with Florio consenting to follow my lead, I relinquished all traces of jealousy, and we melded our voices in one sustained, ravishing bout of ecstasy. Women swooned, gondoliers went wild, and within minutes, the stage was covered with flowers. After four encores, Torani had to leave the harpsichord and beg the audience to let the opera proceed to its finale.

My mission didn't give me time to savor the triumph. As Ministro del Teatro, Signor Morelli was obliged to host a reception to celebrate the close of the opera's run. This gathering at his *palazzo* suited my purposes exactly. By the time I had changed and seen to a few last-minute details, it was after midnight and most of Morelli's guests had arrived. I looked for the master of the house as Annetta and I mounted the stairs to the torchlit portico, but Morelli was not greeting his guests in person. Fabrizio was attending the tall double doors at the entryway. I didn't recognize any of the other servants who were collecting hats and cloaks, minding candles, or serving food and drink. As I had assumed he must, Morelli had hired them for that night only.

The main reception hall was ablaze with light from hundreds of wax tapers. Their flames reflected off the shiny terrazzo floor and the carved marble frieze running around the upper walls. A few tapestries hung from a molding below the frieze, but the focal point of the great hall was a broad alcove that served as a podium where a harpsichord and a few second-rate violins were tearing through a tinkling minuet. Four slender columns divided the semicircular podium and supported a railed balcony above.

The Savio, attended by Messer Grande on one side and his dowdy wife on the other, was holding court at the hall's arched entrance opposite the musicians' podium. His face was beaming with pride as Venice's leading aristocrats approached him to praise *Cesare's* splendid run. Judging by the credit he took, a person would have thought the old military man had been composer, librettist, designer, and director all rolled into one.

The mistress of the *palazzo*, dressed more somberly than I had ever seen her, moved from group to group, stopping to issue a word of welcome to each richly dressed party. I recognized several older men among the guests as Brethren who had been present at the last meeting of the Temple of the Golden Seraphim. When I caught Isabella's eye, she gave me a sad, little smile and came sailing over.

"Are the preparations for your mysterious show in order?" she asked.

"I believe so."

"Oh goody, I love surprises. Anything to liven up this dull crowd."

"It should certainly accomplish that," I replied, keeping my smile as bland as possible.

After circulating a bit more, I spotted Morelli hovering around the serving table. He was eyeing the guests as if he expected to catch them filching expensive tidbits to carry away in their pockets. I avoided our host for the while. I would not be ready to speak to him until Torani gave me a sign that all was ready. Carpani was also easy to avoid. The clerk was sitting against the wall with some black-gowned dowagers, twisting his hands and nervously patting his cheap wig, looking positively lost without either of his notebooks.

While waiting for Torani's signal, I let Rosa engage me in conversation. She had already made a pretty apology for stealing my mask in the San Benedetto garden, so we were friends once more. Her cavalier, Bassano Gritti, was absent. He had finally switched his affections to the dancer that Madame Dumas had mentioned. Florio had joined us by the time Torani appeared at a side door and gave me his nod. Morelli was just approaching. Though Florio and I stood side by side, the nobleman turned his back to me as he addressed my companion.

"Signor Florio, I was hoping you would favor my guests with a few songs. With *Cesare* concluded, it may be our last opportunity to hear the voice that has kept us so royally entertained these past weeks."

I sent Florio a wink over Morelli's shoulder. The singer let a pained expression cross his face; he massaged his throat with one hand. "How kind, Ministro, but I regret I must decline. Our last encore strained my vocal cords and I find myself unable to sing a note." He gestured toward me. "But I am sure Tito would be glad to take my place."

Morelli scowled. His guests expected the singers to entertain them; it was a tradition that Morelli would break at the peril of his treasured social position. But Florio was pleading indisposition, and Emma had decided to skip the reception altogether. As *secondo uomo*, I was next in order of importance. Morelli acknowledged me with a sour expression. "I suppose you have something prepared. You singers always do."

"Oh, yes, Excellency. I've prepared something your guests will find most interesting."

The nobleman moved to the center of the reception hall and clapped his hands. The babble of conversation and laughter gradually lulled. Men lowered their wine glasses and women snapped their fans shut. "Good friends and honored guests," Morelli declaimed, "I have the pleasure to present one of Venice's favorite singers, a *castrato* of singular talent, Signor Tito Amato."

All eyes turned toward me. I crossed the salon and stepped onto the orchestra's podium, but instead of producing music to accompany a song, I addressed the servants. "For the special treat that I have arranged, the room must be darkened. Put out the candles—hurry now—out in the foyer, too."

The footmen hired for the party heeded my command, but Fabrizio shot me a venomous look and hurried to his master's side. Morelli had blanched as white as Luca's body in the Doge's storeroom. I could almost read the nobleman's thoughts. He knew I was up to something, but his guests were smiling and whispering among themselves, clearly anticipating a novel amusement.

Should he order the footmen to stop, thus disappointing the crowd? Or go along with whatever transpired? Morelli looked around the darkening hall and gave Fabrizio a tiny shake of his head. The proud aristocrat had decided to see it through!

"Signor Morelli," I cried, descending from the podium. "As our host and most excellent Ministro del Teatro, you should have the best view. Stand here by me and prepare to be amazed." I took a position several lengthy strides from the alcove, then bowed to the Savio and his shadow, Messer Grande. "Attend him, Excellencies, if you please." The three men moved to my side. The Savio and Messer Grande showed bemused expressions, but Morelli worked his jaw back and forth like a man suffering from a particularly vicious toothache.

A few women giggled nervously as the vast room filled with dark shadows. I sent up a silent prayer. I didn't want even to guess what the consequences would be if my plan failed.

Just as the last candle winked out, a hissing sound came out of the darkness above, and tongues of silvery-blue flame shot out from the tops of the podium's pillars. I heard a chorus of horrified gasps and the sound of chairs being overturned as the musicians rushed to see if their roof was on fire. I raised my voice: "Calm yourselves, it's all part of the show."

Very slowly, with infinite grace, a fantastic figure uncurled itself from behind the balcony's rail. Amid bright sparks, a slender form sheathed in shimmering gold stretched to full height and stood as still as a statue. Wings fashioned of hundreds of glittering feathers capped its shoulders, and a mask of seraphic countenance hid its face. I smiled; Liya had outdone herself.

In the spectral light of Aldo's erupting pyrotechnics, the Savio and Messer Grande parted their lips and stared in astonishment. Morelli's gaze locked onto mine. Beyond anger or hate, it was a penetrating ray of pure loathing. As murmured "oh's" and "ah's" sped around the hall, I broke the nobleman's gaze and craned my neck toward the ceiling. With Torani and Aldo manipulating guy wires from the deserted room behind the balcony, Liya mounted the railing and stepped out into thin air. My beautiful Jewess could have had a calling as a theatrical performer. Without a hint of fear or awkwardness, her golden figure seemed to hover in space before she spread the Seraph's wings in a few dazzling passes over our heads. My heart swelled with pride as she spiraled down and came to rest squarely in front of Morelli.

Though the hall was filled with hundreds of guests, not one human sound was audible above the sputtering hiss of the fire pots. It was as if the room was holding its collective breath, totally focused on what the golden apparition would do next.

Light from the blue flames danced across Morelli's face—a mask of cold, disciplined fury. I wondered what the nobleman must be thinking as he faced a copy of his own deceitful creation. Now that he knew I had plumbed the secrets of his temple, his brain must be reeling. What else did I know? How much could I prove?

Liya delivered her lines with steely precision. "I have descended from the heavenly realm with a burning truth that will not be denied. A murderer prowls this hall, the hall of his illustrious ancestors. He parades before you in the guise of an upright citizen but his mask of virtue hides a foul secret."

Morelli's face contorted. When Liya paused for breath, he threw up his arms, suddenly sounding very much like Dr. Palantinus. "This is nonsense. I didn't authorize this lunatic charade. Get some light in here. Fabrizio, where are you? Someone remove this woman and this fool of a eunuch at once."

Morelli's words broke the spell. Around us, everyone started chattering at once. Liya spread her hands uncertainly; her wings drooped to brush the floor. The Savio glared at her under his shaggy brows. As the fire pots began to run out of fuel and the room darkened again, Messer Grande seized my arm. "I'll call my boys to deal with this one," he said.

"No!" I whirled out of his grasp and leapt to Liya's side. I wielded the force of my voice like a weapon. "Listen to us. Leonardo Morelli is not what he seems. By day he plays the proper patrician, but by night, he masquerades as a Magister called Dr. Palantinus. He hired Luca Cavalieri to help him hoodwink the rich and superstitious at the Temple of the Golden Seraphim. Some of you in this very room have been duped by their false Seraphim scheme. Morelli killed Luca when the painter tried to extort money from him."

My voice screeched in anger. "You are a murderer, Morelli. You killed Luca and set a mob on Isacco Del'Vecchio to hide your evil deed. Admit it. Tell the truth for once in your life."

Morelli stared at me with the glittering, overbright eyes of a madman, but he didn't speak.

Another high voice rang out. "Tito knows what he is saying. I've been to Palantinus' temple. Morelli is a rogue and a charlatan." It was Florio, but he was the only one to speak up for me.

Morelli regained his composure. Though he had never been on the stage, he was a showman through and through, and he was giving the performance of his life. In imperious tones, he said, "How dare you accuse me of such nonsense, Amato? When they clipped your balls, they must have damaged your brain as well. You've let yourself become so besotted with the painter's murder that you've destroyed your career and everything else you possess."

The Savio nodded darkly and I felt Messer Grande's strong fingers digging into my arm again.

It was time to play my last card. Messer Grande twisted my arm behind my back, but I used my other to point toward the hall's arched entrance. I threw the nobleman a challenging smile and raised my voice to a carrying, crystal-clear pitch. "If you won't submit to your own oracle, then heed the truth from your next visitor."

Chapter 29

A woman screamed, then several others.

I couldn't blame them. The sight at the archway was enough to make the breath catch in my throat, and I knew what to expect.

Coming toward us, moving smoothly and silently over the polished terrazzo, was an impossibly tall, dark figure. A cowled garment concealed its face and every part of its form except for one hand. That glistening white member was streaked with an oily, green film and pocked with tiny scabs, like something dead that had decayed in water. The apparition held a branched candelabrum at arm's length.

Messer Grande relaxed his grip on my arm, eyes bulging and mouth agape. At my other side, the Savio whispered hoarsely, "What on earth?" Morelli remained silent, a rigid figure of bottled-up rage.

I glanced at Liya. She had pushed her golden mask to the top of her head. Her own face was calm and composed. I heartened when she sent me a small, sideways smile.

With a rustle of black robes, the towering figure glided to a halt a few paces from us. The hideous hand moved the flaming candles from side to side to inspect our little group. We all shrank back when an unearthly whisper issued from the unformed blackness that should have been a face.

"Signor Morelli," the figure intoned. "We meet again. You're looking well. Murder must become you."

I trained my eyes on the nobleman. Morelli swallowed hard and seemed barely able to force his words past his lips. "This is just another trick. Another theater person got up in fancy dress. Show your face and end this farce."

Emitting a stench of stagnant canal water, the ghostly horror merely burbled a deep laugh in reply.

Morelli raised a sneer. "You can't fool me. I know who you are. You must be Tito's friend, that Englishman who hangs around the theater like a great dolt who doesn't have anything better to do."

"What? He's not talking about me, is he?" Gussie stepped out of the crowd that circled the pool of light around us. Annetta clutched his arm and drew him back.

The faceless figure laughed once more. "Wrong again, Morelli. But it is at the theater that we last met. Can't you guess who I am? Don't you know me? We were so close. Just a few short weeks ago, you had your hands around my neck, choking the life out of me."

The hood fell away as if by magic. A ghastly visage sprang from its folds—slick, pasty flesh; dark, matted hair; and a damp collar and neckcloth torn loose from a bruised throat. A hideous flap of bloody scalp hung down over one ear. The decomposing features were familiar to all of us.

"Luca!" Morelli's proud patrician mask fell away. He looked like a frightened child awakened by a nightmare. "No, it's impossible. You can't be here," he blubbered. "You were dead. I saw your body in the palace storeroom." Morelli drew back against the Savio's stalwart bulk, spreading his hands in front of his face, voice rising to a horrified whine. "You were dead. I know it. I made sure. I rolled your body out of the boat and watched it sink beneath the water."

"There," I yelled. Messer Grande dropped my arm. He and the Savio traded a startled look. I couldn't resist gloating. "There you have it. Do you believe me now—now that you've heard it from the murderer's own mouth?"

Morelli leaped like a stag bounding from a thicket. The Savio lunged and grabbed the back of his jacket, but Morelli wriggled away and the Savio was left holding an empty garment. The guests who had watched the flying Seraph and hooded phantom in frozen awe suddenly panicked. Someone started a stampede for the archway. Screaming aristocrats stumbled and tripped in the darkness.

Luca's specter yelled, "This way," then took off. I dove into the crowd to follow. Barely conscious of Liya on my heels, I pushed scurrying bodies aside, straining to keep pace with the light from the phantom's lurching candelabrum.

Somehow we made it out of the reception hall into the foyer. The crowd was fighting its way through the tall, narrow entry that led out to the waiting gondolas. Morelli had turned the opposite way.

I can't recall ever taking part in a stranger chase. As the desperate nobleman sprinted into the depths of the *palazzo*, the foul-smelling murder victim, trailing his black cloak and wisps of smoke from the now extinguished candles, strove to close the gap between them. Following, I pumped my long legs with a winged Seraph on one side and a very confused Messer Grande on the other. The aging Savio, bright medals dancing on his heaving chest, brought up the rear.

We pounded up one stairway, then down another and another. Morelli and his closest pursuer suddenly disappeared into a side passage. Liya, Messer Grande, and I crashed into each other as we all tried to round the corner and squeeze into the narrow corridor at the same time. The police chief swore furiously as he ripped Liya's delicate feathers from his gold uniform buttons and pushed her aside. By the time we reached the open door at the end of the passage, the Savio had caught up with us.

Beyond the doorway, voices clashed in anger. We stepped into the room. It must have been Morelli's private study *cum* library. Bookshelves stretched from floor to ceiling on three walls. The fourth held an ornately carved cabinet and a wide writing desk flanked by a pair of standing lamps. Morelli had wedged himself between the desk and a bookcase like a cornered animal.

Silvio Cavalieri, Luca's look-alike brother whom Gussie had fetched from Padua, deposited the candelabrum on the desk and flung his black cloak aside. It puddled on the flagstone floor like a spill of tar. Silvio stood tall in costume boots atop thick, built-up soles. With his features so like Luca's and the corpse-like cosmetic effects created by Benito, he could have been a specter from the pits of Hell.

"You thought you could get away with it," he said savagely, stabbing a grisly finger toward Morelli. "Just strangle Luca and go on with your life like nothing happened. But Tito found you out. You'll pay for my brother's murder. They'll hang you from a gibbet on the Piazza and I'll be watching from the front row."

Messer Grande hitched up his belt and approached Morelli with a determined step.

"No, stop. You can't take me away," the cowering nobleman gasped. "I'm a Morelli. My family has been in Venice since the relics of St. Mark were enshrined in the Basilica. How can you even think of arresting me?"

The Savio was leaning against a bookcase with his hand to his midsection. Still huffing and puffing, he said, "You dumped Luca Cavalieri's body in the lagoon. We all heard you admit it. It looks like Tito was right. The Jew didn't kill Luca. You did."

Messer Grande curled his lip at me, but began to advance toward Morelli again. I heard the swish of satin skirts behind me. It was Isabella. Pale and trembling, she leaned against the doorframe as if her knees might give way at any moment. Gussie and Annetta appeared right behind her. My friend steadied the noblewoman with a strong arm.

Morelli stood a little straighter. His eyes darted around the room and came to rest on the Savio. "Excellency, I didn't know what I was saying back there. I was startled. Who wouldn't be with all those histrionics going on? Of course I knew Luca was dead. I was there when we viewed his body in the Doge's store-room, you remember. I knew *someone* had tossed him into the lagoon. I didn't mean to say that I had." He extended an open palm to the Savio. "You see, don't you? Amato threw out all this nonsense about false magicians and… what was it, a golden temple? I hardly knew what I was saying. I was… shocked, confused."

Messer Grande halted again, looking toward the Savio for instructions. The old military man frowned and scratched his head. "This whole thing is very far-fetched," he said.

Morelli's eyes brightened. "And scandalous. A singing eunuch from the Cannaregio accusing a patrician of the Golden Book. What is Venice coming to?"

The Savio eyed me dubiously. Patrician blood flowed in his veins as surely as it did in Morelli's. They were brothers of pride and distinction; their ancestors had deliberated together on the Great Council for centuries. Was the Savio going to let their shared social standing override the admission he had heard with his own ears?

Liya must have been thinking the same thing. Wings trembling, she marched up to the Savio and raised her chin. "If the accusation is baseless, why did Morelli run?"

The Savio arched his shaggy eyebrows, questioning Morelli. The harried nobleman took a tentative step forward. He opened his mouth, then shut it. Silvio peeled off the flap of linen soaked with calf's blood that Benito had gummed to his scalp. He flung the rag on the desk in front of Morelli like a would-be duelist throwing down a gauntlet.

Morelli swayed on his feet. He was exhausted and desperate, but he wasn't beaten. He pounded a fist on the desktop. "I won't be questioned by a filthy, wanton Jewess who shouldn't even be outside the ghetto walls. Look at her. She's half-naked. She should be ashamed."

The Savio sighed. "I'm the one who's asking you. I'm willing to listen if you can give me a good explanation. If you deny Tito's accusation, why did you run?"

Before Morelli could form a reply, another voice broke in. "I don't understand," said Isabella as she released Gussie's arm and moved to the center of the study. "What is my husband accused of? What did the show signify?"

I took both of her hands in mine. "Signora, I have no wish to cause you distress, but justice must be served. I believe that your husband is guilty of the murder of Luca Cavalieri."

She furrowed her lovely brow. "The scene painter at the theater? The murder the Jew was hanged for?"

I nodded. Behind me, Morelli snapped, "Lies, all lies. Don't listen to him."

Isabella squeezed my hands. "No, I want to hear. What makes you think Leonardo would do such a thing?"

"Luca had blackmailed others. I believe that he was trying the same trick with your husband. Have you heard of the Brotherhood of the Golden Seraphim?"

She shook her head.

"It's a secret society, with a heavy initiation fee. Your husband created it. As Dr. Palantinus, the Grand Magister, he collects fees for promises of health, wealth, and knowledge of the future."

"But, how? The State Inquisitors would never allow a patrician to charge money for occult activities. Leonardo would have been hauled before the Tribunal."

"Dr. Palantinus is very discreet. He always wears a mask—the beaked mask of a medieval plague doctor. No one would ever connect the exceedingly proper Leonardo Morelli with the charlatan Palantinus."

"But you do."

"Yes, and you helped me." I continued as a puzzled frown spread over her face. "The Jew dazed Luca with a blow from a bronze statue of Venus, but it was your husband that finished the painter off and dumped his corpse in the lagoon. When Luca's body resurfaced, he needed a scapegoat. The tainted wells had already turned the city into a powder keg with a short fuse. Morelli indulged his hatred of the Jewish race by authoring a pamphlet that put flame to the fuse."

I stopped to glance at Liya. Her mouth was set in a solemn line. She gave a small nod, telling me to go on. Isabella's eyes never left my face.

"A mob burned the Del'Vecchios' home and dragged Liya's cousin Isacco away to his death. Gussie and I traced the authorship of the pamphlet to the mysterious Dr. Palantinus. It contained one unique phrase—'Hebrew swindlers who make capons of us all.' Have you ever heard your husband use those words? Others have."

Isabella shuddered. Her breath caught in a sob. She shot one feverish glance toward Morelli, then turned and ran from the room. She knew what those words signified. I imagined that the revelation of her husband's guilt overwhelmed her and that she couldn't bear to look at him another minute. She would probably run to her suite, throw herself on the bed, and flood her pillow with tears. I would send Annetta to check on her later.

The Savio was rubbing his chin. "So, Tito, you believe that Morelli is Palantinus because of some words in a pamphlet."

I swallowed hard. "That's not all. It's a matter of record that his father sold his inheritance to a Jew. Morelli has been hungry for revenge on the Jews ever since."

"Morelli is not the only man in Venice to carry a grudge against the Hebrew race," the Savio countered. He looked Liya's golden sheath up and down, letting his eyes linger on the swell of her hips under the clinging fabric, then directed an apologetic bow in her direction. "Sorry my dear, but you know it's true."

Liya folded her wings tightly around her and gave me an imploring look. Silvio glowered at the floor, his hands balled into fists. Gussie and Annetta shook their heads at the doorway. I felt like tearing my hair from my scalp. "But I tell you, Excellency, Morelli is Palantinus. And he strangled Luca after Isacco felled the painter with a blow from the bronze statue."

The Savio shrugged. "If you could just produce some tangible proof. Where is this statue? A bronze of Diana, is it?"

"No, not Diana," Liya whispered fiercely. "It's a statue of Venus. I was with Luca when he bought it. Isacco dropped it before he ran away from Luca's studio."

"It was not there the next morning." I sighed. "The statue probably went to the bottom of the lagoon with Luca."

"No, not at all." Isabella returned on a dead run, pushing through Gussie and Annetta. "The Venus isn't in the lagoon. I have it right here." Panting, she used her flat palm as a support to display the sculpture before a phalanx of astonished eyes.

The bronze Venus was portrayed in the manner of the ancients, as a nubile nude of sensuous grace, one hand to her upswept braids, the other held modestly before the space where the curves of her thighs came together. I could see why it had reminded Luca so strongly of Liya.

I glanced toward the living Venus sheathed in gold instead of bronze. Her expression had changed from worry to radiance. "Oh, yes," she breathed. "That is Luca's statue."

"Where did you get it?" the Savio quickly questioned.

Isabella moved to one of the bookshelves and indicated a row of tall volumes. "Right here. Leonardo fashioned a hiding place for her behind these books."

Morelli made a sound like gravel bouncing down a metal chute. He would have sprung toward his wife if Silvio hadn't restrained him.

Isabella's eyes were glittering, but not with tears. She wore a triumphant smile. "If you wanted to hide something from me, Leonardo, you should have made a better job of it."

"My study has always been off-limits to you," he growled.

"Your petty dictates have never stopped me for long. Since you and Fabrizio are so often away from the *palazzo*, I have plenty of time to snoop where I choose. I found the Venus a week or so ago. I assumed she was a family treasure that you had tucked away to sell. I thought she was much too pretty to let go, so I removed her to my bedchamber." Isabella finished on a pointed note. "I knew you would never look for her *there*."

"Well, Leonardo." The Savio cleared his throat and regarded Morelli uneasily. "This is a surprising development. I was willing to give you the benefit of the doubt, but surely you can see that having the statue in your possession changes everything. Now, you'll have to cooperate with Ottavio... er... Messer Grande.

We don't want this to be any more difficult than it has to be. I'll see that you're well treated. You don't…"

"Excellency," Morelli interrupted, "don't distress yourself. I have no intention of giving Messer Grande the slightest trouble."

The nobleman seemed to have passed beyond anger and fear. He straightened his neckcloth, adjusted the lace on his cuffs, and stood before us: upright, shameless, and proud. A new dignity had taken possession of his features—a dignity that borrowed nothing from the decaying aristocracy of our diminished Republic.

He raised his chin and addressed me. "I have to congratulate you, Amato. You pursued the truth with a tenacity I never dreamed you possessed. I did go to Luca's studio that night. He was going to tell the Tribunal about the Temple, accuse me of forcing him to stage the Seraphim's appearance under threat of losing his position at the theater. To forestall my ruin, he'd demanded a large sum of money, more than I had on hand. I was going to beg him for more time, but Isacco Del'Vecchio handed me such a perfect opportunity."

Morelli's candor amazed me. What compelled him to talk so freely? Did he need to impress us with his cleverness? I asked quietly, "The statue? Why did you keep it?"

He answered at once. "I originally intended to plant the Venus among the goods in the cart that the Jew wheeled around to the theaters. But when the mob responded to my pamphlet with such enthusiasm, I no longer needed her. I thought it would be safe to sell the statue once the excitement over Luca's death had subsided. In a year or so, the incident would barely be remembered."

While Messer Grande held Silvio back from throttling the nobleman, I posed another question. "When I was pushed through the trap door—was that another *perfect opportunity?*"

Morelli nodded with a crooked grin. "I couldn't resist that one either. Carpani had alerted me about the extra rehearsal. The clerk did his job well—not much went on in that theater that he didn't recount in excruciating detail. I slipped in without being seen and waited until you were alone on the stage. I thought to rid myself of your prying for good, but fortune favored you over me that time.

"However, and in this you must believe me, I hold no further malice toward you, Amato. It's been a good fight, won by a stroke of singular ingenuity. Venice will be talking about the show you put on here tonight for years to come. Yes, you and your friends have brought this sorry remnant of the house of Morelli to his knees. Not bad work for an effete songbird.

"Of course, I might still have had a chance if my good lady had not seen fit to join the fray." He inclined his head toward Isabella, who recoiled immediately. "Ah, a proud woman to the end. So be it."

I could scarcely believe what I was seeing. Morelli's demeanor had become positively expansive. "Allow me to toast your cleverness, Amato. In the cabinet, you will find a decanter and two glasses. Join me in a glass of muscat."

Liya stepped to my side in an agitated rustle of feathers. "Let him save his thirst for the swill they'll give him under the Leads."

"Please, dear girl." The nobleman's voice was smooth as butter. "You will have my life. Allow me this one small favor. In fact, I'd like you to join us in the toast. I'm sure someone could find us another glass."

"I'd eat a canal rat before I'd raise a glass with the likes of you," she spat back.

Morelli made her a weary bow and regarded me with sad, tender eyes. He seemed almost relieved that his long masquerade was over. He nodded toward the cabinet and said wistfully, "It is an exquisite Cerigo muscat."

I opened the cabinet and reached for the decanter.

Liya grabbed my arm. "Tito, no. You can't share a drink with him. He killed Luca."

I shook her off gently and removed the decanter. It was of fine crystal overlaid with a lattice of woven silver and sat on a divided tray that also held two matching glasses. They made a lovely set, perhaps one of the last remaining treasures of a family that had guided Venice through her golden centuries.

"Tito!" Liya said savagely.

"It's all right, Liya. Morelli is the last of his line. A bit of ceremony will hurt no one."

Tipping the decanter, I said, "I won't drink with you, Signore, but I will pour you a glass to bid farewell to the home of your ancestors."

Morelli swept a fleeting, yearning glance over his study, then reached for the wine. He gave me a curious half smile and drained the glass in one great gulp.

Silvio stomped his heavy boots in exasperation. "Your kindness does you no credit, Tito. It's more than Morelli deserves. Do you think that bastard would have allowed Luca a last drink?"

Liya nodded her agreement, regarding me with a cold stare.

I shrugged. I was who I was.

Messer Grande wrinkled his nose and snorted. "What a night! Have we got all the pleasantries out of the way now? Good. Let's get this over with."

He crossed the room and grasped Morelli by the arm. But as Messer Grande pulled the nobleman toward the door, Morelli crumpled like a stalk of wheat cut down by a scythe. He hit the floor, hands frantically clutching his mid-section. The man was in agony—his eyes bulged from his head and yellow froth poured from his lips. Horrified, we all sprang to help, but there was nothing we could do.

His end came mercifully soon. In less than five minutes, Isabella Morelli had become a widow. She made only one comment: "I should have warned you about something like this. Leonardo always did manage to have the last word."

Chapter 30

It was a few days after I had unwittingly placed the quick-acting poison in Morelli's hand. In retrospect, I wasn't surprised that the nobleman had chosen suicide over the humiliation of prison and public execution, I was simply grateful that I had refused his invitation to join him. Gussie and I were strolling along the Riva degli Schiavoni. The afternoon was mild. Bright flowers spilled from window boxes, and fig trees lifted their heads over sun-drenched stone walls. It was a perfect, golden day in June, but the pavement wasn't crowded. Most of Venice's wealthy families, along with the servants who tended to their needs, had made the annual pilgrimage to their summer villas. The city's foreign visitors had also departed for cooler climes. So I was surprised when a sleek, black gondola pulled alongside and a liveried boatman called my name and directed me to the steps of the next quay.

As the broad-shouldered young gondolier steadied his craft, a mass of shockingly red ringlets appeared at the window of the covered cabin. Isabella Morelli raised her face toward me.

"Tito, what a fortunate meeting. I was on my way to the Cannaregio to find you. Get in for a moment, both of you."

I queried Gussie with a glance.

"You go on. I'll wait here," he whispered from the corner of his mouth.

Hesitating a bit, but curious, I boarded the gondola. Isabella reclined against a pile of cushions. She wore a short taffeta bodice of the liveliest blue. Her skirt of the same material billowed around her, and she had tied a jaunty red ribbon around her neck. She gave a throaty laugh. "I see your English friend is still afraid of me. He needn't be—any flirtation with him would be a waste of time. Anyone with eyes can see that he worships your sister."

I nodded. "That is so. Gussie and Annetta plan to be married as soon as my brother returns from his sea journey. We were just discussing what music I would sing at their wedding."

Isabella didn't comment. With an unreadable smile on her face, she simply stared at Gussie through the small window. I felt like I should say something about Morelli's death but hardly knew how to begin. I discarded several inane platitudes before my discomfort prodded me to make a clumsy observation: "I see you're not in mourning."

A wide smile settled on her carefully painted face as she ran her hand over the blue taffeta. "Leonardo's death is not a tragedy. For me, it's a cause for celebration. Being his wife was like serving a sentence as a galley slave. But now I'm free—after all these years of enduring his grim, oppressive presence, I'm finally free to do as I please."

"Still, you're a widow. Even in these careless times, people will talk."

"Let them. I already have a reputation and I wish to enhance it. The more they talk, the happier I will be. I want to be known as the most audacious, the most daring woman in Venice. Leonardo left me very little, but I do have the *palazzo*. Until those old walls fall in on my head, the Palazzo Morelli will be a gathering place for the witty and clever. People of fashionable ideas will flock to my salon to hear the latest satirical epigrams or debate the most scandalous theories. Perhaps I can even persuade Venice's most charming *castrato* to serenade us on occasion."

I bowed my head. "With pleasure, Signora. It is the least I could do. Is that why you were looking for me?"

"No," she answered, rummaging beneath the cushions. "I have something for you."

"For me? What is it?"

She smiled pertly. "Close your eyes and hold out your hands."

I complied. A heavy object filled my palms. Lifting my lids, I beheld the statue of Venus that had sealed Morelli's fate. The bronze had been buffed to a high luster and was nesting in a length of white silk.

"You're giving this to me?"

"It's yours to do with as you please. I enjoyed having Venus preside over my boudoir, but now that I know she bashed someone's head in... well, I thought you might want it to remind you of your successful investigation. Marco, my new gondolier, polished her up for you. He has wonderfully strong hands." She finished with a sigh and a satisfied smile.

"Have you replaced Fabrizio with Marco, then?"

She tossed her head. "I think Fabrizio turned tail and ran the minute your Jewess appeared above the reception hall. No one has laid eyes on him since."

I took my leave of Isabella and watched Marco of the strong hands pilot her boat down the glistening canal into an uncertain future. Before the dashing widow's appearance, Gussie and I had been strolling without a firm destination in mind. The statue provided me with a new purpose. We hailed a gondola and hurried to the ghetto. I wasn't sure how long my resolve would last and wanted to accomplish my mission before doubt overcame me.

Leaving Gussie at the eastern bridge, I passed through the ghetto's wooden gates. It took only a few minutes to locate Baruch's house and to identify the Del'Vecchios' new shop a few doors down. Pincas had strung an array of fine gowns and suits across the front window. He greeted me warmly and personally conducted me to Liya's workroom.

My beloved sat at a table beside a sunny window, stitching a length of silver lace onto a velvet mask. She rose at my approach.

I gestured to her basket of gaudy trims. "I'm surprised to find you working on these—not much call for masks this time of year."

"I'm trying to build up a stock. The fall Carnival will be here before you know it, and I don't want my mother and sisters to run short."

"You speak as if you won't be here in the fall."

She moved to the door, looked down the hall, then drew it shut. "You are right, but this is for your ears alone. My family doesn't know it yet, but I'll be leaving Venice shortly."

My throat went dry and the blood began to drum in my ears. "Leave Venice? Why? With whom?"

"You men. You just can't imagine that a woman could actually travel somewhere on her own." She emitted a short, barking laugh. "I'm going away by myself, and I'm going because Mama and Papa are insisting that I marry this student that one of Nonna's old friends dug up."

"But why must you leave? Can't you simply refuse him?"

Liya went back to her worktable and stood fingering the metallic laces and pleated ribbons. Finally, she patted the front of her apron and said, "I'm going to have Luca's child, Tito. I managed to keep the baby a secret for a while, but Mama found out. If I stay, I'll be forced to marry."

I swallowed hard. "Is he so bad, this student?"

"He has a face like a shriveled melon, beautiful music bores him, and when he thinks no one is watching, he makes scary faces at Fortunata." She crossed her arms decisively. "I won't have him. I'm going. My plans are made."

"Still, how can you make your living with a baby to tend to? You are a brave woman, Liya, but you are being foolhardy," I protested.

Her eyes flashed, but any anger quickly receded. She came toward me and touched my arm. "I know that you are speaking out of concern, but don't worry, I won't be alone for long." She considered a moment, then continued, "A long time ago, when I was just a little girl, I had a nosebleed that wouldn't stop. The doctors here in the ghetto couldn't do anything for me. Finally, in desperation, Mama took me across the lagoon to a wise-woman who lives on one of the secluded islands."

"A witch," I whispered.

"You may call her that if you wish," she answered gravely. "She cured my nosebleed, and I never forgot her mysterious cottage or her healing ritual. After she had given me honeyed wine and biscuits made in the shape of the crescent moon, she put herself in a trance and invoked a power, a goddess that she called Aradia. Think of it, Tito, a powerful, womanly deity. Here in our synagogue, the women are not even allowed to sit with the men near the altar—we are relegated to a gallery at the back. One time, I asked the rabbi if I could learn to read the Torah—he had Papa punish me for even asking the question."

She shook her head at the memory, then continued. "When I heard that Luca had died, I sought out the wise-woman. I was afraid. I wanted her to give me something that would get rid of the baby. She would have if I'd insisted, but she offered a solution I liked much better. She told me of a village of women like herself. They live over on the mainland, in an isolated forest deep in the mountains where they keep to the ways of the old religion. She arranged for them to take me in—me and my baby. That's where I'm going, Tito, and I must leave soon."

"So, you've finally found that place where it doesn't matter who is Christian and who is Hebrew."

She nodded. "The path of the goddess Aradia is far older than either."

Her hand was still on my arm. I covered it with my own. "You have another choice that your wise-woman would never have suggested."

Liya gazed at me questioningly, her lips barely parted. The sunlight picked out highlights on the lustrous black hair that was spilling over her shoulders. I longed to run my hand through it, but instead, I just squeezed her hand a little tighter. Gathering my courage, I said, "I love you, Liya. I can't offer you marriage because my religion doesn't grant that privilege to my kind, but I do offer you my whole heart for the rest of my earthly existence. You don't have to run away to the mountains. You can make your home with me—we can live anywhere you choose. I promise that you and your child will want for nothing."

"You would accept Luca's child?" she asked wonderingly.

I nodded.

"Oh, Tito. I didn't know… I must be a fool, but I didn't realize." She groaned softly and shook her head. "I don't feel the same way. I owe you so much, and you are a dear, sweet man, but I can't pretend and play you false. I can't go away with you. I've made my plans and I intend to stick to them."

Desolate and bewildered, I searched her face for a hint of some argument I could use to change her mind. I found no encouragement there. Liya didn't love me. She was going away and there was nothing I could do about it. Very gently, Liya pulled her hand from mine and pointed to the bundle under my arm. "What is that, Tito?"

I unwrapped the statue of Venus and handed it to her without comment. She gasped, gathered the bronze to her chest, then regarded it with an expression of such tender longing that I felt like an utter fool. How could I have ever hoped to replace Luca in her heart?

I said tentatively, "Isabella gave it to me. I wasn't sure you would want it since it shed Luca's blood, but I remembered how you spoke of it when we were at the pawnshop window. So, if you'd like to have it, the Venus is yours."

"Oh, Tito," she breathed. "Thank you a thousand times over. I asked Silvio for a memento, but he had sent all of Luca's paintings and other things to be sold. I thought I would be left with nothing of Luca except his child."

She hugged the statue again, her eyes closed and a rapt smile on her lips, transported by memories of happier times. It seemed like a perfect opportunity to retreat.

I don't remember leaving the Del'Vecchios' shop or traversing the winding alleys. I came out of my stupor only as I came through the tall, wooden gates and Gussie's concerned blue eyes floated right in front of my face.

"Tito," he asked, "did you talk to Liya? What did she say?"

We were standing on the arc of the bridge. As so often happens at dusk, a breeze was whipping down the canal, gathering strength as the wind off the lagoon funneled through the passages between the buildings. From behind came the heavy thud of the crossbar shutting the ghetto gates. The finality of the sound reverberated through my bones. I turned to see the sentry guards stepping to their posts for the night. I wanted to rush the gates, throw myself at their oaken planks, claw them open with my bare hands—but I knew it would be a fruitless effort. Liya was going away, trusting the magic of the wise-woman over the traditions of her family or the love of a heartbroken eunuch.

Gussie laid a hand on my shoulder. "Tito, are you all right?"

I nodded slowly. I remembered that I, too, possessed a bit of magic. My hand sought the pocket over my heart. I withdrew the veil and stared at Liya's profile in the dwindling light. Though we might both travel far, I swore by everything I held dear that Liya and I would meet again and that I would keep her image next to me until that sweet day.

"Tito?" Gussie was shaking me then. I must have looked like a man awakening from a deep sleep.

"Yes, Gussie. I'll be fine." I threw an affectionate arm around my friend. "Let's go home. Annetta will be wondering what has become of us, and we still have to pick out some music for your wedding."

Author's Note

Secret societies were rife throughout eighteenth-century Europe and the American colonies. Almost exclusively male oriented, most of the organizations mixed fellowship with devotion to the betterment of society along Enlightenment lines. A few were more interested in the pursuit of esoteric wisdom and power. Many influential eighteenth-century figures were members of one group or another: Isaac Newton, George Washington, Benjamin Franklin, Wolfgang Amadeus Mozart, and Giacomo Casanova, to name a few. Freemasonry was, and continues to be, the most prominent of the societies, but Dr. Palantinus' unique blend of quasi-religious and occult beliefs owes more to the Ancient Mystical Order of the Rose Cross, also called Rosicrucians. More information on secret societies of the era can be found in David V. Barrett's *Secret Societies* (Blandford, 1999).

Francesco Florio is a fictional character inspired by historical *castrato* Luigi Marchesi. Handsome, vain, and extraordinarily demanding, this virtuoso's pretentious behavior undoubtedly contributed to the change in public taste that led to the demise of the *castrati*. Henry Pleasants, in *The Great Singers* (Simon and Schuster, 1966), notes that "He insisted on making his first entrance descending a hill and wearing a helmet crowned with plumes a yard high, his arrival heralded by a fanfare of trumpets." Of course, our Tito would never stoop to such self-serving antics.

The first Jews to settle in Venice were from central Europe. After Queen Isabella's expulsion of 1492, many Jews from Spain and Portugal also arrived. Hebrew moneylending activities were welcome when Venice needed loans to finance a war with neighboring Chioggia, but in 1516, intolerance triumphed. A decree of the Republic confined Venetian Jews to a small neighborhood which had been the site of some foundries, *getti*. Thus the first ghetto in Europe was created. The gates were not thrown open until Napoleon's conquest of Venice in 1797. Today, most of the ancient buildings still stand and are the center of a thriving community with its own museum, library, and synagogues.

Special thanks to my husband, Lawrence, for believing in me and putting up with a writer's angst; to all friends and family who offered unflagging support; to Kit Ehrman, for her insightful comments on the manuscript; to the staff at the libraries of the University of Louisville and the University of Tennessee at Knoxville; to my agent, Dan Hooker, for encouragement along the way; and to my editor at Poisoned Pen Press, Barbara Peters.